The first of an ambitious quartet about the descendants of Llewellyn the Great, the Brothers of Gwynedd, *Sunrise in the West* is set in Wales at the time of the Plantagenets. A richly tapestried tale of high romance and low political cunning, it 'presents the complexities of medieval life excellently'.

...ay Times

Sunrise in the West

Edith Pargeter

Being the first book in a sequence entitled
THE BROTHERS OF GWYNEDD

HEADLINE

Copyright © 1974 Edith Pargeter

First published in Great Britain in 1974
by Macmillan London Ltd
Reprinted in paperback in 1987
by Headline Book Publishing PLC

British Library Cataloguing in Publication Data

Pargeter, Edith
  Sunrise in the West. – (The brothers of
  Gwynedd; 1)
  I. Title   II. Series
  823'.912[F]   PS6031.A49

  ISBN 0 7472 0014 9
  ISBN0 0 7472 3003 X Pbk

Printed and bound in Great Britain by
Collins, Glasgow

Headline Book Publishing PLC
Headline House
79 Great Titchfield Street
London W1P 7FN

CONTENTS

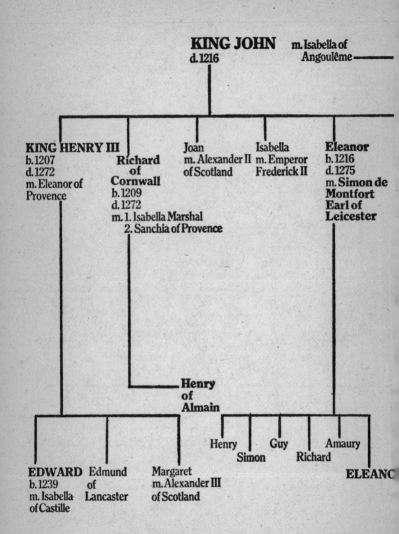

KING JOHN m. Isabella of
d. 1216 Angoulême ——

KING HENRY III
b. 1207
d. 1272
m. Eleanor of
Provence

**Richard
of
Cornwall**
b. 1209
d. 1272
m. 1. Isabella Marshal
2. Sanchia of Provence

Joan
m. Alexander II
of Scotland

Isabella
m. Emperor
Frederick II

Eleanor
b. 1216
d. 1275
m. **Simon de
Montfort
Earl of
Leicester**

**Henry
of
Almain**

Henry

Simon

Guy

Richard

Amaury

EDWARD
b. 1239
m. Isabella
of Castille

Edmund
of
Lancaster

Margaret
m. Alexander III
of Scotland

ELEANO

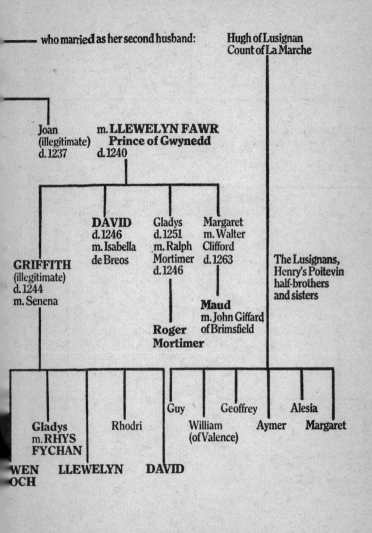

who married as her second husband: Hugh of Lusignan
Count of La Marche

Joan
(illegitimate)
d. 1237

m. LLEWELYN FAWR
Prince of Gwynedd
d. 1240

DAVID
d. 1246
m. Isabella
de Breos

Gladys
d. 1251
m. Ralph
Mortimer
d. 1246

Margaret
m. Walter
Clifford
d. 1263

GRIFFITH
(illegitimate)
d. 1244
m. Senena

The Lusignans,
Henry's Poitevin
half-brothers
and sisters

Maud
m. John Giffard
of Brimsfield

Roger
Mortimer

Guy

Geoffrey

Alesia

Gladys
m. RHYS
FYCHAN

Rhodri

William
(of Valence)

Aymer

Margaret

WEN
OCH

LLEWELYN

DAVID

CHAPTER I

---

*The chronicle of the Lord Llewelyn, son of Griffith, son
of Llewelyn, son of Iorwerth, lord of Gwynedd, the eagle
of Snowdon, the shield of Eryri, first and only true Prince
of Wales.*

My name is Samson. I tell what I know, what I have
seen with my own eyes and heard with my own ears.
And if it should come to pass that I must tell also what
I have not seen, that, too, shall be made plain, and how
I came to know it so certainly that I tell it as though I had
been present. And I say now that there is no man living
has a better right to be my lord's chronicler, for there is
none ever knew him better than I, and God He knows
there is none, man or woman, ever loved him better.

Now the manner of my begetting was this:
My mother was a waiting-woman in the service of the
Lady Senena, wife of the Lord Griffith, who was elder
son to Llewelyn the Great, prince of Aberffraw and lord
of Snowdon, the supreme chieftain of North Wales, and
for all he never took the name, master of all Wales while
he lived, and grandsire and namesake to my own lord,
whose story I tell. The Lord Griffith was elder son, but
with this disability, that he was born out of marriage. His
mother was Welsh and noble, but she was not a wife,
and this was the issue that cost Wales dear after his
father's death. For in Wales a son is a son, to acknowledge
him is to endow him with every right of establishment

and inheritance, no less than among his brothers born in wedlock, but the English and the Normans think in another fashion, and have this word 'bastard' which we do not know, as though it were shame to a child that he did not call a priest to attend those who engendered him before he saw the light. Howbeit, the great prince, Llewelyn, Welsh though he was and felt to the marrow of his bones, had England to contend with, and so did contend to good purpose all his life long, and knew that only by setting up a claim of absolute legitimacy, by whatever standard, could he hope to ensure his heir a quiet passage into possession of his right, and Wales a self-life secure from the enmity of England. Moreover, he loved his wife, who was King John's daughter, passing well, and her son, who was named David, clung most dearly of all things living about his father's heart, next only after his mother.

Yet it cannot be said that the great prince ever rejected or deprived his elder son, for he set him up in lands rich and broad enough, and made use of his talents both in war and diplomacy. Only he was absolute in reserving to a single heir the principality of Gwynedd, and that heir was the son acceptable and kin to the English king.

But the Lord Griffith being of a haughty and ungovernable spirit, for spite at being denied what he held to be his full right under Welsh law, plundered and abused even what he had, and twice the prince was moved by complaints of mismanagement and injustice to take from him what had been bestowed, and even to make the offender prisoner until he should give pledges of better usage. This did but embitter still further the great bitterness he felt rather towards his brother than his father, and the rivalry between those two was a burden and a threat to Gwynedd continually.

At the time of which I tell, which was Easter of the year of Our Lord twelve hundred and twenty-eight, the Lord Griffith was at liberty and in good favour, and spent the feast on his lands in Lleyn, at Nevin where his court then was. And there came as guests at this festival certain chiefs and lesser princes from other regions of Wales, Rhys Mechyll of Dynevor, and Cynan ap Hywel of Cardigan, and some others whose attachment to the prince and his authority was but slack and not far to be trusted. Moreover, they came in some strength, each with a company of officers and men-at-arms of his bodyguard, though whether in preparation for some planned and concerted action against the good order of Gywnedd, as was afterwards believed, or because they had no great trust in one another, will never be truly known. Thus they spent the Eastertide at Nevin, with much men's talk among the chiefs, in which the Lord Griffith took the lead.

At this time the Lord David had been acknowledged as sole heir to his father's princedom by King Henry of England, his uncle, and also by an assembly of the magnates of Wales; but some, though they raised no voice against, made murmur in private still that this was against the old practice and law of Wales, and spoke for Griffith's right. Therefore it was small wonder that Prince Llewelyn, whose eyes and ears were everywhere, took note of this assembly at Nevin, and at the right moment sent his high steward and his private guard to occupy the court and examine the acts and motives of all those there gathered. David he did not send, for he would have him held clean of whatever measure need be taken against his brother. There was bitterness enough already.

They came, and they took possession. Those chiefs were held to account, questioned closely, made to give hostages every one for his future loyalty, and so dispersed with their followings to their own lands. And until their departures, all their knights and men-at-arms were held close prisoner under lock and key, and the household saw no more of them. As for the Lord Griffith, he was summoned to his father at Aber, to answer for what seemed a dangerous conspiracy, and not being able to satisfy the prince's council, he was again committed to imprisonment in the Castle of Degannwy, where he remained fully six years.

In those few days at Easter, before the prince struck, the Lady Senena conceived her second son. And my mother, the least of her waiting-women, conceived me.

My mother came of a bardic line, was beautiful, and had a certain lightness of hand at needlework and the dressing of hair, but she was never quite as other women are. She was simple and trusting as a child, she spoke little, and then as a child; yet again not quite as a child, for sometimes she spoke prophecy. For awe of her strangeness men fought shy of her, in spite of her beauty, and she was still unmarried at eighteen. But the unknown officer whose eye fell upon her among the maids that Eastertide had not marriage in mind, and was not afraid of prophecy. She was young and fair, and did not resist him. She spoke of him afterwards with liking and some wonder, as of a strange visitant come to her in a dream. He took her in the rushes under the wall hangings in a corner of the hall. The next day the prince's guard rode in, and he was herded into the stables among the other prisoners until all were dismissed home. She never saw him again, never knew his name, or even whose man he was, and from what country. But he left her a ring by way of remembrance. A ring, and me.

That same night, for all I know that same moment, in the high chamber at Nevin, in the glow of vengeful

4

hope and resolution, the Lord Griffith got his third child and second son upon the Lady Senena. Certain it is that we were born the same day. Nor was the lady more fortunate than her maid. For six years she saw no more of her husband, for he was held fast in the castle of Degannwy, over against Aberconway, and she here in Lleyn, on sufferance and under surveillance, kept his remaining lands as best she could, and waited her time.

At the beginning of the year of Our Lord, twelve hundred and twenty-nine, in January snows, in the deepest frost of a starry night at Griffith's maenol of Neigwl, we were born, my lord and I. The Lady Senena named her son Llewelyn, perhaps in a gesture of conciliation towards his grandsire, for beyond doubt it was in her interests to woo the prince, and she had more hope of winning some favour from him in the absence of her husband's fiery temper and haughty person. Certain it is that she did bring the child early to his grandfather's notice, and the prince took pleasure in him, and had him frequently about him as soon as the boy was of an age to ride and hunt. With children he was boisterous, kind and tolerant, and this namesake of his delighted him by showing, from the first, absolute trust and absolute fearlessness.

As for me, my mother named me after that good Welsh saint who left his hermitage at Severnside to travel oversea to France, to become archbishop of Dol, and the friend and confidant of kings. As I have been told, that befell some five hundred years ago, and more. Perhaps my mother hoped for some sign of his visiting holiness in me, his namesake, for I had great need of a blessing from God, having none from men. I think that at first, when she found her innocent was with child, the Lady Senena made some attempt to discover who had fathered

5

me, that he might be given the opportunity to acknowledge me freely, according to custom, and provide me when grown with a kinship in which I should have a man's place assured. But my mother knew nothing of him but his warmth and the touch of his hands, not even the clear vision of a face, much less a name, for it was no better than deep twilight in the hall where they lay. And those who had visited, that Easter, were so many that it was hopeless to follow and question them all. And the ring, as I know, she never showed. For even to me she never showed it until I left her for the last time.

It may be that had not the prince's raid put an end to all play he would have looked for her again, and not grudged her his name, whether he meant a match or no. But that bold stroke put an end to more things than my mother's brief love, and I was fatherless.

They tell me, and I believe it, that in those first years in Lleyn I was the constant companion of the young Llewelyn, that we played together and slept together, and that sometimes, even, I was the leader and he the follower, and not the other way round, as I should have judged invariable and inevitable. But this part of my life lasted not long, and the memory of it which I retain is of a sunny, disseminated bliss, void of detail. It ended soon. When I was five years old one of the Lady Senena's grooms took a fixed fancy to my mother, and offered marriage, and though she was without any strong wish one way or the other, she did always what her mistress desired, and to the lady this seemed a happy way out of a problem and a burden. Others aforetime had been caught by my mother's beauty, but all had been frightened away by her mute and mysterious strangeness. This man – he was young and strong and good to look upon – wanted her more than he shrank from her. So she was married to him, she acquiescing indifferently in all.

Me, as it proved, he did not want. Before marriage, though he knew of me, I had counted for nothing. But now that he had her, and could in no wise move her to any show of passion, whether of love or hate or fear, or get from her any response but the calm, uncaring submission she showed him always, he began to look round everywhere about her for whatever could touch where he could not, move where he was but suffered, strike a spark where his fire and tinder failed. And he found me.

That year I had with him I do remember still, as one remembers a distant vision of hell. I have been hated, and that most thoroughly. What he could do to avenge himself upon me he did, with every manner of blow and bruise and burn, with every skill of keeping me from the sight of my betters and the company of my prince-playmate. Whatever comforted me he removed, or broke, or soiled and ruined. Whatever I loved he harmed, so that I learned to hide love. And though he never maltreated me before the Lady Senena, he took a delight in letting my mother see my misery. He thought by then that she had not that core of life in her that others have, to make any voluntary action possible, and that she could do nothing to save me.

That he did not know her is not a matter for wonder, for I think none ever did know her, certainly not her son. She was a secret from all men, and she held more possibilities than any man thought for.

When the Lord Griffith had been six years in prison he made an act of submission to his father, and was released, and restored at first to the half of his old lands in Lleyn, and then, when he continued in good odour, to the whole of that cantref. It was the occasion of great joy to his wife and her court, life was set in motion again in the old manner, and it was a time for asking favours. My mother knew the moment to approach her mistress, and did so in my interest, though thereby losing me. For she begged her lady to take me in charge for my protection, and said that she had a great wish to see me lettered, and a priest.

Now the Lady Senena was herself royal, for she was great-granddaughter to Rhodri, lord of Anglesey, and came of a race which had been lavish in gifts both to the old Welsh colleges of lay canons and the new Cistercian abbeys and Franciscan friaries. Therefore she had but to indicate, to whatever community she thought best, her wish that I should be accepted into care and taught, and it was as good as done. She placed me with the lay canons at Aberdaron, in her own Lleyn, and gave a generous sum for my endowment there. And thus I escaped my purgatory and got my schooling at her expense, and her name was shield enough over me, even if the brothers had not been the saints they were.

Nevertheless, I wept when I parted from my mother. But then I thought of her husband, and I did not weep. And Nevin was not so far that she could not visit me now and again, or I her. So I went without more tears, though a little afraid of the strangeness before me. I was then six years old, within a month. It was shortly before the Christmas feast.

Now the clas at Aberdaron was one of the best regarded and richest of all the colleges of North Wales, which were themselves the flower of all the land, unsullied by Norman interference. For it lay on the mainland directly opposite the blessed isle of Enlli, that men begin now to call Bardsey, and there the hermits have kept the old austere order pure to this day, and the very soil is made up of the bones of thousands of saints. Those who would withdraw to Enlli to die in holiness must come by Aberdaron. There they halt and enjoy the hospitality of the canons, and bring with them all the learning and piety and wisdom of mankind to add to the store. There could be no better place for a boy with a great thirst for knowledge. Even one who came with no such thirst could not choose but quicken to the fire of those visitors passing through.

There were twenty lay canons then at Aberdaron, and three priests, besides the abbot: a strong community. Because of the great number of travellers entertained there, the enclosure was large and fine, and there were many officers, among them, besides the scribe, a teacher. Into his hands I was confided. I slept in the doorway of his cell, and later had a cell of my own beside him. I had my share of work about the lands the canons tilled, according to my age, and I took my part in the services of the church, and learned my psalter in Latin by heart. But in the time that was left to me I had never enough of the marvel of studying, and once blessed with the first letters I ever learned, could not rest from adding to them. Finding my appetite was genuine, and not feigned in order to please, my teacher Ciaran took very kindly to me, and came as eagerly as I to the lessons we had together. In opening books to me, he opened the world, and he was good and gentle, and I loved him and was happy. From him I learned to read and write in Welsh and in Latin, and later also in English. And I began to help the steward who kept the books and accounts, for these values and amounts and reckonings were also strong enchantment to me.

Six years I spent thus in the purest peace and serenity, and all this while the world without went on its way, and the news of it came in to us like the distant sound of the waves on the shore, ominous to others, but no threat to our haven. The things that were told to me seemed like stories read in one of Ciaran's books, vivid

9

and alarming, but not real, so that even alarm was pleasure. For the stories of the saints are full of terror and delight, no less than the legends of heroes that the bards recite to the harp.

So I heard that after the return of her lord the Lady Senena, in her joy at the reunion, again conceived, and her third son was born in the spring of the following year. A fourth followed a year later, David, the last of her five children. But whether she named him after his uncle, with that same hope of softening her lord's fortune which had prompted her to give her second son the name Llewelyn, I do not know. There was peace then between them, the prince had enlarged the Lord Griffith's lands greatly, adding to the whole cantref of Lleyn a large portion of the lands of Powys, designing, I think, to leave him with an appanage which should recompense him for the surrender of his wider rights by Welsh law, and reconcile him to becoming a loyal vassal of his brother. But it was not in his nature to see beyond his own wrong to a larger right, and he knew only the title of Gwynedd, and could not envisage Wales, for all he quoted Welsh law. A man is as he is. The Lord Griffith was a fine man, tall and splendid to look upon, fully as tall as his father, and he was of great stature, though gaunt, where Griffith was full of flesh. He was openhanded to a fault where men pleased him, and too quick to lash out where they displeased. He was hasty in suspicion of affront, and merciless in retaliation. He was readily moved by generosity, and lavish in returning it. He never forgot benefit or injury. But he could not see beyond what helped or hurt him and his, and that is a small circle in a vast world, too narrow for greatness.

Doubtless he loved, but never did he understand, his father, that Llewelyn who is rightly named the Great.

This last child of theirs, the boy David, touched my

10

own fortunes nearly. For my mother had at last conceived by her husband, and brought forth a still-born girl three days before her lady bore her boy. And since the Lady Senena was low with a dangerous fever for two weeks after the delivery, and my mother was heavy with milk and yearning, she naturally became wet-nurse to the royal child. I had lost my sister, but I had a breast-brother, a prince of the blood-royal of Gwynedd, seven years and more my junior. This came early in my peace, and moved me deeply. I thought much of this helpless thing drawing its life from my mother, who had given me life also, and of whatever this mysterious thing might be that we two shared. And the bright, resolute, fearless creature who shared the stars of my birth with me, and who had been my fellow before I knew what royalty was, had fallen away from me then, and was almost forgotten.

I had been four years at Aberdaron, and was approaching my tenth birthday, when first we heard from a pilgrim bard that the great prince had been taken with a falling seizure. It was as if the earth had shaken under us. True, the attack was not severe, and had done no more than weaken him in the use of one arm, and draw his mouth a little awry, but we had never thought of him as being subject to age, like lesser men, even though he was now in his sixty-fifth year, for his vigour seemed to reach like a potent essence into the furthest corners of the land, and inspire even those, like me, who had never seen him in the flesh. Truly that flesh was now seen to be mortal. And the shudder of foreboding that shook most of Wales became a tremor of anticipation and hope to those who had sided with Griffith and were biding their time with him. And not only these, for beyond the march in England they surely licked their lips and tasted already the pickings the dogs find after the lion is dead.

Him they had let alone now for four years, and would let alone while he lived, with all his conquests rich and fat about him, for they dared not tempt again the force they had ventured too often already to their cost. But with the great prince gone, and an unknown, or untried at least, in his place, then they would close in on all sides to snatch back, if they could, the many lands they had lost to him.

It was the first time that I had ever considered how those who felt as England felt towards us could hardly be anything but enemies to Wales; and it caused me some uneasiness even then, but being so young, I did not apply it too closely to those I had known and served all my life. And soon I forgot the qualm it had cost me, in thinking of other things. For towards the end of this same year – I think it was on the 19th of October, and the place I know was the abbey of Strata Florida, a foundation beloved of the prince and always faithful to his house – there was called a great assembly of all the princes of Wales, and there every man among them took the oath of fealty to David as the next heir. Then indeed we felt that death had moved a gentle step nearer to our lord, and none knew it better than he, or felt less fear of it for himself, or more for Wales. Doubtless he knew better than any how the marcher lords were sharpening their knives, and what a load his son would have to bear.

Now I cannot say whether this ceremony at Strata Florida so inflamed the mind of the Lord Griffith that he took some rash action to assert his rights, or whether the Lord David, armed with so formidable a support, moved against him in expectation of just such a defiance, but certain it is that at the end of this year Griffith was stripped of his lands in Powys, and left with only his cantref of Lleyn, and that by order of his younger brother. By which it was made clear to all that the Lord David had already assumed a part of his royal privilege before his father's death, and that undoubtedly with his father's knowledge and sanction, for no son in his right wits would have reached to take any morsel of power out of those great hands but by their goodwill and grace. And surely the lords along the march, who had lost so much to Gwynedd these last twenty years, were counting days and mustering men already. Prince David had King Henry's word to accept and acknowledge him, and none other, and doubtful though King Henry's troth might be, if it held for any it would hold for his nephew, his sister's son. She, that great lady, her husband's right hand and envoy and counsellor all her days, was dead then more than two years, and buried with all honour and great grief at Llanfaes in Anglesey. She had but one son, though her daughters were married into all the great houses of the march, for better assurance. Yet there remained the Lord Griffith, and he was irreconcilable. And the year following there was sudden bitter blaze between those two brothers, the confiscated lands held hostage being insufficient to keep the elder in check, rather goading him to worse hostility. And before the year was out we heard that David had taken his brother prisoner, and his eldest son Owen with him, and lodged them in the castle of Criccieth under lock and key.

This Owen Goch – 'the Red' by reason of his flaming hair – was the Lady Senena's first child, and being nearly three years older than I, was then approaching thirteen, only a year away from his majority. And I suppose that it seemed a folly to shut up the father and leave in his place a son on the edge of manhood, round whom the same discontents could gather. The girl Gladys came next, a year before Llewelyn. She would not present the same danger, and the younger boys were but children as

13

yet, and could be left with their mother at liberty. Thus for the second time that household was broken apart, and the lady was left to protect her own and manage her family's affairs alone. But she was not molested in her home at Nevin, and the boy Llewelyn, they said, was welcome always at his grandsire's court, and spent more than half of his time there, very gladly, for there was life there, and hunting, and riding, and all the exercise and company a lively boy loves. Nor did his mother hinder, even when she knew that he was much in favour with his uncle David, who was childless by his wife Isabella. The boy was too young, said his mother, to understand, and could not be guilty of disloyalty to his house, and surely it was well to have one child covered by the protection of royal favour, a warranty against the loss of all, if the greatest must be lost. But I think, knowing or unknowing, she was using this boy to go back and forth in innocence and keep her informed of what went forward at Aber, while she waited for the prince to die. For she knew, none better, that there was a well of sympathy for Griffith's case, and that its time for gushing would not come while the lion yet lived. And she had learned how to wait with dignity, and in silence.

Yet I am not sure, even then, how right she was to trust in the innocence of her son Llewelyn. For even without art, news can flow two ways. And at what age art and wisdom begin is a mystery, and at what age those who will some day be men achieve the courage and the clarity to judge and choose and resolve, that is a greater mystery. And this was no ordinary child, with no ordinary grandsire. And they namesakes. There is magic in names.

Howbeit, on the tenth day of April of the year twelve hundred and forty the great Prince Llewelyn, feeling the heavy darkness draw in on him again, and this time

14

believing it an end, had himself conveyed into the abbey of Aberconway, which he loved and had shielded so long, and there took the monastic habit, after the manner of great kings going to their judgment. And wrapped in this blessed cloth he died on the day following, and there his great body lies buried. And doubtless his greater soul has room enough now, even beyond that reach he had in this world. For he was the true friend and patron of the religious, wherever they preserved the purity and austerity of the faith, and whatsoever he did was done with grandeur and largeness of mind, and for Wales, which he loved beyond all things.

So David ap Llewelyn was Prince of Aberffraw and Lord of Snowdon in his father's room. And in May of that same year he attended King Henry's council at Gloucester, became a knight at the king's hands, after the English fashion, put on the talaith, the gold circlet of his state, and did homage for Gwynedd, pledging himself liegeman of the king of England as overlord, saving only his sovereign right within his own principality. All which had been many times done before, and was no surrender of any part of his due, but his own side of a covenant, of which the reverse was King Henry's sworn acknowledgement of his firm status as prince of North Wales. And the other great magnates of Wales did homage in their turn on the like understanding.

What did not appear was how wide a gulf yawned between the two conceptions of what that status meant. It was not long before all those lords marchers who had lost land to Llewelyn, however long ago, and all those border Welsh who held themselves aggrieved at surrendering to him commotes and castles forfeited for disloyalty, or taken in open battle, began to resort to law and to force, demanding from David the return of

15

losses they would not have dared reclaim from his father. Thus the earl of Pembroke went with an army, in the teeth of the lord of that cantref, to rebuild his lost castle of Cardigan and plant a garrison there, while lawsuits came thick and fast over Mold, and Powys, and the lordship of Builth, which came legally to David as his wife's dower, but not without all possible resistance from her de Breos kin. Any and every disaffected lord, English or Welsh, who could bring a legal plea for the possession of land lost to the father, fairly or unfairly, turned now to rend the son. And King Henry, always maintaining his good faith in recognising his nephew's status, connived at all the activities of those who were bent on plucking his principality to pieces.

Nor was he so rich in solid friends on the borders as his father had been, for the line of Earl Ranulf, Llewelyn's lifelong ally and sympathiser, was extinct in Chester, and that earldom had gone back to the crown, laying bare all the north-east of Gwynedd to the assaults of the enemy.

David in this storm, perhaps not all unexpected but breaking upon him too soon, did his best to delay, after the English fashion, those lawsuits the English brought against him, and as a better instrument to his hand, chose rather than law to submit the impleaded lands to a council of arbitrators nominated from both sides, with the Pope's legate in England at their head. But this measure also he found to be acting against him, and fell back once more upon delay, sending excuses for failure to attend the meetings of a commission he now saw to be no more than a dagger in King Henry's hand. For this whole issue had now been channelled through the king and his council, making a quarrel between two countries rather than between mere men at odds over land. Thus he held off the pack for a year, his envoys, his father's old, able men, going backwards and forwards many times and using every art of persuasion and disruption, but in the end to no purpose. For King Henry saw that he had many allies, so many Welsh princes being either disaffected over land, or aggrieved by Griffith's captivity and disinheritance, and that all that was obstinately being withheld from him by legal means he could acquire by force at little cost, something he dared not attempt beforetime. Having summoned David to appear before the commission at Montford on the Severn in June, and well knowing that he would not come, he made preparations for an attack in arms. And David, though he had word of the martial movements behind the summons, had no way left open to him but to absent himself, and let what must follow, follow.

I tell all this not as I saw it then, being little more than a child, and without understanding of many of the tidings I heard, but as I understood it later, when I had seen more of the world than the clas at Aberdaron. But I was not so young or so ignorant that I could not feel the threat as touching even me, when they spoke of the king of England moving into the marches at the end of July with a great force of men in arms, and setting up his court in Shrewsbury. For what could he be doing there in the borders but preparing the undoing of Gwynedd? Shrewsbury was a great way off, further than I could then imagine, but not so far that the English could not reach even this last corner of Lleyn with fire and sword if war once flared.

Yet I had no notion that events outside our enclosure and our fields and coast could ever touch me as a person, or draw me out of this haven I had grown to love and think of as my lifelong home.

They came for me on the last day of July, two grooms

of the Lady Senena's household, bringing a third pony for me.

I was raking the early hay in the field above the shore, about noon, when Ciaran sent one of the brothers to call me in, for I had visitors with the abbot. A clear, bright day I remember it was, with a fresh breeze bringing inland the strong, warm scent of kelp from the beach below me, and the southward sea innocently restless, sparkling with the sun and its own motion. So beautiful a day that I went unwillingly, even believing it would be only for an hour, I who have never seen Aberdaron again.

Abbot Cadfael was waiting for me in the antechamber of the guest-house within the enclosing wall, and with him two men in the Lady Senena's livery. I saw their horses in the stable as I passed, not blown nor sweated, for it was no long ride from Neigwl, where the lady then had her household. The younger of the two riders I did not know. The elder it took me some minutes to know for my step-father. I had not seen him for six years, half my lifetime, and he was changed by double as many summers and winters, for men age by curious lurches and recoveries, now standing still in defiance of time for a dozen years, then sliding downhill by a decade in one season. These years with my mother had been his breaking time, for I think she had won, without fighting, that long battle between them. It was not that she could not love, but that he could not make her love. There was grey in his shaggy dark hair, and his face was hollow and hungry, with deep-sunken eyes. He had been a very comely man. Yet in one thing he was unchanged. I saw by the way his eyes hung upon me in silence that he hated me as of old. But it is one thing I can never forget to him, that as long as he lived he could not cease from loving her. And when I was old enough to understand

18

that purgatory aright, and had myself some knowledge of the pain of love, then I forgave him all, for he was paid over and over for any injury he ever did me.

'Son,' said Abbot Cadfael very gravely, 'there is here a call for you to go out from among us, to another duty.'

At that I was clean knocked out of words and breath, as if one had attempted my life, for Aberdaron was my life, and I had thought it should be so always. I knew by rote already the vows I was to take, and waited for the time without impatience only because I was sure of it. And in one sentence all was taken away from me. I went on my knees to him, and when I could speak I said: 'Father, my heart is to this life and none other. My home is here, and all that I am is yours. How can I go hence, and keep any truth in me?'

He looked at me closely and thoughtfully for a long time, for I think I had not spoken as he had expected of a boy twelve years old. But he said only: 'Truth is everywhere, and your truth will go with you. Child, you were but lent to us a season, and she who lent you requires you of us again. It is not for you to choose, but to accept with humility. I have no right to deny you, nor you to refuse.'

I would have wept, but not with those deep eyes of my mother's husband watching me, for I still hated him then as he hated me. And I knew that the abbot spoke truth, for the Lady Senena had been my provider and protectress all these years, and by rights I belonged to her, and not only could not, but must not refuse her commands. She could cut off my endowment and have me put out of this refuge when she would, but that I knew she would not do. For though she was austere and hard of nature, she was also faithful to whatever she undertook, and would not avenge herself upon an underling. Therefore my debt to her was all the greater, and whatever she asked of me I must do. But to discover, if I might, the magnitude and the duration of my loss – for even losses can be regained after years – I questioned humbly after the cause of my recall.

'That,' said he, 'I cannot tell you. I have received the indication of her wishes, which are that you should return at once with these men, and rejoin your mother at Neigwl. It is your mother's wish also. They have need of you, and to be needed and to fill the need is the greatest privilege in life. Bearing God and his grace in mind always, go and give as you may. There is nothing to regret.'

I asked him, quivering: 'Father, if God will, may I come back?'

He raised his old, weak eyes from me, and looked beyond those men who had come to fetch me, out through the wall of the anteroom, through the high wall of the enclosure, and as far as the inward eye can see. 'Come when you may in good conscience, son,' he said, 'and you will be welcome.' But I knew by the sad calm of his face that he did not expect to see me again.

I asked him for his blessing, and he blessed me. A little he questioned me as to my knowledge, and the skills I had gained to take away with me, and commended me to maintain them all diligently. Then he kissed and dismissed me.

I put together what little I had, my copy of the psalter, a spare shirt, my ink-horn and pens, and the few little brushes I had for illuminating. And I said my farewell to Ciaran, so barely that the poverty of words hung heavy on me all the way, and I doubted if he knew what I had within me unsaid, but doubt it not now, so long afterwards. Nor doubt that he prayed for me without ceasing, as long as he lived. And then we went. By the upland road we went, turning our backs on that blessed sea that leads outward over the watery brightness to the beauteous isle of Enlli, where the saints are sleeping in bliss. We went towards the rib of Lleyn, that leads into Wales as an arm leads into the body; from rest into turmoil, from peace into conflict, from bliss into anguish. Side by side we rode, my mother's husband and I, and the young groom a few paces behind us. And for three miles of that ride we never said a word for heaviness, however bright was the noonday sky over us.

I had not been on a horse since the day I was brought to Aberdaron, pillion behind a groom, for the brothers of the pure communities abjured not only women, and the eating of flesh, but also riding on horseback. And I was awkward enough, and before we reached Neigwl sore enough, on that broad-backed hill pony, but I kept my seat with some pleasure, and my head high and my back straight with more obstinacy, riding beside this man who hated me, in such mourne silence. I had then no fear of him, and that was surprising to me, though I knew the good reasons for it. He dared not now touch me, if he had been sent to bring me to the Lady Senena. She would expect to see me in good health and good heart, moreover, I was now of an age to speak out volubly against any ill-use. Yet he was double my size, and hate might prove stronger than caution. There was more than wisdom restraining him from laying any hand on me, more even than the witness trotting behind us. He saw now no gain, not even any satisfaction, in killing me. I began to be a little curious about him, and a little in awe of him, as of the tragic and the accursed, from that moment. It is not far from awe to pity, but it was so far then that the end was out of sight, my stature being low, and my vision short.

I asked him, as we breasted one green crest of the

hills, and looked upon another valley: 'What does she want with me?'

He said: 'She?' and looked darkly into the sunlit distance, and terribly smiled.

'The Lady Senena,' I said, suddenly trembling, because I had not known so clearly until then that for him there was only one she.

'You're wanted,' he said grimly, 'because she will not go without you.' And that was the same she, his, not mine.

'Go where?' I asked. In all these years she had visited me only three times, for to her a journey, even of twenty miles, was a traverse of the world. Yet she had not wished me back, or tried to uproot me out of my green garden of books and vegetables and saints, content to have me content, and still in the same cantref with her. 'Where is it she must go,' I cried out to know, 'with me or without me? How far?'

'Ask the lady,' he said. 'I'm but the messenger. I go where I'm sent, like you. All my task is to bring you.'

'But you know,' I said, insistent.

'I've heard a name. It might as well be the holy city of Jerusalem. I never was beyond Conway,' he said, 'in my life, what are names to me?'

So I asked him nothing more, for he was as lost as I was. Only after a while I asked for my mother, if she was well, and he said, well, so dourly that I ventured to ask no more as long as we rode together.

There was nothing strange to be seen round the llys at Neigwl, when we came there. In the village and the fields men were working as ever, and there was no more bustle than usual even inside the walls. It was always a lively place. But when we came to stable our ponies I saw that there were more horses within than ever I had seen there in the old days, or even at Nevin, and moreover that there were great bundles and saddle-bags already packed and waiting, covered over with hides and stacked along the wall. If there was no great to-do at this hour, it was because the Lady Senena's plans, whatever they might be, had been made some while since, and now only awaited the right moment for execution.

My mother must have been listening for the sound of hooves, for she looked out from the hall as we clattered across the courtyard, and came hurrying to kiss me. She had a child by the hand, a boy about five years old, who clung to her confidently, and stared up at me with shining curiosity. Very dark he was, with broad cheekbones and wide eyes of a blue like harebells, soft and light, under straight brows as black as his blue-black hair. He was tall for his age, and well-made, and of a bold beauty, and he gazed at me unwaveringly in silence, for so long that I was forced to be the first to turn my eyes away. And I knew this boy for my breast-brother, the youngest of the Lord Griffith's four sons, who bore his detested uncle's name of David.

A second boy, a year or so older, came trailing out from the hall after them to stare at us from a distance before he made up his mind to come close. He approached a little sidelong, hesitant and unwelcoming in his look. This one had something of the colouring of Owen Goch, but as though bleached and faded in the sun, for his hair was of a reddish straw-colour, and his cheeks pale and freckled. When he saw my mother kiss me he came the rest of the way across the dusty court to us in a rush, and laid hold upon her skirt as if to assert his ownership and my strangeness. But in a moment, as she only gave him her free hand without a glance, and continued speaking with me, he lost interest in us both, and looked round for other entertainment, and pulling away his hand again, ran off after one of the maids who passed from the kitchens with her arms full. The youngest stood immovable and watched, saying never a word, and missing nothing, until my mother leaned down to him cajolingly, and turning him after his elder, urged him to go with Rhodri, and Marared would give them some of the honey cakes she was baking. And then he went, at first composedly, and then breaking into a hopping dance of his own, to which he seemed to want and need no audience.

This was the first time that ever I saw the two youngest of the brothers of Gwynedd.

My mother drew me with her into the store-room, I think to be out of sight of her husband when she embraced me, and there she held me against her heart, and said over and over: 'I could not go without you! How could I? I would not go so far and leave you behind.' Then she held me off from her to search my face more earnestly, and asked, almost as if in fear, whether I had been happy at Aberdaron, and whether I was not glad rather to come with her, and travel so far into the world. And I swallowed my regrets, since there was no sense in two of us grieving when only one need, and told her that I was her dutiful son, and I willed to go with her wherever she must go, though God knows I lied, and I hope forgives me the lie. Could I have had my way without hurt to any other, I would have begged a fresh pony, all stiff and sore as I was, and started out on the instant back to my cell and the unfinished haymaking, and my master Ciaran. But since that could not be, for neither she nor I was free, or had any support but in the Lady Senena's service, I comforted her as best I could, myself uncomforted, and asked her where it was we must go, and for how long a time, to make it necessary that I should be recalled. For often enough the court moved between three or four maenols, but none so distant that it implied a parting between us.

'We are going further,' she said, 'very far. She has sent couriers ahead days ago, to have changes of horses ready. And we leave tonight, after dark.'

'But why after dark?' I questioned. 'And where do we go?'

'Eastward,' she said, 'to England. But in secret. No one outside these walls must know.'

'To England?' I said. 'What, all? The children, too?' A foolish question, as I saw, for it was because the children were to be of the party that she, their nurse, must go with them, and would and must take her son with her. And if the lady was thus preparing to remove herself and what family she had about her furtively into England, it could only be into King Henry's care, and there could be but one reason. No wonder the expedition was being mounted by night, and in the expectation of a long exile. How long, the king's army and the Welsh weather must decide. Only dimly did I grasp the meaning of this move, but she did not question it at all. What the lady ordered was her law. 'How many go?' I asked her. 'She and the children, and we – how many more? The steward? And a guard? She'll never ride unprotected.'

'Twenty are gone ahead,' my mother said, 'to make ready and meet us along the way. Three officers ride with us, and ten more men.'

A large party to make so secret and desperate a move. She did not mean to appear before the king of England without some remnants of royal state.

'And Llewelyn?' I said, for I had not seen him yet about the llys. 'Is he in this, too?'

'He is on his way now, he should have been here already. She sent for him yesterday from Carnarvon. And you are to go to her,' she said, 'and she will tell you what your part is to be. Go to her now, she will have heard you are here, she does not like to be kept waiting.'

So I went, for indeed that lady was not one to be trifled with, especially with so grave a business in hand. But as I turned to go on past the hall to the lady's apartments, my mother suddenly called after me, in the child's voice that suited so ill with this learned-by-rote business she had been expounding for me, and with the most hushed and bitter awareness of having somehow offended: 'Child, forgive me – forgive me!'

I went back to her, greatly shaken, and held and reassured her that my only wish was to be with her, that I had no reluctance or regret, while my heart wept in me for longing. There was something deep within my mother that understood more than other men do, while all the shell of her mind was without understanding.

Then verily I went. The Lady Senena was sitting in a great chair in her solar, with a coffer before her, into which she was carefully laying away small packets of valuables, while her steward came and went with certain parchments and consulted with her, discarding some for burning, and adding others to those she would take with her. When I came in she looked up, and I louted to her, and signified that I had come, in duty bound, in answer to her summons.

She was not a tall woman, nor beautiful, but she had a great dignity about her, and was accustomed to being respected and obeyed. She had thick brows that all but met over her nose, and made her seem to frown, and her voice was cool and strong, so that I had always been in some awe of her, and still was, however good she had been to me.

'So you are here,' she said, considering me. 'Have you spoken with your mother?'

I thought it best to know nothing but what the lady

herself chose to tell me, so I said: 'Madam, I have, and she sent me here at once to hear what your wishes are.'

She began then to question me closely about my studies, and all I had learned at Aberdaron, and what I told her seemed to content her, for she nodded repeatedly, and twice exchanged glances with her steward and they nodded together. I was indeed more forward in letters than most about her court, and might be of use as a clerk, she said, but in particular I was to earn my place, since her children's nurse would not go without me, as groom and attendant to the young princes. I said I would do my best in whatever work she chose to give me, and go wherever she willed that I should go.

'You do not ask me where,' she said drily.

'Madam, if I am to know, you will tell me.'

And tell me she did, and set me to work then and there, helping the steward to sort out and burn those parchments she did not need, and wished not to leave behind her for others to see. For my eyes were younger and sharper than the old man's, and even in the bright summer the light was dim within the room. So it happened that I was crouched by the hearth-stone, feeding rolls of vellum into a sluggish fire, or laying out those harmless and only once used for cleaning, when there was a rush of loud young footsteps outside, and Llewelyn flung the door wide and came striding in.

I saw him first only as a dark figure in outline against the brilliance of the day outside, and saw him so, in stillness, for a long moment, for he had halted to get his bearings in the dimness of the room, after his ride under that radiant sky. Then he came forward to plump heartily down on his knee and kiss his mother's hand, though so perfunctorily that it was plain he saw no reason for more than ordinary filial respect, and knew nothing as yet of why she had sent for him. And very straightly he went to it and asked, as though, whatever it was, he would see it done, and then be off again to whatever employment she had interrupted.

'I came as soon as I could, mother. What is it you want of me?'

The flames of my small fire, burning up to a brief flare as I forgot to feed it, lit him clearly as he bounded up from his knee. He was then no taller than I, though afterwards he shot up to gain half a head over me. But he was sturdier and squarer than I, and perhaps because of this, perhaps because of that glowing, carefree assurance he had, being born royal, he seemed to me my elder by a year or two, though I knew that to be false. He wore no cloak in this high summer, he had on him only his hose and a short riding-tunic of linen, that left his throat and forearms bare, long-toed riding shoes on his feet, and round his hips a belt ornamented with gold, from which a short dagger hung. And wherever his skin was bared he was burned copper-brown by the sun, so that his thick brown hair seemed only a shade darker. He looked at the coffer his mother had on the table, and at the pieces of jewellery and the documents laid away in it, and his smile of pure pleasure in sun and motion and his own vigour faded a little into wonder and puzzlement.

'What are you doing? What is this?'

'I sent for you,' she said, 'to come home to your duty. Tonight we leave here on a journey. If I have not consulted you before, you must forgive me that, for it was necessary. I could not risk any accidental betrayal, it was best the secret should remain within these walls until all was ready. It is ready now, and we leave here tonight. For Shrewsbury.'

He echoed: 'Shrewsbury?' in an almost silent cry of astonished disbelief. When his brows drew together so, they were almost as formidable as hers, and very like. 'Mother, do you know what you say? King Henry is on his way from Gloucester to Shrewsbury this moment, with all his feudal host. Bent against Gwynedd! Did you not know it? Whatever you could want in Shrewsbury, God knows, I cannot see, but this is no time to stir about it.'

He was slow to understand, though she had told him bluntly enough. And after all, perhaps my experience had made me a year or so older, not younger, than he when it came to probing the political moves of his noble mother. Or he was too near and fond, in the unthinking way proper to his youth, and I, kinless, fatherless, dependent, saw from outside and saw more clearly. Yet when the truth did dawn upon him, he spoke from a vision which I had not, and did not yet comprehend.

His face had sharpened in the unseasonable firelight. I saw all the golden, reflected lines along his bones of cheek and chin quiver and draw fine and clear. He was not smiling at all then. He said: 'Madam, let me understand you! Is that your reason for riding to Shrewsbury? To meet King Henry?'

'I am going,' she said with deliberation, and rising from her chair to be taller than he, 'to confide your father's cause and yours to King Henry's hands, and ask him for justice. Which you well know we have not had and shall not have from any here in Gwynedd. The English in arms will restore us our rights. I am resolved to stake all on this throw. We have been disinherited and insulted long enough. I will have your father and your brother out of prison and restored to their own by the means that offers.'

'You cannot have understood what you are doing,' he said. 'You could not talk so else. The king of England is preparing now, this very minute, to attack our country, our people. You want to make our right in Welsh law one more weapon on the English side, to slaughter Welsh-men? Your own kin? You will be siding with the enemy!'

'You talk like a child,' she said sharply, 'and a foolish child! I have waited long enough for Gwynedd to do justice to my lord, your father, and talk of enemies is hollow talk to me. We are disinherited, against all law. I am appealing to an overlaw, and make no doubt but it will hear me, and do right.'

'You cannot do right to my father or any,' he cried, blazing up like a tall flame, 'by doing wrong to Gwynedd! To Wales!'

'You talk of fantasies,' she overbore him, looming against him like a tower, 'while your father rots in Cric-cieth, a reality, deprived of what is justly his. And you dare talk to me of right! We are going, and tonight. Go, sir, do as you are bidden, go and make ready, and no more words. I did not send for you to teach me my duty, I know it too well.'

Long before this I would gladly have crept away if I could, but I dared not move for fear of reminding them that I was there. And even he, I thought, wavered and blanched a little before her, for in his father's absence she was the law here, and he was still two years short of his manhood, and could not act against her will. Yet I think now he did not give back at all, and even his hesitation was nothing but a hurried searching in his unpractised mind for words which might convince with-out offending.

'Mother,' he said, low and passionately, 'I do know my father's case, and know he asks but what he feels his right. But I tell you, if I were in his place, rather than get my sovereignty at the hands of King Henry, I would make my full submission to my uncle David as his loyal vassal, and put myself and every man I had into arms to fight for him against England. There should be no factions here when a war threatens, but only one cause, Wales. Do not go! Go rather to Criccieth, and beg my father to remember his own father, and the greatness he gave to Gwynedd, and urge him to offer the oath of fealty to his brother, and come out and fight beside him. Even at his own cost, yes! But I swear it would not cost him so high as you will make it cost him if you go on with this. Do not go, to make traitors of us all!'

She had heard him thus far only for want of breath and words to silence him, and found no argument, for they had no common ground on which to argue. But then she struck him, on the word she could not endure. The clash of her palm against his cheek was loud, and the silence after it louder, until she found a laboured, furious voice to break it.

'Do you dare speak so to me? You have been too long and too often at your uncle's court, it seems! You had better take care how you use the word traitor in this house, for it may well echo back upon your own head. You have been spoiled at Aber! They have bought you, foolish child as you are. Now let me hear no more from you, but go and make ready. You are the eldest son of this house at liberty, and should be doing your duty as its head.'

He stood unmoving, his eyes fixed upon her angry face, and he had grown pale under the sunbrown, so that the marks of her fingers burned clear and red upon his cheek. After a long moment he said, in a voice quiet and even: 'You say truth, and you do well to remind me. I am the eldest son of this house at liberty, and I will do my duty as its head. Have I your leave to go and set about it?'

'That is better,' she said grimly, and dismissed him with no greater mark of forgiveness than that, for she was much disturbed, and still angry. Nor did he ask any.

31

He went out as abruptly as he had come, and the back view of him as he passed from dark to bright in the doorway did not look to me either tamed or penitent.

I saw him again towards dusk, when we brought in the stock. For all must go forward as usual and seem innocent after we were gone. He had chosen a horse for himself with care, and tried its paces about the courtyard, and professing himself but half satisfied, rode it out and round the llys to make certain of his choice. I had been sent out to bring down a flock from the hill grazing, north of Neigwl, and I came out of a fold of the track close to where the road swung away to the north, towards Carnarvon and Aber.

He was walking his horse up the slope over the grass, away from Neigwl and the sea, and when he came to the road he halted a moment and looked back, motionless in the saddle. Thus, his back being turned to me, he did not see me until the first yearling lambs came down into the corner of his vision, and made him look round. He knew then that I was from the llys. Perhaps he did not know whether I was in the secret, or perhaps he did not care. He looked at me calmly, and did not recognise me, but he knew that he was known, and that I, whoever I might be, was reading his mind.

That was a strange moment, I cannot forget it. He sat his horse, solitary and grave, examining me with eyes the colour of peat pools in the sun. He had brought away with him nothing at all but the horse, and a cloak slung loosely over his linen tunic. Whatever else was his he had left behind, to be taken or abandoned as others decided, for valuables are valuables, and we were going where we might soon be either in need or living on English bounty. He wheeled his horse and walked it forward deliberately some few paces along the road northwards, his eyes never leaving mine, and suddenly he was satisfied, for he smiled. And I smiled also at being read and blessed, for his confidence was as open and wide as the sky over us.

He said to me: 'You have seen nothing.' Confirming not ordering.

'Nothing,' I said.

'And I know nothing,' he said. That, too, I understood. The Lady Senena could never be told, nor perhaps would she believe it if any tried to tell her, that the son who would not go with her to England would not send out an alarm after her, either, or betray her intent in any way, having made his own decision yet still allowing her hers. No, it was for me he said it, that I might be satisfied as he was satisfied, and feel no guilt in keeping his secret, as he felt none in keeping hers. And that was no easy way to take, alone, for a boy twelve years old.

He shook the reins, and dug his heels into the horse's flanks, and was away from me at a canter along the track towards the north. He had ridden much, and rode well, erect and easy, as I would have liked to ride. I watched him until he breasted the next rise and vanished into the dip beyond, and then I took the lambs down to Neigwl, and said never a word to any of that meeting.

So when the dusk was low enough, and the hour came for our departure, when the sumpter horses were loaded and sent ahead, and the litters for the lady and her children stood ready, and the horses were being led out saddled from the stables, there was great counting of all the heads, and the word began to go round: 'Where is Prince Llewelyn? Has anyone seen him?' No one had, since he took out his chosen horse to try its paces. We waited for him more than an hour, and men hunted in every possible and impossible place about the maenol, while the Lady Senena's face drew darker and bleaker and angrier with every moment. But he did not come, and he was not found. He was the eldest man of his house at liberty, and he was gone to do his duty as its head, according to his own vision.

Even when she cried out on him at last that he had turned traitor, had abandoned and betrayed his own mother and brothers, I said no word. Unable to understand, she would have been unable to believe that he could go on his own way and not block and prevent hers. She feared pursuit, and therefore every hour became more precious, and she ordered our departure in great haste, and extended our first forced ride as far as Mur y Castell, where her advance guards had fresh horses waiting for us. She would not risk taking the old Roman road across the Berwyns, but had planned a route further south, to give all David's favourite dwellings a wide berth, and our first rest was at Cymer. Thence, with a greatly increased company, we made two easier days of it by way of Meifod to Strata Marcella, and crossed the Severn at a ford below Pool.

And all the way she complained bitterly of her second son's treachery and ingratitude, until she went far to make her daughter Gladys, who was his elder by a year, hate him and decry him even as she did. Being the only daughter, this girl was very dear to her, and much in her confidence. Yet I think there was so much of grief and smart in their blame of him that even hate had another side, and in their softer moments they could not choose but wonder and harrow over old ground, marvelling how he had come to that resolution against all odds, incomprehensible to them, and blameworthy, but surely hard indeed for him, and therefore honest. And this all the more when the journey was nearly over, and no breath of suspicion or pursuit followed us. For if he had not garnered all the favour he could by setting his uncle's huntsmen after us, what was his own welcome likely to be after our flight was discovered? He was known to have been summoned by his mother, and obeyed and returned, the very day of the defection. The revenge that could not reach his mother might fall on him for want of larger prey. And sometimes those two women, a moment after cursing him, wondered with anxiety how he was faring now, and whether he was not flung into Criccieth with his father and his brother.

As for me, I learned painfully to ride, if not well as yet, doggedly and uncomplainingly, I tended the two little boys, I wrote one or two letters of appeal for the Lady Senena to such English lords as she best knew by contact or reputation, urging her cause, and I did whatever clerking there was to be done by the way. But familiar as I became with her argument, I could not forget his. And for which of them was in the right, that I could never determine. For both were honest, and both spoke truth, though they went by opposite ways. Yet being of the party that went one way, I heard now nothing but this side of the case, and matter repeated again and again without opposition grows to fall naturally on the ear. So I doubt I veered with the wind, like other men older than I, and came to be much of the lady's way of thinking before we reached Shrewsbury, which we did, with safe-conducts from the king's council, on the fourth day of August of this year twelve hundred and forty-one.

CHAPTER II

This Shrewsbury is a noble town, formidably walled all round and everywhere moated by the Severn, but for a narrow neck of land open to the north, for the whole town lies within a great coil of that river. It has three gates, two of them governing the bridges that lead, one eastwards deeper into England, one westwards into Wales, and the third gate lies on the tongue of dry land, under the shadow of a great castle. I have seen larger towns since then, though none fairer. But when we came in by the Welsh gate, over that broad sweep of river and beneath the tall tower on the bridge, that August day in the heat, I saw such a town for the first time in my life, and thought it more marvellous than I can tell. For we in Wales had then borrowed very little from this crowding English life that pressed in on our flank, that used coined money, and markets, of which we had scarcely any, and lived in stone houses that could not be abandoned at need, for they were too precious, and grew ordered crops that tied men to one patch of soil. And above all, few of us had ever seen what the English called a city.

The Lady Senena had sent her steward ahead to deal with the bailiffs of the town, being armed already with a recommendation from John Lestrange, who was sheriff of the county. And we were met at the gate, and conducted to a great house near the church of St Alkmund (for this town has four parish churches within its walls) where we were to be lodged. There was fair provision for the lady and her children and officers within, and those of her escort and servants who were married were given the best of what remained, while the young men had reasonably good lying in a barn and storehouse in the courtyard. And it was mark of some respect that our party got so much consideration, for Shrewsbury was crowded to the walls. King Henry and his court and officials had been in the town three days, and many of his barons and lords were installed with him in the guest halls of the abbey of St Peter and St Paul, outside the walls by the English gate. The chief tenants and their knights were quartered in the castle, or wherever they could find room in houses and shops inside the walls, and the main part of the army, a great host, encamped in the fields outside the castle foregate.

But this numbering, vast though it was, was but the half of the stream that had poured into Shrewsbury. There were plenty of clients eager to enlist King Henry's favour, besides the Lady Senena. All those marcher lords who had lost land to Llewelyn the Great, and had been trying through legal pressures to regain it from his son all these past months, had come running to the royal standard, waiting to pick the bones. Roger of Montalt, the seneschal of Chester, who had been kept out of Mold for many years, Ralph Mortimer, who had trouble with his Welsh neighbours in Kerry, and Griffith ap Gwenwynwyn, who laid claim to most of southern Powys by right of his father, these were the chief litigants. This Griffith ap Gwenwynwyn was a man twenty-seven years old, and had been but an infant when his sire lost all to Llewelyn of Gwynedd. He was married to Hawise, a daughter of the high sheriff, John Lestrange, who had three border counties in his care, and was justiciar of Chester into the bargain, a very powerful ally. The English called this Welsh chief Griffith de la Pole, after the castle of Pool, which was his family's chief seat; and indeed, this young man had been so long among the English that he was more marcher baron than Welsh chief, let alone the influence of his wife, who was a very strong and self-willed lady. But apart from these, there were not a few of the minor Welsh princes here to join the royal standard, some because they felt safer owing fealty to England than to Gwynedd, some with grievances of their own over land, like the lord of Bromfield, some because they upheld the Lord Griffith's right, and had conceived the same hope as had his lady, some in the hope of snatching a crumb or two out of David's ruin for themselves, with or without right. Which was cheering indeed for the Lady Scnena, who found herself not without advocates and allies in this foreign town.

But if the outlook was bright for her, it seemed it was black enough for David, with all this great force arrayed against him, and in this summer when the world was turned upside-down. For scarcely ever was there a year when the rivers sank so low, those waters on which Gwynedd counted for half her defence. There had been no rains since the spring, the sun rose bright every morning, and sank cloudless every night, pools dried up, and swamps became dry plains. And all those supporters of the Lord Griffith whetted their swords and watched the skies with joy, waiting for the order to march.

The Lady Senena sent a messenger at once to the abbey, to ask for an audience of the king, and his officers appointed her to come on the twelfth day of August. So we had time enough to wait, and to draw up in detail the petition she intended to present, together with her proposals for an alliance which should be of benefit to both parties. This kept her steward and clerk busy for some days, and I was employed to help in preparing fair copies of the clauses, for I had learned to write a good clear hand. I had also to help my mother take care of the two young princes, for now it was part of my mother's own duties to be waiting-maid to the Lady Gladys, so that I came in for much of the work of minding the little boys. And as they were full of curiosity and wonder at this strange and busy town, I was able to go with them sometimes about the streets, gaping at everything as simply as did the children, for it was as new to me as to them. So many fine buildings, such shops and market stalls, and such a bewildering parade of people I had never imagined. Those four noble churches were of stone, the houses mainly of timber, but large and splendid, the streets so full of life that it seemed the whole business of the kingdom had followed the court here, and London must be empty. And all the while this blue, unpitying sky over all, very beautiful, very ominous.

When the day came, the lady had her daughter, who was growing up very handsome, dressed with great care to adorn her beauty, and the two little boys also made as grand as might be. Rhodri, the elder, was a capricious and uncertain-tempered child, but not ill-looking when he was amiable, and David had always, even then, at five years old, a great sense of occasion, and could light some inward lamp of charm and grace at will, so that he truly shone, and women in especial were drawn to him like moths to flame. I do not know why it was, for I paid him no more attention than I did his brother, but David was much attached to me, and it was because he would have me with him that I was of the party that went before the king.

We went on foot, for it was not far. Only the Lady Senena and her daughter rode in a litter, for it was not fitting for them to arrive at the king's audience on foot. The road was by a fine, curving street that dropped steeply to the bridge on the English side, where there was a double gate, the first a deep tunnel in the town wall, and after it a tower set upon the bridge itself, of which the last span was a draw-bridge. And beyond the bridge, where a brook ran down into the river, the abbey mills stood, and the wall and gatehouse of the great enclosure loomed bright in the unfailing sunshine, with the square tower of the church over all. We went in procession over the bridge and along the broad road to the gateway, and so to the guest-houses where King Henry kept his court. In the anteroom his chamberlain met us, and went in before us to announce the lady.

She took the petition, carefully inscribed and rolled and sealed with the Lord Griffith's private seal, which she kept always about her, and marshalled us in order at her back, and so we went into the glow and brilliance of the royal presence, she first and alone, her daughter after her with my mother in attendance, Rhodri led by the steward, and I with David clinging to my hand. And of all of us he was the least awed and the most at ease.

It was a great room, draped with tapestries and green branches and bright silks, and full of people. The lady halted just within the doorway, and so did we all, and made a deep reverence to the throne. Then, as we moved forward again at the chamberlain's summons, I lifted my eyes, and looked for the first time upon King Henry of England, the third of that name.

He was seated in a high-backed chair at the dais end of the hall, with a great plump of lords and secretaries and officers on either side of him; a man not above medium tall, rather pale of countenance, with light brown hair and beard very carefully curled, and long, fine, clerkly fingers stretched out along the arms of his chair. He was very splendid in cloth of gold, and much jewelled. I saw the glitter before I saw the man, for he was like a pale candle in a heavy golden sconce, and yet he had some attraction about him, too, once I could see past the shell. I suppose he was then about thirty-four years old, and had been king from a child, among courtiers and barons old, experienced, greedy, and cleverer than he, and yet many of them were gone down into disaster, and he was left ever hopeful among the new, who might well prove as ruinous as the old, but also as transient. He had a kind of innocent shrewdness, light and durable. I never knew if it was real or spurious, but it made for survival. He had, as it turned out, other qualities, too, that taught him how to shed others and save himself, as slender trees give with the wind. But that was not in his face, it remained to be learned in hard lessons by those less pliable. That day he smiled on us with great gentleness and grace, and was all comfort and serenity. The only thing that caused me to tremble was a little thing of the body, that he could not help. He had one eyelid that hung a little heavier than the other, drooping over the mild brownness of his eye. It gave me a strange shock of distrust, as though one half of him willed to be blind to what the other half did, and would take no responsibility for it hereafter. But that was an unjust fancy, and I forgot it soon.

He was gracious, he leaned forward and stretched out a hand to the Lady Senena, and she sank to her knees before him, and took it upon her own hand, and kissed it. And that she knew how to do without losing one inch of her stature or one grain of her grandeur, as plain as she was, and the mother of five children, in this court full of the young and beautiful. He would have lifted her at once, but she resisted, retaining his hand in hers. She lifted the roll of her petition, and held it up to him. And whatsoever I have been, and however shaken between conflicting loyalties, I was wholly her man then. And the child clinging to my hand stood the taller with

41

pride, and glowed the more brightly.

'My liege lord,' said the Lady Senena, 'I pray your Grace receive and consider the plea of a wife deprived of her lord by his unjust imprisonment and more disgraceful disinheritance, wholly against law. I commit myself and my children to your Grace's charge, as sureties for my lord's and my good faith and fealty to your Grace. And I ask you for the justice denied elsewhere.'

As he took the roll from her, and as expertly had it removed from his hand by a clerk almost before he touched it, he said: 'Madam, we have heard and commiserated your plight, and are aware of your grievances. You are in safety here, and most welcome to us. You shall be heard without hindrance hereafter.' For there would be no bargaining here, this was a time for measuring and thinking, before the fine script I had put into those clauses came to be examined by older, colder eyes than mine. But he raised her very gallantly, and sat her at his knee on a gilded stool they placed for her. And she, though I swear she had never played such a part before, played it now with so large a spirit that in truth for the first time I loved her. She folded her hands in her gown like a saint, and only by the motion of her head beckoned us forward one by one.

'I present to your Grace my daughter Gladys....'

The girl bent her lissome knees and slender neck, very dark and bright in every colouring and movement, and kissed the king's hand, and lifted her long lashes and looked into his face. It was curiosity and not boldness, but I saw him startle, attracted and amused. The young one saw nothing but a man's fair face smiling at her, and smiled in response, marvellously. She hung between woman and child then, the child having the upper hand. And truly she was very comely, more than she knew.

'My son Rhodri. Your Grace is advised already that

my eldest son, Owen, is prisoner with his father, in defiance of all honour.'

'I do know it,' said the king. 'Child, you are welcome.' Not a word of Llewelyn, the second son. He could not advance her cause here, he was put out of mind, as though he no longer lived.

'My youngest son, David.'

I loosed his hand, and gave him a gentle push towards the throne, but he did not need it, he knew all that was required of him, and went his own God-given step beyond. He danced, there is no other word, to the step of the throne, and laid his flower of a mouth to the king's hand. He looked up and smiled. I heard all the women there – they were not many, but they were noble and of great influence – breathe out a sound like something between the sighing of the sea and the cooing of doves, for he was indeed a most beautiful and winning child. And the king, amused and charmed, lifted and handed him gently to his mother, and he stood by her unabashed and looked all round him, smiling, aware of approval. I drew back very quietly into the shadows, for I was not needed any more, not until he remembered and wanted me, and that he would not do while his interest was held. He had never been happier, he knew every eye was on him, and every lip smiled on him, even the king's. For Henry left a finger in his clasped hand, and withdrew it only when the hand relaxed of itself, and let the royal prisoner go.

They say he was a fond, indulgent father to his own children, though apt to tire of their company if they were with him long, and to grow petulant if they plagued him. His son and heir was then just past his second birthday, and the queen had a second babe in arms, but these were all left behind in the south, and I suppose it was pleasant to him to play gently for some minutes with a pretty child of whose company he could be rid whenever it grew irksome. For in that audience he spoke as often to the boy as to his mother, and got his answers just as readily. He asked after his adventures on this great journey, and David chattered freely about the ride, and about the wonders he had seen in Shrewsbury. And when he was asked what he would be and do when he was grown, he said boldly that he would be one of the king's knights. His mother gave him a swift, narrow look then, as doubtful as I if that was said in innocence, for clever children, even at five years old, know very well what will please. But since it did give pleasure she said no word of her qualms, then or afterwards. There is no harm in accepting aid where you find it.

So this open audience went very well, and gave promise for the closed conference which was appointed to follow the next day, and the Lady Senena made her withdrawing reverence and led her procession back to its lodging reasonably well content.

And for the hard bargaining that went on at this council at the abbey, the earnest after the show, I was not present, and cannot speak as to what passed. There were present at first only the Lady Senena and her steward on our part, and on the part of the crown King Henry himself for a part of the discussion, and with him his chancellor and his secretary. And after the terms were agreed certain of the marcher barons and the Welsh chiefs were called in to approve and to sign as guarantors. But the terms themselves I do know, for I was set to work making fair copies before ever the agreement was made public, two days later. They seemed to me curious enough, for I knew nothing of money, the minted money they valued, and could not conceive of a man's liberty and rights being reckoned in terms of the round pieces of metal they struck here in this town.

Yet so it was, for money entered into every transaction. After all their conferring, King Henry undertook, in the campaign he intended against the prince of Gwynedd, to bring about the release of the Lord Griffith from imprisonment in consideration of the sum of six hundred marks, and to restore him to his rightful share of the inheritance for three hundred more, one third of the whole sum to be paid in coin, and the remainder in cattle and horses. And a commission of lawful appraisers was to view the stock so rendered in payment, when they were delivered to the sheriff here in Shrewsbury, to make doubly sure that their value was equal to the sum due. To this document many of the marcher lords and Welsh princes also added their signatures as security. And the Lady Senena placed herself and her children under King Henry's protection, and her two youngest sons specifically in his charge, as hostages for her and her husband's future fealty.

Whether she was fully content with this arrangement I do not know, but it was the best she could get, and I think she felt secure that it would be of short term and soon resolved, and the restoration of half Gwynedd to her lord would make payment a light matter. For she listened with great eagerness to all the talk within the town, and paid attention to all the news she could get of the king's preparations, which indeed were impressive. And the season still continued bright without a cloud, and the rivers shrank into mere trickles in the meandering middles of their beds, even the Severn so low that a man could ford it where no fords were at other times. So all men said it was but a matter of marching into Wales, and the elusive warfare the Welsh favoured and excelled at would be impossible, for an army could go in force where normally marsh and mountain stream would prevent. And in a month all would be over.

And for once men said truth, for in a month all was over.

We stayed in our lodgings in Shrewsbury, King Henry's pensioners, when the army marched. After they were gone, the town seemed quiet indeed, but with a most ominous quietness, and for some time no news came They marched to Chester, where the nobles of the north with their knights were ordered to join the muster, and from there advanced westwards into Tegaingl without hindrance, and reached the river Clwyd, which was no let to them, and crossed the great marshes that surround Rhuddlan dry-shod as on a drained field, so rapidly, that Prince David was forced to withdraw or be cut off from his mountains. But even the mountains betrayed him, for they provided him neither rain nor cloud nor mist to cover him. Such a season had never been known in Snowdon. He razed to the rock his castle of Degannwy, on the hither side of Conway, when it was plain that he must abandon it, and he kept his army from the direct clash which must see it shattered. In the end he preferred to sue for peace rather than continue a war which could not be won, but only lost with great bloodshed or with none.

At Gwern Eigron on the river Elwy, the twenty-ninth day of August, the prince of Gwynedd made a complete surrender on terms to the king, and in King Henry's tent at Rhuddlan the pact was confirmed two days later. And a hard and bitter meeting that must have been between these two, uncle and nephew but very much of an age, kinsmen and enemies. And very hard and bitter were the terms of the surrender, though David kept his rank and the remnants of his principality.

Rumour of the end of the fighting came back to us in Shrewsbury early in September, while the army was still at Chester. The Lady Senena sent daily to the sheriff or the bailiffs for news of what most concerned her, her lord's fortunes, and I well remember the day when her steward came back from the castle glowing with the details at last. She was in the hall when he came, and I was taking down for her one more letter of the many with which she had throughout continued to solicit the favour of the powerful, especially those lords who held along the northern march. Therefore I was present when she received the word for which she waited.

'Madam,' said the old man, flushed with joy and importance, for it is always good to be the bearer of news long-desired and wholly welcomed, 'the Lord Griffith is freed, and handed over to his Grace at Chester, and your son with him. They will return here with the king's Grace within the week.'

She clasped her hands and coloured to the brow with delight, like a young girl, and said a fervent thanks to God for this deliverance. And fiercely she questioned him of those other matters, for she was a good hater as well as a loyal lover.

'And the terms? What becomes of all those impleaded lands, Powys, Mold, all those conquests held from their father? Does David give up all? All?'

'All!' he said. 'Everything Llewelyn Fawr took by force of arms goes back to those who claim it. Montalt gets back Mold after forty years. Gwenwynwyn's son will be set up in Powys, and Merioneth returns to Meredith's sons. All the Welsh princes who used to hold directly from the crown are to come back to the crown. Everything he fought for, he has lost!'

A strange thought came into my mind then that I was not listening to a Welsh princess and her officer speaking, but to English voices exulting over a defeated Wales.

'What, all the homages that belonged to King John are to come back to the crown again? A great loss!'

And I thought how the Gwynedd she looked to see divided now by force between the Lord Griffith and his brother was shrunken by all those fealties, and marvelled how she could be glad of it, even for her lord's own sake, for surely he was also a loser, or at best stood to gain only a meagre princedom. But she saw no false reasoning.

'And David will pay!' she said with passion. 'The expenses of this war, also! King Henry will not let that go by default.'

'Madam, he is to give up the whole cantref of Tegaingl, and Ellesmere also, these go to the crown. And there will be a further payment in money, a heavy fine.'

'His justice returns on his own head,' she said. 'And will my lord truly be here within the week, shall I see him again?'

'Madam, he is already with the king, they return together. Your son also.'

'And what provision is made for him? What lands are allotted to my lord?' She shook suddenly to a frightening thought. 'He'll hold them from the king, in chief? Not from David! Say not from David!'

'Direct from the crown, madam. It's agreed that the question shall be determined by his Grace's own court, according to Welsh custom or strict law, as may be decided. Our lord will be there to speak for himself.'

'Then no division is yet made. No,' she said, but with some doubt and reluctance, 'I see there could be no judgment yet. It is a matter for the court, in fairness. Then all will be well. And I did right to come. I tell you,' she said, for her humbly, 'sometimes I have wondered. Am I now justified?'

'Madam,' he said, 'my lord is on his way back to you and to his children, and the Lord Owen with him. What other answer do you need? They are free, and you have freed them.'

She was so abashed, and so glad, that briefly she shed tears, she who never wept. And she called the children, and told them their father was coming in a few days. At which David only stared and pondered with little understanding, for he hardly remembered his father.

I remember also the day that they came. All the citizens of Shrewsbury were out on the streets to see the army return, though the main body of men did not enter the town walls. But the king and his officers and barons rode through from gate to gate, from the castle to the abbey, where they halted again for two nights. The house where we lodged was very close to the street where they passed, and we went down into the crowd to watch, while the Lady Senena and the Lady Gladys had a place in the window of a burgess's house overhanging the route, and took the children with them.

That was a brave show, bright with pennants and surcoats and colours, the horses as fresh and fine as the riders, for there had been no great hardship or exertion in that brief war, no armour was dinted, and no banners soiled. We saw the king go by, a fair horseman, and at his fairest when he rode in triumph, for he swung ever between the rooftops and the mire, higher and lower in his exaltation and abasement than ordinary men, and this was an occasion unblemished by any doubts. I had not yet learned to know the faces and devices of those closest about him, though they all looked formidable enough and splendid enough to me. I saw them as a grand cavalcade of bright colours and proud faces, not as men in the manner that I was a man. Or almost a man, for I had not yet my years. These lived on another level. I knew no parallel for it in Wales, where no man felt himself less a man than another, or bridled his tongue for awe of the great. Great and small surely we had, and every man knew his place in the order, and respected both his own and every other soul's, but not with servility. In this land I felt great wonder and pleasure, but I was never at ease.

I stood with my mother and her husband – for I never thought of him as father to me in any way – among a hot and heaving throng, pressed body hard against body, watching these great ones ride by. And suddenly my mother gave a soft cry, and struggled to free a hand, and as ever, to touch me, not him. And never did this happen but he was aware of it, and I aware of his awareness, as a pain most piercing and hard to sustain. But she never knew it, as though what he felt could in no wise touch her. So she handled me eagerly by the shoulder in his sight, and cried: 'He is there! It is true, he's free!'

I doubt if I should have known the Lord Griffith for myself, for I had not seen him since I was five years old. He rode among a group of lords not far behind the king's own party, on a tall, raw-boned horse, for he was a massive man, full-blooded and well-fleshed, and had lost no bulk in his imprisonment. He towered almost a head over King Henry, and though he was white in the face from being so long shut away from the sun, he looked otherwise none the worse in health, and was now, like his lady, in very good spirits. At whose expense he was provided for this ride, both with clothes and mount, I do but guess, yet take it that as yet all he had came from King Henry. For he was fine in his dress, and his hair and beard, which were reddish fair like Rhodri's colouring, very elegantly trimmed. Close behind him rode a big boy of about fourteen, massively made like his father, but his thick crop of hair, which was uncovered to the sun, was fiery red, almost as red as the poppies in the headlands of the English fields. And that was Owen Goch, the firstborn son.

They passed by us, pale from their prison but bright with joy in their triumph, and people pointed them out for the Welsh princes, and waved hands and kerchiefs. The Lady Senena sat at her upper window motionless and silent, with tears on her cheeks, but her daughter leaned out and shook a silk scarf streaming out on the breeze, and called down to the riders so shrilly and joyfully that the Lord Griffith looked up, and saw his womenfolk weeping and laughing for pleasure at seeing him again live and free and acknowledged joint-heir of Gwynedd. Then the men below waved and threw glances and kisses as long as they were within sight, their chins on their shoulders, until the curve of the Wyle took them away, and the women embraced each other in floods of tears, and hugged the two little boys, and urged them to wave and throw kisses after their father's dwindling figure. For this was but the public presentment, and soon, when King Henry was installed at the abbey, there could be a private reunion even more joyful.

So it went that day. 'There goes one, at least, who has got everything he prayed for,' said my mother's husband, as we struggled back out of the crowd in the street, and drew breath in the courtyard of the house. And so we all agreed, except perhaps my mother, who went in to her mistress very thoughtful and absent, though she said no word.

We waited, and looked for the Lord Griffith to come to us and take up his dwelling in this same house, but instead a page came from the court in the abbey bearing a message from him, desiring his wife to remove herself and the children and all her party, to join him there. And so she did, proudly and in haste, for it seemed that her household was to be of the king's own circle. It was therefore in a guest apartment at the abbey that she at last embraced her lord, and he took his children also into his arms.

I think she had hoped, somewhat against reason, for a quick return to Wales, but she conceded that he spoke good sense when he said that this could not be done overnight. There would be no return until the question of the equitable division of lands had been settled, and that could only be by discussion, and under King Henry's patronage, and would take time and patience. Did it matter, when the end was certain justice? And she owned that indeed they owed everything to the king, and must abide his judgment, as the homage for the lands granted would be due directly to him. And first, said the Lord Griffith confidently, it was fitting and necessary that they should move south to London in the king's train, as was his wish, for thither the defeated David must come the next month, according to the agreement, to appear before a council of the king's magnates and ratify the peace. And at that the Lady Senena was well content, for she longed to see that humiliation visited upon her lord's rival and enemy.

'Let him eat the hard bread he has doled out to others,' she said vengefully. 'And we shall sit among the king's honoured companions, and watch him swallow it.'

So when the king dispersed the middle English part of his muster, and moved on southwards to London, all our party went in his train, just as she had foreseen, and she and her lord and her children were favoured with King Henry's frequent notice and conversation on the journey, and their comfort attended to by his officers wherever we halted by the way. A daily allowance was made for their maintenance, generous enough for all expenses, until the Lord Griffith should be established in his own lands and as the king's vassal. And in due time David ap Llewelyn came, as he had promised, in what state was left to him, to meet with King Henry's council on the twenty-fourth day of October. And if his bearing was proud enough, and his person gallant, yet his humiliation was as deep as even the Lady Senena could have wished, for the king made still new inroads on what remained to him, demanding that Degannwy be handed over to the crown in payment of the expenses of the war, and David had no choice but to submit even to this deprivation. Everything he had pledged he made good. Roger of Montalt got back his castle of Mold, Griffith ap Gwenwynwyn took possession of his father's lands in Powys, the king's lieutenant in the southern march garrisoned Builth, Degannwy passed to the crown, and the king began the building of a new castle at Diserth, near Rhuddlan, for the better containing of his half-ruined neighbour. Everything the Lady Senena had foreseen came to pass, but for one particular.

Neither she nor the Lord Griffith witnessed the despoiling. Very richly and comfortably they were lodged in London, when they reached that city, and their generous allowance continued, enough for all their needs. But their apartment was high in the keep of the Tower of London, that great White Tower, and their privacy well guarded by chosen attendants, though none of their choosing, behind safe lock and key.

It was done so smoothly and plausibly that it took her more than a week to realise that, in spite of all the smiles and promises, she had but rescued her lord from a Welsh prison to fling him into an English one. The king's whole train took up residence in the Tower – for this tower, as they call it, is a city in itself – as soon as we came to London, and there King Henry kept court some days,

53

while the southern part of his host was dispersed again to its own lands. So there was no occasion to wonder that all our party were quartered there, too, the royal children in a small house within the green, with my mother and me in attendance, and my mother's husband as groom and manservant, the Lord Griffith and his lady in a well-furnished apartment in the great keep. The men she had brought with her as escort from Wales were withdrawn to the guardrooms with the garrison, the steward and the clerk had a small lodging in another corner. And thus we were distributed about that great fortress, within easy reach one of another, yet separate. But the whole place being, as it were, one vast household, there was no occasion to wonder, or to question the host's use of his own house and his arrangements for his honoured guests.

For two days no one of us felt any need to look beyond the walls, for we had this new and strange world to examine, and it did not appear until the Lord Griffith made to ride out and take a curious look at London, on the third day, that the gates were impassable to him. The guard turned him back, without explanation but that he had his orders, which it was not for him to question. The Lord Griffith applied forthwith to the officer, with the same result, and then, still in good-humour, for he suspected nothing but a mistake, or some misapprehension as to who he was, to the lieutenant. The lieutenant entreated his patience, but the order did indeed apply to him, for the king was concerned that he should not yet adventure his life in the streets, where he was not known to the citizens, and might be all too well known to some stray Welshman embittered by the recent war, for many such worked and studied in the city, and some who favoured David's cause would certainly be gathering in preparation for his coming. This he accepted as a compliment, that the king should be at such pains to guarantee his safety, however this kindly care limited his movements for a while.

But some few days later he enquired again, growing restive, and on being refused exit without his Grace's own orders to the contrary, requested an audience with the king. But it seemed King Henry had withdrawn for a few days to Westminster, having unfinished business with his council there.

Perhaps he had, for at this time it may be he had not quite made up his mind where his best interests lay. If that be true, in two days more he had come to a decision, for that day the Lord Griffith was stopped not at the outer or the inner gate, but at the door of his own apartments. Two officers, unknown to him, unimpressed by him, perfectly indifferent to his protests, informed him that they had orders to allow the Lady Senena to pass in and out as she pleased, that she might visit her children when she would, take exercise, spend her nights either here with her lord or below in the house where her family was lodged. But that he was to remain within these rooms. They no longer cared to pretend that it was for his own protection. Whatever he needed for his comfort should be provided, the maintenance the king paid him would continue, he should not want for service. But he was not to pass the door of this chamber.

Nor did he, ever again.

It was she who raged, protested, harried every official she could reach with her complaints. He had known captivity before, and recognised its familiar face instantly, and knew his own helplessness. Nor had he the refuge she possessed, for a time at least, in disbelief. If she could get to King Henry, if she could but speak with him in person, all this grotesque error would be quickly set right. She had his promise, somewhat of the price he had asked she had already paid, she would not believe that he knew how her husband was used, or would countenance it for one moment when he did learn of it. So she went valiantly from man to officer, from officer to minister, always put off, always persisting, passed from hand to hand, never getting any answers. As for her husband, he let her do what she would, but he expected nothing.

And as long as she continued resolute, indignant and bold, she never reached King Henry's presence, for he well knew how to protect himself from embarrassment. Still he was at his palace at Westminster, and when she begged to be received by him there, he was unwell, and could see no one. Then she grew cunning, and came mildly with a request for some minor concession to her lord's comfort, and King Henry, receiving these reports of her tamed and pliant, granted her an audience, and talked with her affably of the Lord Griffith's health, promising her the amenities she asked. But when she took heart and spoke of freedom, and of a promise given, the king, still smiling, looked the other way, and the audience was over. Then she, too, knew that she wasted her pains.

She did not go back at once to her husband, for she was too bitter and too deeply shaken. She came to us to shed her grief and rage. For then she believed that she understood what had happened to her and hers.

'They are in conspiracy together,' she said, 'uncle and nephew, the one as false as the other! This was all agreed between them, behind what was written into this peace. David, since he must, would give up what he could not hold, and give it up with the better will since he was promised then, he must have been promised, his brother should never take from him the half of what was left. This is what they have done to him between them!'

There were many, as I know, who thought as she did. But I cannot believe it was so. All defeated as he was, and helpless, what persuasion had David to induce his uncle to prevent Griffith from claiming the half of his shrunken realm? None! There was nothing he had to offer in return, and King Henry gave nothing for nothing. No, I think there was a more private argument that swayed that devious personage. I do believe he had meant to do as he had promised, but after his return to London had considered again, more carefully, what might follow. For if he set up Griffith in the moiety of Gwynedd, thus forcibly removing the worst emnity between these two brothers, and turning them into neighbours of one blood who must both make the best of straitened circumstances, might they not, once the old bitterness had receded by a year or two, come to consider that they had a mutual interest in enlarging that realm to its old borders? And had they not, together, the backing of all the Welsh princes, a solidarity David had never enjoyed? Nor could there soon be such another summer, traitor and vindictive to Wales. Yes, after his fashion I think King Henry reasoned wisely enough. For if he held Griffith in his power, not so vilely used as to alienate him incurably, he could be held for ever over David's head, the strongest weapon against him should he ever take arms again for his lost lands. One move in rebellion, and Griffith could be in Chester with English arms to back him, and hale away half the Welsh princes to his side as before. No, while Griffith lay here in the king's hand, like a drawn sword, David could not stir.

I am the more firmly convinced of this by all that King Henry did in the matter thereafter. On the one hand, he took every precaution to secure his prisoners more impregnably. It soon occurred to him that a vigorous woman like the Lady Senena, who had had the courage and decision to act once for herself and appeal from Wales to England, might have it in her yet, given a suitable focus for her cause, to appeal as fiercely from England to Wales. She could not make use of her husband now, except as a distant symbol, not apt for rousing men to arms, but there was still Owen Goch, his father's image and now, by Welsh custom, a man. Thus with every personal flattery and consideration, but implacably, Owen Goch was removed from our household, upon the pretext of providing more suitably for his father's heir, and made prisoner in a room high in the keep, like the Lord Griffith himself. True, he was allowed exercise within the walls, but with a retinue which was in reality a guard, and armed. The younger boys were thought no threat, and could be let run on a loose rein. And the lady, while her chicks were cooped here – all but one, and that stray was neither heard of from Wales then nor mentioned in England – would not forsake them. Also, all the Welsh men-at-arms were gradually dispersed from the Tower. Some, I know, took service with the king's men, some, I fancy, vanished when David drew the rags of his royalty about him and rode again for home. Only we who cared for the children were left. No doubt we seemed harmless enough. Even the servants who waited on Griffith and his lady were now English. The old steward they let alone until he died in the winter, for he was past sixty years. And the clerk vanished to some new service, I never knew where, for I was considered able enough to shift for us all, should there be need of any drawing of documents in Welsh and English thereafter. Thus we were stripped of the reminders of our own land.

But on the other hand, the king was by no means inclined to alienate us in other ways, once he had us tightly secured. For as soon as he was aware that the

Lady Senena had fallen into some state between resignation and despair, and accepted her fate, she was invited very often and as of right into the queen's company, and became a minor figure of this court. And since she could do nothing about her deprivation, she took what she could get and made the best of it, and as I believe, those two strong-willed, resolute women got on well together by reason of their likeness, where had they met on truly equal terms they might have clashed resoundingly for the same reason. But the queen could be generous and warm without condescension to one who was not a rival, and the Lady Senena could take with dignity from one she felt to be at once her creditor and debtor. The Lady Gladys, too, with her budding beauty, became an admired figure among the young women of the queen's retinue, and was much favoured by her, and after some months whispers began to go round that a good match might be made for her. As for the two little boys, they went in and out freely among the other noble children about the court, and being very young, soon took this lavish state for their right, and forgot the more austere customs and habits of Wales. David in particular, with his beauty and his winning ways, was made much of by the noblewomen, and became a favourite even with the king. And surely this imprisonment seemed to them rather an enlargement, for never had they been so indulged and lived so finely.

Thus King Henry hedged his interests every way, keeping his puppets close under his hand, but treating them with every consideration and make-believe honour that should maintain them sharpened and ready for use at need. And their efficacy was made plain, for that year ended with no word of any unrest in Wales, and all through the two years that followed the same heavy quietness held. David of Gwynedd knew only too well

59

the sword that dangled over his head, and he went peacefully, minding his lopped princedom and biding his time, with never a false move.

As for us, what is there to tell? We lived a life unbelievably calm on the surface, but it was a furtive, watchful calm, in which all but the children moved with held breath. Yet no man can live for ever taut like a strung bow, and I remember days when indeed this life of ours seemed pleasant enough, comfortable and well-fed as we were, and like the children we drew perilously near to being content with it.

But not the lady. She closed her lips upon her great grievance, but in her heart she thought of nothing else. I think she hoped at first that David would blaze up again in revolt, and cause her husband to be taken hastily out of his cage and sent with a strong force to draw off Welsh allegiance from him. But as the slow year wore away, and the uneasy peace held fast, she lost hope in this, and fretted after some other way. And she took into her confidence the only Welshman left her, but for myself, still a boy, and that was my mother's husband.

It was fitting that those two should cleave together, for next to her, and doubtless the Lord Griffith himself, whom now we never saw, my mother's husband was the unhappiest among us. For that slothful ease of mind under which the rest of us laboured in this well-furnished prison was impossible to him. There was no taste but wormwood ever in his mouth, and no weather but winter and cold about him, his torment being perpetual, for my mother was ever before his face and by his side, and even in his bed, and at all times submissive and dutiful, and at all times indifferent to him, and by this time he was assured, whether he admitted it or no, that there was nothing he could do, between this and death, to change her or himself. He had her, and he would never have her. Her hate he could have borne, but as she could not love, so she could not hate him. She was now thirty-four years old, and even more beautiful than as a girl, and he could neither live happily with her nor without her.

So it was some relief at least to his restlessness when the Lady Senena began to employ him as news gatherer for her about the Tower. I was not in their confidence, but I saw that he spent much of his time wandering about the fortress, observing at what hours the guard was changed at every gate, and when the wardens made their rounds, and every particular concerning the daily order of this city within a city. To this end he made himself agreeable and useful to the guards, and made himself out, surely truthfully enough, as weary and discontented for lack of work, so that after some weeks he had a few regular familiars among them who were willing to use him as messenger, and would talk freely to him. So patiently was all done that there were some he might truly call his friends. From them he brought in morsels of news from Wales more than were to be heard about the court, where the Lady Senena might pick them up for herself. Also, being very wise with horses, he made himself well accepted in the stables, and was several times among the grooms who went out to buy or to watch at the horse sales at Smithfield on Fridays. And as I know, after the second such occasion the Lady Senena gave him money for some purposes of her own.

It was late in the autumn of the year twelve hundred and forty-three when he came back from the outer world after a trip to buy sumpter ponies, and was closeted a while, as was usual, with the lady. It was as they came out into the hall where I was sitting with my mother and

61

the children that he turned and looked again, and closely, into her face, and said: 'Madam, I have heard mention made of your son Llewelyn.'

It was the first time that name had been uttered openly among us since we had left Shrewsbury, though what she had told her lord in private I do not know. She halted as though she had turned to ice, and in her face I could read nothing, neither hostility nor tenderness.

'What can the horse-traders of London know of my son Llewelyn?' she said, in a voice as impenetrable as her countenance.

'From a Hereford dealer who buys Welsh mountain ponies, and trades as far as Montgomery,' he said. He did not look at her again, and he did not speak until she asked.

'And what does this dealer say of my son?'

'Two drovers came down from Berwyn with ponies. They told him they were bred on their lord's lands in Penllyn. And the name of their lord was Llewelyn ap Griffith. He lives, madam, he is well, he has his manhood, and he is set up on his own lands.'

'Set up by his uncle,' she said, so drily that I could not tell whether there was any bitterness there, or any wonder, or whether she was glad in her heart that he should be living and free, and in some sort a princeling, or whether she grudged him all, and chiefly his freedom. 'So he got his pay,' she said, 'for betraying me, after all. Why else should David give him an appanage, and he with so little left for himself?'

My mother's husband said bluntly, for he had the Welsh openness with those he served: 'Madam, if he had betrayed you we should never have reached the border. Do you think one well-mounted courier could not move faster than we did, with two litters and a gaggle of children? He got his commote for soldier service. These men of his said he was in arms with his uncle at Rhuddlan.'

'There was no blood shed there,' she said sharply, 'and little fighting.' But whether she said it to belittle what he had done or to reassure herself in face of a danger she had not known one of her children was venturing, I could not be sure. And then she said in a muted cry, gripping her hands together: 'He was not yet thirteen years old!'

Then I knew that for all her hard front, and the bitterness that tore her two ways where he was concerned, she still loved him.

That winter came and passed in mild, moist weather, with scarcely any frost but a sprinkling of rime in the mornings, washed away by rain or melted by thin sunshine long before noon. And I noticed that daily the Lady Senena watched the skies and the wind, and bided her time, and was often private with my mother's husband for short whiles. In February, when for the first time the true winter came down a fair fall of snow and then iron frost to bind it, it seemed to me that their eyes grew intent and bright, as though they had been waiting only for this. And when it held all the last ten days of February, with every day they drew breath more easily and hopefully, and spoke of the weather as though it held more meaning for them than for us, how the word went that the great marshes of Moorfields, outside the north gate of the city, were frozen over hard as rock, but with overmuch deadening snow for good sport, so that the young men who went out there for play were forced to sweep small parts of the ice for their games. And I thought how this way from the city would be the quickest and most secret, once that marsh was past, for the forest came close on that side. But they told me nothing, and I asked nothing.

The last day of February matched all those before. My mother's husband went out from us in the afternoon, and did not come back with the night, but the Lady Senena came in the dusk from visiting her lord, and told us that she would spend the night in the lodging with us, for the Lord Griffith was a little unwell, and she had entreated him to rest, and the guards not to disturb him again until morning.

What she told my mother I do not know, but those two women slept – or at least lay, for I think much of the night they did not sleep at all – in the same bed that night, and I know they talked much, for I heard their voices whenever I stirred from my own slumber. The girl had a little chamber of her own, and the boys slept as children do, wholeheartedly and deeply. I lay in the dark, listening to those two muted voices within, that spoke without distinguishable words, my mother's pitched lower, and now that I heard them thus together, far the calmer and more assured, and the lady's tight, brittle and imploring, like one lost in prayer. I doubt she was not heard.

Towards dawn she slept. When the first light began I was uneasy with the silence, and I got up and pulled on my hose and shirt and cotte, and went stealthily and lifted the latch of the high chamber, to be sure if they breathed and lived. For sleep and silence draw very close to death.

There was a wick burning in a dish of fat, paling now that a little light came in from the sky. My mother lay open-eyed, high on the pillows, her face turned towards me as though she had known before ever I touched the latch that I was coming. She held that great lady cradled asleep on her breast like a child, and over

64

the greying head she motioned to me, quite gently, to go back and close the door. And so I did, and in a few moments she came out to me.

At this time I was already taller than she, but she was so slender and straight that she had a way of towering, not rigidly or proudly, but like a silver birch tree standing alone. She had only a long white shift on her, and her arms were bare, and all her long, fair hair streamed down over her shoulders, and hung to her waist. In this harsh frost, now twelve days old, she seemed to feel no chill. And I have said she was beautiful, and strange.

'Make no sound,' she said in a whisper, 'but let her sleep, she has great need. Samson, I am not easy, I cannot see clear. Somewhere there is a death.'

Daily there is a death waiting for someone, for one who departs and others who remain to mourn. But she looked at me with those eyes that missed what others see and saw what others miss, and I knew that this was very near.

I was afraid, for I understood nothing, though something I did suspect. I asked her: 'Mother, what must I do?'

'Take your cloak,' she said, very low, and peering before her with eyes fixed as it were on a great distance, 'and go and look if there is anyone stirring about the keep, or under Lord Griffith's windows.'

So I wrapped my cloak about me, and crept out shivering into the icy morning, where the light as yet was barely grey, though very clear, and still full of fading stars. It was too early for anyone to be abroad but the watch, and I knew their rounds, even if they kept to them strictly, and on such mornings I had known them none too scrupulous about patrolling every corner, preferring the warmth of the guardrooms. I went softly, keeping under the walls of the houses, and left their shelter only when I must. I could see the great, square hulk of the tower outlined clear but pale against the sky, and beyond it, across the open ground, the tooth-edged summit of the curtain wall, and the ruled line of the guard-walk below its crest. All the grass was thick and creaking with rime, the bushes that stood silent and motionless in the stillness rang like bells when I brushed too close, and shed great fronds of feathery ice on my hose and shoes. I drew closer, circling the rim of the ditch and avoiding the main face where the great door-way was, and the ditch was spanned. There was such a silence and stillness that I should have heard if another foot had stirred in the crisp snow, but there was nothing to hear. I was the only creature abroad.

The Lord Griffith's apartment was very high at the rear part of the keep, with two small windows at the base of one of the corner turrets. I made my way round by the rim of the ditch, which was deep and wide, and for the most part kept clear of briars and bushes. Every-thing was quiet and nothing strange, until I came under the part where his dwelling was, and looked up at those two round-headed windows, set deep in the stone. And hanging from the ledge of one of them I saw a dangling line of knotted cloth, no more than two or three yards long, that seemed to end in a fringe of torn threads, light enough to stir in the high air while the coil above hung still. My eyes were young and sharp, and this frayed material I knew for a piece of brocaded tapestry such as might furnish the covering of a bed, or wall-hangings.

Then, halfway to understanding, I looked below, and at first saw nothing stranger than a stony outcrop break-ing the level of the ditch's grassy bottom, under the window, for this, too, was covered thick with rime. But as I looked I knew that it was no stone, but a man, humped heavily upon one shoulder and half-buried in the ground, and about him the rope that had broken and let him fall had made serpentine hollows in the snow and then made shift to heal them with its own new growths of hoar-frost. The pool of darkness under and about him I had taken for a shelf of level shale, for it was so fast frozen and sealed over with rime, but it was his blood. And at first I had thought this body was headless, for he had so fallen that his head was flattened and driven into his shoulders.

The Lord Griffith, ever a big and well-fleshed man, had grown heavier still in his enforced idleness, too heavy for the ancient and treacherous drapings of his bed to sustain him. His hopes and his captivity were alike over. He had escaped out of his prison and out of this world.

CHAPTER III

———————

There was nothing I or any but God could do for him any longer. All I could do was creep back, shivering, to the living, and tell what I had seen. For when the warders of the Tower discovered it there would be such an outcry that we, shocked and stricken as we were, had no choice but to be prepared for it, and ready and able to meet all that might be said and done. Thus, that I might know the better what I was about, I came to hear the rest of it in haste.

The rope she had contrived to take in to him, doubtless coiled about her body, for the warders examined all the gifts she carried to the prisoner, had proved too short at the test, and he had eked it out with the furnishings of his chamber. Unhappy for him that he secured this makeshift part of his line to the upper end. If he had trusted only the last few yards to its rotten and deceitful folds he might have fallen without injury, and made his escape. As it was, my mother's husband, shivering in the cold on the outer side of the curtain wall, had waited in vain until there was no hope left, and he must take thought for his own life, for he could not re-enter the Tower gates without condemning himself, if the plot was discovered. So there would be no shrouded travellers riding out at Moorgate with the first light, across the frozen marsh into the forest. Or at the best, only one ...

Somehow the thing passed over us, and we endured it. There was no sense in blaming wife or children, or the servants who served them, in face of a grief that could not now be remedied. We watched out the time, owned to nothing, told nothing we knew. And they took him up, that great, shattered man, and gave him a prince's mourning and burial, for King Henry was as anxious as any to be held blameless, well knowing that there would be those who suspected him in the matter of this death. But I know what I saw, and what was after told to me. Moreover, after our lord himself, there was no man lost more by this disaster than the king, for with Griffith dead he had no hold to restrain David, and no fit weapon to use against him. It was the end of his fine plans, as it was of ours. There was nothing he could do but begin over again, and mend his defences as best he could.

My mother's husband did not come back, and though he was quickly missed, and certainly hunted, they did not find him. But for more than a month we waited in anxiety, for fear he should be dragged back, for him they would not have spared, having found the line he had secretly secured from a merlon down the outer face of the curtain wall in a secluded corner, for his lord's escape. It seems to me that all had been very well done, but for that too-short rope, for late though he must have left his own flight, yet he got clean away with both the horses he had provided, for they made enquiry everywhere after good riding horses stabled for pay and abandoned, and none were ever reported. Though truly the coper who had such a beast dropped into his hands masterless and gratis might well hold his peace about it.

Afterwards, when we spoke of this lost venture again, for at first there was a great silence over it, they spoke also before me, being the last man they had. For two husbands were lost, one living and one dead, and they were left with only me, a man according to Welsh law by one year and some months. And freely they said in my hearing the deepest thoughts of their minds and regrets of their hearts, and strange hearing they were. For those two women were changed from that day. The Lady Senena, who had never doubted her own judgment and rightness, was saddened into many misgivings and questionings, and sometimes she said:

'It was I who killed him. Not now, but long ago. I might have prevailed on him to accept a second place, to be content as his brother's vassal, and he might now have been alive and free both, and a man of lands, too. But I was as set as he on absolute justice. Is it now justice God has dealt out to me?'

Now much of this I remembered, as men remember the burden of an old song, familiar but without a name, until it came to me that she echoed the entreaties of Llewelyn, that last day before he left her to go to his duty. But I never reminded her, and I think she did not recall where she first heard this prophecy: 'It would not cost him so high as you will cost him, if you go on with this.' She had cost him life and all, but what profit in telling her so?

And my mother, who all these years had lived with that other man, had lain in his arms, cooked food for him, washed for him, been pliant and submissive to him, and all without letting him set foot over the doorsill of her mind and heart, and often without seeming to know that he lived and breathed beside her, she took to listening with reared head every time the guard passed, or if voices were raised in the courtyards, her eyes wide and her breath held, until she was satisfied that they had not found and hauled him back, bloodied and beaten, to answer for his loyalty with his life. And when this time was past, still she would say suddenly over the fire at night:

'I wonder which way he took, and where he is now?'

I told her he would certainly make for Wales, for his repute was clean there, and he would not want for a lord to take him into service. And I said that he must be safe over the border already, out of the king's reach.

But that was not all that ailed her. For as often as the night was cold she would be wondering if he had a warm cloak about him, and when the spring storms came it was: 'I hope he has a roof over him tonight, and a good fire. He takes cold easily.'

Also, where she had always called him by his name, which was Meilyr, and only now did I begin so to think of him, as a man unique and yet subject to fear and pain and cold like me, now she never spoke a name, but said always: 'he'. 'I wish he took better keep of himself, I doubt he'll be out even in this weather.' 'He never liked leaving Wales. I pray he has comfort there now.' And once she cried out in enlightenment and distress: 'I was not good to him!' And once, in wonder and awe, she said as if to herself: 'He loved me.'

Now when the news of the Lord Griffith's death reached Wales, as news from England did almost as fast as the east wind could blow that way, the manner and suddenness of it, the circumstance that it took place, like a blow aimed at Wales itself, on St David's day, the injustice of the imprisonment which had brought it about, all these combined to make him a hero and martyr, who perhaps had been neither, and also to give to his whole story a fervent Welsh glow that turned every enmity against England, and quite misted over the old dissensions between Griffith and his brother.

Long afterwards I heard an old bard at Cemmaes singing a lament for Griffith, made at his reburial at Aberconway, and hymning the great grief and indignation of the Lord David at this untimely cutting-off. And I

71

was still young enough to make some mock of his singing, for I said that David had had good reason to be
glad of the deliverance, for it set him free to strike afresh,
and with a united Wales at his back now, for his right.
And the old man, though he did not deny it, was undisturbed.

'For,' said he, 'have you room in you for only one
view at a time, and do you never look both forward and
back together?'

I said that there was something in what he said, but
nevertheless such extravagance of grief over a brother
he fought with all his life, and whose removal eased his
way to glory, was strangely inconsistent.

'When you have half my years,' he said, 'you will have
learned that where the human heart is concerned there
is nothing strange in inconsistency. Only what is too
consistent is strange.'

So it may be that there was truth in the story that
David grieved sincerely over the fate of his half-brother,
and nothing contradictory in the fiery vigour with which
he took advantage of it.

They had only one leader this time, not two, and only
one cause, not two. Barely nine weeks after the Lord
Griffith died, the Lord David had entered into an alliance with all the Welsh chiefs, but for those very few,
like Gwenwynwyn's son in Powys, who were more English marcher barons in their thinking than princes of
Wales. And before June began they were in the field,
stirring up the spirit of revolt in every corner of the land,
raising and training levies, and making rapid raids almost
nightly across the border, and into that part of Powys
that bordered Eryri, the citadel of Snowdon, the abode
of eagles. King Henry's castle of Diserth, built after his
bloodless victory of three years before, was in some

danger of being cut off from Chester, whence all its supplies and reinforcements must come, and by mid-June the whole of the march was in arms.

But David did more, for he formally repudiated the treaty made under duress with King Henry, and sent an envoy with letters to Pope Innocent stating his case, and appealing for support in maintaining the independent right of Wales. This did not come to light until later in the year, when the king was greatly startled and incensed to receive a writ from the abbots of Cymer and Aberconway, as commissioners for the pope, summoning him to appear at the border church of Caerwys, to answer the charge that he had discarded the promised arbitration in his dispute with David, and resorted wantonly to war, thus procuring by force what should only have been decided, perhaps differently, by discussion and agreement. I spoke with a clerk who had been in council when this writ was delivered, and I vouch for the terms of it on his word. And I have heard it said, though for this I cannot vouch, that the one particular factor which most enraged David, and put it in his mind to resort to the pope, was a rumour reaching him that King Henry, in his casting about for a fresh hold on what he had gained, after the restraint of Griffith was removed, had secretly considered having his elder son Edward, the long-legged four-year-old who ran wild about the stables with our young David, declared Prince of Wales. It may be so. If he was not cherishing this intent then, he certainly did so later. And if true, it was justification enough for tearing up the treaty.

Howbeit, the king naturally did not go to Caerwys, but merely made haste to send fresh letters and envoys to Pope Innocent on his own account, putting his own case, no doubt very persuasively. Yet this ploy filled up the latter months of this year, and caused him to walk

73

warily until he got the answer he wanted, transferring the case once again from Welsh to English law, the English purse being the heavier. So Wales gained half a year in preparing for the battle to come.

At first the defence was left to the wardens of the march, for Henry still preferred to concentrate on compiling his evidence for the pope, and sharpening for use the only subtle weapon he had left. He withdrew Owen Goch from his prison, took him into his own household, and nursed his ambition and ardour until he prevailed upon him to swear allegiance to England in return for the king's support in winning his birthright.

The Lady Senena was no longer so innocent as to believe that she could repose any trust in King Henry's faithfulness, but she had still a shrewd confidence in his self-interest, and indeed it seemed that his need of Owen at this pass was urgent enough to ensure his good behaviour towards him. She therefore made no objection when her son eagerly accepted the king's offer, and willingly swore fealty to him. But in private she advised him to be always on his guard, and in particular to acquiesce until he found out what the king had planned for him. 'For,' said she with a grim smile, 'either Shrewsbury or Chester, at need, is nearer to Wales than the Tower.'

This Owen the Red was then seventeen years old, and with every day more like his father in appearance, very well-grown and already more than six feet tall. He was not ill-looking, but less striking than the Lord Griffith by reason of a certain too-emphatic sharpness in his features, where his sire's for all their impetuosity and pride had been good-humoured. Owen had all his father's rashness and arrogance, but lacked the warmth and generosity with which he could turn back and make amends. His body bade fair to grow as wide, but his mind and nature never would, they closed against other men in suspicion and ready for jealousy.

It may be that his imprisonment, first in Criccieth and then in London, had done something to narrow him, but I think it did not change, but only aggravate, his tendencies. Certainly it had not been arduous here in England, however he had chafed at it, and it had done nothing to teach him patience or humility. The first offer of sovereignty in Gwynedd had him reaching for it greedily. I think King Henry did not have to exert much persuasion to get him to promise homage for it. And if the fulfilment of his hopes and the wearing of the talaith were delayed, he got something by way of earnest at once, for he was very richly fitted out with clothes at the crown's expense, and provided with a horse and a small retinue to go with him, suitable to a native prince coming home.

The place chosen for his bid was Chester, the nearest strong base to Eryri. And since he must set out squired and escorted almost wholly by English retainers, and with an officer of the king to supervise and direct his efforts, he had need of someone who could write well both in Welsh and English, and Latin, too, if need arose. And there was no one but me. So I became clerk and squire to Owen the Red.

My mother had lost her childlike look since Meilyr fled from London. I know not how it was, but she had grown more comfortable and ordinary, and as though in some way nearer. Much as I had loved her, and she me, being embraced by her, touching her, walking with her had been like touching a picture or a carving, but now she was flesh. And very hard it was for me to leave her, but she willed it so, for she was wholly devoted to the Lady Senena's household, having lived for this family all her days. So I said submissively that I would go.

'And think,' she said, sitting with me that last night, after the children were asleep, 'how close this town of Chester is to the commote of Ial. He was born there, west of the Alun, he may well have gone back there. Surely if he hears that the Lord Owen is in Chester and calling up his men, he will come to him there.'

Hearing her was like another echo in my mind. For she had but one 'he' who needed no naming.

I said: 'He may well.' But did we know whether he was alive or dead?

'It may be,' she said, 'that you will meet him there.'

'And if I should,' I said, 'have you any message to him?'

She sighed, saying: 'It is too late. I shall never see him again.' And I think she was a little sad, but with her it was not easy to know, for there was always a withdrawn sadness about her, and where its roots lay, even now that her feet trod the same earth with the rest of us, I never could fathom.

On that last evening before we rode from London she took out, from the box where she kept her few ornaments, a plain silver ring with an oval seal, a deep-cut pattern of a hand severed at the wrist, holding a rose. I had never seen it before, nor, I think, had any other person among us, except, perhaps, her husband. She put it on my finger, and bade me take it with me, for it was my father's, and who knew? – it might yet bring me in contact with him. And that was the first and last time that she spoke of him to me, at least in all the time I had been of an age to understand and remember. It was long since I had even given a thought to that unknown man-at-arms who had fathered me, and when first she said 'your father' I own I took her to be referring to Meilyr, even though she had never before called him so. But then I knew that of him she would only have felt it needful to say: 'It was *his*!' Yet the first man who took her I do believe she loved, however briefly, and the second, the one to whom she was lawfully given, I doubt she never did, not even then, when his absence was ever-present with her as his presence had never been. For indeed she was always a strange woman.

So I promised her I would wear it, and did so, I confess, with some pride, as though I had acquired with it a place in some legitimate line. And the next day I kissed her, and set out.

It was no easy matter being clerk and personal servant to Owen Goch, for he had grown accustomed to the English ways after his recent heady novitiate at King Henry's court, and required that servants should be servile, while I had still the Welsh habit of speaking my mind freely even to my masters. Familiarity he would not stomach now, but cut it off short, with lashing reproof, or if his mood was ill, with a ready blow, so that I learned to keep my distance in word as well as fact. But once this was accepted, we got on well enough on such terms as he dictated and I endured with an equal mind. It was less wise of him to use somewhat the same tone and manner with the English fighting men who surrounded him, or at least the lower ranks among them, for he knew well enough how to moderate his pride with the knights and their commander. But Owen, ever over-sanguine, felt himself within grasp of the talaith that should have been his father's, and he would be a prince in every part.

To John de Rohan, who was in fact his guard and keeper rather than the captain of his escort, I am sure he ranked rather as a kind of engine of war on two legs, an expensive but hopefully valuable weapon, somewhat irritating and cumbersome to manipulate about the country, but effective once brought to the proper spot.

I was of an age then to get more profit from adventuring about the world, and in that summer weather I used my eyes and ears to good effect, and found great pleasure in the pageant of man and season and countryside. And often for days, and ever longer as time passed, I forgot my mother and the Lady Senena, and the life we had left behind, and so, I am sure, did Owen Goch. I knew well enough, if he did not, that we were no more free than we had been in the Tower, but it was hard to believe it while we rode in the sunshine thus, and fed well and lay comfortably at every day's end.

We got a ceremonial welcome in Chester, all that Owen could have wished, for they hoped much from him. John Lestrange, the warden of the northern march, received us and saw us installed in a fine lodging, and there was set up the office that was to busy itself about drafting proclamations and appeals to the Welsh, and circulating them throughout the Middle Country as far as Conway, and by means of various agents, even deeper into Eryri. I came into my own there as Owen's best scrivener in the Welsh language, for though he had a fine flow of eloquence like most of his house, he was not lettered beyond the signing of his name. Very fine proclamations we drew up between us, and I was kept busy copying the long pedigree of my young lord, and setting forth his claims and his injuries, King Henry's tender care for him and concern for his just cause, and the peace and benefit that might accrue to Wales if they did right to him, and rallied to his standard against the uncle who shut him out from his inheritance. Throughout all those parts of Wales which were held under the crown these were read and distributed and cried publicly. And where the crown had no sway they were insinuated by whatever agency de Rohan could discover and use.

So the last of the autumn passed, with only one drawback, that we got no result for all our labour. And for myself, I did not see these efforts of mine go out with a single mind or a whole heart, seeing at whose expense and for whose profit this matter was really undertaken. For here was Wales contending against England, and a Welsh prince was seeking to win away as much as he might of Wales to a side which, Owen or no Owen, could only be called England's. And surely there was a part of me that drew relieved breath as every day passed, and still barely a man, and none of substance, took the bait we put out and came to declare himself.

Then Owen, unhappy with this state of affairs, for he had counted on making a strong appeal to all those chiefs who had taken his father's part, at least did something for those few Welsh who were brought in prisoner, for he suggested that they should be offered grace and aid if they would either convert to his banner, or better, go back into Wales as agents for him. But such as accepted this surely took to their heels gladly when they were released to their own country, and did no recruiting for us, and such as elected to join the king's forces did so to save life and limb, and were of little worth, their hearts being elsewhere.

Most of that winter we passed in Chester, but when the hardest of the weather was over we moved out nearer to the salt marshes and sands of the Dee, to the king's manor of Shotwick. I think by then King Henry had given up the idea that Owen could be of much use to him at this stage, but still he required him as a puppet to be produced and give his proceedings a cover of justice when he put an army into the field in earnest, as now he had determined to do. For the Welsh revolt continued vigorous and successful. In February a certain Fitz-Mathew, who was in command of a force of knights controlling the southern march, was ambushed and killed in a hill pass near Margam, and most of his company shattered. And if King Henry could rejoice over one bloody engagement near Montgomery, where, as we heard, three hundred Welshmen were drawn into a net from which they could not escape, and there slaughtered, he was soon grieving again for the loss of Mold, for David stormed and took it at the end of March. That could not pass. With Mold in David's hands again there was no safety for the royal castle at Diserth, it might be cut off from its base of Chester at any time. The king knew then that there was nothing for him to do but call up the whole muster of his knighthood service, and launch a full campaign with the summer, and he began at once to send out orders to his justiciars to collect provisions for his army.

We spent most of that year at Shotwick, for the king would not risk using Owen in the field, though he did entertain and display him at Chester when he came there in August, and halted his army for a week. Then they moved on to the banks of the Conway, and the king began the building of a great new castle on the rock of Degannwy on the east bank, to provide protection from a distance both for Diserth and Chester. They remained in camp there, busy with this building, until the end of October.

Now it chanced that that year the winter came down early and like iron, before autumn was half over, fighting at last for Wales. The whole month of October was bitter and bleak, full of frosts and gales and snow, and in that camp by the Conway they froze and starved, killed and died, with no mercy on either side. The king's army was far too strong to be attacked in pitched battle, which in any case we Welsh never favoured, and it managed to keep open a supply line back to Chester, as well as bringing in supplies by sea from Ireland. But ships are flimsy against such storms as came down that year, and some foundered, and one at least was run aground by a clumsy steersman in the sands on the Aberconway side, and fought over bitterly by both armies, but the Welsh got away with most of its cargo. Their need was at least as great, for the king had landed troops from Ireland in Anglesey and captured or despoiled the late crops there. But King Henry went on doggedly with the building of his new castle, and the work grew rapidly.

One of the few Welsh soldiers who had embraced Owen's cause was our courier back and forth to this camp at Degannwy, and brought us grim accounts of what went forward there, how the English had raided the abbey of Aberconway, across the river, stripped the great church of all its treasures, and fired the barns, how they had given up taking prisoners, and slaughtered even the noblemen who fell into their hands, until David took to repaying the murders upon the English knights he captured. Nightly the Welsh made lightning raids in the darkness, killed and withdrew. And daily the English, after every skirmish, brought back into camp Welsh heads as horrid trophies.

These things he told us, and I could not forbear from watching Owen's face as he listened, for these were the heads of his kinsmen, over whom he desired to rule, and whose support he was wooing. But he was not of such subtlety as to question deeply what he did, and saw no further than the right that had been denied his father and was still denied him.

'And I'll tell you,' said the messenger, steaming beside our comfortable fire, 'one they have killed, though he was brought in prisoner after an honest fight, and that's the youngest of Ednyfed Fychan's sons.' This was the great steward who had served Llewelyn Fawr and now David, in all some forty years of noble, wise dealing, without greed for himself, and with the respect of all. And he was now an old man. 'Hanged him,' said our courier, 'on a bare tree, high for the Welsh to see. And that David will never forgive.'

Sometimes I had wondered, as I did then, about this man, whether he was not carrying news two ways, and not all to the English side of Conway, for he was a bold and fearless creature, as he proved by his many journeys across that torn and tormented country, and would not change his coat simply to buy a little security.

'Yet he cannot hold out long now,' Owen said, wringing hard at the hope that was always uppermost in him. 'Last time he gave in without much blood spilled, and now they tear each other like leopards, and he gives no ground. Surely he must be near surrender. They feel the cold, too. They have lost half their winter store, they must be as hungry as we, they cannot continue thus for long.'

I saw then the small spark that lit in the man's eyes when Owen spoke of 'they' and 'we', and I understood him better.

'Last time,' he said, 'the season played false. Now the winter comes early and true as steel. And he has a list of loyal chiefs behind him, as long as your arm, such as he never had before. There's a name high on the list,' he said, eyeing Owen all the while, 'that will be known to you, the name of Llewelyn ap Griffith.'

Owen jerked up his head to glare across the fire. 'He is there? In arms?'

'He is there. In arms. And very apt and ready, too, in the teeth of cold and hunger.'

'You have seen him?'

'I have. Close about his uncle very often, but he is trusted with a command of his own, and they do tolerably well in a night raid. With no son of his own he had good need of such a nephew.'

I felt the sting of every word, though they were not aimed at me. And I leaned back into shadow that I might smile, no matter how bitterly, unnoticed. But I think that man knew. His voice all this while was level, mild and dutiful. And as I have said, Owen was not a subtle person, nor, for that matter, a sensitive listener.

'I can but give you my judgment,' said our courier when he left us. 'There'll be no surrender. Not this year.'

Nor was there. And at the end of October King Henry realised it and made the best of it. He could no longer sustain his exposed position, with such numbers to feed. But he could and did raise Degannwy to a point where it could be garrisoned and supplied, by sea and land, before he ordered withdrawal. It was understood that this campaign was to be resumed and finished, with total victory and Eryri conquered, the following year. But that had been the understanding also this year, and God and his servant, the cold, had disposed.

The king also set up a new justiciar in Cheshire before he went south, one John de Grey, and gave him orders what was to be done by way of strangling Wales indirectly, since he could not do it honestly with his hands. Trade with the land was to cease, totally. In particular there were certain things Wales could not provide herself, as salt, iron, woven cloth, and a sufficiency of corn, and these at least could be denied her.

Then he went south with his army.

An idle winter we passed that year, waiting for the battle-time to come round again, though to my mind fighting is an ill use for the kindly summer. After the early frosts and snows the weather proved less severe, and we had good riding there above the Dee when the salt marshes were hard and firm, and for want of real employment spent much time in the saddle. True, de Rohan's guards were always close, our household was all English, and there were archers among the escort, who could as well bring us down, if we showed a disposition to play King Henry false, as ward off Welsh attack from us. And to tell truth, it irked me that I should have to expect execution from either side at the first free move, as though I had no real place of my own, and no cause, anywhere in this world. But if it irked Owen, he gave no sign. All his impatience was for the seasons to turn, so that the king's unwieldy muster could be on the move again, and hurry to bring him his princedom. He fretted all the winter, gazing westwards.

As for me, I was in two minds. I had been too long in the service of the Lord Griffith's family to feel at ease when my vision showed me black, or even a dubious shade of grey, where they saw white. Yet I was not happy with the letter of the law, and the narrow knife-edge of justice that was slitting so many Welsh throats to uphold a Welsh prince's right. And I had been glad in my heart of the iron winter that had caused the king to withdraw before he suffered worse losses than those already sustained. And I was glad now of every storm-cloud that threatened, and held back the new campaign. Even so, this waiting had to end.

It ended as none of us had expected. On the last day of February a messenger came riding from Degannwy, and turned aside to cross the Dee and come to Shotwick for a fresh horse before hurrying on to Chester. It was pure chance that Owen and I were out in the mews when he came, and so we heard his news before he took it in to de Rohan. For Owen, ever greedy for any word from the west, began to question him at sight, and the rider – he was an Englishman of the garrison, and known to us – saw no reason for denying him.

84

'My lord, the case is altered with a vengeance,' he said, big with the import of what he carried. 'You've lost a kinsman and an enemy, and what's to come next is guessing, but it's thought in Degannwy we're a great leap nearer getting by luck what we failed to get last year by fighting. We got the word yesterday, and from a sure source: the Lord David's dead!'

'Dead!' cried Owen, and paled and glowed, tossed by a tangle of emotions like a leaf where currents meet. 'My uncle dead? In battle? There's been fighting, then, already?'

The man shook his head, stripping the saddle-cloth from his steaming horse and letting a groom take the bridle from his hand. 'In his bed, at Aber. The sweating sickness did what we failed to do by the Conway. He's dead, and Gwynedd in disarray. They've taken his body into Aberconway, to lie by his father, and the bards are tuning their harps over him. And I must get on to Chester, and let Lestrange know.'

And he went in haste to the house, while the grooms led in his blown mount and began to rub him down and water him sparingly, and saddle a replacement for the ride to Chester, which was no great way. But Owen took me by the arm in mute excitement, and drew me away into the mews, out of earshot.

'Samson,' he said in my ear, quivering, 'saddle up now, for both of us, while they're all taken up with this news. Openly, as always when we ride. Saddle up and lead the horses out, and not a word to anyone. Now, while he's setting their ears alight within!'

I was slow to understand, for he was not wont to be so decisive, and his whims usually made more commotion. I said foolishly: 'What do you mean to do?'

'Slip my collar, now while I may, and ride to Aber. Do you think I'll sit back and let King Henry pluck

Wales like a rose from a bush, while she's lost for a leader? If my uncle's dead, childless as he is, Gwynedd is my inheritance. I am going to claim it. Get the horses! Quickly!'

'Thus?' I said, 'without clothes or provisions?'

'If we carried a saddle-bag they'd know, fool!' he said, I own justly.

So I went as he had said, where they were bustling about the courier's beast, and with no concealment or haste, though losing no time, either, I saddled the horses we usually rode, and led them out. The sun was breaking through early mist and cloud at the rise of a fair day, good enough reason for us to change our minds and ride, and unless the grooms thought to come out and watch us depart, how could they know that this time we had no escort riding behind us within easy bow-shot? We had been there among them so long, and seemed so content to leave our future to them, that I think their watch must have been slack enough for some time before this, had we realised it. And within the house they had ears for nothing but the news from Aber.

We mounted and rode, and no one loosed a shout after us. And give him his due, Owen walked his mount down the gentle slope and into the coppice that gave the nearest cover, riding as loose and easy in the saddle as if he meant nothing more than a little lazy exercise over the salt-flats. But when the trees were between us and the manor he set spurs to his horse and steered a course that made good use of ground cover, putting several miles behind us before he uttered a word or drew rein.

'God give us always such luck!' he said then, drawing breath deeply. 'I had not thought it would be so easy. We'll need to cross the Dee above Hawarden, and give Mold a wide berth. Degannwy, too! I won't be rounded up by English or Welsh short of Aber. If they follow, they'll keep to the roads, they'd not be safe else. But we'll do better and move faster. Better than owing any rights of mine to King Henry, now I'll take them for myself, and owe him nothing.'

I thought, as he did, how easy this beginning, at least, had been, and how we might have ventured the attempt, with better preparation, long ago if he had been so minded, and how we had never so much as considered it. The case was changed now, and not only because David was gone, but because Llewelyn remained, already a magnate, acknowledged, followed in war, there on the spot to catch the talaith as it fell, and with it, very logically, the consent and approval of all the chieftains who had followed his uncle into battle. For he was the only prince of his blood there to take up the burden and the privilege. And he the second son! Yes, Owen had good reason for the frantic haste he made on that ride.

We had good going between Dee and Clwyd, and crossed the latter river at Llanelwy, and nowhere did we excite any interest more than other travellers, for Owen was plainly dressed. Beyond Clwyd we took the old, straight road they say the Romans made, keeping well away from the coast and the castles, and prayed that they had not discovered our flight in time to send a fast rider by the direct road to Diserth, to start a hunt after us. But we saw nothing of any pursuit. Once we made a halt and took food at a shepherd's holding in the uplands, and got rest and fodder for our horses, but Owen would finish this ride before night, instead of breaking the journey, so we set out again as soon as the jaded beasts could go, but now in somewhat less haste, for at least we breathed more freely here.

We crossed Conway at Caerhun, and took it gently on

the climb beyond, through the pass of Bwlch y Ddeufaen and along the great, bare causeway over the moors. When this track brought us down to sight of the sea we were but a few miles from Aber, and land and sea were growing dark. But the night came clear and bright with stars, and I could still see, across the vast pale stretch of Lavan sands, and the deep water beyond, the long, jutting coast of Anglesey, and the solitary rock of Yyns Lanog, an island of saints as holy as our own Enlli.

We came where the wall of the llys reared beside the track, under the shoulder of the mountains and staring across the sea. I had never before been in Aber, the favourite court of Llewelyn Fawr and his son, the noblest home of this noble line, and I was moved and awed, so grand was the soaring height of the mountains on one hand, and the sweep of the open salt-marshes on the other, melting into the distant glimmer of the sea. It was then so nearly dark that I could not see the timber keep on its high motte towering over the wall, or the roofs of the many buildings within, but the wall ran tall and even beside us until we drew near to the gate, and figures rose out of the dark to halt us. They were calm and made little sound, for they were on their own ground, in the heart of their own homeland, and the court they guarded was in deepest mourning for a chief dead as surely in battle as if he had perished by the Conway red with blood, with his slain heaped around him.

'Where are you bound, friends, by night?' the officer challenged us, and took Owen's horse by the bridle, for we were so nearly foundered by then, or our beasts were, that he knew well enough where we were bound, and turned us in towards the gate without waiting for an answer.

That vexed Owen, weary as he was, for he had forgotten the free ways of Welshmen. He took the man's hand by the wrist and ripped it from his rein and flung it aside. 'Take care whom you handle!' he said. 'I am Owen ap Griffith. Best stand out of my way. I am here to consult with the royal council of Gwynedd and with Ednyfed Fychan, the high steward. Send and let them know that Owen Goch is broken free from imprisonment in England, and come to take up the charge that belongs to him.'

The officer stood back and looked up at him long by the light of the torches his men had brought forth. He was a local man, most likely born in the tref outside the gate of the maenol, and he went bare-legged in the cold and in linen clothing, with only a light leather jerkin on him by way of body-armour, and a coarse cloth cape over his shoulders. He had a great bush of black hair, and another of beard with red in the black, and eyes like arrow-points in the torchlight.

'Ride in, my lord Owen,' he said, when he had mastered the look of us and memorised it. 'But slowly, and my runner will be before you. Follow him to the hall, and ride softly past the lady's apartments, for she's in mourning for her lord and ours, and it's late to trouble her tonight. I'll send word to the Lord Llewelyn that his brother is come, and doubtless he'll be ready to receive you.'

All the household of Aber, the young men of the warband, the archers and men-at-arms gathered about the great hearth in the hall, the maidservants, the scriveners, the bards, the children huddled cosily in the skins of the brychans by the wall, fell silent and watched us as we went by. In the vast, blackened roof the wisps of smoke hung lazily circling like the eddies of a sluggish river, and rivulets crept upwards to join it from the pine torches in sconces on the walls. The smell of resin and wood-smoke clung heavy and sweet. I think there had been music before we entered, and a murmur of voices, but where we passed there was stillness and silence.

So we were brought into another room, smaller and withdrawn behind hide curtains, where a brazier burned. The walls were hung with tapestries, and skins of bear and wolf were laid on the beaten earth of the floor. The lost imprint of the hand of King John's daughter lay softly on all in that chamber. The torches burned in tall holders of silver, but they were few and dim, only enough to light the way for those passing through, for who had leisure to sit down over wine or warm his feet at a fire in Aber at this time? The young men of the bodyguard, having conveyed their lord with grief and solemnity to Aber-conway, might lie down and sleep until they received other orders, but all the solid men of the council must be in almost constant debate over the desert he had left behind, the legal rights of his young widow, the state of readiness of the land for King Henry's next move against Gwynedd, now that its buckler and sword was laid low, with no son to take up the fight after him, not even a daughter to bear princes hereafter.

There was one great chair, higher than the rest on the dais by two tall steps, and carved and gilded. And I had half-expected that Llewelyn would be braced and ready for us there as on a throne already claimed. But the room was empty and silent. We waited some minutes, Owen with mounting impatience and rising gorge, before the curtains swung behind the dais, brusquely and suddenly, and a young man came shouldering through and let the hangings swing to behind him. I have said it was dim within the room, dulling even the red of Owen Goch's hair. The boy came forward a few quick steps before he halted to peer at us, standing there a foot or so lower than he stood. The light of the torches was on him, we saw him better than he could distinguish us.

I knew him to be but two months past seventeen then, for so was I. He had shot up by a head since last I had seen him, and stood a hand's-breadth taller than I, but well short of his brother, and his shoulders were wide and his limbs long, but he carried little flesh upon him. His face was I remembered it, all bright, gleaming lines of bone starting in the yellow light of torches and candles, with those fathomless peat-pool eyes reflecting light from the surface of their darkness. And the longer I gazed, the younger did he seem, this boy burned brown with living out of doors in all weathers, so that even in winter, in the long evenings shut within walls, his russet only fined and paled into gold. But what I most remember, beyond the careless plainness of his dress, which was homespun and dun, is the healed scar slashed down the inner side of his left forearm, and its fellow, a small, puckered star under the angle of his jaw on the right side, mementoes of Degannwy in the frost six months ago; and with that, the slight reddening and swelling of his eyelids, that might have marred him if I had not known it for the stigma of private weeping, some two days old.

He said clearly: 'They tell me there is one here claims to be brother to me. Which of you is he?'

I own I thought at first that this was policy, a move to affront and repulse the returned heir, but then I recalled that it was seven years since these two had stood face to face, and those perhaps the most vital seven years of Llewelyn's life, all the time of his enforced growing-up, under angry pressures in which Owen Goch had had no part. I do believe that he was honest. For never have I known him go roundabout of intent, but always straight for his goal. And before Owen could blaze, as he was willing to do, Llewelyn came closer, voluntarily surrendering whatever advantage he had in the height of the dais, and swinging down to look at us intently. I saw his eyes dilate and glow.

'It *is* you!' he said. 'I had thought it was some trick. Well, what's your business with me?' And after a pause, very brief and chill, he said: '—*brother*!' as though he tried the savour of the word on his tongue, and found it very little to his taste.

'My business is hardly with you,' said Owen, stung and smarting, 'but with the council of Gwynedd. You know me. I *am* your brother, and since you will have me say it, your elder. The prince of Gwynedd is dead, and there is no heir to succeed him. And mine is the next claim.'

'You must forgive my being slow to recognise you,' said Llewelyn. 'I have been so long brotherless here, when I could well have done with a brother. Yes, the prince of Gwynedd is dead. No doubt you came to mourn him, you should have halted at Aberconway for that. As for an heir to succeed him, the council are in some dream that they have one ready to hand.' He drew back a short step, and looked Owen Goch over from head to foot and back again, and his face was bleak, like a man wrung but unwilling to weep. 'Who gnawed through your leash,' he said bitterly, 'you or King Henry?'

At that Owen began to smoulder and to threaten a blaze, and but that he found himself somewhat at a disadvantage here, there would have been an outburst on the spot. 'What are you daring to charge against me?' he cried. 'If the king's men could have got their hands on me this day, do you think I should not have been dead by now, or on my way back to the Tower? He had no part in my coming.'

'So you say. But you have been his lapdog too long to be easily credited, and it makes good sense that he should toss you in here at this pass to break Gwynedd apart for him, so that he can devour piecemeal what he found too big to swallow whole. Strange chance,' said Llewelyn hardly, 'that offered you a way of escape now, after keeping the doors fast shut on you so long.'

'Well for you,' flamed Owen then, 'who have never been a prisoner! Can you not understand that I have been dogged at every step, never gone from room to room without a shadow on my heels, or ridden out without archers at my back? I broke loose as soon as I could, and I am here, and it is *my* doing – none other's!'

'A year too late,' said Llewelyn. 'Where were you when your masters sacked the church at Aberconway? Where were you when they hanged Edynfed's boy, the child of his old age, high on a tree by the shore of Conway, and stood Welsh heads in a row to freeze along the edge of the tide? Do you think,' he said, 'that we have not your fine proclamations by heart, every word? We know where you were, what you were doing, how you were living princely while we sweated and drowned and died. And we know who paid for it all, the very clothes on your back! And we know what you pledged for it, the future of Gwynedd and of Wales! To hold direct from the king whatever he could get for you!'

The blood had crowded dark and blue into Owen's face. 'You know, none so well,' he said thickly, 'that your mother and mine pledged that for our father, and for me after him, while we were still prisoners in Criccieth. What say did I ever have in it? I was no sooner out of one dungeon than into another.'

'And was it she who repeated the pledge, and signed your name to it, two years ago in Westminster? Oh, we have our intelligencers, too, even in King Henry's court. Who threatened you with rack and rope then? You jumped at it willingly. To get your few commotes of

Wales you were ready to help him set fire and sword to the whole.'

'I wanted no such warfare! Was one side to blame for that bitter fighting more than the other? I did nothing but promise natural gratitude and loyalty for the restoration of my right ...'

'Your right! Your *right*!' said Llewelyn through his teeth. 'Can you see nothing on earth but your right? Has no other man any right, except you? The right to be Welsh, tenant to a Welsh lord, judged by Welsh law, living by Welsh custom? You would have given over your own people to the king's officers to tax and plague and call to war service like the wretched English. Do you expect a welcome for that?'

'Yet it *is* my right,' said Owen, setting his jaw, 'and the council cannot but uphold it. I am the eldest son of our father, and the next direct heir to Gwynedd, and I stand on that right. And if you have complaints against me, so have I against you, and against him that's dead, for he deprived our father of his birthright and his liberty, and you – you turned traitor to your own family and sided with their enemies.'

'I sided with Wales,' said Llewelyn. 'Your grandsire and mine had a vision of Wales that I learned from him, Wales united under one prince and able to stand up to all comers. There's no other way of fending off England for long. I went with my uncle not against our father, but against England, and sorry I was and am that we could not all stand together. Now you come running with the same old ruinous devotion to a right that will dismember Gwynedd, let alone Wales, and feed it to your king, whether you mean it or no, gobbet by gobbet until he has gorged all. And if I can prevent you, I will.'

As Owen had grown redder and angrier, and fallen to plucking at his sleeves with shaking hands, so Llewelyn

94

had grown ever more steady and quiet, as though he took the measure of an enemy who was seen now to be no great threat to him, and in time might even come to lose the complexion of an enemy. He had a way of standing with his feet planted a little apart, very solid and very still, like one set to withstand all winds and pressures from every quarter and remain unmoved. A moment he looked into Owen's congested face, then: 'And I can!' he said with certainty, and turned on his heel to walk back towards the door from which he had come.

To Owen, I think, it seemed that he had said his last word, and that with undisguised contempt, and meant to go away from us without another glance. But I think his intent, having found out all he needed to know in order to determine his future course, was merely to call in his chamberlain, and commit his brother to the care of the servants for board and bed, for even between rivals and enemies hospitality could not be denied or grudged. However it was, he turned his back squarely, without a qualm, as he had turned his face towards us without compromise or evasion. And as he took the first long steps, Owen made a curious small noise in his throat, a moan too venomous for words, and plucking out the dagger he wore at his belt, lunged with all his force after his brother's withdrawing back, aiming under the left shoulder.

I had been standing a little behind him, unwilling to move or make sound or in any way be noticed during this scene, indeed I would gladly have been away from there if I could, for there was no room for a third in that exchange. But now I had good reason to be grateful that there had been no escape for me, for surely, if only for those few moments, Owen meant murder. And even so I was slow to catch the meaning of the sudden rapid motion he made, and snatched at his sleeve only just in time to hold back his arm from delivering the blow with full force. The point of the dagger slid down in a long line, dragged to the right by my retarding weight, cut a shallow slash in the stuff of Llewelyn's tunic, and clashed against the metal links of his belt. Then I got a better hold of Owen's arm and dragged him round towards me, and in the same moment, feeling the rush of our movements behind him even before he felt the shallow prick of the dagger – for there was almost no sound – Llewelyn sprang at once round and away from us, whirling to confront the next blow.

But the next blow was not aimed at him. The opportunity was already lost, Owen turned on me, who had robbed him of it, or saved him from it, I doubt then if he knew which for pure rage. His left hand took me around the throat and flung me backwards, and my hold on his arm was broken, and I went down on my back, winded and shaken, with Owen on top of me.

I saw the blade flash, and tried to roll aside, but the tip tore a ragged gash through my sleeve and down the upper part of my arm, between arm and body. His knee was in my groin, and I could not shake him off. I saw the dagger raised again, and in the convulsion of my dread one of the tall silver candle-holders went over, crashing against a chair, and spattered us with hot wax. I closed my eyes against that scalding shower and the glitter of the steel, and heaved unavailingly at the burden that was crushing me.

The weight was hoisted back from me unexpectedly, and I dragged in breath and looked up to see what had delivered me. Owen was down on one hip, a yard and more aside from me, glaring upwards under the tangle of his hair, and panting as he nursed his right wrist in his left hand. And Llewelyn, with the dagger in his grasp, was stamping out a little trickle of flame that had spurted along the hair of one of the skin rugs, and righting the fallen candlestick.

He was the first to hear the buzz of voices outside the room, and the latch of a door lifting. He flung the dagger behind him into the cushions of one of the chairs, and reached a peremptory hand to Owen's arm.

'Get up! Do you want witnesses? Quickly!'

I had just wit enough to grasp what he wanted, and shift for myself, though lamely, at least quickly enough to be on my feet and well back in the shadows, my arm clamped tight against my side, when they came surging in from two doors. The inner one by which Llewelyn had entered admitted an old, bearded man, once very tall but now bent in the shoulders and moving painfully, and a younger man, perhaps himself as much as fifty, who propped his elder carefully with a hand under his arm. At the outer door the guards looked in from the hall, coming but a pace or so over the threshold, and I saw the maids peering over their shoulders in curiosity and alarm.

Llewelyn stood settling the tall candelabrum carefully on its feet and straightening the leaning candles. He looked round at them all with a penitent smile, and said, looking last and longest at the old man, whom I knew now for that Ednyfed Fychan whose fame almost matched his lord's: 'I am sorry to have roused the house with such a clatter. A mishap. I knocked over the candles. There's no harm done but a smell of burning.'

Whether they entirely believed I could not tell, but they accepted what he wished them to accept, and asked nothing. He kept his face turned steadily towards them, and only I could see the slit in the back of his cotte, and the one bright blossom of blood where the point had pricked him.

'Goronwy,' he said courteously to the old man's son,

'will you take the Lord Owen in charge, and have food and a lodging prepared for him? He has had a long ride, and is weary. And, Meurig, make sure his horses are well cared for.'

The guard drew back obediently into the hall and closed the door. Owen, moving like a man indeed very weary, half-stunned by what he had done and the resolute way it was being buried and denied before his eyes, stepped forward unprotesting, and went where Goronwy ap Ednyfed led him. The old man, standing straighter now that he stood alone, but so frail that I seemed to see death, a good death, looking peaceably over his shoulder, looked at Llewelyn, and briefly at me, and back, without wonder or doubt, at Llewelyn.

'All is well?' he said, in the clear, leaf-thin voice of age.

'All is very well. There is nothing to trouble you here.' He smiled. 'Leave us. You can, with a quiet mind.'

When they were all gone but we two, he made me sit down close to the warmth of the brazier, and himself slipped away for some minutes, very softly, and came back with another cotte on him, and warm water in an ewer, and linen, and helped me to peel the torn sleeve back to the shoulder from my bleeding arm. The gash was shallow but sliced, and had bled down into my waist as I hugged it against me to keep it from being seen. Ashamed to be so waited on by a prince of Gwynedd, I said I could very well bind it myself, and he told me simply and brusquely that I lied, and foolishly. Which I found to be no more than the truth when I obstinately made the assay, and he took back the task from me, tolerantly enough, and made very neat and expert work of it.

When it was done, and I would have risen and withdrawn from him, conceiving in my weariness and con-

98

fusion of mind that he was done with me now, and wondering sickly what was to become of me, and whether I had not put myself clean beyond the limits of mercy in Owen's household, I who had no kinsmen here in any group to take me in, he bade me sit down again, and himself sat long with his chin in his fists, gazing at me intently. And after a while he said abruptly:

'You could have made your master the master of Gwynedd. Why did you interfere? You came here with him to serve his interests, did you not?'

'Not that way,' I said, and he looked at me sharply, and a little smiled.

'Well, plainly you cannot now return to him. He would either make an end of his unfinished work, and kill you, or else discard you and leave you to fend for yourself.' He leaned a little closer, and moved the torch to cast its light more directly on my face. 'I know you!' he said. 'You are the boy at Neigwl – the boy with the sheep!'

It was the best part of five years gone, and he had not forgotten. I owned it, remembering how he had looked at me then, and found himself content.

'And you never told?' he said.

'No.'

'Neither did I,' he said. 'I knew then you would not. Afterwards, when it came out that my mother had taken the children and fled, my uncle asked me outright if I had known of it beforehand, and I told him the truth. And he said to me that if I could make as solitary a choice as that, well calculated to bring down on me the anger of both sides, then I was a good man for either side to welcome and value, if they had the wit. That is what he was like, at least to me. And he's gone! Fretted away to skin and bone in his bed in seven short days of fever! And my brother comes galloping to pick the bones!'

He got up from his chair suddenly, and turned to walk restlessly between the brocaded wall and the shrouded doorway, to hide the grief and anger of his face, for even if he remembered me with warmth, this was a private passion. To do justice, all the more because it might bring him some shade of comfort, I said what was true: 'He did come of his own will. The king and his officers had no part in it, we took the moment when they were shaken and distracted, and we ran. I don't say it could not have been done earlier. I do say the way offered then, and suddenly, and he jumped at it.'

'I take your word,' said Llewelyn, still pacing. 'I would not take his! Brother or no, it sticks fast in my gullet that he comes running now, when God knows we have troubles enough, even united, and with King Henry ready to prise his sword-point into every chink of disunity we shall crumble away like a clod after frost. But that's none of your doing,' he said, shaking himself clear of the greatest shadow that hung upon him, and turning again to face me and consider me sombrely. 'It seems,' he said, 'that you made a kind of choice of your own, a while ago. Are you willing to abide by it?'

I caught his meaning, and my heart rose in me for pure pleasure. I said: 'My lord, more than willing!'

'If you enter my service there is none here will challenge or offend you, not even Owen. He will learn that he dare not.'

'But, my lord,' I said, much afraid that this unlooked-for offer might yet be snatched away from me, 'he has my pledged fealty.'

'I will ensure that he shall release you. If he values you no more than shows in him, he will not care overmuch, and his grudge against you – as I remember him, he bore grudges! – can be bought off. What were you to him? In what service?'

I told him then what I could do, for I think he had taken me simply for manservant and groom; and when he heard that I could read and write in Latin, English and Welsh, was now a fair horseman, and even had some mild practice in arms, though never otherwise than in play and exercise, he was astonished and pleased, and in pleasure he lit up into a child's unshadowed brightness.

'You are what I need,' he said gladly, 'for I do well enough in Welsh, and have some Latin, but in English I go very haltingly. You shall teach me better. And you can also reckon, and have copied documents at law? English law I must learn to know, if I am to understand my enemies.'

'My lord,' I said, still a little afraid of such good fortune, 'I know very well that you must have clerks about you who have served your uncle well and will do as much for you, and I do fear that what you are now offering me is offered out of too much generosity for a very slight service I could not choose but do you. I would not wish to take advantage of a moment when gratitude may seem due, but only to take and hold a post in your service if I deserve and am fit for it. Take me on probation, and discard me if I am not worth my place.'

And at that he laughed at me, frankly and without offence. 'You also make very lofty speeches,' he said, 'and I may yet make good use of your eloquence, but I am not obliged to take your advice. There is the small matter of a life I owe you.' The laughter vanished very suddenly. He said seriously: 'He meant killing.'

'I have good reason to know as much,' I said, shaken by the recollection. 'And to remember that that debt is already paid, and with somewhat over.'

'So much the better, then,' he said, 'that you and I should remain close together, close enough to go on bandying the same small favour about between us the

101

rest of our lives. Yet if you do refuse me, I can but offer you my hospitality here as long as you choose, and a horse to carry you wherever you will thereafter. But I had rather you would not refuse me.'

It was ever his most disarming gift that he had a special humility, the very opposite of his youngest brother, and never took for granted that he should be liked, much less loved. Confident he was of his judgments and decisions, but never of the effect he had on those about him, and I swear he did not know that by then there was nothing within my giving or granting that I could have refused him. So there was eternally renewed pleasure in making him glad. And I said to him: 'With all my heart, if it were for that reason only, I will come to you, and be your man as long as I live. But it is not only for that reason, for there is nowhere in this world I would rather take my stand than here in Aber, and no one under whom I would more gladly serve than you.'

So it was sealed between us. And he put away ceremony, and began to speak of finding me food, and a bed, and fresh clothes to make away with the blood-stained cotte I wore, for we wanted no rumours and curiosity about the llys concerning an ill encounter between the brothers, to add to the load of uncertainty and disquiet the court already bore. And last, as we were about to leave that room, he asked me: 'One thing I have forgotten – I never asked your name.'

I said it was Samson.

At that he gave me one quick, bright look, and began to say: 'I once knew another Samson....' And there he halted abruptly, and looked again at me, very closely and in some wonder, and for a while was not sure of what he thought he saw.

'Not another,' I said. 'The same.'

'You? Was it you? My mother had a tirewoman was

left with a child ... You are Elen's son?' He did not wait for an answer, for now he was all but certain without any word for me. 'Yes, you could well be! But then, if you are my Samson, I saw you here at Neigwl that day, bringing down the sheep, and I did not know you again!'

'You had not seen me,' I said, 'for more than six years, and you saw me then but a moment.'

'Yes, but there's more to it! I never thought of you then, nor dreamed it could be you. They sent you to Aberdaron long before.'

'When your mother fled to England,' I told him, 'my mother would not go without me. They sent to fetch me back that very day that you saw me.'

'And I had thought they would make a canon or a priest of you, and now I get you back thus strangely and simply. I have not forgotten,' he said, the deep brown of his eyes glowing reddish-bright, 'the years we were children together. We had the same birthday, the same stars. We were surely meant to come together again. I missed you when they sent you away. And now you come back with an omen – the dagger that strikes at one of us strikes at both. We are linked, Samson, you and I, we may as well own it and make the best of it.'

To which I said a very fervent amen, for the best of it seemed to me then, and seems to me now and always, the best that ever life did for me, whatever darkness came with the bright.

Thus I became confidential clerk and secretary to the Lord Llewelyn ap Griffith, prince of Gwynedd.

CHAPTER IV

There was never any mention made of what had befallen between Llewelyn and Owen, and that was at Llewelyn's wish and silent order. For the situation of Gwynedd, even though King Henry held back from committing an army to so positive an adventure as the previous year, was weak, exhausted and in disarray, and every additional burden was to be prevented at all costs. So this matter of the rivalry between those two was put away. Llewelyn did it as disposing of a difficulty, and Owen was very glad to do it, since it reflected no credit on him either in the treacherous attack or in its ruthless defeat.

I was present at the meeting of the council, the last but one such meeting Ednyfed Fychan ever attended, there in the hall of Aber. The old man, waxen and frail but with his long and honourable devotion burning in his eyes, presided at the table, his son Goronwy on his right side. The old man had hands that lay on the table before him like withered leaves, and a voice as light and dry as the autumn wind that brings them down, but a spirit like a steady flame. I will not say that there was no high feeling between the brothers at that meeting, for they urged their claims hard after their own fashion, Owen with the more words and the louder voice, since very strongly he felt himself at a disadvantage as the new-comer, and under some suspicion of being King Henry's willing pensioner, Llewelyn in very few words but bluntly and bitterly. But perforce they listened, both of them, to the arguments of the council, for there was no future for any man in claiming the sovereignty over a ruined land. And there was not a man present there, by that time even I, who did not know how grim was the plight of Gwynedd, however defiantly she stood to arms.

'Children,' said Ednyfed, in that voice like the rustling of dried leaves, 'there is no solution here but needs the goodwill of both of you. For past question the Lord Owen is his father's eldest son, nor was he to blame for his imprisonment in England, since it stemmed from imprisonment here in Wales, before he was of age. And he has given us his word that he made his escape when he might, to return here to his own land and take up the defence of Gwynedd. But the Lord Llewelyn, younger though he may be, is known to all here, has never set foot in England, and has fought faithfully for our lord and prince, David, without personal desire for his own enlargement, for never has he asked lands for himself, though lands have rightfully been granted to him. The Lord Llewelyn's wounds speak for him, those who served under him at Degannwy speak for him. He needs no advocate here. And therefore I say to him first, and after to his brother, that the land of Wales has great need of all the sons of Griffith, not as rivals but as brothers, if the land of Wales is to live. Children, be reconciled, divide Gwynedd between you only to unite it in your own union, for unless you fight together you will founder apart.'

This was his matter, if not his words. Indeed, I think he had to use, and repeatedly, many more words to hold this balance. And his son ably backed him, for the minds of these two worked almost as one. Moreover, there was no alternative to what they advocated. Those two, with whatever doubts and misgivings they felt, agreed to divide Gwynedd between them, in order to hold it as one against England.

Among his share, when the division of commotes was arduously worked out, Llewelyn kept his old lands of Penllyn, to which he had become attached as being his first appanage received from David at his majority, and there we spent much of that summer at his court of Bala, though he came several times to Aber to pay visits to his widowed aunt, Isabella, for whom he had some fondness. I saw her several times before she withdrew into England in August, a slender, dark, sad girl, never truly at home in Wales even after sixteen years. She had been but a child when they married her to David, and without him, and lacking children, she had nothing now to bind her to this land, for she was a de Breos by birth, and all her kin were Norman. As a widow she was entitled under Welsh law to a part of the royal stock, and in August these cattle and horses were shod and taken away by drovers to the lands of the earl of Gloucester, and into his protection the lady followed them very shortly after. Her mother had been one of the daughters and heiresses of the Marshal estates, and through her the castle of Haverfordwest came to Isabella, with lands in Glamorgan and Caerleon. So she was provided for amply, and passed out of our lives.

There remained to be decided in this year how Gwynedd should deal with the still outstanding issues between Wales and England, for though the full feudal host was not called out against us this summer, yet we were still in a state of war, and the king's wardens of the march and others were free to make inroads where they could. The council argued for caution and waiting, for the last year's main corn harvest had been lost in Anglesey, and stocks were low for feeding an army in the field. Nor was this a fat year for crops. Better to make the castles secure and provision them well, and be content to hold fast what we held. So we did, and as well for us. At least we lost few men, and no territory, if we gained none.

Yet there was one happening in the late summer that painfully displayed our weakness and helplessness. King Henry had installed one Nicholas de Molis as custos of his castles of Cardigan and Carmarthen, and this was an energetic and ambitious person who had formerly been seneschal in Gascony. During these summer months he launched a successful campaign in South Wales, greatly consolidating the royal holdings there, and then, swollen with this triumph, crossed the Dovey with his army and marched them north through Merioneth and Ardudwy to the Conway valley, and so without hindrance to join the garrison at Degannwy. There was some heat between Owen and Llewelyn once again over how to meet this impudent march clean through the middle lands of Wales, for Owen was ever fierce and rash, and thought every man a coward who was not ready to rush upon a superior host with him. But as for Llewelyn, it was clear to him that this army, in such circumstances, hardly dared delay its passage by essaying much diversion or damage on the way, and that the Welsh forces could be more effectively used where they were finally most needed, in keeping the Conway and ensuring the stronghold of Eryri itself should be held inviolate. He therefore advocated the usual Welsh tactic of withdrawing our people and valuables into the hills, and suffering the intruders to pass, while denying them everything that was movable by way of provisions. And the council sided with him. Thus de Molis reached Degannwy, which in any case was strongly held, but we massed our defences there opposite the castle, and threw back all his attempted raids from that vantage-point. Never once did he get across the river, and of bloodshed that year there was very little.

Howbeit, this unimpeded march, which had crossed

lands untroubled by an English army for a century and more, had showed all too clearly how thoroughly King Henry had the more accessible parts of Wales in his power, and how little we could hope to do against him if he decided to put his entire host into the field. And there was very earnest discussion in council as soon as the winter began to close in, and raids and skirmishes ceased. For the drain on the land was remorseless in labour, resources and livestock, and two more such years would be hard to endure.

And that was the last council of all for Ednyfed Fychan, and the last service he did to the land he had served lifelong. Llewelyn spoke his mind, with what reluctance and grief I knew, for we had talked of it beforehand. And he bore to be called timorous by Owen, for whose opinion he cared little, so long as Ednyfed's ancient eyes watched him steadily and did not disapprove.

'There are but two choices before us,' he said, 'and the first is to continue as we are, at war but without fighting, so far as we can avoid it. True, we can hold our losses in bounds by these means, so long as the king also holds back from fielding his host against us, but such a country as ours, barren of grain, wanting salt and a hundred other things that are now denied us, can bleed to death slowly and find that death as mortal as any other. And should King Henry decide to make an end, with such stocks as we have now, and so stripped of allies, fight as well as we might, we could not prevent the quick death from sparing us the slow. And the other alternative – to be blunt – is surrender. I call it so, that we may not imagine its countenance as any more comely than it is. We sue for a truce, and ask for terms of peace, and on the face of it we may reject them if they bite too deep, but to be honest, we cannot afford even to play hard to please. And I am for the second way.'

Owen cried out indignantly that this was abject surrender.

'I have said so,' agreed Llewelyn grimly.

'If you are ready to bow your neck to King Henry's foot, I am not,' protested Owen.

'Times are changed,' flashed back Llewelyn, for he was human, and almost as quick to hit out as his brother, 'since you bowed your neck low enough for his gold chains and his ermine. Not long since, your head was in his bosom, now you have less trust in his mercy – or at least his caution – than I have. Our mother and sister, our brothers, are still in his court and under his protection, and he'll hold back from putting us too openly to shame, for the sake of his own face. Not that the draught will be any the sweeter for that, but there'll be a cloak of decency. He has his pretext – Prince David was his enemy of some years' standing, whom he was sworn to bring to book. We are the innocent inheritors, to be plundered, yes, but not picked clean to the bone or made mock of, provided we behave ourselves seemly. You have nothing to fear.'

Owen flared that it was not he who was fearful, that he was willing to put all to the issue, that there was a time for valour.

'So there will be,' said Llewelyn, with a spark of golden anger in his eyes. 'It is not now. Fortitude, perhaps. And patience. And humility.'

Then Ednyfed spoke. He set before the council all the state of their arms, men and stores, and their nakedness of trustworthy allies, for in Wales then it was every chief for himself, and those who were not demoralised by the too close presence of marcher neighbours, or royal castellans armed with carte blanche to raid and despoil, were quarrelling among themselves, or had been seduced by the king into promising their homage directly to him in return for his protection. Not now, not for many years, could that unity be restored which had almost been perfected under Llewelyn Fawr. And at this present time, he concluded, it was a different service and a different heroism that was required from the grandsons of that great prince.

There was no man there who was happy with the verdict, and some disagreed, and many doubted and feared, but the sum of opinion was that there was no choice but to send at least for a safe-conduct to Chester, and despatch envoys to ask John de Grey for a truce, and a meeting with King Henry to discuss permanent terms of peace.

We came out from the hall, after that council, to a grey and cloudy eve, for it was December, and the dark came early. In the chill air of the courtyard the old steward drew breath deeply, and heaved a great, wavering sigh, and fell like a drifting leaf into his son's arms. They carried him to his bed, and both the princes were with him through the dark hours, and in the first light of dawn he blessed them, and died.

Goronwy, his eldest son, was distain of Gwynedd after him, and Llewelyn's bards made mourning songs for the father, and songs of praise and hope for the son, hymning their noble line as worthy to give birth to great and illustrious kings.

It was Tudor ap Ednyfed, the second son, who went to Chester in the first place, armed with the royal safe-conduct, to negotiate a truce with John de Grey, the justiciar and the king's representative on the border. And later, in mid-April, Owen and Llewelyn received further safe-conducts for themselves and their parties, to meet King Henry at Woodstock. There on the thirtieth day of April a very hard peace was made, too hard for all the civility and ceremony to do much to soften it. And those two, who rubbed each other raw did their sleeves but touch, endured to ride together, to stand together before a curious court, and to keep each his countenance calm and resolute through all, at least in public. I know, for I was of Llewelyn's party, and I witnessed all, and greatly I admired the stern control they kept upon themselves when the need was greatest.

They were forced to give up much, in order to keep at least the heart of their land. All that Middle Country from Clwyd to Conway, the four cantrefs of Rhos, Rhufoniog, Tegaingl and Dyffryn Clwyd, was lost to them, and they renounced all claim to it. Also at last they surrendered Mold. King Henry maintained that the homage of all the minor chiefs of North Wales belonged directly to him, and ensured that any such chiefs who had been adherents of his cause against their own country should be securely established in the lands they claimed. In return for so much sacrificed, Owen and Llewelyn were acknowledged as the lawful princes of all Gwynedd beyond the Conway, but they had to do homage to the king for their lands, and to hold them of him as overlord by military service.

But they got their peace. And it did endure for several years. Trade was delivered from its ban, imports flowed in again. Sad, slow gains to set against such losses, but Wales had been bled into weakness, and needed time to grow whole again.

Thus being received into the king's grace, those two took their places for a few days among the magnates of the court. The queen received them, and among her noblewomen was the Lady Senena. That meeting, being matter for the nobility and not for clerks, I did not see, but as I have heard, she kissed her eldest son with warm affection, and her second son with markedly more reserve, even coldly, for she could never quite forgive him for taking his own way, and still less for being, as she secretly suspected he was, in the right. However, he had made his peace with Owen, she made peace silently with him, and there were never any words either of reproach or reconciliation.

As for me, when I heard that the Lady Senena was in the queen's retinue, I went with an eager heart to make enquiry where she was lodged, for I thought my mother would be there with her. But the lady had left her daughter and her younger sons in London, and my mother was there in attendance on them, so I could not see her. For from Woodstock we rode for the border, and for home.

Those were years of labour and husbandry, and with little to tell, for we had a kind of peace that left us no field for action on any wider front than Gwynedd, and there Llewelyn occupied himself doggedly in raising stock and crops and making his lands as self-sufficient as he could. Owen surely fretted more and did less, for he had his father's lordly impetuosity and restlessness, not made for farming a cantref, nor was he infallible in choosing his officers. But except when the council met in full session we saw little of him, and what I most remember of the remainder of this year of twelve hundred and forty-seven is a steady drawing closer to my lord, until I was hardly ever from his side.

'I had thought,' I said to him once, when we spoke of that first visit to England, 'that the Lady Senena would come home now and bring your sister and brothers with her. Why does the king still detain her?'

'She is still a hostage,' said Llewelyn sombrely, 'though I doubt if she knows it. Hostage for Owen's good behaviour and mine. Not until we've kept his sorry peace another year or two will he let go of my mother. When he's sure we are tamed, then he'll unlock the doors for her. But whether she'll choose to walk out is another matter. For all my father's death, she's grown used to the comfort of an English court now, and to English policies, too. For Owen, if he asked her, she might make the effort to take up her roots again and replant them here. But Owen won't ask her,' he said with a wry smile. 'He wants no elders lecturing him on his duty or telling him how to run his commotes. And for me I think she would not stir.'

There was a one-sided effect of this peace with England, in fact, that continued, though without direct attack, the work of undoing what remained of the unity of Wales. For Gwynedd's submission and the tightening of the royal grasp on the Middle Country made many another small princeling consider that it might be safer to make direct contact and peace with this king, and many did so, settling thankfully under the shelter of his cloak. These he used against those who still continued recalcitrant, and divided and ruled in most of the southern parts of Wales. And by this time there was no one so hot in condemnation of those who voluntarily allied themselves with England as Owen.

Towards the end of the autumn he came riding into Bala, where we were busy making sure of the last of the harvest, for we had there some good fields, and had been at pains to extend them. Owen was full of news, having received letters from England, and fuller still of patriot rage.

'Do you know what she has done? Without a word to us, let alone asking our leave!'

'By the look and the sound of you,' said Llewelyn, watching the gleaners raking the last stubble, 'she would not have got your leave if she had asked it. What she?

113

And what has she done to set you on fire?'

'Why, our mother, of course! Have you heard nothing? She has married our sister, at King Henry's expense and with his goodwill, as if the girl had no male kin to be responsible for her! And to one of the king's Welsh hounds, one of the first of the pack, Rhys Fychan of Dynevor.'

This Rhys Fychan was son to Rhys Mechyll, of the old heart-fortress of Deheubarth, and had come to his inheritance when his father died, three years gone. I suppose at his accession he was about eighteen, which was my lord's age and mine when Owen came with this word, and he had had many difficulties to overcome, an ambitious uncle and a hostile mother not the least of them, so that he had done well to survive and keep his hold on his own, and it was no marvel to Llewelyn or to me that he had made his peace with England and done homage to King Henry a year previously. His was an old and honoured line, going back to the great Lord Rhys, whose last and least descendant was not to be despised as a match. But Owen was Welsh now from the highest hair of his head to his heel, and intolerant of everything tainted with English patronage.

'She might have done worse,' said Llewelyn mildly, and stood for a moment staring back into his childhood, for the Lady Gladys was little more than a year older than he, and came between those two brothers, but he had not so much as seen her for six years. 'She must be turned nineteen,' he said, pondering, 'and he's hardly two years older. And he was there at court last year, paying his respects, and not a bad-looking fellow, either. What would you have? If he took her fancy, and she took his, what could be more natural? I wish them heartily well.'

'The man is a traitor,' said Owen, smarting. 'And she must know it, as our mother surely does! But she grows old, she forgets with what intent she went to England. She has taught our sister to turn with the wind.'

I will not deny there was something in what he said, had it come from one less compromised himself. For whatever human creatures undertake, however purely, with whatever devotion, the ground turns under them and brings them about, facing where they never meant to face, and hard indeed it is to keep a clear eye to the north, and right oneself from such deflecting winds. And the Lady Senena had suffered much, and was weary, so that now I saw what Llewelyn had seen without effort, by pure instinct, how she was lost to us, and lost to her old self, the whole ground having shifted under her.

'Oh, come!' said Llewelyn tolerantly. 'We live among realities. Rhys Fychan is a man caught in their devil's web and doing his best with what he has, just as we are. God knows, there may come a time when we have to treat him as an enemy, but his is no case for hatred. Or overmuch righteousness!' he said, and gave me a smile, knowing Owen would never take the allusion. 'Much less our sister's! If she likes him, God give her joy of him. At least he's her own age, and belike every bit as innocent.'

Owen stamped off to the stables in dudgeon, to see his horse cared for, and left us to follow when the last cart was drawn in. He had no interest in such occupations.

Llewelyn walked beside me with wide eyes fixed upon the bowl of Bala and the mirror of the lake beyond. 'She is my only sister,' he said, marvelling, 'and I do not know her, or she me. Samson, what have we done with our childhood, or what have others done with it, to leave us strangers now?'

The next event of note I remember during these years of slow recovery is the bringing home of the Lord

Griffith's body, in the year following the peace of Woodstock. When a year had passed since that treaty, in exemplary quietness and submission on our part, Llewelyn judged that the time might be ripe to advance an intent he had always cherished since his father's death.

'For,' said he, 'King Henry may be satisfied by now, surely, that we have passed our probation, and the granting of a matter so small to him, especially where it touches the church, may appear very good policy.' For his estimate of the king, which proved accurate enough, was that he was an amiable person apart from his crown, and by no means bloodthirsty, but where his royal interests were concerned liable to look all round every concession or request in suspicion of hidden disadvantages, and incapable of any gesture large and generous. And often, in searching so narrowly for the insignificant march that might be stolen on him, he failed to see his best and truest interest when it was large under his nose. 'If he can read any malevolent intent into an act of filial piety,' said Llewelyn, 'let him argue it with ecclesiastics better versed in piety than he is. Or, for that matter, than I am!'

So first it was put to the council, who approved it to a man, Owen most loudly and perhaps with the most surprise and chagrin that it was the unfilial son, the deserter of his family's cause, who put it forward, rather than he, the fellow-sufferer with his sire in Criccieth and in London. And then the formal letters were drawn up, with all ceremony, both to king and archbishop, and committed to the willing and reverent hands of the abbots of Strata Florida and Aberconway, and a splendid escort provided to bring them to Westminster. For with all the abbots of the Cistercian houses Llewelyn was ever on the warmest terms of friendship and regard, like his grandsire before him, and the very echo of that name stood him in good stead.

To these letters, which were sent in the name of both brothers, and to the persuasions of the reverend abbots, King Henry listened, and saw that it could reflect nothing but radiance upon him to accede to the request, while he parted with nothing but the body of a broken tool, and might even a little salve his conscience and silence persistent rumour concerning that death by being gracious now to the remains. He therefore gave his permission and countenanced the removal of the Lord Griffith's corpse from its alien resting-place, and the abbots brought the prince's coffin in slow and solemn procession home to Aberconway, and there interred him with all appropriate rites beside his father and his half-brother. So those two sons of Llewelyn the Great lay together in peace at last.

It was four years more before the Lady Senena came home to Wales. Reassured by so long a period of calm and enforced order in Wales, King Henry declared himself willing to equip the lady and let her take her two remaining children to receive their allotment of land under Welsh law, even the youngest being now of age. It suited very well with the king's designs that even what he had left us of Gwynedd should be parcelled out among as many rival lords as possible, for the more and the more trivial the titles to land there, the less likely was any kind of unity in the future. And it suited well with the Lady Senena's old-fashioned leanings that ancient right should be observed at all costs. She was not yet old, being but five and forty, but experience and care, and especially the long years of being eaten by a sense of bitter grievance, had aged her greatly, and she longed to see all her sons established before she retired into the secluded life which was now increasingly attractive to

117

her. So the agreement was made that Rhodri and David should receive lands of their own, though the supreme rule over Gwynedd remained as before with their two elder brothers. And in the early summer Owen and Llewelyn sent an escort to bring their mother and brothers home.

Doubtless King Henry was also spared a considerable expense once they were gone from his court, and that was some relief to him, for he had difficulties of his own with his council and magnates over his expenditure, and to be able to point to one economy was at least a step in conciliating them. So all in all it suited everyone, though I am sure the Lady Senena felt pain by then in any upheaval in her life, and suffered doubts and depressions of which no one else knew, unless it might be Bishop Richard of Bangor, who accompanied the royal party on their journey, making one of his rare visits to his see.

This Bishop Richard had formerly been a strong supporter of the Lord Griffith's cause against David. After the treaty signed at Woodstock he had forsaken Gwynedd and preferred to make his home in the abbey of St Albans, and came only now and then to visit his flock. But in England he had taken an interest in the fortunes of the Lady Senena and her family, and she had a great respect and reverence for him, though many found him a difficult and thorny priest. Doubtless she was glad to have his support and consolation in setting out on this return journey to her own country, after eleven years of absence.

It was at Carnarvon that the princes received their mother and her retinue, that court being convenient to the commotes the council had agreed to give to Rhodri and David, and also to the bishop's own town of Bangor. Both Owen and Llewelyn rode out a mile or two on the road when they got word that the cavalcade had been sighted, and I went among their companions, for

Llewelyn knew that I was eager to get sight of my mother after so long, and bade me leave whatever work I had to do, for it would not spoil with keeping.

It was a slow procession we went to meet, for they had made a fair distance that day, and the horses were tired. The bishop, like the lady, rode in a litter, being already in his elder years, and frail. But a bright spark of blue and white played and darted about the group, now spurring ahead, now whirling to make a circle round them, now dancing along the green verge of the road on one side, now on the other. Restless and eager, this one young horseman fretted a silvery lace of movement about the slow core of the party, hard put to it to restrain himself from outrunning them all and coming first to Carnarvon.

He saw us, and for one moment reined in abruptly, on the crest of a hillock by the roadside. Then he came at a canter, and wheeled broadside before us, his eyes sweeping over us all, eyes the misty blue of harebells, and yet bright, under straight black brows. His head was uncovered and his breast was bare, the linen shirt turned back from his neck, for the June sun was hot. The wind had blown his blue-black hair into a tangle of curls, and stung a bright flush of blood over the cheekbones high and wide like wings.

So I saw my breast-brother again, smiling and eager, no less beautiful than when he charmed the ladies of the court at six years old.

He found Owen easily, and cried his name aloud in a crow of pleasure, and reining very lightly and expertly alongside, flung an arm about his eldest brother and kissed him.

'You I'd know by your hair among a thousand,' he said heartily, 'and glad I am to see you again. But Llewelyn was not red, and it's longer, I might shoot wide.' He

119

laughed with pleasure, for whatever he did he did with all his being. His eyes roved, touched me for an instant and wavered, flashing with a recognition that must wait its time. He walked his horse forward to where Llewelyn waited, smiling but not helping him, for he was too careless of his dress to be known for the prince by his ornaments. 'Yes! Not by your hair, but I know you!' He reached a long brown hand and touched very lightly the star-shaped scar at the angle of Llewelyn's jaw. 'My mother – *our* mother told me, when she came from Woodstock. Did you think she had not noticed? You,' he said, 'among ten thousand!' And he reached both arms, loosing the reins, and Llewelyn embraced him.

When the kiss was given and received, they drew apart, those two, and gazed at each other with something of wonder and curiosity, of which this quick, brotherly liking was but the blunted point. For they had been eleven years apart, and David now was but sixteen. And they said the most ordinary of words, because no others then would have had any meaning, their need of mutual exploration being so great.

'Our mother is well?' said Llewelyn, looking over David's shoulder towards the approaching litters.

'Well, but weary. Bear it in mind, for she'll never admit it, and draw the celebrations short tonight. Give her a day or two, and she'll be arranging all our lives for us,' said David irreverently.

'And Rhodri?'

'He's there, riding beside her litter. We took it by turns, but he has more patience than I. Rhodri is very well, only a little tired of the bishop's supervision. He minds him, I do not. It pleases him better,' said David, 'not to be minded. Where would he find matter for homilies, if we were all like Rhodri? Will you go and meet them?'

So we moved forward again towards the approaching procession, watching the gold-tinted dust eddy upwards, glittering, from the hooves of the horses. And as we went, David laid a hand softly on Llewelyn's arm, and said in his ear, but not so quietly that I did not catch the words: 'Pardon me if I leave you a moment. There's one here I must greet.' And without waiting for a reply he edged his horse very delicately from between his brothers, and brought him sidling and dancing alongside my pony on the edge of the escort.

'Samson ...? You are Samson, I could not be wrong.' He curbed his horse in such a way that we two fell aside and a little behind, and did it very smoothly, until there was space enough between us and the rest for us to talk openly and alone. And for my life I could not understand this compliment he was paying me, though I felt it pierce to my heart. As he had a way of doing, for good or evil.

'I am indeed Samson,' I said. 'I did not think you would remember me. I am glad from my heart to see you home.'

'I own,' he said, 'we have been apart some years now, and I was not very old or very wise, to remember well. Yet how could I forget *you*? We had one kind nurse, and she was yours, and only lent to me. Oh, Samson, I dearly loved her! How can I say what I need to say? My mother has it in charge to tell you, and I would spare you and her.' He saw how I was straining ahead to try and see into the open litter, from which the curtains were drawn back fully to let in light and air in the radiant June. And he laid his hand on my arm and held me hard. 'Don't look for her!' he said. 'You'll not find her.'

I turned then to look at him fully, and the blue of his eyes was like the pale zenith of the sky over us, almost blanched with pity. Then I understood that I had lost her, that Meilyr, wherever he was and if he still lived,

121

had been robbed of her whom he had never had but in a barren leash of law. And the strangest and best thing then was that this boy beside me, who could laugh, and play, and charm the hearts out of brothers and strangers alike, had tears in his eyes for her and me.

'If we had sent you word,' he said, 'it could have come only a day or two ahead of us, it was better to bring the grief with us, and share it with you. She died three days before we left London, of some fever, God knows what. It made such haste with her, she was gone in a night. My mother labours and frets with it, let me tell her that you know. And if I have done my errand ill, forgive me! She's buried there in London. We did all we could do.'

I told him I had no doubt of it, that I was grateful, that he need not be in any distress, for this was to be his day of reunion. I said I had lived without my mother now for some years, that no man nor woman can be kept for ever by love, that he should reassure his own mother that all was well, that all was very well. Nevertheless, he kept his hand touching my hand upon the bridle until we came up with the litters. And it was a mile and more on the way home to Carnarvon before he was riding again in flying circles about us, and laughing into the wind.

Thus my mother's few poor possessions came back to me at the Lady Senena's hands, and she spoke with regret and affection of the years of service Elen had given to the royal children, and there was no distress between us, the boy having done her office for her. And so unlikely a messenger of mourning never lived, except that birds can sing in cloudy weather as loudly and bravely as in the sun. For he was like a darting king-fisher over a stream, wild with delight in his own energy, youth and brightness, preening himself in the new clothes

122

provided for his home-coming, and inquisitive about everything that had once been familiar, and now had to be learned anew. And once, in the brief time while she was most softened and welcoming to me, the Lady Senena caught my dazzled eyes following his flight, and said to me, half in admiration, it seemed, and half in warning: 'Do not think him as light and shallow as he seems. He is as deep as the sea off Enlli, and as hard to know.'

I thought her partial to Rhodri, as indeed she was, for in his childhood he had suffered occasional illness, and so attached her to himself more anxiously than any of his brothers. Moreover, he was of a somewhat dour temperament not unlike her own, and she understood him better than the youngest and most wayward of her brood, whose alien brilliance reached back to his grandsire.

I watched them often, during those few days spent at Carnarvon, as they sat side by side at the high table in hall, for that was the first and only time that I saw all those four brothers of Gwynedd together, grouped like a family about their mother. And very earnestly I studied all those faces, so like and so unlike, for all had something of both parents in them, but all shaped that essence differently. Owen Goch most resembled his father, being the tallest and heaviest of the four, with florid, russet face and opulent flesh. Only his dark-red, burning hair set him apart. He was very strong, and a good man of his hands, though too ready with them in and out of season, like the Lord Griffith before him, and with the same hot temper. With weapons he was fearless, but too rash and therefore a little clumsy. And for all his ready furies he also, as Llewelyn had once said of him, bore grudges which he never forgot, so that often I had wondered how he contrived to put away the memory of being worsted and having the dagger wrested out of his hand, that night at Aber, and how he could stomach that defeat and work mildly with his brother in court and council. As for me, he had never given me a reminder of it by word or look, hardly met my eyes since that day, and I had kept out of his way to avoid touching, even by the sight of me, a spot that might still be sore. Yet I felt some shame in doing him what I thought must, after all, be an injustice.

Llewelyn, sitting beside him, was well-nigh as broad in the shoulder, and not much shorter, but brown and lean and hard, for he lived a rough outdoor life by choice, as often involved with cattle and fields as with court and council. Eryri is a harsh, stony, untilled land, yet it has fields in some sheltered valleys that can be made to bear beans and pease, if not corn, and he had good reason to remember the winter of hunger after the rape of Anglesey. His brown face, all bone and brow, looked lively and good-humoured in company, and sturdily thoughtful in repose. My lord at this time was twenty-three years old, body and mind formed fully, and both under large and easy control. Often I was aware that he was consciously waiting, and employing his days to the best effect until his time came, for he knew how to wait.

Rhodri was the slenderest of the four, but of resource in getting by device what he could not get by force. His face was fair and freckled, a condition usual with hair of such a light, reddish colour. As a child I remembered him as capable of spite, and capricious in his likes and dislikes as in his interests, blowing all ways in one day, and in and out with everyone about him too quickly to follow his turns. Beside those other three he seemed of light weight, but that weight might be thrown into the scale so wantonly as to upset all. At the manly exercises which showed David at his burning best Rhodri was but

124

mediocre, though he could hold his own with the lump. He was attentive and gentle with his mother, who loved him dearly, and fretted over him constantly.

And David sparkled and shone upon all, the youngest and the most radiant, for to him everything was new and strange, and he was about to enter into the possession of lands of his own, and bright with the excitement of it. He, of them all, knew how to approach all, though his calculations were civil, heartening and kind. And I loved him for the wisdom of which his mother had warned me, for deep he was, as the sea, but better governed, and more sparing of poor men.

Both those young princes were full of the news of the English court, and both talked like men of the world, familiarly naming far places, and great men whose dealings came to us in Wales only as distant legends, though we knew they lived and moved in the same world with us, and could bring about changes that effected our lives, too. The more voluble and loud was Rhodri, the elder, who looked upon David still as little more than a child. But what David had to say was more sharply perceptive, and often critical.

'King Henry has a finger in so many affairs abroad,' Rhodri said, 'I doubt he has no time or attention to give to Wales nowadays. He's very close with Pope Innocent, since he took the cross, two years ago. You knew of that? It eased his situation with Innocent that the old Emperor Frederick died. It was all very well having a sister married to the greatest man in Europe, even if he had had other wives before, and kept hundreds of concubines, as they say, in his court in Sicily. But since the pope has turned against the whole house of Hohenstaufen as the devil's brood, it's well to have Isabella safely widowed, and the whole adventure forgotten.'

'He bids fair to have trouble enough with the sister's

husband he still has,' said David, 'and nearer home. There's been the devil to pay ever since Easter, with the Gascons charging the earl of Leicester with God knows what mismanagement in their province, and the earl on his defence, and hard-pressed, too. King Henry hit out at him more like an enemy than a brother – he never could keep his temper when he felt himself measured against a larger man. Earl Simon never raised his voice but once, and then but for a moment.'

'You speak too impudently of his Grace,' said the Lady Senena frowning. 'And what do you know of the matter, a child like you?'

'Everything,' said David, undisturbed. 'I was there in the abbey refectory four days running when the fighting was at its best. I heard them at it.'

'You?' she said indulgently. 'And how would you get admission to a grave court hearing? You are making up vain stories.'

'Edward got me into the room with him. I was curious, and put it into his head. It all ended in a compounded peace,' said David, 'as everybody knows, but Earl Simon had the best of the argument, to my way of thinking. True, he brought it on himself, for from all I hear the man is mad who believes French law and order can be imposed on Gascons. He never understood them, and they would not abide him. In the end the king has imposed a truce, and promised to go himself to Gascony next spring, or to send Edward, and Earl Simon has given up his command voluntarily, on his expenses being paid. They got out of it with everyone's face saved by having Gascony formally handed over to Edward, for he's to have it as part of his appanage in any case. And the earl has gone back to France for the time being, free of his province. He never wanted it in the first place,' said the boy positively. 'He wanted to go on crusade with

126

King Louis, and only gave it up because King Henry begged him to take charge in Gascony. And all it's done is cost him a great deal of money out of his own purse, made him hated in the south, and spilled a whole sea of bad blood between him and the king.'

'You have no right,' said the Lady Senena severely, 'to speak so of either the king or the earl. It would do you more credit if you showed a greater respect for your elders.'

He smiled at her placatingly, but he was unmoved. 'They are men,' he said, 'like other men.'

Now this Earl Simon was a French nobleman of the de Montfort family, who had come into the earldom of Leicester by right of his grandmother Amicia, there being no male heir left in England to the Leicester honour. He was the second son of his father, but his elder brother Amaury held by his French possessions, and surrendered the English right to the next in succession. And this young man had not only come to take up his estates in England, but taken the eye and the heart of King Henry's widowed sister Eleanor, so that she married him, and to that marriage the king was privy. The story caused much scandal, for the lady, who was but sixteen when her first husband died, had rashly taken a vow to remain chaste for life, and for love of Earl Simon she broke that vow, against all pressure upon her from chaplains and archbishops, and wed where her heart was. But all this happened when I was but a child, and I had the story only long afterwards, while we were close to the court in London. King Henry had always geese that were swans, and Earl Simon was high in his regard then, but when he found that the match had brought his own countenance into some disrepute with the clerics the king was affrighted, and though he made no break with his new brother I think he held that embarrassment greatly against him thereafter, and never quite forgave it, so that any new dissension between them had in it the seeds of greater hostility than appeared in the matter itself.

'So Edward's to have Gascony,' said Llewelyn, musing. 'Is it just a way of getting out of the difficulty with no broken heads, do you think, or is the king setting him up already in a court of his own? He's barely turned thirteen.'

Rhodri was confident that it had been but a convenient close to the dangerous dispute with Earl Simon, allowing him to withdraw honourably and gracefully, though doubtless it had been intended that some day young Edward should indeed rule the Gascon possessions. But David shook his head at that, very sure of himself.

'This is but the first move in another game. King Henry has a great many other lands marked down for his heir, and very soon, too. He's being fitted out with a great appanage in readiness for his marriage, though only a handful of people even at court know of the plan. You've heard there's a new king in Castille? This Alfonso has a half-sister, only a child as yet. King Henry is making the first advances to marry Edward to her.'

'And takes you into his confidence before he even sends proctors!' scoffed Rhodri. 'Don't listen to him, he's flying his hawk at the sun!'

'King Henry may not,' said David, unperturbed, 'but Edward does. Where else should I get it?' He looked round with a sudden flashing glance at us all, and said in a lower voice: 'And there's more, and nearer to us. King Henry intends his son shall have all the crown's lands in Wales, into the bargain.'

Curbed and hemmed in as we then were, it sounded no worse than what we had already, and offered promise of something better, for if a separate court and council were set up for the crown's Welsh lands there was a hope, at least, that the administrators might draw upon experience and wisdom from among the better marchers, who knew how to deal with their Welsh neighbours as with men deserving of respect. The Welsh tenants under the present jurisdiction of the justiciar of Chester had complaints enough, that their customs and laws were disregarded, that they were being increasingly squeezed under heavy taxation, and that unjustly administered into the bargain, their lands bled to help supply London, while London turned a deaf ear to their needs. So we heard what David reported thoughtfully, but kept open minds concerning the event.

In the middle days of July, having set up Rhodri already on his portion, we brought David with ceremony home to take possession of his lands in Cymydmaen, in Lleyn, that very commote from which the Lady Senena had set out with her children for Shrewsbury, so long before. The lady went with us, escorted still by Bishop Richard of Bangor, that small, soured, querulous priest, who was desirous of seeing right done to all the brothers before he returned to his see, and thence to his chosen retirement in St Albans.

So we rode back, all together, over the inland roads and the rolling pastures to Neigwl, and came in sight of the sea, pale almost to whiteness in the bright sunlight, with the island of saints gleaming offshore, Enlli, where the holy come to die and be buried in bliss. When we passed by that spot where we had met on the evening of the lady's flight, Llewelyn turned his head and looked at me, smiling, and I knew that he was seeing a boy coming down from the fields with the lambs, as I was seeing a boy on horseback, who turned to look a last time at the home he was forsaking.

But David, who rode between us, reared up tall in his

saddle to gaze with bright and hungry eyes down into the walls of the maenol that was now to be his court, the first over which he had ever ruled alone. There were his servants, his councillors, his cattle and horses, and in the hills and trefs around, his tenants, his men in war and peace, owing him service according to Welsh law.

'And all this is mine!' he said, but softly, only for our ears, seeing it was a child's cry of triumph and delight, not fitting the public utterance of the lord of a commote. When we brought him down to the gates, to give his hand to all those who came crowding to attend him, then he was princely and composed enough, and did all with lordly dignity. Nevertheless, that day I think he was utterly fulfilled and content.

So, at some bright peak of their lives, must all men be. The grief is that it lasts not long.

CHAPTER V

King Henry, just as David had said, went in person into Gascony the following year, and there he found it by no means so simple as he had supposed to put right everything he claimed the earl of Leicester had put wrong, for that Count Gaston of Béarn whom he had expected to find a grateful and affectionate kinsman, having championed him in his complaints against the earl, turned out a difficult and rebellious vassal, as obdurate against the king himself as against his viceroy, and there was great to-ing and fro-ing of letters between Bordeaux and England before the king got all into control, the troubles in those distant parts, and the matter of his son's marriage, keeping him absent all the following year.

During this long absence his queen, together with his brother Richard of Cornwall, acted as regents in his room. And it was they who summoned David to court in the first week of July, shortly after the king's departure, to do homage to them as the king's proxies for his commote of Cymydmaen. He had held it then for a year, and I think his pleasure in it was still keen, if he had not received this friendly call back to a wider and more worldly court. Moreover, this was to the queen, with whom he had always found great favour because of her son's attachment to him. He had less fondness for the king, indeed to some degree he showed a certain disdain for that less resolute and dependable personage, though he had been much indulged by him. Certain it is that he received the summons joyfully, almost like one startled out of a comfortable but confining dream to his real waking life. He made great preparation, and provided his party royally for the journey, intent that there should be none about the queen's person more splendid than himself and his retinue. This I bear witness, having visited him on my lord's business shortly before he left for England. I think indeed, however gilded and jewelled, no young man more beautiful graced the court that year, or any year. And so thought many a Welsh lady he left behind him, and I doubt not many an English lady who greeted him.

Who first had his favours I do not profess to know. But by this he was no stranger to women. Nor did any ever complain of him, save perhaps of his absence.

I think the Lady Senena would have liked to travel with him to court on that occasion, but he was not so minded. He was fond of her, but fonder of his own new and heady freedom and dignity, and it must be admitted that she was a managing woman. He persuaded her that his commote of Cymydmaen could not flourish in his absence without a touch as firm as hers, and that there was no one to whom he would so happily confide it, and that sweetened her exclusion from his party. So if he was ruthless in ridding himself of her company, at least he did it in a way that flattered instead of affronting.

Thus he went south from us at the end of June, in great splendour, at least to our eyes. Llewelyn laughed to see how fine he had made himself, and how formally attended, but without unkindness, for the boy was still only seventeen, and in his pride and determination to outshine the nobility of the English court he was making a stand for the good name of Wales, however childishly. Indeed, he laughed at himself, but never relaxing his resolve to show like the sun. And always he had this seeming ability to stand aside from himself and make a mockery of what that self did in all solemnity, either part of him as real and formidable as the other. So he went to his reunion with the queen and the earl of Cornwall, and with Edward, his play-fellow.

He did not come back until the end of July. Most of his escort he sent on ahead to Neigwl, and himself, with only a few attendants, came visiting to us at Carnarvon. He was lively and full of news, but as it were something distracted, as though but half his mind had returned with him, and the remaining half lagged somewhere on the way, reluctant to catch up with him. And he spoke – I noted it, and so, I know, did Llewelyn – of the queen, and Richard of Cornwall, and the two boys Edward and Edmund, and other of that company, very familiarly yet not with any air of boasting his familiarity. Had it been Rhodri we should have seen him plume himself as he spoke. David used their names as simply and naturally as ours, and only from time to time seemed to catch the strange echo of his utterance, and to be startled and shaken by it. For it was that very familiarity that was so strange. And then his eyes would open wider in their blue brilliance, and look round the solar where we sat, at every skin rug and smoky hanging, as though starting out of a dream, or falling headlong into one.

'And this Castillian marriage,' Llewelyn questioned intently, 'that goes forward?'

'So Edward says. At least his proctors are appointed, before the king left England, and they're busy dealing now over terms. If the marriage and the treaty come to fruit, then Alfonso could be the best protector of King Henry's interests in Gascony, where he's in very good odour with even the Béarnais.'

'I'd as soon see King Henry still on thorns, and looking towards Gascony,' Llewelyn said drily, 'as comforted and easy in his mind, and looking my way. The less care he

133

has to lavish on me, the better.'

'Take heart, then,' said David, 'for as fast as he gets out of one morass he's into another. He's barely got clear of the whole dangerous race of the Hohenstaufen, from Barbarossa down, than he swings too far towards the pope in his relief, and finds himself mired to the knees in the opposite swamp. Innocent hates that family and all who are allied to it, and his one desire left in life is to uproot the last of them from the kingdom of Sicily, and set up an emperor more to his taste. Last year he began sounding out candidates for the honour of supplanting him. He began with the earl of Cornwall, but our Richard took very little time to refuse the compliment. As well try to pluck the moon out of heaven, he said, as turn Conrad out of Sicily. King Louis's brother thought a little longer about it, but the answer was the same. And now, it's rumoured, Innocent has mentioned the matter cautiously to King Henry, with young Edmund in mind. The king has not closed with the offer yet, but trust me, he's too deeply tempted and too incurably hopeful to resist, if a firm offer is ever made. It would mean paying off the pope's debts in the enterprise to date – well above a hundred thousand marks, they say – and putting troops into Sicily. If he can so much as land them there! But it might induce Innocent to commute his crusading vow to undertaking this act of cleansing nearer home. All in all, there are those at court who are mightily disturbed about the prospect, for to them it looks like the short road to ruin. Not many are wise to the danger yet, but Richard of Cornwall is, since it was first offered to him, and he had good sense enough to refuse. So you may rely on it, King Henry is more than engrossed in his own plans, and soon will be in his own troubles.'

He said all this without flourishes or hesitation, not

afraid to speak as statesmen and councillors do. And while his wits were thus engaged in this enlarged world, peopled by popes and emperors and the paladin brothers of kings, his eyes were brilliant and his cheeks flushed, as though he entered into a kingdom of his own.

'I see,' said Llewelyn, between amusement and wonder, 'you have not wasted your time in England. Is it Edward who discusses these intimate matters with you? Before the king's own council know them?'

'I use my eyes and ears,' said David, and smiled. 'And given a certain sum of knowledge, more follows without questions asked or answered. As, for instance, that if King Henry does indeed want to pursue this latest hope, he can hardly get far with it while he's still at odds with the king of France, and it needs no prophet to judge that sooner or later there'll be an accommodation. Those two will be friends yet, trust me.'

'I had rather they stayed enemies,' Llewelyn owned. 'I breathe more easily so. But you could be right, and I'll bear it well in mind. If my enemy has no enemies elsewhere, how shall I thrive? Go on, tell me what you have heard concerning this Castillian marriage. A great appanage, you said, to set the prince up as a married man. Gascony, that we know of. What else? There'll be equally large endowments nearer home.'

'It's no way certain,' said David, 'what they'll be, for there's no decision made yet, no more than talk. But they say he'll have Ireland. And Chester and its county, and most likely Bristol, too. And Wales, all the crown possessions here. The Middle Country, the castles of Diserth and Degannwy, the lordships of Cardigan, Carmarthen, Montgomery and Builth. Maybe the three castles of Gwent. But nothing's yet certain.'

His face, intent and bright, said that nevertheless it was known to him, as surely as if it had been sealed already. And Llewelyn saw that certainty in him, and sprang upon it.

'But you had this from Edward!'

David acknowledged it, but with reserve, for Edward's father was an ever-hopeful, light and changeable man, and what was not yet made public could be taken back unsaid.

Said Llewelyn: 'I begin to see this boy, this Edward of yours, as a shape that threatens my plans. Chester and Bristol, that's my northern march and the southern one, too. Gwent and the Middle Country, spears into my side. While they stayed with Henry, did they matter quite so much? Henry shifts. This son of his has an immovable sound about him. I would I knew as much of him as you know. God knows I need it, for Edward is the future. And like to live? Yes, surely, you spoke of his rough health, he's for a long life. Talk to me of him,' he ordered, and his voice was urgent and low. 'Tell me all that you know, all that you feel concerning him. Shut your eyes, if you will, and forget I am here. Show me your Edward!'

I know of no one to whom such an order could be easy to obey. It closed David's mouth as though some curse had sealed it, but that was only for a while. He shut his eyes, to me an astonishment, for he rebelled by nature against all such suggestions, and in a little while the tight, bright lines softened in his face, and he did begin to speak of Edward. Softly and haltingly at first, then as if in a dream, with curious happiness and eloquence, so that he seemed to be speaking only to his own heart. He had known this boy, three years younger than himself, for some ten or eleven years, and the king's second son, Edmund, had never made any great mark in their companionship, Edward's bent being always, as it seemed, towards those somewhat his elders. For he was a strong, clever and serious-minded child, able to grapple with those more grown in body and more tutored in mind. And past doubt, as we heard from his own lips, David had been involved in both loving and misliking him, the prince being adventurous and gallant to a degree, willing to match himself against his older comrade, yet able to revert into royalty when outmatched or displeased. A strange child, well aware of his destiny from early years, but proud, too, of his body and its competence, of his mind and its brightness. There was a certain largeness and warmth in him then, that would take a tumble and never grudge it, provided no one laughed. But from what I heard out of David's lips, as he talked blindly from behind closed eyelids, sometimes smiling and sometimes grim, I would not have given much for any who outmatched the prince constantly and innocently, unaware of offence, and trusting to have their own magnanimity reflected in his. For there are those who cannot abide to be any but first, and can afford to throw away one lapse, or two, as largesse, but never more than one or two, for after that the sin is mortal.

When he had talked himself out of breath and words, and into some deep, private place of recollection and discovery, David opened his eyes, and they were wild and a little affrighted, as though only now, with the return of vision, did he realise all that he had revealed. As though the first person he saw was the Edward he had painted for us, his back turned, walking steadily away. For surely he had never before looked inward and examined what he knew and felt of his royal companion, and now that he did so, the very depth and width of his knowledge frightened him, and his having shared it went beyond, and in some way horrified and shamed him.

'What have I done?' he said in a dismayed whisper. 'I have said too much. What right had I to strip him so for you?'

'You did no more than I asked you,' said Llewelyn, smiling at him with astonished affection, 'and did it very well. If I needed a portrait, I have it.'

'But to bind him hand and foot, and stand him in front of you naked!' David cried, twisting and knotting his hands.

At that Llewelyn laughed, and flung an arm rallyingly round his shoulders and shook him. 'I did not see him so! Far from it! Very well and richly clothed in his own abilities you showed him to me, and well worth looking at, too. You're too tender of your loyalties. Faith, I think you've come back to us more an English courtier than a Welsh prince!'

He meant no more than the lightest of touches, and yet it went in like a barb. David shook off the arm that held him and bounded to his feet, white-faced with passion.

'You dare say so to me? You dare? I am as much Griffith's son as you are, and no one, not even a brother, can use such words to me and not be called to account. Is it my fault if I grew up at King Henry's court? You think I've turned my coat for Edward's favour? Every drop of blood in me is Welsh, as Welsh as yours, as royal and as true!'

Llewelyn was too taken aback by this outburst to get his breath for a moment. He stood open-mouthed, the rallying laughter still on his lips, and a great astonishment in his eyes. And before he could retort either with indulgent mockery or blunt and forcible reproof, David had caught himself a little back from us into shadow, as if to hide, turned one wild and angry glance like the sweep of a sword to hold off both of us, and flung out of the room.

'Now what in God's name ailed him,' Llewelyn demanded, gazing after him, 'to take me so desperately in earnest? Does he know so much of his Edward, and so little of me?'

I said no, that he knew well enough, had known even while the words were pulsing hotly out of his throat, that the sting he had felt had never been delivered but in his own mind. But if that was comfort to Llewelyn, it was oddly discomfortable to me. For if, in his unguarded moment, David had been so ready and quick to resent the imagined charge of a divided and shifting allegiance, it was surely because his own heart had already accused him. Llewelyn had touched a wound that was already waiting, open and painful. More, for I had seen the boy's face as he leaped to his feet, and I was sure that if he had not shown his prince to Llewelyn naked and bound, naked and bound he himself had suddenly seen him, and that cry of his: 'What have I done? I have said too much!' was his own recognition of an act of treason on one side, barely a moment before he felt himself assailed by the like accusation from the other.

It seemed to me then that we had none of us given enough thought to the stresses under which those two younger ones laboured, thus translated so late back to their own land, when all their most formative years had been spent in another, and that in innocence, protected and indulged, when they were too young to understand the agonies and wrongs that had brought them there. What they now knew and professed, and even understood, they had never been forced to feel. And Rhodri, perhaps, was centred so shallowly in himself as to be proof against too much thought, but David was subtle, brooding and deep.

Llewelyn had been thinking much as I had, for he said soberly: 'He's newly back, and it comes hard, I daresay. But it will pass. Give him a month or two to settle down at Neigwl, and he'll be too busy and content to look

139

back towards Westminster. All the same, better not make that journey too often, the cost comes too high.'

I asked if I should go after him, for the disquiet and desperation of his face as he left us tormented me, and he was fond of me, and would not bite too viciously if I offended him. But Llewelyn said no.

'Let him alone. He'll come back of his own will, and better so.'

And so he did, before many minutes were past, entering almost as abruptly as he had left us, and taking his stand before Llewelyn, within touch and in the fullest light of the room, with a clear face and wide-open eyes, only a little flushed in the cheeks now after his bitter pallor.

'I ask your pardon,' he said outright and easily, 'for being so ill-humoured. It was foolish to think you meant any evil.'

'Call quits,' said Llewelyn, 'for it was a very feeble joke. That's one subject I shall know better than take lightly again. Faith, it was like putting a torch to tinder!'

'And over as quickly,' said David, with a trace of bitterness, before he hoisted his shoulders and laughed. 'If a real enemy sets light to me you shall find I burn both hot and slow.'

So suddenly and vehemently he made his peace, and they went out together to the mews with David's arm about Llewelyn's neck. But at times he did revert to this flare thereafter, always without warning, and always as one excusing himself, saying how he grudged it that only Llewelyn, of the four brothers, had fought and starved for Wales, while he fattened in comfort as a pampered child at the English court, and how this sense of having been cheated out of his morsel of glory made him sore to touch on that point. So that sometimes I questioned within myself whether it was indeed so soon and safely over, or whether he brooded still in his heart, keeping his trouble to himself. And above all, whether what he revealed of it was the true core, or whether he went about, unknown to himself, to dress it more acceptably for our eyes and his own.

But Llewelyn, who seemed to be most wise in his youngest brother, took him peaceably as he came, and made no to-do, letting him alone with his own good heart and good sense to find his way aright. And when David thus spoke of playing the child in England while Wales bled, and not even chafing at his helplessness for want of understanding, Llewelyn would say bluntly that he need have no regrets, for the true struggle for Wales had not yet even begun, and he had plenty of time in the years ahead to make his name as a paladin.

Once I asked him, when we were alone, if he truly meant this. For we seemed then to be so securely pinned down in our restricted lands, and yet so tolerated and accepted in this limited state, that I could not see how we could again be brought into conflict with England. King Henry was utterly absorbed in his Sicilian plans and his son's marriage, in the business of bringing to an end his long enmity with France, in settling Gascony for Edward and resigning himself to relaxing all hold on Normandy. His face was set constantly eastward, not westward. It seemed that he had no thought for us, and no intent to trouble us further. And if he had no will to make war, we had no means, or means so slight that the attempt would be madness.

'As yet,' said Llewelyn. 'Yet even now we are not so unready as you may suppose. Still, I grant you there are stones in the way.' He mused for a moment on the greatest and most immovable of these, but went on without naming it. 'It will, it must, come to war in the end, the art will be in choosing the time. For this most

141

marked stress upon Wales, in Prince Edward's appanage, with the earldom of Chester held fast by the crown for him, and Bristol in the south, this is a new threat, whatever its appearance in the documents. His is not meant to be any parchment title. This is a planned move to tighten the royal grip upon Wales. The time will come when we must fight to regain what we have lost, if we are not to find ourselves fighting hard to keep even what they have left us. It cannot stand long as it is. They will take all from us, or we must regain all from them.'

I had learned to have great faith in his judgment, and I knew by his face and his tone that he was in strong earnest. Yet it seemed to me, considering the cautious stillness in which we had lived now such a number of years, that our situation rendered action as impossible to us now as before the peace of Woodstock.

Llewelyn shook his head. 'No! The king's officers are doing our work for us, we need not lift a finger yet, they win friends for us right and left. This la Zuche who holds the Middle Country in his grip, and has sworn to bring it under English control for all time, is worth an army to me. I could not so soon have convinced every knight and lord and tenant in the four cantrefs of his Welsh blood, and his need to remember it, as this man has done. I could not have united all those quarrelling borderers as he has done, in one patriot hate of England and her officers and all her works. He calls recruits for me out of the ground like corn from seed. The time will come when I need only to go and reap the harvest. And a little success there could call back to their allegiance great numbers of those princes elsewhere who offered King Henry their homage out of fear. Success breeds true and fast. Only,' he said, and looked out long over the sea towards Ynys Lanog, for we were riding by the salt-flats of Aber, 'there must also be unity at the top, or we split and fall apart.'

I was in his close confidence. He spoke with me as with his own soul, and I with him as I had wit, for all my intent was to be of help to him if I might, in whatever enterprise he undertook, whether it was the better draining of a piece of upland bog that might be made to grow food, or the training of the falcons of Snowdon in which he delighted, or the glorious recovery of all the lost lands of Gwynedd, or, yet more wonderful, the reaching forward strongly into his grandsire's dream of a single and splendid Wales under one prince, which I knew to be also his dream. My will was always to see with his eyes, to divine his desire, and to lend whatever might I had to help him achieve it. Therefore I said without conceal: 'The stone in your way is the Lord Owen. God knows I mean no ill against your father, but he had no such vision, and neither has his eldest son. With a great work to be done, he is not the partner you would have chosen.'

In this I was astray, for I believed he had young David in mind. And I think he saw my meaning, for he gave me a long, dark but smiling look, and answered only: 'There are many men in this land I will gladly have as allies and officers, and I hope friends. None I would choose as a partner. The time I have waited for is coming. Slowly, but it is coming. And what I have to do, Samson, can only be done alone.'

'How, then,' I said, willing to follow him into any extremes for that vision, 'will you dispose?'

'In his own good time, and with whatever instrument he chooses, God will dispose,' said Llewelyn.

But the quietness and the waiting continued yet two years, and Llewelyn made no complaint, but went on with his work in orderly fashion.

David visited us but little, busying himself with his lands in Lleyn, though I think with less joy than formerly. For the first lustre was gone from possession, and after his return to his old royal haunts the llys at Neigwl looked poor and rustic to him, and Cymydmaen shrunken and wild. I speak with the wisdom of hindsight, for we knew nothing then of any discontent and unrest in him, and thought it well that he spent so much time on his own lands, believing he cherished and improved, rather than fretting and brooding. Llewelyn had never but once seen the English court, and that was in somewhat diminished state at Woodstock, never at Westminster, and its glories had been as a front opposed to him, never as a warmth enclosing him, such as they had been to David. I, who had seen somewhat of London, though as a servant to my child lords, should have understood better the force of the contrast between David's two estates.

I did not, and the more blame to me.

We took good care, those days, to get regular news of all that went forward about King Henry's court. In February Prince Edward's portion was published, and contained all that David had said: Ireland, but for a few places held in reserve, Chester and its county, Bristol, where his exchequer and offices would be based, all the crown possessions in Wales, the Channel Islands, Gascony entire, with the island of Oléron. A vast endowment. The Welsh grant included even a part of the coast north of Cardigan, so that the powers of England closed their claws on Eryri from every side. And one Geoffrey Langley, a king's officer heretofore best known for his harsh dealings in the law of the forest, was given the Middle Country to milk for his masters, for they held that it could be made to yield a far higher revenue for the prince than it had so far produced. I doubt Langley in the first six months of office did more even than Alan la Zuche had done in several years, to make good Llewelyn's words concerning the raising of an army of embittered Welshmen who waited only for a leader.

We had full reports also, and none so slow in reaching us, either, of the marriage in Burgos. Prince Edward crossed over to Gascony a little before his fifteenth birthday, which fell on the seventeenth day of June of that year, twelve hundred and fifty-four. The queen travelled with him, and also Archbishop Boniface of Canterbury, uncle to the queen, one of those kinsmen of hers from Savoy who were causing so much jealousy and resentment among the English nobility, together with the king's Lusignan half-brothers, his mother's sons by her second husband, who came swarming over from Poitou to make their fortune by rich marriages in England. These foreign kinsmen were one of the chief causes of complaint against King Henry, and brought him into great difficulties in later years, but he valued and favoured them in spite of all blame.

The marriage plans were completed at leisure during the summer months of June and July, and then the prince's party moved on to Burgos, and there King Alfonso knighted him, and towards the end of October the child Eleanor, the king's half-sister, was married to the heir of England with all ceremony in the cathedral of Burgos. Then King Alfonso formally renounced all claims to Gascony, having acquired a close interest in it by another way which suited him well enough, and cost no warfare and no bad blood. For his influence was great with both King Henry and King Henry's son. The prince took his little bride back into Gascony with him, and there they stayed for a full year before coming home to England.

And there was more still to confirm all that David had told us. For King Henry on his way home after the marriage determined to make the first advance towards that composition with France which would set him free to pursue the Sicilian enterprise on his second son's behalf. King Louis was returned at last from his crusading adventures in the east. King Henry sent envoys to him, and solicited a meeting, a personal acquaintance such as could be sealed into friendship. And at Chartres King Louis met him most graciously, and conducted him to Paris, where he was royally entertained, and the queen's Provençal family were brought together in a grand reunion. For this King Louis was more than commonly wise and kind in personal matters, very skilled in turning to pleasure and ease a first meeting that might have been hard and painful. So those two met, and the seed was sown which should bring about a full settlement, a treaty of peace and harmony between their countries, formerly in enmity.

Nevertheless, as Llewelyn had said, a compounding between those two kings boded nothing of benefit to us, for our enemy's rear was thereby secured, and he could turn his attention all the more freely to Wales. Yet such are the chances of the time, it fell out otherwise. For always there is some unforeseen mercy, or unexpected chastening, waiting to be manifested.

The Christmas feast that year was chill and bright and windy. Contrary gales kept King Henry from landing at Dover until the day after St Stephen's, and went driving down the coast of Wales like silver lances, cold as ice. And yet the skies were cloudless and full of stars, most beautiful to see, and there was but a little snow, that dried up in the frost and blew like white dust about the flats. For we kept the feast at Aber, after the old fashion.

We lacked only Rhodri and the Lady Senena at that feast. For Rhodri had at that time a certain lady who

146

took up all his attention, and kept him at home in his own llys, and the Lady Senena, though she made her stay mainly with David at Neigwl, having spent so much of her married life there and having a fondness for the spot, had journeyed in the autumn into the south, to pay a first visit to her daughter Gladys at Dynevor. Between that castle, willing subject to King Henry, and our princedom of Gwynedd, there was no contact, though before the Lady Senena came home to Wales the two princes, at Llewelyn's urging, had offered to Rhys Fychan and his house a compact of mutual aid and support, which remained, unhappily, no more than a parchment pledge, since the members of that house could not even agree among themselves. Yet I know that Llewelyn had blessed his mother's journey, and sent greetings in all kindness to his sister, whose stiff loyalty to her husband he did not any way blame. But no word came back, as he looked for none.

In the brightness of the day the brothers rode much, and by night in hall there was good food and drink in plenty, and good harping, for our bards were famous, and so was Llewelyn's patronage, so that many singers came from other parts to entertain in his hall, and none ever went away empty-handed or discontented with his reward. That Christmas we saw David in uneasy mood, either wildly elated and gay, or withdrawn into a black depression. And often his tongue bit sharply, but both his elders, seeing how deeply he had drunk, bore with him goodnaturedly, and always he sprang back into the light in time to disarm us all. So though it was unusual in him, we thought nothing amiss.

He came to me late in an evening in the little chamber where I kept the rolls, and did my writing and reckoning on Llewelyn's business. I had left the hall early, having some matters waiting for me, and thinking this the best hour to withdraw and see the work done. There were certain complicated cases to be heard in my lord's commote court, two concerning the removal of boundaries, and also a matter of some wreckage cast up by the sea on the edge of the church lands of Bangor, the goods being in dispute between prince and bishop, for Bishop Richard was a contentious and obstinate man. Llewelyn relied on me to have all the needful information tabled and ready to his hand. True, he had also his chaplain and official secretary, but the clerking was left to me at my lord's wish, and it was I who accompanied him when he rode out to preside in all his district courts.

Over this labour David came in to me, alone, and stood by me for a little while reading over my shoulder. He was flushed with wine, but quiet, and very well able to carry what he had drunk with grace, as commonly he did.

'Samson,' he said, after a while of silence, 'you know Welsh law as well as any man here. Tell me, what is the law concerning the succession to a crown?'

'You know it as well as I,' I said, and went on writing, for I had much to do. 'The wise prince names his successor while he's well alive, and sees to it that he's accepted by all.'

'And if the prince is less wise, and never names an edling to follow him?' he persisted in the same low and deliberate voice.

'Then his realm is liable to division among all his sons. But in practice it's far more like to go by consent to the eldest, and see some minor lands given to the others.'

'True,' he said, 'but that's not Welsh law, and you know it, it's a convenience borrowed from the English. Four sons with an equal claim are entitled to fair shares of the inheritance.'

'If they care to stand on their rights, and tear apart what has been laboriously put together,' I said, still paying him little heed, 'they may say so. But with a greedy neighbour waiting to pick off their portions one by one, I would not recommend it.'

'Why, they could still work together and fight and plan together,' he said, 'each for all, could they not? And listen to me, if that is good Welsh law, and English law says the eldest takes all, and gives what he chooses and sees fit to the younger, then by what strange law, neither Welsh nor English, have we apportioned Gwynedd? Samson,' he said reproachfully, seeing I still laboured to round off a word, 'you might at least look at me! Time was when you were kinder.' And he laid one long hand flat over the blank part of my parchment, and prevented me from continuing.

I looked up into his face then, perforce, sighing for my lost time, and he was smiling at me, but darkly, with only the glimmer of mischief in his eyes, for his mouth was petulant and sad.

'Am I your breast-brother, or no?' he demanded, and sat down beside me, leaning against my shoulder.

'You are,' I said, 'and my prince, and at this moment a little drunk, and more than a little perverse. And I have work to do.'

'It will keep an hour. And I am not so far gone in wine as you imagine. Listen, Samson, for I'm in earnest. If law is to be respected, why have we neither gone by the old way, and parted everything fairly among us, nor openly adopted the new way, the English way, and given all to the eldest? By what rule can we claim this settlement was made?'

'There were but two heirs here,' I said, 'when the Lord David your uncle died.' Though truth to tell I might have gone further, and said that there was but one.

'The council recommended them to share equally and rule Gwynedd together, and they consented, and so they have done to this day. All of which you know, so why torment me with such questions when I am busy?'

'If we other two were elsewhere,' he said, 'that was no fault of ours, and should cost us none of our rights. And seeing we were elsewhere, was our fosterage with King Henry so different from any lawful Welsh fostering in the old days, when young princes were put out to grow up with lordly families? When it came to the succession to a crown, do you think every such lord did not back his own fosterling for the honour, and every fosterling make play with his foster-father's power and influence? Supposing I chose to call my royal foster-father to back my claim? And my princely brother, newly made lord of most of the borderlands?'

His voice was wilful, soft and mischievous, and I knew he was but plaguing me. But there was a kind of restless malevolence in such teasing that vexed me, as much for his sake as my own, for it showed all too well he was not happy. So I put down my pen with a sigh, and turned to him.

'Well, I see you must talk out your fill of nonsense, for you mean none of it. Both you and Rhodri were set up with very reasonable portions as soon as you came back to Gwynedd. You hold the lands your father held before you—'

'A part of them,' he said.

'True, then, let us be exact, a part of them. Good land, however, richer than the rocks of Eryri. I thought you were very happy with Cymydmaen,' I said, 'what has made you so restless suddenly with your lot?'

'Oh, Samson,' he said, twisting his shoulders impatiently, 'I am cramped! So narrow and poor a life, how can I settle to it? I could do so much! I know what is in me, and I want my due.'

'Have you spoken of this to your brothers?' I asked him.

'Oh, Samson, do you not see I need your good word there? Llewelyn will listen to you, if you speak for me.'

I still did not believe that this was anything more than a black mood of frustration in him, one of the last echoes of his discontent when he remembered London and the glories of that court. Surely he needed to be rid of it, and as well pour it out upon me as venture a rougher welcome from his elders. But his need would be met when he had cleansed his breast at my expense, and slept off this evening's wine, which, as I knew, he did lightly and vigorously, rising fresh as a lark in the early morning. So I told him simply that I would not be his advocate, because I was not of his party, much as I loved him. I said that neither his plea nor mine would move Llewelyn, for reason enough, because he dreaded and would resist to his last breath the further partition of Gwynedd, which he felt in his heart and blood must be one to survive. I said that the dismemberment of the land, into parcels princed but locally and with no outward eye, would mean nothing but the sly swallowing of each portion in turn by England, until all were devoured. Which could mean nothing but loss and ruin to all. I said that only a single, united Wales could hold its own, in the end, with an England perhaps equally subject to faction, but infinitely stronger, not in courage or grandeur, but in resources of food, materials, weapons and men. I told him, lastly, that Llewelyn had once asserted in practical fashion his own faith in this great, hopeful unity, when it meant that he accepted a lesser part, and surrendered his father's legal right, and his own after it, to fight loyally for the uncle who dispossessed them. And I said that in like manner he, David, might most honourably stand to it as captain of the household guard to Llewelyn now, for the present penteulu was growing elderly, and there was no one on earth I would rather see keeping my lord's head than this, his favourite brother, and my own breast-brother.

By the time I had ended this, and I am ashamed of it when I remember, my right hand was softly reaching again for my pen, and my left was smoothing the parchment and turning it stealthily, ready to continue writing. Which, though he never lowered his great harebell-blue eyes from my face, nevertheless he saw. He had listened unmoving to every word I had said to him, those eyes devouring me, and though I swear he had not so much as quivered, yet he seemed to have drawn back from me very slowly, by some foot or so of charged air, and to have receded into shadow. I remember now his face fronting me, the flush of wine misted over in shade, the broad, high bones of his cheeks and the narrowed, ardent angles of his jaw touched by gleams of light from the torches, and those eyes, like blue lakes, their depths concealed behind the shallow reflection of the sun.

'Well,' he said, 'well! I have listened dutifully, have I not? I see you are his man.' He had ever a very low and beguiling voice, and used it like an instrument of music. 'Well, I do believe you honest towards us all,' he said, 'and I will think of what you have said. But I should never have plagued you so, and I will no more. You may go on with your work now.'

And he got up from his place beside me, and turned to the doorway. And truly I put down my pen, confounded, and would have called him back if I could, though I did not know why. For he went very gently and serenely, as though he had bled out of him all those humours that tortured him and disquieted him. And in the doorway he turned, and smiled back at me with all his youthful sweetness, and said:

'My brother is a lucky man!'

And with that he went out from me. And the next day he rode for Cymydmaen with all his retinue, gaily as ever, and kissed me on departing, very warmly. He said not a word of what had passed between us, and he embraced Llewelyn with particular fervour and affection.

It was past Easter before I saw him again.

In the spring Owen Goch came visiting to Aber twice. On the second occasion, shortly after the Easter feast, David also rode up from Neigwl to join us for some days, in his best and most dutiful humour, full of his activities in his own lands, and willing to ask for advice and listen to it when given. It was not until after he had left us again that the quarrel broke out between Owen and Llewelyn that altered everything in our lives. The boy himself had raised not a word of any grievance, nor seemed to be cherishing any, rather to have put away from him all his regrets for his English glories, and to be bending all his energies to the right running of those lands he held. He was gone, and we were merry enough in hall at the day's end when Owen leaned to my lord, and said suddenly:

'These young brothers of ours – have we done right by them? I tell you, I am not easy in my mind.'

Llewelyn was somewhat surprised to have such a subject launched out of a clear sky, and gave him a long, considering look, though he was smiling. 'Taking things all in all,' he said, untroubled, 'we did exceedingly well by them. We kept, between us, something to bestow on them, at least, and have kept them undisturbed in the possession of it ever since. They might have been still landless and in exile. I am by no means ashamed of my part. You must weigh your own conscience, mine's light as air.'

I am sure he meant no reference to old quarrels and jealousies, but his tone had a certain bite, for he anticipated what was in the wind. But Owen took quick offence, and flamed as red as his hair.

'We have been told before, brother, of your exploits in the October war, while the rest of us sat by good roaring fires eating King Henry's meat. That's old history – or old legend, I doubt! There needs no repetition of that story here. Leave your praise to the bards, who do it with a better grace. I am talking of justice.'

'God's life!' said Llewelyn, laughing. 'I meant no such vaunt, as you should know. You and I between us, I said, have secured them the undisturbed possession of what is theirs, whether by fighting or good husbandry or sound policies, what does it matter? You say, have we done right by them. I say, we have. We – not I!'

'But I think not,' said Owen, jutting his great jaw. 'And it's time we spoke of it now in earnest, for they're no longer boys under tutelage, but young men grown, and will be in need of proper endowment, fitting their rank as princes ready to marry and father families. What's one commote, even the fattest? It belittles their birth to have so poor an establishment.'

'It belittles mine,' said Llewelyn, looking far past his brother, and narrowing his deep eyes upon a distance I could only guess at, 'to sit here squeezed into the narrow measure of Gwynedd beyond Conway. Well, it seems it is not the lot of any son of Griffith to know content. What is it you want of me?'

'Not here,' said Owen Goch, and looked about him with meaning, for I was but two places from my lord's right hand, and Goronwy as near on the other side of them, and chaplain and chamberlain close, and half the

154

household guard and the retainers in the lower part of the hall within earshot. There was noise and talk enough under the smoky timbers of the roof to cover the conversation at the high table, but Owen knew the power of his own voice when his temper was inflamed, and wanted no public dispute yet. Nor, I thought, did he yet intend to draw in the judge of the court, until he had sounded out his brother and had some sort of understanding with him. For if they two agreed, the more open discussion could be decorous and peaceable, and the officers and councillors would listen with respect, even if they demurred. For those two brothers, even the hotter and less governable, had practised this manner of restraint with success now for eight years, though they loved each other no better than the first day. Llewelyn was right, saying that between them they had preserved what could be preserved of Gwynedd, and that was great credit to Owen, for he was the one who took most hurt from containing his passions.

'Not here,' said Owen, 'but in private.'

'Very well,' said Llewelyn, 'we'll withdraw early.'

He waited only for the harper to make an end of his playing, and the wine to circulate freely at the end of the meal, and then made a sign to the silentiary, who struck the pillar of the hall opposite the royal seat with his gavel, and signified that the princes desired to retire. And the hall rose to pay respect to the brothers as they left the high table and withdrew into Llewelyn's private chamber.

'Come with us, Samson,' said my lord, passing by my place. 'Let us have a witness.'

I would as lief he had chosen some other for the honour, but I knew why he did not. There was no other man in that court who knew what I knew about the first meeting of those two at Aber. Things could be said before me, if it came to the worst, that must not be heard, for Gwynedd's sake, by Goronwy or any other. Never unless the times changed for us all, and Gwynedd grew too strong to be torn by any minor dissensions. So I followed into the inner room, and closed the heavy door upon the renewed hubbub of the hall, drawing the curtain over it to shut out even the notes of the harp.

'Now,' said Llewelyn, 'say your say, in as few words as you will.'

There was wine set for them on a table there, and drinking horns, and the candle-bearer had made haste to place lights at their coming. To justify, in some sort, my presence, and signify that I was a servant in formal attendance, I served them with wine, and drew back into shadow from the lighted place where they sat down. There was a small fire of split logs in a brazier, for the April night was chilly, and the kernel of flame and the scented curl of smoke made a barrier between them.

'We are four brothers,' said Owen, 'of whom all have rights in law. When you and I parted Gwynedd between us there was no other here to dispute our rights, but that time is past. We are at peace, and our brothers wait for us to do them justice. I want a fit and proper partition of our common inheritance, fair shares for all.'

'I admire,' said Llewelyn, 'your generosity, but not your wisdom. Are you willing, then, to give away half of what you hold? Or have you in mind that I should surrender all?'

'It would mean each of us surrendering some part of our holding,' said Owen. 'It need scarcely be half. But it is not right or just that David and Rhodri should have only the crumbs, and I say the whole of Gwynedd must be divided afresh.'

'And which of them,' Llewelyn asked shrewdly, 'put you up to be spokesman? And what reward did he propose for you, to compensate for what you will be losing?'

Owen began to fume, and to drink more deeply to feed his fire. 'I need no prompting,' he said haughtily, 'to show me where I am compounding injustice. I know the old law, and so do you, though you may close your eyes against it. I say there must be a proper partition made.'

Llewelyn laid down his drinking-horn with a steady hand. 'And I say this land shall be parcelled out no more. This endless division and redivision is the ruin of Wales and the delight of her enemies, since they can feed fat on one commote after another, while every little princeling shivers and clings to his own maenol, trusting to be spared while he lets his neighbour be dispossessed, and fool enough not to see it will be his turn next. My answer is no. Nor now nor ever at any future time will I be party to dismembering my land.'

'Take care!' flared Owen. ' I can very well take it to the council over your head. I made concessions enough for the sake of peace, I, the eldest son. If it come to a reassessment, I shall not again be so easy.'

'Ah!' said Llewelyn, fiercely smiling. 'Now I begin to see what reward you expect. It is not the rights and wrongs of Rhodri and David you have on your mind, it is the hope of a revision, on new terms, at a council where you can hold me up as the grasping tyrant who will not do right, and end by asserting your seniority, and getting your hands on the lion's share. It would be worth sacrificing something to the young ones, would it not, to be rid of me? Them you might dominate, me you know you never will. What you want of me is not my consent to this idiot proposal, but my refusal, and a court at which you can arraign and dispossess me. If I will not go by the old Welsh way, then you will concede something – oh, very reluctantly! – and agree to what I seem to desire, the practical way of setting up the eldest son as single overlord and keeping Gwynedd one! Out of my own mouth I am to be snared! Go to the council, then, try your influence. You will find they will not sell you Llewelyn so cheaply. Make the assay! I will abide it. You have put your plan and your conscience before me, I have said no. Take it further, and let them declare which of us they value more.'

Owen came to his feet in loud indignation, protesting that he had no such devious thoughts in mind, that he came honestly, prepared to reduce his own state in order to do justice to his brothers, and that there was no man living had the right to cast such accusations in his teeth, far less Llewelyn, whom he had accepted as an equal to his own detriment. Yet I could not help feeling that he made too much noise and fury about his defence, and that he was, in some curious and secret way, not displeased with the way this interview had proceeded.

'What justification can you have,' he said with deep injury, 'for charging me with seeking to be rid of you, when I have worked faithfully with you all these years?'

'The justification,' said Llewelyn, 'of a dagger in my back once! Or have you forgotten, as I have not? Now, it seems, comes the second knife you had concealed about you – but no doubt, not until I turn my back again. Strike, then, what do I care? You will get a very different reception than you expect from the council of Gwynedd.'

Until that moment, I believe, Owen had been satisfied with his answer, and had truly intended what Llewelyn had divined as his purpose. If he was to bring up again the whole matter of sovereignty in Gwynedd, it had to be done in a way which was plausible, such as this scruple over Welsh law and a fair portioning, and also in a way which displayed him in the better and

158

more virtuous light, and placed Llewelyn in the situation of a man accused. It was, in theory, a sound enough plan. But the absolute security of Llewelyn's voice shook him to the heart. For the first time he began to be afraid of putting it to the test, for fear it should react against himself. I saw the tremor of doubt and dread go over his face, and his acted rage break uneasily into a real fury, the only refuge he had when he lost his certainty.

'I will not stay in your house,' he cried, 'to suffer insult upon injury.' And he flung away from us and out at the door in terrible haste. And though he did not gather his retinue and ride that night, in the early hours of daylight next morning he and all his folk were gone.

When we were left alone, Llewelyn said to me, softly and wearily: 'Come and sit down, Samson, and bring the wine with you. God knows I need it. Would you have thought this was brewing? After all this time?'

I said what I believed: 'He'll take it no further.'

'To the council? No, I think not. He is not sure enough of his welcome, though why my confidence should shake his I cannot see. If he was to give up so easily, why and how did he bring himself to begin?'

I said, which was true, that the Lord Owen was not a very subtle or clever man, and did indeed begin things he could not finish. And at that Llewelyn laughed, with real amusement, but the next moment frowned in deep puzzlement. 'That is true. And to do him justice, this assay had a certain devious skill I would not have expected from him. It was more like him to take fright halfway, and let it drop. He'll say no word, to Goronwy or any, not even his own counsellors. We shall hear no more of it.'

In this he was right, for April passed into May, and May into June, and not a word was said more concerning the partition of Gwynedd. It was in a very different way that we heard again of Owen's quarrel.

In early June we were at Bala, in Penllyn, and in the second week of that month a messenger came spurring from the west in great haste, with despatches from Carnarvon for Llewelyn. Goronwy haled him in to the prince at once, for his horse was lathered and his news urgent.

'My lord,' he said, spent for breath as was his beast, 'I come from your castellan at Carnarvon. There's treason afoot in Lleyn! The Lord Owen has gathered all his fighting men in arms, and means to move against you before the month's out. The letter tells all, and how we got the news so soon, I hope soon enough to serve well! And my lord, there's more yet! A shepherd who remembers you from a lad has slipped away from Neigwl to warn us – the Lord David is putting his own household guard into the field along with his brother's men, the two of them have conspired to make war against you.'

Llewelyn uttered a brief, bitter sound between a laugh and a shout of pain, and struck his hands together with the parchment in them, the seal newly broken.

'David, too! He has corrupted the boy, into the bargain. This is his way out of the deadlock, is it? David! This is certain? No possible mistake?'

'None,' said the messenger heavily. 'It was one Peredur brought the word. He said you would know him well, my lord.'

'So I do, and trust him. And he's safe in Carnarvon now?' he asked urgently.

'No, my lord, he went back. He said if he stayed with us it would be known, and they would hasten the attack. He was out in the upland pastures, he trusted to make his way back again without question.'

'I pray he may! Goronwy,' said Llewelyn, unrolling his castellan's scroll between his hands, 'send my penteulu here, and bid him call the muster before he comes. In one hour we'll hold council. I want the captains present, too.' He had a standing guard of a hundred and forty men, and could call up many more at need, and there were good allies on whom he could draw, among his chief tenants. 'See to the messenger,' he said, and dismissed the man with his commendation. 'And have three more ready to ride as soon as we have held council.'

All went forward then according to his will, for his men understood him, and he knew his own mind, which is great comfort to those who follow and serve a prince. So the ordered frenzy of preparation made no great noise or excitement, however strange the event that had launched it. And Llewelyn, in one still moment, leaned for an instant on my shoulder, and drew breath to think, and select, and see his way plain.

'It is not ill done,' he said, catching my eye, and responding with a tight and thoughtful smile. 'It is very well done. There was no way in which I could have dismissed him with a clear mind and a clean heart, however he hampered and vexed me. Now he has written his own dismissal.'

'Yet Owen's forces and David's together,' I said, 'are a formidable army.'

'I am not afraid of the issue,' he said. 'Owen is. He takes up his quarrel with me in the only way he dare. He was afraid to put it to the judgment of the wise, but in avoiding the council he has judged the case himself, and given me best. He may draw his second dagger, but it will be no more effective than his first. Once I overlooked the stroke, for the sake of Gwynedd. Now I will repay it, with a vengeance, for the sake of Wales. Only,' he said, and suddenly his voice ached, and I knew with what pain, for I shared it, 'I wish he had not dragged the boy into it. I wish he had let David alone!'

Not until that moment had I thought to look back, and compare those two, Owen with his hot, impetuous, blundering bravery, and his stupidity that undid all his better qualities, and David in his lustrous, secret, restless brilliance, deep as the sea off Enlli, and as hard to know. And I was flooded with a burning doubt and a terrible dismay, recalling now how David had gone from me, that night after the Christmas feast at Aber, closing up his affection from me because I had answered him as Llewelyn's man, I to whom he had come for warmth and counsel in his extremity, for so I now knew it had been. Which of those two minds, I questioned my own heart, was more like to have conceived that circumambient approach, tempting Llewelyn with a proposal to which one of them, at least, knew he would never consent? Which of them was more capable of the snare thus baited, to arraign Lewelyn out of his own mouth before Welsh opinion? Or, when he was unmoved, and showed his strong contempt for the trap, unmanning Owen and frightening him away from the attempted challenge, which of them had the force and boldness to transfer the attack to this clash in arms, a shorter and surer way to the same end? The tongue that could not have seduced Llewelyn would know how to work upon Owen.

Yet I knew nothing, there was nothing certain in this, only within me a hollow place full of doubt, wonder and pain. It could as well be true that David's restlessness and unhappiness had left him easy prey to Owen's dangerous solicitations, and caused him to wish to end his self-torment at all costs, even by this extreme road. I had no evidence to show, no certainty to share. And I held my peace. It was bitter enough to Llewelyn to know his youngest and dearest brother had been beguiled into turning against him. Why should I twist the knife in

162

him by suggesting that it was David who had done the beguiling?

But if I could not accuse David, neither could I defend him. I said: 'I am coming with you. I can use a sword now as well as some who earn their bread by it. I will not let you go to Lleyn without me.'

'I should like nothing better,' he said, and smiled again, for this grief was also the opportunity of his life, and there was no way he wanted to go but forward. 'We have the same stars,' he remembered, 'you and I. We shall stand or fall together.'

But the manner and tone of his voice was such, that our standing together was assured.

CHAPTER VI

We rode from Bala in the morning early, in the bright June weather, and we rode light, for it was full summer, travel pleasant and fast, and living easy. We had with us the full number of the household guard, one hundred and forty archers and lancers, and some five and twenty knights mustered from the chief nobles, those who habitually followed the court in its progresses, and those tenants who could readily be reached by messenger in so short a time. For it was Llewelyn's intent to move the battlefield, since battlefield there must be, as far westward as possible. Since they could not very long be unaware of our movements, the rapid use of these first two days was invaluable to us, to transfer the field nearer their borders, and select the ground where we might wait for them, rather than letting them, once they knew we had word of their gathering, take their stand on ground of their own selection, and there wait for us to make the onslaught.

We went with all our lances and harness blackened, for the sun would find a blade over miles of country if the enemy had look-outs posted in the right places, though we did not expect such forethought until we drew nearer to their lands. We, for our part, had runners out before us to form a chain as far as the western hill-roads Owen would use to come at us, so that news could be passed along from hand to hand, and keep us informed of all that went on in the camps of Lleyn. Thus we knew when Owen began to move, and knew we had time to spare, for we had been quicker in the launching than he. And having a night to pass, we drew aside to camp near Beddgelert, where Llewelyn and his officers had lodging with the brothers, and heard services in the church.

In the shining dark of the summer night he went out, taking me with him, and made the round of his men encamped within the enclosure, speaking a word here and there of criticism or commendation, and again I saw the good reasons that made him confident of the issue. For all was calm and orderly and eager, and all his men spoke with him as knowing their business very well, and trusting him to know his. Truly all his waiting had not been to no purpose, nor those years wasted or fretted away without profit.

Our second messenger came in before midnight, with word that the household armies of Owen and David had massed at Nevin, and would move up into the plain of Arfon with the dawn. There were some among the cottagers of those parts who had no great reason to love Owen, and were well-disposed towards Llewelyn, and our forward riders had made contact there without danger. So we got some estimate of the numbers the two had mustered, and together they amounted to somewhat more than we had with us.

'No matter,' said Llewelyn, 'we shall need no reinforcements. We are enough to deal.'

He spoke also, as we walked back together in the night, of David, though not naming him.

'He is shamefully misled,' he said. 'Surely I have been traduced to him, and he thinks I grudge him advancement. Owen will have gone to him with some lying version of what was said between us, wanting to make use of him. Faith,' he said ruefully, 'I made the arrows for him to shoot, for indeed I did roughly refuse what was asked, how can I deny it? Yet that was not the way. I would most gladly use the boy, to the full of his powers, when the time offers, and trust him with much. But not that way!'

'When he comes to himself,' I said, 'he will know and understand it.'

'There is a battle between us and that day,' said Llewelyn grimly, 'and I must and will win it, whoever goes down. Yet I pray God David may come out of it whole. I wonder did Owen go also to Rhodri? Though Rhodri is a blab-mouth, and would have let out the secret, besides being no great help in a fight. Maybe he thought it better to leave him out of the reckoning.'

'Or it may be,' I said, 'that Rhodri refused him.'

'Then all would have been out, for he would have betrayed Owen to me as surely as he would betray me to Owen were the matter opposite. Rhodri, given a choice, will keep clear of trouble. Doubtless he would like a larger portion, but not at that risk.'

'Did you ever think,' I asked him as we went in, 'that it would come to this?'

'I waited,' said Llewelyn, 'for God to dispose. And He has disposed. And God forgive me if I boast myself before victory, and bear me witness I will not vaunt myself after it.'

Then he went in and slept. At dawn there was a brief council with his captains, and after it we moved south by Glaslyn water, round the roots of the great mountains, for in that valley no long-sighted look-out could find us, and over the uplands our movements and our few colours might have been visible over miles, even with our steel blackened. Where we left the river and turned west, a third messenger met us, and confirmed that the armies of the two brothers were moving up the easy coastal plain of Arfon, towards the border pass of Bwlch Derwin, where once Trahaearn ap Caradoc defeated Griffith ap Cynan at the battle of Bron yr Erw, and drove him back into Ireland for refuge, before he fought his way home into Gwynedd to avenge the shame by overcoming and killing Trahaearn. But that was long ago, soon after the Normans came. Much was changed at their hands, but the rocks and passes of Eryri were not changed, and by that same road Owen must come.

'By this,' said Llewelyn, 'unless Owen is a bigger fool than I think him, they should know that we are in arms and on our way to meet them.'

'They do know,' said the man, 'but not by which way we come, or how close we are. No question, they'll accept battle wherever we happen to run our foreheads against theirs. And they are in good conceit of themselves, and sure of their fortune.'

Said Llewelyn, but in a manner almost devout: 'So am I.' And indeed all that day he moved and disposed as one bearing consciously, in pride and humility, the burden of his own future, which was the future of Wales.

We who were mounted made a stay near the old place of the Romans by Glan-y-Morfa, to let the foot soldiers overtake us and get an hour of rest. Then we went on towards the great thrusting head of Craig-y-Garn, towering above Dolbenmaen. Here we had the lower, rolling hills of Lleyn on our left hand, and on our right, beyond this sheer crag, the higher peaks and lofty moors stretching away for miles towards the north, bare rock above, heather and bracken and peat-moss below. Here the mountains are not so high as round Snowdon itself, yet high and bare and bleak enough, and in the uplands between the peaks the black marshes fester, and the dark-brown peat-holes reflect the sun from within their circling reeds like long-lashed eyes, the colour of my lord's. The strong, steel-bright bones of his face always called to my mind the rocks of Snowdon, and his eyes those silent lakes between.

Our road avoided the lower ground here, and kept upon the shoulder of the mountain, circling Craig-y-Garn, and crossing brook after brook that came tumbling down from the ridge on our right hand. Thus we climbed towards the watershed, and into the scrub woods that grow in the sheltered places of the pass of Bryn Derwin. And there we took our stand, with our forward look-outs keeping watch down towards Arfon, and the body of our host drawn back in two small cavalry bands flanking the woods, and arrayed where they had the advantage of the slope on either side the way, and passable ground for their advance. The lancers were drawn up in the pass, where it was somewhat sheltered on either hand by low trees and bushes. And the archers climbed in four small groups among the rocks, two to the left, two to the right, and on either side one group higher than the other. There was broken cover there to hide them, and dun as we were, lacking the show of banners and armour, we melted well into that landscape, without even motion to make us visible at any distance.

That was the first time that I had ever worn mail corselet or sword in earnest, though I had some years since taken to exercising at play with Ifor ap Heilyn, who was the best swordsman about the llys at Carnarvon, and he thought fairly well of me for one coming late to the game, and a clerk into the bargain. I was well-grown and strong and had at least a quick and accurate eye, if not the true dexterity of wrist to match it. Nor was I afraid, though I do not know why. Neither in play against my betters, who could bruise if they wished, nor now in the pass of Bryn Derwin was I afraid, but for a corner of my mind that dreaded, against my conviction of blessing, for the issue, and for Llewelyn.

He kept me at his side, with the knights on the right flank, and I was glad. For where he was, was where I willed to be, for good or ill. Nor did he ever send me away from him at any trial or danger, for he read my mind plainly, and held me so in his grace that I might have what most I wanted.

We waited until past noon, before the fore-runners sent back the signal that Owen's army was in sight below the pass. We had not taken the extreme forward position possible to us, commanding the entire downward slope against them. And I think that Llewelyn had avoided this error, and sacrificed its advantages, to prevent their seeing us too soon, assessing the odds too cautiously, and abandoning, with some plausible pretext, the offered combat. For though he had not provoked nor sought this trial, now with all his heart he desired it, and intended it to come to an issue this day, and not to continue hanging over him for more long years, before he was set free to pursue his purpose and his fate.

Then we saw them rise out of the trough beyond, in the gentle bowl of the enclosing hills, first their plumed heads, for they were prouder and more Norman than we, and had exulted in the array of their knighthood, though neither of them was then knight. The long frontal line rose slowly out of the ground, marching in close order, the horsemen first, with that dancing gait horses have on a gradual climb, first their bowing, maned heads coming into view, then the rippling shoulders, and the horsemen sitting erect and swaying to the movement. I have heard music like this motion. And behind the riders we saw the bright heads of the lances splinter in the sunlight, and the faint golden dust like a gilded mist hanging about the foot soldiers.

They saw us, and knew us, across some extended bow-shot of rock, gravel and turf. The long line checked and hung still, staring. Not in surprise, for we might well have cropped up at any point of this onward journey, though perhaps they had not looked to meet us so soon. They stared like hawks fixing before the stoop, measuring mass and distance. And even I saw that they were more in numbers than we, perhaps by thirty to forty men.

Thus these two armies stood confronting each other in the sunlit afternoon, motionless and at gaze, just out of reach one of the other. And Llewelyn said, ranging the line of horsemen ahead for the figures best known to him: 'I will not draw on my brothers without due challenge given. Hold your shots, archers, but cover me close.' And he rode forward some twenty paces before his front rank, and sitting his horse there alone, shouted before him in a great voice:

'You are looking for me, Llewelyn ap Griffith? Who comes here in arms against me, and for what purpose? Peace or war? Speak now, or strike now!'

I saw the light flicker of movement in the still ranks ahead, and cried out a warning he did not need, for he had as good a judgment of the range of the short bow as any man in North Wales. The men of the north were by nature lancers and throwers of the javelin, and our archery as yet felt more at home with the short bow than with the great long-bows the southern men used, drawn to the ear. This arrow loosed at my lord fell a dozen paces short, and struck humming in the turf. He never gave a glance at it, but he laughed, and cried powerfully towards his brother and elder, there in the centre of the foremost rank fronting him:

'I accept your answer, Owen! Come on, then! I am waiting for you!'

He wheeled his horse, turning his back fully on them, and as he moved back to us and to his chosen place, so did they move forward, breaking into the fast and fierce rush the Welsh always used, even against horsemen and fully-armed knights, trusting in agility and speed to strike a first damaging blow, and if forced to draw off in flight, able by reason of their lightness to outdistance pursuit, and find time even to harry it, seizing every chance to turn again and do more devastation. Llewelyn well knew they were hot on his heels, but he had time to order all before they struck, opening his ranks at the impact to take in such as penetrated, and make sure they never drew off again, and signalling the alert to his archers, in cover up the slopes on either side.

Our lancers formed close, butts braced into the ground, the first rank kneeling, the second standing. Owen's horsemen, too ill-disciplined to temper their speed to the footmen's pace – though some clung to their stirrups and were carried with them – struck that wall of lances, and did no more than make its centre shake for a moment. Then the rushing spearmen struck after them, and foot by foot our centre gave slowly back to draw the whole mêlée inward, and it became a hand-to-hand struggle there, edging always a little back towards the east.

We with the two small companies of horsemen remained drawn aside on either hand, a little up the sloping ground, and the rush of the attack was so wild and single that it crashed full into the centre between us like a hammer-blow, leaving us stranded on the flanks. Above us the archers shot a first volley, and a second, into the mass, wounding several horses, and churning the whole into a threshing confusion. Then Llewelyn gave the sign, and we charged down from either side into the shouting, bellowing tangle of horses and men, crushing it between our two matched thrusts.

The battle at Bryn Derwin lasted but one hour in all, from the first clash to the breaking and flight of the remainder of Owen's army. As for me, all I saw of it after the first attack was a turmoil of hand-to-hand fighting, almost too close for damage, where I was flung hither and thither by the swaying of the battle, and glimpsed now one enemy fronting me, now another, without, I think, doing harm to any beyond a scratch or two. But I kept close at Llewelyn's quarter, covering his flank as best I might. I know he singled out Owen's plumed helmet as he led our downhill charge, and drove straight at it. His lance struck his brother's raised shield full, almost sweeping Owen out of his saddle, if the shaft had not shivered and left him still force enough to regain his seat. Then they had swords out at each other, but Owen's horse, slashed by a chance blow, and shrieking, reared and wheeled, plunging away from the fight. And other riders came between, loyal to their prince, to fend us off.

This mêlée was brief. The foot soldiers knew defeat first, and drew off as they could, and scattered. Then a few of the horsemen also fled, some were already unhorsed and wounded, some yielded. Only a handful, at the very moment of our downhill charge, had wheeled to meet the attack on the other flank, driving vehemently up the slope to clash with Goronwy's detachment. And these continued fighting tooth and nail when all else was over, even when they knew their fellows had broken and run, and there was nothing to be gained.

So intent was I on this tight whirlpool of motion on the slope opposite that I never saw the moment when Owen Goch was pulled from his horse, half-dazed, and pinned down in the turf under the weight of three or four of our spearmen. Two more led aside and quieted the maddened, trembling horse. But we watched the small, obstinate battle on the hillside, reduced now to two enemy horsemen, of whom one was gradually hedged off from his fellow and surrounded. The other spurred his beast obdurately higher up the slope, clear of immediate reach, and instead of attempting flight, whirled again to drive at us who moved below him. He circled and wove as he came, whirling his sword about him on all sides to fend off attack. Young and tall he was, and slender, but steely, and he drove his horse with hand and spur and knee straight at Llewelyn. And his visor was raised, and I saw that it was David.

His face I could see from eyebrows to mouth, brow and jaw being cased by his helmet. So I saw the smear of blood along one cheek, and the gleam of sweat outlining his bright, lean bones, and the black of his lashes like a soiled frame for two eyes so fixed and pale in their blueness that they looked tranced or mad. Straight at Llewelyn he drove, and leaned in the saddle, and swung a round, mangling stroke at him with his sword.

Llewelyn never reined aside or lifted his own weapon, but stooped under the blow, took David about the body in his left arm as the horse hurtled by, hoisted the boy violently out of saddle and stirrups, with a jerk that spilled one long-toed riding shoe, and flung him down, not gently, into the turf, where he lay sprawled and winded, the sword wrenched out of his hand and lighting far out of reach. There he lay, panting for breath, his chest heaving under the fine chain-mail and the soiled white surcoat, his wide-open eyes reflecting the blanched summer sky.

'Do off his helm,' said Llewelyn, gazing down at him with a hard face and veiled eyes. And when it was done, and the black hair matted with sweat spilled into the grass, he lighted down from his horse and took the boy by the chin, and turned his face roughly up to the light, searching right cheek and left for the gash that bled, and sustaining without acknowledgement the blue, blank stare that clung all the time with wonder and rage upon his own face.

'Are you hurt?' he said, plucking his hand away and standing back a pace or two.

Still heaving at breath, David said: 'No!' He said nothing more, but turned his face haughtily away from being so watched and inspected. And in a moment more he braced his fists into the turf and raised himself, and turning a little lamely on to his knees, thrust himself unsteadily to his feet, and stood with reared head and empty hands before his brother and conqueror. He stood very close. And I, who also had drawn close into my place at my lord's left hand, saw his lips move, and heard the thread of breath through them, as I swear none other there did, except Llewelyn.

'Kill me!' entreated David. 'You were wise!'

His eyes rolled up into their lids, and his knees gave under him. Down he went in a sprawl of long limbs into the grass from which he had prised himself, and lay still, angular and sad, like a fallen and broken bird.

'Take him up,' said Llewelyn to the captain of his guard, 'and have his hurts seen to. Look well to him! Bring him as soon as you may to join us at Beddgelert. But gently! I look to you to deliver him whole and well.'

We took up our wounded, none of them in desperate case, and our dead, of whom there were, God be thanked, but few, and also made disposition for the care of those wounded and killed upon the other part, for from this moment Llewelyn was sole and unquestioned prince of Gwynedd, as he had always meant to be, and ruled alone, and those who had been loyal to his brothers as their lords had but done their true part, and deserved no blame, but rather commendation. They were now his men, and he wanted no waste and no vengeance, but rather that their truth to him should be as it had been to Owen and David. Why harass or maim what in the future you will need to lean on? So all those who were willing to abide the verdict of the day and give their troth to Griffith's son were despatched freely back to their trefs, and sent about their daily business without hindrance or penalty. And doubtless that word went round also to any who had fled and remained in hiding, so that they came back to their homes and took up daily living as before. There was no killing after Bryn Derwin. But at Beddgelert, where the good brothers of the settlement, saints after the old pattern as at Aberdaron, cared for the hurts of the living and said devout offices for the dead, there was a thanksgiving, subdued and solemn. Llewelyn had said truly, there was no vaunting after victory. The matter was too great for that.

I think he spent all that night in the church. For once I was dismissed. There was no man with my lord that night of the twenty-fourth of June. But doubtless God was with him, who had moved a hand and set him up in the estate he had so greatly desired, and not all for his own glory, but for that dream that went with him night and day, of a Wales single and splendid, free upon its own soil, equal with its neighbours, unthreatened and unafraid.

He had always about him this piercing, childlike humility, that walked hand in hand with his vast ambition. For the more he succeeded in exalting the dream, in whose pursuit he was strong, ruthless and resolute, and seemed a demon of pride, the more he marvelled and was grateful within him that he, all fallible and mere man as he was, should be made the instrument of a wonder. And I do know, who was his teacher many years in English and Latin, how eagerly and earnestly he studied to improve, how poorly he thought of his own powers, and how he chafed at his progress, but humbly, expecting no better. And I believe I tell truth, saying

175

that when he came out to me from the church of Beddgelert on the morning after Bryn Derwin his eyes were
innocent of sleep, but not of weeping.

After the practical matters had been taken care of,
the weapons refurbished, the horses tended, the men
rested, then we came to the question of the defeated.

They brought in Owen first and alone before my lord,
according to the wish of both of them, for Owen had
much to say in his own cause, and Llewelyn was ready
to listen. Though I think his mind was already made up,
for though some among his own council afterwards
blamed him somewhat for his hard usage of Owen upon
one offence, they did not know what cause he already
had to distrust his elder, and hold him guilty not once,
but twice, of the intent of fratricide. Nor did he ever tell
that story in his own justification, and since he willed it,
neither did I. But when those two spoke together, they
understood each other.

Owen came in between his guards, limping and defiant.
He had brought away from Bryn Derwin nothing worse
than bruises, but his harness was dashed, and his surcoat
soiled and torn. He was not bound, but sword and dagger
had been taken from him, and even in desperation he
could do no harm.

'We were two, somewhat ill-matched I grant you, who
had worked in a yoke together many years,' said
Llewelyn, looking him steadily in the face, 'and if you
have chafed at it often, that I can understand, for so
have I. But I did not take up arms, and come against
you as against an enemy. Why have you done so to
me?'

Owen looked him over from head to foot with a
smouldering stare from under his fell of red hair. 'I came
to you in good faith,' he said, 'asking for justice for our

brothers, and you would not hear me, or join in what I proposed. Truly I bore with you for years, but with our peace undisturbed for so long, and unthreatened now, I thought it a great wrong to hold Gwynedd together thus by force, on the plea of King Henry's enmity. I urged what I thought right, and you refused me. I put it to the issue of arms, wanting another way.'

'There was another way,' Llewelyn said. 'I myself told you that you were heartily welcome to take the matter to our council, and ask them for a judgment. You preferred the judgment of the sword. Have you any complaint of the answer the sword gave you?'

Complaint, perhaps, he had, but his sheer unsuccess he could hardly urge against Llewelyn, and he did not think to blurt out what I had half expected, the direct accusation against David. For such a man as Owen Goch can never perceive, much less admit to others, that his aims and actions have been directed, persuasively and derisively, by another person, and that person his junior, and still looked upon almost as a child. So he was voluble about the unselfishness of his intentions, and his generous indignation against Llewelyn's unreasonable obduracy, but never said: 'It was not my idea, the boy worked on me!'

In the end he began to draw in his horns, and if not to plead, at least to offer a measure of submission.

'I have done nothing of which I am ashamed. Yet any man, the truest of men, may be in error. I don't ask to be readmitted to the old equality. If I was wrong to resort to arms, let me pay for that fault, but in reason. My life may still be of service to you as it is dear to me ...'

'Your life,' said Llewelyn coldly, 'is as safe with me as mine has been with you. Safer!'

'My liberty, then! You have your victory, keep all the

fruits of it. I accept the second place under you. I pledge you my word.'

'I cannot take your word. Nor has any man in Gwynedd a second place from now on, above his fellows. I do not believe you could ever accept that truth, and I do not intend you should ever again be able to disrupt this land. There is nothing I can do with you but hold you prisoner perpetually, out of harm's way and out of mine. I commit you to the charge of my castellan at Dolbadarn, and I set no term to your stay there. It may depend,' he said sombrely, 'on others besides you and me. Take him away!' he ordered, and Owen went out from him stunned and silent, for he had tasted imprisonment already, passing several years of his young life behind bars, and even I, who knew him dangerous and disordered, too erratic to be trusted, felt pity for him.

This castle of Dolbadarn was among the most inaccessible and impregnable in the land, being set on a great rock between two lakes among the mountains of Snowdon, and hard indeed it would be to conceive and execute an escape from it.

'Let David come in,' said Llewelyn then.

They brought him in between them, not a hand being actually laid on him. I do not know how it was that he was always able to emerge from any rough and tumble, any privation, even from being hunted shelterless through the mire, looking a thought more polished and pure than any that came against him. But so it was, his life long. He bore the mark of one shallow wound down the left side of his neck, and was bruised about one cheek, and he moved with a little more care than usual to maintain his presence and grace, for he was stiff with the fall Llewelyn had given him. But what I noted in him at once was that his eyes were quick, live and easy, that had stared up at his brother in the field, in the moment of realisation of what he had done, blanched and stricken. And the voice that had barely found breath enough to husk out its anguished warning then came meekly and mellowly now, again ready to beguile, as he said:

'I am here, and I know my fault. Dispose of me as I deserve.'

It fell upon my ears like a strange echo, as though his intelligence had taken that smothered cry of dismay and prophecy, and translated it into this deceptive submission, asking again for his deserts, but with intent to escape, not to embrace them. Then I was sure of him in my own heart, though proof there was none.

'But I entreat you,' he said, with eyes downcast and voice subdued, 'to show mercy on my brother, and hold him less guilty than I. It was on my behalf he made this stir. I own I did complain that I was starved of my due. I take the blame upon me.'

All this he said with slow, deliberate humility, as though it cost him pain he knew well-earned, and yet so simply and innocently that it gave me no surprise to see that Llewelyn accepted all as the chivalrous gesture of misled youth. It is an art to tell truth in such a way that it cannot be seriously believed.

'You did not complain to me,' said Llewelyn hardly. 'Why not? Do not pretend you went in such awe of me that you dared not make the assay.'

'No,' admitted David, and raised his head and opened wide those clear eyes of his upon his brother. 'You never gave me cause to fear you. Only cause to be ashamed, in your presence, to admit to such a grievance. But to him I could, without shame.'

He said no more. I think he was feeling his way, for he could not know what Owen had said of him. But if that was his difficulty, Llewelyn said then what eased him of his load:

'But why did you listen to him, when he urged war against me?'

'Out of ambition and greed,' said David readily, sure now of his ground. And the hot blood rose in his cheeks, perhaps in the surge of relief that filled him, but it answered well for penitence and shame. 'I have no defence,' he said, and stood in submission. I do not know if he had hoped to be forgiven so lightly as to regain his liberty on the spot, but Llewelyn was not so deluded as that, nor could he afford the gesture.

'Ambition and greed are poor recommendations for a brother,' he said. 'Can you promise you are cured of them by this fall, or must we expect another attempt?'

'To what purpose,' said David steadily, 'if I did promise, promises being so cheap after such an act? At some future time, when I have purged my offence, I trust to *show* you whether I am cured.'

'You will have time enough and leisure enough to consider it well,' said Llewelyn grimly, and forthwith committed him, also, to imprisonment in the castle of Dolbadarn, among the crags of Eryri. And David, as decorously as he had entered, went out between the guards without complaint. I would have wagered he had come to a satisfactory judgment then that it would not be for long. The droop of his head was eloquent of resignation, and that manner of pride that saints have in embracing their trials as just, and not beyond their bearing.

'Let him cool his heels for a year or so,' said Llewelyn when he was gone. 'It will do him no harm. But for him there may well be a use in the future. Did you see how he came at me yesterday? How he stood off half a dozen good men, surrounded as he was? One born fighting-man, at least, our father bred.'

'You have done right,' said Goronwy ap Ednyfed

gravely. 'His offence was too gross to be overlooked. And he is not a child, he knows what he does. But yes, I own he is gallant enough. He may do you good service yet, if you can keep him from Owen Goch.'

'We'll take care of that,' said Llewelyn.

I was busy with my lord about all the letters he found needful after this great change, the first and most difficult of them being to the Lady Senena, who was then at Aber, when one of the guards came to say that David, before he was taken away to Dolbadarn, entreated that he might see me for a few moments. Llewelyn hesitated, but then said yes, go to him, for he respected the tie that was between us two on account of my mother Elen, whom David had truly loved. So I went to the cell where he was guarded, and they shut me in with him.

'Don't be afraid,' he said, grinning at the sight of my wary face as I sat down with him, 'I will not ask you to intercede with Llewelyn for me. That's not my purpose. I wanted only to see you, once before I go, since it may be a long while before I have the chance again. And perhaps to discover if you would come – and if he would let you come. And both I know now. I am glad you have not shaken me off as utterly damned.'

'There is only one who can damn you,' I said, 'and that's yourself.'

'And I came near it, did I not?' He caught my doubting eye, and the defiant smile left his face, and he was unwontedly grave. 'You think I am still playing the devil now, I saw it in your face. A speaking face you have, Samson – or I know how to read it. As you read mine, all too clearly. But what would you have? I am nineteen years old, I want my freedom, I want to escape punishment if I can – who but a liar says anything else? Threaten me with pain and punishment, and I will do all I may to avert it. To a point, at least,' he

181

said, frowning over his own words as though finding his way through a labyrinth. 'There may be a place and a time when I cannot escape the doom I've brought down on myself, and when all there is left to do is stand erect and let it fall on me without a cry. But not when it's Llewelyn who threatens. Tell him, if you love him – you do love him, do you not? – tell him not to be too easily appeased, not to melt towards me too soon, not to forgive too recklessly, if he wants to hold me. But tell him – no, do not tell him, only bear with me if I tell *you*! – that he *could* hold me, better than any other, if he can keep the respect I bear him, as well as the love. But if he lose the one, the other is not enough.'

'I am not empowered,' I said, for I still distrusted this seemingly artless bleeding of words, 'to offer you any hope of a short sentence or an early release. Nor am I willing to do what you take such good care not to ask, and plead for you.'

At that he laughed, not quite steadily, and threw his arm about my shoulders and leaned his head against me. 'Fair, sweet Samson, how did you come by so much knowledge of me? And how is it that I still escape you when you have almost grasped me? No, I want my freedom, but not at that price. And with you I play no tricks. Will you believe that? Never, never! Because it would be useless, for Elen gave you her sight. And because I want no such dealings between you and me.'

'In the name of God, boy,' I said, 'I understand you not at all, for nothing can explain to me why you did this thing to both your brothers. Oh, something of what ailed you I do know. You were restless and wretched when you came back from court, all we had here became small and rustic and mean to you, your world too narrow for your energy. All this I know, and it explains nothing. You are far too sound in wit to think doubling your lands would satisfy you, or provide you the kind of field you wanted for your soul to work in. Was it pure mischief only, the will to destroy others because you could not have what you desired? And to destroy which of them? You have made Llewelyn now, and undone Owen, but not even you could have foreseen that end. What was it you intended?'

'Do I know?' said David, ruefully sighing into my shoulder. 'Owen would have come to it in the end, even without me. I bore no more ill-will to him than I did to the sword I drew on Llewelyn. And cared for him as little, I suppose. Do I know what drove me? Yes, I do know! A child's reason! Llewelyn had taken from me something I thought of as mine, and like a child deprived I struck at him.' He shifted his head, and his eyes blazed into my face, and I knew what it was that had been stolen from him. 'Does the child care then whether he has a dagger in his hand?'

I heard again in my mind his voice saying softly: 'I see you are his man!' I remembered his particular affection for me from a child, when I was his slave and familiar. And I knew for how much I, too, had to answer in this matter. He had come to me in his torment of frustration, and I had wanted nothing but to get on with the work I did for his brother. We are all victims one of another. Yet I took comfort in this, that the present trouble had passed with no great damage, rather a hopeful issue, and I was warned now, and could be on guard for both of them. For both I loved. And this being an occasion for speech and not for silence, I told him that his reason, reason enough and forgiven at this moment, was no reason hereafter, for he was my breast-brother, the only one I had, and that was a life-long tie, and dearly welcome to me. That I loved him, and should not cease from loving him. I did not say: 'no matter what folly or what

183

wise wickedness you commit in the future', for it seemed better to assume that this spleen was now ended.

He embraced me, between laughing and weeping, and pressed his smooth forehead against my breast, shaking with this sorrowful mirth. 'Oh, Samson,' he said, quivering, 'always you do me good! Always you leave something unsaid. Must I not promise to amend?'

I told him that love had no right to demand amends.

'You should have been left at Aberdaron,' he said, 'to work out your doom. You would have made a most formidable priest. A little more, and you would have me on my knees, promising an amended life – if I were subject to penitence!'

He had recovered that secret, baffling assurance that set me, like other men, at a distance, and I thought that an ill ending, my time with him being almost spent. Therefore I said what otherwise I would have kept to myself.

'You are as subject to penitence,' I said, 'as I, or any other creature. Why else did you cry out to my lord, whom you had so wronged: Kill me! You were wise!?'

He stiffened in my arms, and his forehead froze against my heart. The words he knew all too well, he did not know until then that I had heard them, for indeed they were but a breath, a thread in the wind. He shrank into himself, drawing by secret, slow degrees away from me, and closing as he went those channels of affection and comfort he had suffered to open between us. When he raised his head from me and sat back, his face was in the chill of a deliberate calm, and he smiled at me with veiled eyes.

'A stunning fall indeed I must have had! Did I verily say so? I thank God my brother did not take me at my word, I have a fancy to go on living many years yet.'

I had overstayed my time already, and the guard was

at the door. He was withdrawn from me as never before, and it was I who had driven him.

'I am glad,' he said as they opened the door upon us, 'that my brother has you to read for him where he is unlettered. He will need you!'

The prisoners were gone from us, haled away under escort into the wilds of Snowdon, and we in our turn moved away to our various duties, the chosen castellans into the lands Owen and David had left masterless, my lord and his court back to Bala first, and then, following the letter I had taken down at Llewelyn's dictation, to Aber on the northern coast.

'She will have had time,' said Llewelyn, with somewhat sour good-humour, 'to sharpen her claws.'

The Lady Senena gave us, as he had foreseen, a dour welcome. She had become stout, and was less active than of old, her hair was grey, and at times she spoke of retiring to a hermit's cell, as many other royal women had done in their old age, but I think her energy, however confined now into the activity of the mind, was too great ever to allow of such a withdrawal. Could she have ruled a large household of nuns, that might have provided her what she needed, but the anchorite's life was not for her. She kissed Llewelyn in greeting, but it was as like a blow as a kiss, and when he rose from his knee and relinquished the hand he had saluted with equally perfunctory devotion, she looked him up and down with those deep eyes, under black, locked brows, in so formidable a fashion that he smiled suddenly, remembering another such occasion, when she had thought herself in command of him, as perhaps she thought now.

'What is this you have been doing with my sons?' she said pointblank.

'Which sons, madam?' he said, in a voice patient and equable, for there was neither profit nor pleasure in quarrelling with her, but even less in submitting to her. 'Your second son I have been making into the prince of Gwynedd. That should please you, it was a title you coveted for the father of your sons.'

'And at what a cost!' she said. 'Two of your brothers shamefully used, arraigned like felons and cast into prison. Is that brotherly?'

'Was it brotherly in them to muster an army secretly and come against me in war, without challenge or justification?' he said mildly.

'I want to hear nothing,' she said fiercely. 'You'll tell but one side of the story.'

'You mistake, madam. I will tell neither. I am under no obligation to refer what I see fit to do to you, or to any but my council. Those orders I please to give will be carried out, by you as by others. In courtesy I wrote to you all that you needed to know. If that is not enough for you, enquire of others. Me you will not question.'

All this he said very placidly, but with such authority that she was moved to withdraw into a lengthy silence, while she examined him afresh, and made a more detached assessment of what she saw. Her hands, which were grown knotted and thickened at the joints with the stiffness of middle-age, folded together in her lap, and lay clasped and still.

After a while she said, as if beginning again, and in a voice very little more conciliatory, but still with a new note in it: 'You cannot leave them in Dolbadarn, it is too remote and bleak.'

'Remoteness is its virtue,' he admitted readily. 'That, and the staunchness of the castellan. But they shall be well looked after, I promise you. We cannot, perhaps, provide all the luxuries Owen enjoyed in King Henry's prison, but we'll see to it he's warm and fed.'

'I should prefer,' she said, 'to see as much for myself. I shall visit them in Dolbadarn at once.'

At that he smiled, though grimly. 'No, mother, you will not. Not for six months or more will you be let into Dolbadarn. And even then you will not be left alone with either one of them. I have too sound a respect for your stout heart and sharp wits to allow you even the narrowest chance of letting loose my brothers and enemies on me again so soon. I have work to do before I take the slightest risk of another Bryn Derwin.'

She fumed at this, and said that it was monstrous a brother should not only make captive his brothers, but rob their mother of the very sight of them in their most need and hers. And yet I had the thought in me all the while she scolded him that there was in her voice a note of strange content, almost of pleasure. And he, it may be, felt it in his heart also, if he did not discern it with his ear, for he laughed aloud suddenly, and stooping, caught up her hand again, and kissed her heartily on the cheek, she still glowering but making no demur.

'Oh, mother,' he said, 'if you but knew it, you and I are as like as two peas, and if you rail at me you are but storming at a mirror. Where do you think I got the stubbornness that makes you so angry? Or the force that I need to make Gwynedd great again? Now, make peace with me, for you cannot win if you make war!'

And though for a long time after this she did her best to get concessions from him by trickery, and nagging, and even by seeking to shame him with her portrayal of a poor woman robbed of her children -- though tears she could not command, or even feign with any conviction – she never could move him, for always he smiled and refused her, or, if he was preoccupied, failed to notice her, which was worse. But for all that, it seemed to me she liked him better, now that he was her master and she without privilege or influence, than ever she had liked him before, and in their cross-grained way they achieved a cautious, respectful companionship, neither ever admitting it.

For at the end of the six-month delay on which he had insisted, it was he who offered her an escort to take her to Dolbadarn, before she had asked it. And it was she who volunteered him, very gruffly, her troth that, however much she desired and hoped for their release, she would not convey into the castle with her anything that could help the prisoners to escape, or in any way connive at such an attempt. And he took her word without hesitation, and bade her go in freely and alone to her sons, with whatever gifts she pleased, for her bond was enough for him.

A busy year we had of it, we who served Llewelyn, that year of his accession to power. From the autumn he began to send us out with overtures of friendship to all the independent princes and chiefs of middle and southern Wales, to exchange news and views, to collect what reports we could of feeling everywhere, not only towards Gwynedd, but towards England, too. He had even a man in Chester, and very close to the justiciar's household, who sent word of all that went on in the Middle Country and the marches, where discontent and distrust were almost as hot and widespread on the English side the border as on the Welsh. For the men of the four cantrefs were close to revolt because of the iniquitous exactions of the royal officer, that same Geoffrey Langley once of the forest courts, and his arrogant overriding of Welsh law and customs, while even the marcher lords watched this essay in turning marcher country into tamed English shires, bound by county administrations, with deep suspicion, aware of a threat to their own palatine powers.

'What did I say?' said Llewelyn, watching this seething unrest with satisfaction and hope. 'The man recruits for me better than I could do it myself.'

But when at length the angry Welsh tenants of the Middle Country went so far as to send a delegation to him, inviting his sympathy and advice, and plainly hoping for his leadership, he counselled patience and stillness a while longer, for the time was not yet ripe. Moreover, the autumn was then drawing to a close, and winter coming on, and though he had no objection to undertaking winter campaigning if the need arose, yet he had not stores enough in barn and hold to feed an army in the field this year.

'You have borne it some years now,' he said, 'it is worth waiting a little while longer to take the tide on the flood. What I counsel for this time is that you wait for Prince Edward's first visit to Chester, for as I hear, he's back in England some ten days ago, and has brought home his new young wife to Windsor. Let him at least have time to show whether he has wit enough to listen to Welshmen on Welsh affairs, and respect their manner of life, and put some curb on his officers, who have no such respect. And in the meantime, with another breeding season to come, and another harvest to be sown and reaped, make sure of every grain and every bean you can, and look well to your beasts. And so will I. Then, if he will do nothing to lighten your load, you are in better case to lighten it for yourselves.'

And though they went away disappointed, and were not, perhaps, all provident enough to pay heed to what he said, yet some surely remembered, and thought no harm to be as ready as a man may be, whether for a good or an evil outcome.

This news of Prince Edward's return we had from our man in Chester, who was a smith, and a skilled horse-doctor, often employed by the justiciar himself and the officers of the garrison. Through this man all the news of the court came to us. So we heard that King Alfonso of Castille, King Henry's new ally, had an ambassador at court discussing the next moves to be taken in their treaty of friendship. He was still anxious to secure King Henry's promise to join him in his crusade against the Moors, but the feeling among many of the court officials was that this expedition would never take place, or at least not with Henry's aid, for he was hoping to have his crusading vow further commuted to the pursuance of his Sicilian adventure. Though there was a new pope now, this Alexander would certainly hold him to his bond over Sicily, but if that kingdom could truly be achieved it would count to Henry as a crusade, while absolving him from the expense and inconvenience of sailing for the Holy Land, or even crossing the middle sea to Africa. And the prospect of making good his vow at a profit, instead of a loss, must appeal greatly to Henry, who was always optimistic, and always, in intent, thrifty, though his economies usually cost him dearer than if he had spent freely.

'But he has no hope in the world,' Llewelyn said roundly, 'of ever enjoying the kingdom of Sicily. And he's committed to paying off the papal debts incurred in the war already, under pain of excommunication. It bids fair to cost him more than sending troops to Jerusalem. And Pope Innocent with his own armies had little enough success against the Hohenstaufen, why should King Henry expect to do better?'

'So a great number of the king's magnates are thinking, too,' said Goronwy drily, pondering the smith's des-patches. 'It seems there's a deal of unrest over the whole project, it's bringing King Henry's very government into question. His brother had the good sense to decline the honour of pulling the pope's cakes out of the fire for him, only to see Henry fall into the trap in his place, and flounder in deeper and deeper now he begins to show signs of wanting to get out. This whole matter may yet be serviceable to us.'

'Yet it's been the cause of a friendly advance towards King Louis,' Llewelyn said dubiously, 'and that's no benefit to me.'

'That's barely begun yet. It will take years to bring them to terms, if that's what they do intend. And if both keep their eyes fixed upon Naples and Sicily,' Goronwy said reasonably, 'so much the better for us here in the west.'

So we took comfort, but cautiously, in these distant doings of which we began to understand something, at least, during that winter. The old Emperor Frederick, Barbarossa's grandson, dead some years, had left a young son, Conrad, to inherit his crown and his feud with the papacy. Now Conrad also was dead of a fever, some months before Edward's marriage in Burgos, so that throughout that year the project of setting up young Edmund in his place must have seemed reasonably hopeful. But there was another son, of a kind those nations call bastard, one Manfred, who had been named as heir to his brother in the event of the direct line being extinguished, and who had been regent for Conrad in Sicily, and this Manfred was said to be very strongly in possession of the disputed kingdom, and would certainly not be easily displaced.

Very strange these names seemed to me, and much I wondered about those far-off cities and plains where the armies of emperor and pope contended and tore each other, and the still more distant land where that same

Frederick, the wonder of the world, had treated with the paynims for the deliverance of the holy places of Christendom. It seemed more than a world away from the rocky pastures of Eryri, and yet the battles and complots of those great men sent echoes even into our mountains, and ripples into the mouths of our rivers.

'I have a crusade of my own,' said Llewelyn, turning his back upon such dreams, 'nearer home.'

And with all his might he pursued it. While the days were favourable he was busy about the better equipping of his fighting men, and in particular the raising of companies of well-mounted and well-armed horsemen, which had never been the custom in Wales, though his grandsire had also made good use of knights in his day. Llewelyn would have as many as he could mount, and procured good horses, able to carry heavily-armed men, wherever he could happen upon them. He encouraged the smiths, also, to make more substantial armour, both mail and some plate, than we were accustomed to, and took great interest in the training of archers and fletchers. And beyond these matters, he studied the making of siege engines, and had workmen build him arblasts, mangons and trebuchets, all things foreign to our usual manner of warfare, for the siege was something we rarely attempted in force, preferring to pass by and isolate castles rather than storm them. For the English by custom feared being shut out of walls, and we, when pressed, rather feared to be shut within them.

'My grandsire knew the use of these devices,' he said, 'and profited by them, too. God knows my uncle had little enough chance to use them, he was always the besieged. And in the end we may hardly need them. Effective they may be, but slow to move around the country they surely are. You could lose a battle elsewhere while you shifted these into position about a castle. But

192

let's at least have them. Who knows, there may be a need some day, and we have timber enough.'

And one more thing he would have, and that was a fleet. 'Not again,' he said, 'shall they sail round from the Cinque Ports or put over from Ireland, and burn our corn in Anglesey while we starve.' And he collected skilled men, shipwrights and others, and at his court of Cemais and at Caergybi, in the sheltered waters between Anglesey and the island, he founded boat-yards, and had them lay keels and begin to build him small ships, such as could be put in commission quickly, some masted, for rapid sailing, and a few built for rowers, and sturdy enough to have trebuchets mounted in the middle aisle between the banks of oars. There were coastal fishermen enough to man such craft, men wise in winds and tides. He took delight in this work, and went often to see the progress made.

And in the dark winter nights, when we were shut indoors perforce, we read together in Latin and in English, debated law, and heard music, the great poetry of the bards in hall, and my little crwth in the high chamber when he was weary, for I had learned to play for his pleasure and my own.

So passed the first year of his unchallenged rule in Gwynedd, and the spring and the summer came on again, and we were a long stride nearer to readiness.

During that following spring there came a distant kinsman into Gwynedd as a dispossessed fugitive, who was to prove thereafter a very formidable ally, though at times a wayward and unreliable one. This was that Meredith ap Rhys Gryg who was younger brother to the late lord of Dynevor, Rhys Mechyll, and uncle to Rhys Fychan, who had married the Lady Gladys. There had always been rivalry between uncle and nephew, and as a youth Rhys Fychan had been kept out of his lands for some time by his uncle, who possessed broad lands and many castles in the same region of Wales. And by way of vengeance, now that he was established firmly in the favour of the English, and no longer afraid of his kinsman, Rhys Fychan had enlisted the help of his marcher neighbours and the royal forces in South Wales to oust his uncle from all his lands and drive him into exile. It was a mark of my lord's growing standing and influence among the Welsh chiefs that Meredith should flee into Gwynedd and make straight for Llewelyn's court, and there both ask for asylum and offer his services in war. And Llewelyn took him in gladly and graciously, not all for policy, for there was much that was likeable about Meredith, and of his courage, daring and ability in battle there was no doubt.

He was a thickset, sturdy, bearded man in his late fifties, loud-voiced and genial, good company at table and a notable singer. As a swordsman he was famous, and for the sake of his lost lands he was a good hater of the English, and an eager conspirator in council when the issue of England came into consideration. I think Llewelyn was in no need of a spur, for all his patience, which some took for timidity, yet Meredith surely confirmed him in all he had in mind to do, and weighed down the balance in favour of action when it might otherwise have hung level. So his coming was an omen, his loud voice among us like a trumpet sounding to battle.

He had, however, one implacable enemy among us, and that was the Lady Senena, who was a whole-hearted champion of her daughter and her daughter's husband, and therefore found only satisfaction in Meredith's expulsion, and was greatly affronted that her son should welcome him into Gwynedd as an ally. For these family relationships with their hates and loves were the trammel

194

and bane of Wales as they were of the marches, and indeed, from all I could ever learn, of England and France and those troubled realms beyond the sea no less. And the more the great laboured to make dynastic marriages, the more they tied their own hands, and put into other hands knives for their own backs. Their history and ours was ever a chronicle of such expulsions and revenges, the tide of fortune flowing now this way, now that, and never safe or still. But the ladies and the waiting-women about the llys at Aber had reason to thank Meredith for some relief, for while he was with us the Lady Senena withdrew in dudgeon to Carnarvon, and her strict and increasingly cantankerous supervision of the household was withdrawn with her.

Doubtless Meredith thought her a harridan, as she thought him a villain, neither being of a temper to acknowledge that there may be some substance even in an opponent's viewpoint, and some justice in his complaint. So it was as well that they should be separated. Surely that lady was destined always to be torn in pieces between those people she loved most, for now she saw her son, the one who had least obeyed or supported her, but also the one who had best fulfilled in his own person the ambitious dreams she had cherished for her line, preparing undoubted rebellion against the English, under whose protection her dear daughter, with her husband and children, enjoyed the peaceful possession of their estates. It may be that she confessed, in her own heart though never to any other, her sad responsibility for these divisions, for if she had stayed in Gwynedd and maintained, in the teeth of all deprivations, the loyalty of her family to Wales, they might now have been all in unity upon one side, if not in total harmony. And it may also be that she had learned somewhat from all these trials, for whatever her own hope in the matter, she kept silence, and gave no warning to any party of what the others intended, but retired into her own helplessness, determined not to do further harm where she doubted her ability to do any good.

So the year went on, with due attention to lambing, and the cultivation of the fields, and the hope of harvest, and the building of boats and fashioning of armour. And in the high summer Prince Edward as earl of Chester paid his first ceremonial visit to that city and shire, and sent out formal proclamations announcing his coming, and appointing times and places where he would receive the homages due to him in the four cantrefs of the Middle Country. He came to Chester on the seventeenth day of July, and towards the end of that month he was conducted by the justiciar and his officers on a tour of his Welsh possessions, making a stay of two or three days at his castle of Diserth, and again at Degannwy, where the chieftains and tenants of the region once Welsh would attend to offer him their fealty.

'Now,' said Llewelyn, reading the smith's despatches with the first spark of excitement in eye and voice, 'we shall see of what he is made.' And when some of the men of Rhos and Rhufoniog sent secretly to ask him whether they should attend or no, he advised without hesitation that they should. 'For,' said he, 'it's well always to see for yourselves whether he means justly by you or not, and whether he has wit and understanding to listen to you, as well as ears to hear you.'

So they went, and we had more than one report thereafter, hopeful and doubtful both. For this was, they said, a very comely and upstanding young man, very tall for his years, which were just seventeen, and in audience gracious and welcoming to all, so that they had been encouraged to open to him their grievances, though with care, and ask hopefully for a more considerate tenderness towards Welsh custom, which was daily flouted. All which he had heard with debonair patience, though whether any of it had sunk in, or whether it was to him the mere tedious business of making a royal appearance, the more cautious among them were not prepared to say. As we heard, there was a great train of young nobles in attendance on him, very gay and frivolous, more interested in the pretty tourneys the prince held in Chester than in the administration of the four cantrefs or the welfare of their inhabitants. There was much money spent on the lavish entertainment and courtly show of those round tables and jousts in Chester, by all accounts, and the prince himself was a very fine lance already, and could hold his own with any who came.

'Before the winter,' Llewelyn prophesied, following this pageantry from a distance with a calculating eye, 'he may well be wishing he had again every mark spent and every lance broken. He will need them.'

The royal party left Chester and rode south on the third day of August. Whether the prince had made any easy promises, or whether the hopeful among his tenants had deceived themselves into believing that he had, I cannot be sure. But for some weeks after his departure there was an expectant quiet, while they waited for the meeting between benevolent lord and dutiful vassals to bear the good fruit it should. Only in September did they begin to give up hope of betterment, for Edward was gone, seemingly, without a glance behind, or a thought to spare for remembering them, and the exactions of the chief bailiff continued as before, and the acts of tyranny in the enforcing of English law, county law, upon Welsh commotes, without regard for local feeling or respect to tradition.

'Let be,' said Llewelyn, when the young men of the

bodyguard grew impatient, and looked to him expectantly, 'a month or two yet, till the corn's all in, and safe stored. If an army's to starve this coming winter, it shall not be mine.'

By the same token he took particular care to see to the late autumn salting of the slaughtered beasts that had not fodder for the winter, for he had been buying in salt as much as he could get. And this last was still in the doing when the unrest in the Middle Country broke out into scattered acts of rebellion, and two of the high men of Rhos crossed the Conway and came riding to Aber to appeal for Llewelyn's aid.

'For,' said they, 'we cannot live longer in this fashion, deprived of our right as free Welsh landholders, our young men forced to give armed service to the English, and our land taxed to keep our own people in chains. Come and make Welsh land Welsh again, for we will die rather than go on in bond to Langley and his kind. Come and lead us, and we will be your people, in war and peace the same.'

Llewelyn knew his hour then. The season was ripe, the supplies assured, and of winter fighting we Welsh, better prepared and equipped than usual, had no fear. Moreover, we were also better informed on one point than our visitors, for we knew from the smith of Chester that Geoffrey Langley had left that town for Windsor, where Prince Edward kept his court, to render due account to him of all his Welsh lands in the north, believing the Middle Country, if not pacified, securely bound, and helpless to do more than thresh in its chains. And when the prince rose before his council and his guests, very pale with recognition and desire of his destiny, and very bright with the assurance of his own election, we all knew that the waiting was over.

'Go back and tell all those who sent you to me,' he

said, 'that I am coming, that I am with them. I, too, have waited for Wales to be Welsh again, and what I can give, and what I can do, towards that end, that I promise you. Go back and tell your people that one week from today I shall cross the Conway and break out of my own bonds, which I have suffered as long as you. And until then, for your sons' sakes, keep the fire damped low, that the blow may fall harder and more suddenly when it comes. When I bring my army across the river, then send me your young fighting men. And by the grace of God I shall make them the instruments of liberty, and bring, God helping me, the most of them safe and free back to you.'

After the Council dispersed, place and time having been appointed and all the needful preparations discussed and put in train, Llewelyn drew me aside with him, and said to me, glowing, for that meeting had been strong wine to him: 'Samson, will you ride with me? There is yet one more thing I must do, to be ready for this day that's coming, and I would have you with me when I do it, for no one has a better right.'

I said gladly that I would go with him wherever he willed, though his intent I had not then divined, nor did I until we turned into the uplands short of Bangor, riding southwards. Then I knew. And he, sensing the moment when the knowledge entered me, turned his head and smiled.

'You do not ask me anything,' he said, inviting question.

'I would not by word or look prompt you to anything, or presume to advise or censure whatever it is in your mind to do,' I said. 'Whatever it may be, the judgment is yours alone. And in your judgment I place my trust.'

'That was one of your loftiest speeches,' he said, mocking me, 'and if you had no personal hopes or fears of what I may be about to do, you would not need such high-flying words. I am going to war. I have room for a good fighting brother who hardly knows what fear is. Provided, of course,' he said grimly, 'he is on my side! I propose to ask him.'

'Him! Not both, then,' I said.

'One, as I remember,' he said, 'did his best to kill me, once.'

'Both, as I remember,' I said, 'have done as much, and with equal ferocity.'

'One to my face, and one behind my back. I see a small difference there,' he answered me mildly. 'There is also a nagging doubt in me concerning the one who rode at me head-on like a mad creature. Was he indeed trying his best to kill? Or to be killed?'

He saw that I was startled, for indeed I had not considered how apt this conclusion might be until this moment. 'Did you think I had not caught what he said to me?' he asked gently. 'I heard it, and so did you. No other. It was as well. There were knots enough to be undone, after that affray, without having to explain David to other men.'

I told him then, honestly, that it had never entered my head to think that David had been seeking to run upon his own death. Nor could I truly believe it now, no matter what he had cried out against himself when he was half-stunned and wholly dazed. And yet Llewelyn had planted a doubt in me that would not be quieted thereafter. He, with his open and magnanimous charity, put the best construction on what David had said and done, able to envisage without too bitter blame a thwarted and restless young man tempted to strike for power even against his brother, and finding no difficulty in the shame and self-hate that caused him to invite

200

retribution afterwards. A simple enough David that would have been. But I was sure in my heart that the David God had visited upon us was in no way simple. Nor had he cried out to his conqueror: *'Kill me, you were justified!'* but: *'Kill me! You were wise!'*

'Well, let it lie,' said Llewelyn, humouring me because he saw me troubled. 'He is young, he called himself ambitious and greedy, but I think it was for glory and action more than for land, and glory and action I can offer him in plenty. We'll make the assay, at least, and hear how he will answer.'

I did not urge him to offer the like opportunity to Owen Goch, for I could not in good conscience make such a suggestion. So when we rode down out of the hills to the neck of land between the two llyns, with the sunset light heavy and bright as fire in the water, and climbed the winding path up the great rock on which Dolbadarn castle stood, he bade his castellan bring forth to us in the high chamber only David.

He came in stepping with soft and wary delicacy, like a cat, and stood blinking for a moment in the full torch-light, for doubtless his own cell, though provided with what comforts were possible, was but poorly lit in the dark hours. He was, as always, very debonair in his apparel, imprisonment could not deface his beauty or his gift of freshness and cleanliness. But he was thinner, and had a hungry look, like a mewed hawk, or a horse starved of exercise. Recognising us, he smiled, even at me, as though we had parted only yesterday, and the best of friends.

'It's long since you honoured me with a visit, brother,' he said. 'And to bring Samson, too, that was kind.'

Llewelyn bade him sit, and he obeyed without comment or thanks. I saw that his face was somewhat haggard, the eyes blue-rimmed like bruises. He had put on a good front, but he was sadly fretted with his confinement, for surely he was one bird never meant to be caged. Llewelyn looked him over closely, and said with compunction: 'I think I have done worse to you than ever you tried to do to me. Do you eat? Do you sleep? Have you had wants that could have been met, and have not asked? What sort of pride is that?'

'Do I look so ill-cared-for?' said David, injured. 'I had thought I made a very fair bid at being what a prisoner should. It takes a while to get into the way of it, but I think I have it now. You may be better pleased with me the next time.'

'If you are in your right wits now,' said Llewelyn directly, 'there need be no next time.'

I saw the small, wary flames of doubt, and desire, and calculation kindle in David's eyes, and from cool burn into vehement heat. Until then he had been on his guard against us and against hope, clenching all his longing and frustration tightly within him lest it should show in voice or face. Now he began to quiver, and with bitter force stayed the trembling, too proud to let us see how desperately he desired his freedom.

'Even in my right wits,' he said carefully, 'I am not good at riddles. If you want me to understand you, you must speak as plainly as to a child.'

'Some time since,' said Llewelyn, 'when for good enough reason I put you here, you declined to promise your loyalty in the future, rightly discounting the force of such a promise, so soon after disloyalty. At some time to come, you said, when you had purged your offence, you trusted to show me by deeds whether you were cured. The time is come now when I need good fighting brothers, when I would gladly have you by my side, and see you put your faith to the proof. If you are so minded.'

'Something has happened,' said David, in a dry

whisper, and moistened lips suddenly blanched white. 'Tell me what you mean to do with me.'

He still was not willing to believe that he had any voice in the matter, but as Llewelyn spoke, telling him in simple words exactly what was toward, the colour ebbed and flowed in his throat like a wind-lashed tide, and slowly reached his cheeks, burning over the high bones. His eyes shone bluer than speedwells. I saw him swallow the dry husks of fear that silenced and half-strangled him, and in the piteous hunger and thirst that seized him he looked younger than his twenty years, he who had looked dauntingly critical and knowing at five years old. He did his best to restrain the hope that was devouring him, and not to grasp too soon at the vision of his freedom. But his heart was crying out aloud in him to rise and go, like a falcon clapping its wings.

When it was told, he sat with his arms tightly folded across his breast and hands gripping his shoulders, as if to hold in that frantic bird until the cage was truly opened, and the clear sky before him, while his dark-circled eyes burned upon Llewelyn's face.

'And you will take me with you?' he said, still fearful of believing.

'If you are of our mind, if you will take up this warfare like a man taking the cross, and be faithful to it, yes, then come with us. And most welcome! You need have no fear of that.'

'And I may come forth? Into the light of day again?'

'Into the dusk of a chilly evening, and with a long ride back in the dark,' said Llewelyn smiling, 'if you say yes at once.'

'Tonight? Dear God,' he said, beginning to shake and to shine with the intensity of his joy, 'the midnight will be brighter than anything within here.' And he cast one wild, glittering glance all round the great chamber, and a stony, gaunt cavern of a place it was, for all its rugs and hangings. 'Oh, I would say yes, and yes, and yes, to whatever you please, only to get out of here. Don't tempt me with too much, too suddenly. This, at least, I must not do lightly, nor you, either. There must be something to pay.' He started suddenly forward out of the chair where he sat, and went on his knee in front of Llewelyn, and lifted his hands to him, palm to palm, so that his brother, surprised but indulgent, had little choice but to take them between his own, which he did warmly. 'I make my act of submission to you as my prince and over-lord,' said David, in a voice ragged with passion, 'and I do regret with all my heart those follies and treasons I committed against you. From henceforth I am your man, and you are my lord. And that I swear to you—'

'Swear nothing!' said Llewelyn heartily, and clapped a hand over his lips to silence him. 'Your word is enough for me,' he said, and took him strongly under the fore-arms and plucked him to his feet.

David stood trembling in his brother's hand, half-laughing, yet not far off tears, either, with the excitement and relief of this unexpected deliverance. 'You should have let me bind myself,' he said. 'I thought you had learned better!'

'Fool!' said Llewelyn, shaking him lightly. 'If your word was not bond enough, why should your oath be? Nor do I want you bound. I want you free, and venture-some, and with all your wits about you. And we had best be moving, and take it gently on the road, for you'll find yourself stiff and awkward enough in the saddle after so long without exercise.' Then he leaned and kissed his brother's cheek, and of solemn words there were no more.

So in the onset of the night we took fresh horses, and rode back to Aber under a bright, cold moon, three instead of two.

CHAPTER VII

We mustered at Aber on the last day of October, and on the first of November we crossed the Conway at Caerhun. Llewelyn had mounted as many of his men as possible, amassing great numbers of hill ponies, for speed was at the heart of his plans, and he did not intend the royal castles or the small local offices from which the cantrefs were administered to have any warning of our coming. Beyond the river we split our fastest cavalry into two parts, one to strike directly north-east to the coast, under David, and so sever the Creuddyn peninsula and the castle of Degannwy from all possibility of re-inforcement or supply from Chester, while a part of our little fleet kept tight watch over the Conway sands and the sea approaches, to prevent any ship from making in there to the fortress with food or men. The other half of our horsemen, under Llewelyn himself, swept on as fast as possible to the east, to cross the Clwyd at Llanelwy and push ahead to the coast beyond Diserth, thus isolating that castle, too, in lands once again Welsh. Diserth, not having an approach by sea, could more easily be held fast once it was encircled, nor did we have to sit down around it for so much as a day, for by then the young warriors of Rhos and Tegaingl were up in arms and out to join our slower foot soldiers, who followed hard at our heels, and all that was needed was to furnish them with commanders and the core of a disciplined war-band, and leave them to hold down what we had re-possessed.

It was no part of the prince's plan to waste time and men in attacking the castles, strong as they were, and heavily manned. Nor was there any need, once the garrisons were penned tightly within them and denied any relief. What harm could they do to us? Far better to press onward to the very walls of Chester, and recover all the lost land, thus putting a greater and greater expanse of enemy country between the castles and their base, and securing ever more of our own soil, and ever more firmly. Should it be necessary in the end to reduce the fortresses and raze them, for that there was no haste. No man could now help them without encountering our armies by land or our ships by sea. And though by English measure, and certainly by comparison with the Cinque Ports navy, ours were but poor little boats, yet the mouth of the Conway was better known to our seamen than to the English, and navigable far more easily with our small, shallow craft than with the king's ships.

Of fighting we had some fleeting taste here and there, but disordered and scattered, for the surprise was complete, and even after the first days we moved so fast that hardly a messenger could outride us, and none by more than an hour or two. The garrison at Diserth ventured a sally at us, but mistook our numbers and the nature of their own encirclement, and were glad to withdraw within the walls again with their wounded, leaving a number of dead behind. They came forth no more, but the young men of Tegaingl kept station about the castle and waited hungrily for another clash with them.

Elsewhere, those few places where there was a small force of English stationed made some resistance, but were either overwhelmed and scattered, or drew off and ran for the shelter of Chester. Some minor officers of the royal administration we took prisoners, but most fled, though even some of these, lost in a hostile coutryside, were later either taken, or killed by the people of the villages. We had half expected an army to be put into the field from Chester to meet us, and were ready for a pitched battle should it come to that, but nothing stood before us. We had reckoned, too, on some show of retaliation from the lords of the march, however disaffected themselves, when the Welsh broke out in rebellion, but they sat sullen and vengeful in their own castles, and lifted not a finger to hinder us. And that was the greatest surprise of this entire northern campaign, and perhaps made us too optimistic in similar case thereafter. We were not used to being smiled upon by the marcher barons, our uneasy neighbours.

'It seems,' said Llewelyn, astonished, 'that I had even undervalued the dislike and suspicion they feel towards this new order in Chester. God knows how long it may last, but now they hate the spread of royal power in the borders, it appears, more than they hate us.'

And indeed it was clear, by their continuing complacency even after Geoffrey Langley came rushing back into the county from Windsor, that they held us to be fellow-sufferers, who were now busy fighting their battle for them. Hardly a view that would be welcomed by those who lost lands to us, like Robert of Montalt. But those who were not personally at loss looked on our encroachments with no disfavour, seeing the threat of effective royal administration in the marches recede. There was laughter, rather than tears, along the English side of the border when Langley came back into the county just in time to be chased ignominiously into the safety of Chester.

We had halted for a night in Mold to let David and his force catch up with us, having established what was almost siege order round Degannwy. David was in high feather, and in very fair favour with his men, though I think there were a few among the captains who were wary of him as yet, unsure how much truth there was in his new fealty to Llewelyn. But by the time we were patrolling opposite the walls of Chester he had won them all, for he was dashing, intelligent and without fear in battle, and in his own person, eye to eye, he could charm birds out of the trees.

Everywhere we had passed, the chiefs and princes, restored to their free holding, declared themselves as allies of Llewelyn, and placed themselves willingly in fealty to him. Nor did he seek to keep under his own direct hold any part of what he freed, but set up the high men of that country in possession of their own, or where there was no Welsh claimant by reason of the past history of the marches, but either a marcher lord at distance or the crown itself as sole overlord, bestowed the land upon one or another of those allies of his most able to maintain it, thus keeping the full strength of Middle Country loyalty fixed in his own person. And so within one week, no more, we had freed the four cantrefs, and enlarged Gwynedd to its old bounds, and won valuable allies wherever we touched.

And it was but halfway through the month of November, and so much changed, in our fortunes and in our aims. For this rapid and almost bloodless advance could not but open up the possibility of further conquests.

'It is true enough, as the Lord David says,' said Goronwy in council, 'that it would be waste and shame to halt here, but I am for pressing on for another, perhaps a better, reason. To halt now would be to put in danger even what we have already done. It can be secured only by taking it further.'

'I know it,' said Llewelyn. 'All we have done – though I grant you it was done with less risk and less loss than I had dared believe possible – is to take back what was taken from us by the English crown and bestowed upon the prince. But how long can that or any Welsh land be held safe from England, while Welsh chiefs are divided, and can be picked off one by one? I want back not only the Welsh commotes, but even more the Welsh fealties that have been stolen by King Henry. They count for more than land, for they are the only means of protecting the land. Very well, let us learn from our enemies, and pick off the crown's Welsh allies one by one, now, before King Henry can raise the money to come to his son's aid. Let them learn that it is safer to keep their homage at home, as well as more honourable. I wish no ill to any Welshman who has been pressed and daunted into pledging himself to Henry against his own wish. But I think it time to offer such at least a demonstration of the consequence, and if they cannot learn, to set up in their place those who know of what blood they come.'

For the first step he had taken was so great and so vehement that there was no way of keeping his balance now but to go forward and match that step, checking as he went, until he reached a strong and favourable stay. And so said we all.

That was a wet and stormy winter, but for the most part not severe in frost and snow. Such weather always served us Welshmen well, for it fitted our habit of ambuscade, and night raid, and lightning attack and withdrawal, and was very evil for the massed fighting and ordered battles the English preferred. So we felt confident enough to hold our own, even if they should yet put an army into the field against us. But they did not, leaving all to their officers and allies in the threatened commotes. Langley was not a soldier, and though he had a great enough garrison in Chester to hold that town and county, he was afraid to risk an advance to the west against us, lest he should lose half the force he had, and lay even the border towns of England open to attack. So he kept still and mute within the city, and perforce left the forward castles to fend for themselves. As for Prince Edward, I think he had no money in hand to raise a force of mercenaries, as was becoming the English habit, or even to pay the expenses of mustering the feudal host against us. And his father was as poorly furnished at this time, having his own troubles at home with his magnates. The king's brother, Richard of Cornwall, did, as we heard afterwards, provide borrowed money for a campaign, but the weather and the harassments at home, and the speed of our movements, made all null and void, and the money raised was never even spent. Most vital of all, the marcher barons would not lift a finger to aid the administration they themselves feared. So everything Henry attempted came to nought.

As for us, being so close, and having resolved on carrying the assault against those Welsh princes who had voluntarily allied themselves with King Henry aforetime against their own country, and benefited by their desertion, we swept down from Mold into the two Maelors of Griffith ap Madoc, to the very border of England itself. 'For he forsook the old faithfulness of his house to my grandsire,' said Llewelyn, 'and allied himself with England against my uncle when he was worst beset with lawsuits and wranglings, before ever the war began. And he got a pension out of the king's exchequer for his services, too, and is growing fat in the king's favour.'

'He holds fat lands, too,' David reminded us shrewdly, 'and will have had a good harvest. And if they do succeed in fielding an army against us, there's corn enough in his barns and cattle enough in his byres to lighten their load. Shall we leave him all that plenty?'

So we moved down into the softer land of Maelor and Maelor Saesneg, dispersed the fighting men Griffith ap

Madoc raised hurriedly against us, and sent him running into Oswestry for shelter. We drove off to the west all the cattle and horses we found that were worth the taking, and much of the stored grain passed into the hands of our allies of Dyffryn Clwyd, and what we could not remove we burned in the barns. Before the end of the month we had secured all the northern march as far as the Tanat, and so stripped it of food supplies that no royal army could well live off that countryside to do us annoy. We made some raids even into England itself, towards Whittington and Ellesmere, to make known the power we had to hold what we had taken. But by then I think they needed no more proof.

'I tell you, Samson,' said David to me in the onset of the last night of November, as we rode back from one such raid, the sky to eastward sullen and smoky with our fires, 'I am sorry for Edward! It was not he who penned us on the further shore of Conway, and it is not he who has driven the men of the Middle Country to this fury. But here is he newly installed in his honour, to have it snatched out of his hands before he has even enjoyed it. And I am sorry,' he added soberly, 'for any of Welsh blood who come in his way if ever he does find himself with men and money to take his revenge. For his nose has been rubbed well into the mire,' he said, 'and that was never a safe thing to do to Edward, boy or man!'

I said it was the fortune of war, and other men had had to bear the like with a good grace, not least David's uncle and namesake. For I well remembered the bearing of Prince David at Westminster, when his fortunes were at their lowest.

'Other men,' said David very gravely, 'are no measure for Edward. Neither for the value he puts on himself, nor for the extremes he will use in exacting his price.'

I said that as far as the north-eastern approaches of Wales were concerned, and for this year at least, we had effectively denied him the means to exact anything, even the more legal of the taxes Langley had been levying for him. And David laughed, and owned it.

'But remember what we have scored up against us,' he said, 'for very surely Edward will remember it, every heifer and every grain.'

We drew off westward then to Bala, to rest briefly and reorganise our forces, which had grown greatly with the accession of allies from all sides, so that it began to seem a live possibility that Wales should indeed be welded into one. Llewelyn had sent also in advance to Aber, and had them bring south some of those engines of war he had been preparing and testing.

'We'll take them with us,' he said, 'or they shall follow after us, south into Cardigan. For we'll go and take back Llanbadarn, if we get no further this year.'

This was that part of the Cardigan coast which had also been given to Prince Edward in his appanage, together with the castles and lordships of Cardigan and Carmarthen, formerly part of the earldom of Gloucester, but held back by King Henry after the death of Earl Gilbert, when the other castles and lands of that great honour were regranted to the heir, Richard. Those two strong castles the crown had long coveted, and so took this means of retaining them. And truly if we had set out to invest or storm them we might have wasted all our substance and our men before making any mark upon them, they were so strongly manned. Such fortresses were better isolated, at little cost, like Diserth and Degannwy, than beseiged at the price of long months of bloodshed and tedium together. For us it was ever best to keep on the move. If they could pin us down they might have a hope of dealing with us.

Between us and Cardigan lay the cantref of Merioneth, held by a distant kinsman of Llewelyn, for both were descended from Owen Gwynedd. And this young man was also named Llewelyn, and had but lately come into his inheritance by the early death of his father, who had been an ally of King Henry, and whose loyalty his son, who was not many years past his majority, had assumed along with his lands. We had no great quarrel with him, indeed the prince was loth to harm the boy, but he sat squarely between us and our aim, and moreover, he was himself, however admirably, what we had set out to punish, a willing adherent of England in the teeth of his own birth and breeding, and we could not well spare him and strike at others who were but doing the same as he.

'At least let's send him a herald and offer him the chance to choose Wales,' Llewelyn said, and sent on a messenger to talk with his kinsman. 'Though if he is what I think and hope,' he said to me privately, with some doubt and sadness, 'he'll not change his allegiance now at a breath, when all goes wrong with his master and well for Wales. No, if he comes to us, as he should, it will be later and without leaving a passage open to the enemies of his old lord. It will be of his own choice, and with due warning given, when the scales are not weighted.'

And so it proved, and he was glad and sorry for it. For soon after we had marched across his borders the boy met us in arms, in a narrow valley among the high hills, and for all his forlorn state against so many, would not give place until we broke the formation of his men, and they scattered to save themselves, and in so doing saved their young lord also, for even he had wit to know he could not stop our way alone, and let his friends hustle him away in haste into the mountains. We, for our part, made no haste about pursuing them, and since we pressed on towards the coast, they were forced to withdraw eastward, and I think found refuge in Pool castle after much riding, and there, though still in Wales, were as safe as in the king's court, for Griffith ap Gwenwynwyn was King Henry's man from head to foot, and with him, as yet, we had not meddled. His time was yet to come.

Llewelyn now wrote to appoint a meeting with Meredith ap Owen, to whose rightful holding those lands about Llanbadarn, bestowed by the king upon his son, had formerly belonged. On the way to that meeting, which took place on the sixth day of December of this year of our Lord twelve hundred and fifty-six, some miles south of Llanbadarn, at Morfa Mawr by Llanon, which was a grange of the great abbey of Strata Florida, we conquered without much resistance all that stretch of coast that pertained to Edward, and cast out his officers and garrisons from it. At this same time David, with Meredith ap Rhys Gryg, had made south by a different way, and overrun and possessed the cantref of Builth, while letting alone the town and the castle, which lay on the eastward extreme of the cantref. Thus we all met again at Morfa Mawr, having freed much of mid-Wales. And there came also Meredith ap Owen, true to his time, and greatly moved by so sudden and glorious a change in the fortunes of his country. And there Llewelyn, constant to his policy of securing his allies in their rights, and rewarding their loyalty by making yet greater demands upon it along with great rewards, bestowed upon him the lordship of Llanbadarn and its district, and of the whole cantref of Builth, and Meredith ap Owen gladly received them and acknowledged the prince as his overlord and sovereign.

He was a fine vigorous man, perhaps ten years older than Llewelyn, of grave dark countenance and cool judgment, and as he proved shortly, a formidable fighting man for all his gentle manner, whose allegiance was well worth cherishing.

Thus in somewhat less than six weeks from leaving Aber we had re-possessed and united much of North Wales and mid-Wales, and bound them firmly to Llewelyn as supreme prince, and surely that great man, his grandsire, knew and blessed the achievement. And always the winter weather continued murky, moist and baffling, covering us like a veil from our enemies, and with gales and squalls confounding all that they contemplated against us.

In this two-day stay we made at Morfa Mawr the fletchers and armourers were busy re-flighting arrows and repairing dinted mail, and those engineers who had brought south the siege engines from Llanbadarn caught up with us, having made very good time of it on that journey. We could afford no prolonged rest, for we must make the best use of what remained of this year before the feast of Christmas. And Meredith ap Rhys Gryg, now so near to his own ground and his own castles, fretted even at so short a delay, and looked out always towards the south, where beyond the hills of Pennardd lay the green, rich vale of Towy, and the heart fortresses of Deheubarth. And Llewelyn, seeing him narrow his eyes to gaze so far, and stroke and tug at his bushy beard for want of other occupation for itching hands, laughed and clapped him on the shoulder.

'I have not forgotten,' he said, 'nor am I going back from what I set out to do. Before Christmas you shall be lord in your own lands again. But I have also to remember certain family complications of my own. I have a sister there, and one I would gladly have as a brother if he would come round to our way of thinking. I will not hold back for that, but I want no slaughter if we may avoid it.'

For now we were come to the most vital passage of this war, and one that could not be avoided or postponed. And at night, when we were out alone, walking the outer horse-lines, as he did regularly before sleeping, he said to me, almost in wonder and with some sadness: 'My sister has two boys, and I have never seen them. Fine boys, my mother says. It's a hard thing that I should be a stranger to them, and an enemy.'

But I knew that he would not, for that cause, hold his hand, or let it fall any less heavily on Dynevor, if Rhys Fychan defied him, than on Maelor or Llanbadarn. For he was in no doubt at all where his road lay, and those doubts he had of his own personal actions and intents could not cast any shadow upon the path laid down for him. That he saw always clearly, and pursued it with his might. For there was but one Wales, that must be made truly one if it was to survive. Also he said, more than once on this long and roundabout journey: 'Truly I never knew how various and beautiful was this land of ours!' For like me, he had never before been south so far, never looked out, as we looked now, over Cardigan Bay, or seen the great, rolling, dappled green hills of the south, racing with cloud-shadows like fast ships upon a tranquil sea, so different from the burnished steely crags of Snowdon which were his home. He rode always with wide eyes and a startled smile hovering, between the fighting and the ruling, like a lover discovering ever new and unforeseen beauties in the beloved.

'It may be,' I said, though hardly believing it, 'that Rhys Fychan will be willing to listen to argument, and be reconciled with his uncle.'

'And with his brother?' said Llewelyn, and smiled ruefully. 'I think my sister will not let him, even if he would. But what we did for the boy yonder in Merioneth we'll also do for Rhys, and he must make his own choice.'

Accordingly a herald went before us, though not too far before, for if Rhys had time, and were ill-disposed, he could send for help to the royal garrison of Carmarthen, which was not far away, and it was no part of my lord's plans to attempt at this stage either Carmarthen or Cardigan castle, both of which were very strongly held, and easily reinforced and supplied from the south, where we had as yet no means of intervening, and no effective allies. We marched, therefore, hard on the herald's heels. And when we had reached Talley abbey with no sign of our man returning, Llewelyn smiled grimly, and said that we surely had our answer. From then on, certain in his own mind that the messenger had been detained in Dynevor to avoid giving us warning of Rhys's intentions, he read them no less plainly, and put out before us well-mounted outriders to keep watch against interception, and particularly against ambush.

The hills declined towards Cwm-du, dipping to cross a brook, and on the slight rise beyond the forest began. We were between the trees, in the dim light of a December afternoon, when we heard the distant sound of a horn from the hanging woods somewhere before us, and knew that Rhys had chosen to come out and fight us in the country he knew, rather than wait for us in Dynevor. He had had time to bring out his muster some five miles from his castle. Doubtless he had been warned of our presence in mid-Wales days since, and made his preparations accordingly, so that when the hour struck he had only to march his men out and take the station he had chosen. And in this tangled woodland, even the ground thinly dappled with snow and baffling to the eye, this could be no planned and ordered battle, but a confused hunt, every man seeking his own adversary, and the advantage with those who knew the ground.

'Not half a mile away,' said Meredith ap Rhys Gryg, rearing his grizzled head to catch the note and distance of the horn. 'Will you take station and let them come to you, or meet them moving? There's an assart just over the crest there that would stead us, cleared and abandoned after. They pasture sheep there in summer.' For he was on his own turf here, no less than his nephew, and knew every fold of the hills, and the way the frost flowed and the winds blew.

'If he chooses to stand,' said Llewelyn, 'he'll maybe have taken that for himself. No, we'll go to him. But gently, and roundabout. Forward softly, and wait until word comes back to us.'

In a little while one of the outriders did come cantering back without haste, through the deep mould of leaves off the track, and reported the fruit of his mission.

'My lord, we saw them from the crest, just as they were leaving the open track. The ground beyond dips, not too deeply, but the slopes are steep enough to keep riders to the track, unless they have good reason to leave it. And thickly treed on both sides. They are moving into cover there on either side, to take us between them as we come. Their numbers we could not guess, so many were already hidden, but by the light reflected here and there they've spread themselves widely. And they have many archers.'

'But can use them only close to the track,' said Meredith. 'The woods grow too thickly to give them any field from above. They'll rely on their first few volleys, and then try to ride us down.'

'They can hardly have known how close we are,' Llewelyn said, considering, 'or they would not have ventured the horn. If they think to enclose us, well, we have time to go a little out of our way and enclose them.

Meredith, you know these woods. Take your party up the slope to the right, and work your way above them. You, David, to the left. If you can do it undetected, go forward to the limit of their stand, and when you are there, confirm with each other by a woodpecker's call, and then sound, and close. We shall be at the point of entering their range, if I can judge it aright, and will drive in on them from the track.'

He kept only his mounted men for this party which was to spring the trap, and sent all his archers with the flanking companies. Goronwy he sent with David, and gave the steward the command, to temper David's boldness and audacity with Goronwy's patience and wisdom. And after they had withdrawn into cover and moved well ahead of us, we rode softly on, and having breasted the rise, where there was an open space as Meredith had said, and therefore some limited view ahead, we let ourselves be seen moving down at leisure and sought for the slight shiverings of the bushes that marked where the woods were occupied on either side by more than foxes and deer.

'Two hundred paces, and we're in range,' said Llewelyn to himself, fretting. 'Where is the horn?'

Then we heard the green woodpecker's raucous laugh, far before us, and he uttered a muted cry, and spurred again, to be at the point he desired when the horn sounded, as it did a moment later. And on that he cried the order for which we waited, and our ranks broke apart and plunged to left and right into the trees. The judgment was good, perhaps forty paces or so short, but our impetus was such that we made good that distance, perilously crouched over our horses' necks with swords out, before they well knew what was happening, and spread out among them, choosing each his path and meeting whatever enemy sprang up in his way. The archers were bereft of their targets and helpless from the start. Distantly we heard the clamour and tumult of the two flanking parties, closing in from the slopes. If Rhys had hoped for a surprise, it was he who was taken in his own trap.

The daylight was dim among those trees, but the outlines of powdered snow made it possible to avoid the branches that swept down at us, and preserved a kind of subdued light that was enough to distinguish friend from foe. To do him justice, Rhys fought well, and used his head once he had recovered it, for he drew out such of his horsemen as were able to rally to the horn, and pulled them back to try and block our way, beyond the jaws of the trap now closing about him. But Meredith was swarming down the slope on the one hand, and David on the other, pushing forward as vehemently as Rhys drew back, and being now clear of our confused battle among the trees, their archers could choose their stance and fit and draw without haste or fear, and did great slaughter. Indeed, those on the flanks outran us, and left the way clear behind them for many of Rhys's men, both horse and foot, to get clear away out of the fight by climbing up the slopes and taking to their heels among the trees. But for some time they held their ground bravely enough, and in the twilight and tumult of the woods there was a long and bitter struggle that swayed now back and now forth, without direction, for in such conditions we could but find our marks where they rose at us, and take them one by one. So none of us knew how the others fared, or what carnage was done on either side, until the battle was over.

It was my wish to keep close at Llewelyn's quarter, as always I did, but such was the tangle of men and horses, archers and lancers, among those thickets that I lost him quite. I was busy about the keeping of my own life, where even the shadows swung swords or drew bows at me, and I laboured after him but slowly and without direction. I did not then know what was happening ahead, where David, at his own suggestion but with Goronwy's hearty blessing, had taken the mounted part of their troop far forward under cover of the trees, and occupied the track at Rhys's rear. So when the issue was decided, and the men of Dynevor broke and began to scatter and run from us, and Rhys sought to rally to him all those remaining who could reach his banner, they found David blocking their way back home, and penned between his audacious challenge and the pursuit that massed out of the woods to follow them, they scattered and ran, slipping away singly into the forest, where we hunted them for a while only, and then were recalled by Llewelyn's horn.

Some of those fugitives, breaking away to our right, certainly made their way safely to Carmarthen, where the king's hand was over them. Others, driven eastward instead of west, made for Aberhonddu, and drew off even further, into the security of Gwent. A few managed to get past us in cover, and fled to Dynevor to give the alarm. For Rhys had ventured most of his garrison, and the castle was left defenceless without them.

We rode back, obedient to the call of the horn, in the heavy, late afternoon light, and the ground was crisping under us with frost, the leaves crackling, that had been moist and soft but an hour ago. We mustered to Llewelyn's summons, and salvaged our wounded, who were many, but few in serious case, for that was a battle of wrestling and scratches on our part. Yet there were dead, and not a few. We left them. We could do no other then, for the day was dying above us, and we had a castle to possess. Two, indeed, for David was sent forward to demand the surrender of Carreg Cennen, a few miles beyond Dynevor, while Llewelyn took his main party directly to Rhys's court. And as I know, he had his sister heavy on his mind, she who was but a year older than he, and utterly a stranger and an enemy, and now, for all he knew, widowed and bereaved, her children orphans. For Rhys Fychan was not made prisoner in that affray, nor did we find his body, though we sought for it close about the track until the light was failing. And doubtless many who fled, being hurt and having lost blood, benighted in the forest, died before morning.

Howbeit, we mustered and rode. For however shaken he might be, he was not shaken in his resolve. And before we crossed the last gentle rise and looked down over the broad, gracious valley of Towy it was twilight, and only dimly could we discern, heaving out of the grey-green levels beneath us, the great mound with the river coiling beyond it, a moat to its southern approach, and on the mound the towering shape of Dynevor, the greatest and most sacred of all the castles of the line of Deheubarth.

From that vantage-point it was but a mile. We came with the night, and challenged with horn and voice under the lofty gatehouse, and a trembling castellan, old and surely abandoned to this charge after the active had fled, came out to us from the portal with a flag of truce, and surrendered the castle to Llewelyn.

I remember the hollow sound of the cobbled courtyard under our horses' hooves as we rode in, and the sparse gleam of torches and pine flares in sconces in the walls, and the few frightened domestics who peered out at us from doorways as we passed to the inner court, and drew back hastily into cover if we glanced their way. And the great, empty silence that hung about every tower and every hall like a heavier darkness, so that we knew before we asked that the soul was fled.

The first thing Llewelyn said to the old steward, as he

came anxiously to his stirrup to deliver up the keys, was: 'Where is my herald?'

The man had some dignity in his helplessness, though he was greatly afraid. He said that the herald was within, and safe, that the Lord Rhys had meant him no harm, nor discourtesy to his errand, but had ordered his detention until the army should have marched, when there was no longer anything to be gained by riding out, since he could not overtake the host.

And the second thing my lord said to him was: 'Where is your lady? Tell her that her brother is here, and begs her, of her grace, to receive him.'

Some of the womenfolk had crept out from the doorways to gaze at us by then, all in mourne silence and ready for retreat. A few young boys and old men were left to guard them, and stood as wary and irresolute as they, waiting to try the temper of this new master, of whom doubtless they had heard much, most of it blown up out of knowledge, like tales to frighten children.

'My lord,' said the steward, 'the Lady Gladys is gone. There is no one here but myself to deliver the castle to you, as I was charged to do.'

'Gone?' said Llewelyn, shaken and dismayed, for though in a sense he feared, this meeting, yet with all his heart he had also hoped for it, and to turn it to better account than conquest and dispossession. 'She is in Carreg Cennen?'

'No, my lord, she was here. When the first wounded man came down from the hills, with the news that the Lord Rhys's war-band was scattered and defeated, she had horses saddled, and left at once with her children, and a small escort.'

'What, now?' cried Llewelyn. 'In the frost, and with night coming on? And to snatch away the children, too! Does she think so ill of me that a death of cold in the forest is better than shelter of my giving?' Whatever else he would have complained in his resentment and hurt he caught back and closed within himself. In a voice dry and calm he asked: 'Which way have they gone?'

'Eastward, towards Brecon. She hopes,' said the old man sturdily, 'to find her lord there, if he lives.'

Llewelyn looked up at the sky, where the stars were sharp and steely with frost, and eastward at the rising hills she must cross. 'Very well,' he said, 'since she will have none of me, there's little I can do to aid her.' He looked down at the offered keys, and turned to reach a hand to Meredith's bridle. 'Here is your lord, make your obeisance to him.' And to Meredith ap Rhys Gryg he said: 'Take possession of your castles and your cantrefs, my friend, and I give you joy of them. Dynevor is yours, and by this time, I doubt not, Carreg Cennen also. Cantref Mawr and Cantref Bychan, the great and the little lands, are yours. Look well to them.'

Thus was Meredith restored to all those lands he had held before, together with the appanage of his nephew, of whom we did not then know whether he was alive or dead. And for his part Meredith acknowledged Llewelyn as his overlord, and undertook to be always his faithful ally and vassal.

Then, the night being upon us wholly, we dismounted and went in, and the grooms who remained, together with our men, saw to the horses. Within Dynevor all was in good living order, but with some sign everywhere of that abrupt departure, a coffer open and clothes unfolded in the high chamber, where the lady had hurriedly put together such warm cloaks and furs as she most needed, and left all else behind, even a ring, forgotten, lying by her mirror. And though Llewelyn did not in any way abate his personal care for all the detail of our living, even seeing to it that the kitchens were manned and the proper order of the hall maintained, yet many times that evening he looked out at the darkness and frowned, and said, as if more to himself than any other: 'To take such young children on such a night ride! And by mountain roads, mile on mile without even a hut for shelter!' And again: 'I would go after her, but to what purpose, if she fears me so much, and wants none of me? I should but frighten her into worse folly.'

In the morning early came a messenger from David, to say that Carreg Cennen was ours, surrendered without resistance, and waited only for Meredith ap Rhys Gryg to choose a castellan and put him in charge there, and upon the arrival of his party to garrison the place, David would rejoin us at Dynevor, or repair wherever his lord and brother pleased to send him.

'I please,' said Llewelyn, 'to send both him and myself home, in time to keep the Christmas feast at Aber, as is fitting when we have so much cause for thanksgiving. What we set out to do here is done.' And though Meredith pressed him to stay longer, he would not, but set all in train for the march northwards. 'We'll go by Builth,' he said, 'where we can move fast and freely, and have another good ally. And it may be we'll give Roger Mortimer something to think on with his Christmas cheer, as we pass through Gwerthrynion.'

But me he drew aside, before the bustle of preparation began, and with an earnest face committed to me a special charge. 'I cannot rest,' he said, 'for thinking of my sister and her boys riding friendless through the hills in such weather, for surely they can have but a feeble escort, and with women and children they'll make but slow speed, and may meet God knows what perils. I cannot go after her, she would only fly me in greater anger, it seems, and I must take my army home. But you

– you are not so changed that she will not know you, and you she has no reason to hate or fear. Take ten men, choose whom you will, and take the pick of the horses, for I want you fast and safe, and go and look for her along the roads to Brecon, and offer her safe-conduct wherever she may choose to go. But not like this, running like hunted hares, that I cannot abide. If she will not meet me, see her safe into Brecon, for her word should give you a courier's right to get safe out again. But if she will come, bring her north with you, and reassure her she shall have all possible honour and respect at my court, and her children also. They are princes of my grandsire's and my father's blood, and dearly welcome to me. Bring her if you can. Bring me word of her if you can bring no more. And say that I am sorry we were ever divided.'

I wondered, and then did not wonder, that he chose to send me rather than David, who equally would know and be known to the Lady Gladys. But David was a prince of the royal blood of Gwynedd, and should he venture his head into a castle held by the English, might not get out again so easily as a mere clerk of no importance to them. And Llewelyn, not to speak of the risk to David, would not give them a hold upon anything that could be used in bargaining against him. It was strange that he had so shrewd a grasp of the devious mind of King Henry, whom he had met but once, and under great stress. But without hate or bitterness he had always a very accurate understanding of his opponent. With other opponents, later and of greater malevolence, he was less expert, having no such qualities within himself as those he was required to combat in them, and having to guess at malignant strengths instead of weaknesses, for which latter he had always a humble man's compassion and generosity.

So I said, glad beyond measure to be so trusted by

him, that I would do all I could to be of service to the
Lady Gladys and to him, and would find her if I could,
and if I could, induce her to come home to his court.
That phrase pleased him, for he would have liked to
believe she might look on it as a home. He had it always
in his mind that he might have been the death of her lord,
against whom he bore no malice, but whose challenge
he could do nothing but accept.

'Do not come back here,' he said, 'for we shall be
gone. But make your way northwards to Cwm Hir, for
we'll make a halt at the abbey there. And if we're gone
from there, they'll furnish you with horses and provisions,
and come after us to Llanllugan and Bala on your way
to Aber. Somewhere along the road you'll overtake us.
For,' he said very sombrely, 'if you do not find her today
or tomorrow, I fear she is lost to us both. And when you
are certain of that, then come, even without her. For
you I cannot spare.'

Then I kissed his hand, which was rare between us,
and always at my will, and I went.

CHAPTER VIII

I took with me as guide one of Meredith's drovers, a man named Hywel, who knew that countryside from Dynevor to Brecon and beyond like the lines of his own hand, and we rode hard over the first stages of the journey by the nearest and openest road, for the Lady Gladys had a night's start of us, and to the castle of Brecon it was but a matter of twenty-seven or twenty-eight miles cross-country. My hope was that with the night and the cold coming on, she would have taken the children but a part of the way, to get them safe out of our shadow as she thought, and then sought shelter until daylight in some homestead, for after our Welsh fashion the households there were scattered widely rather than grouped in villages, and hospitality would be given without question to any who came benighted. So I trusted by pushing quickly over the first ten miles either to be ahead of her, and intercept her nearer Brecon, or at worst to overtake her before she withdrew into its walls.

It was barely light when we rode, and the sky was heavy and leaden-grey with the threat of snow, but in the night there had been only sharp frost, and riding was easy. We climbed out of the vale of Towy, up on to the hill ranges where Hywel led us, half heath and half forest, according as the ground folded and the winds swept it. For wherever there was a hollow or a cleft, there the trees grew dark and thick. Twice we encountered shepherds, and twice passed homesteads, and wherever there was creature to ask we asked for any word of our party, and at the third asking, at a hut in an assart of the heathland, we got an answer. They had passed that way indeed, some hours into the darkness, and halted to ask milk for the children, and a warm at the fire. The woman of the house had begged them earnestly to bide the night over, but they would not. She knew her lady, and was in no doubt what visitors she had entertained at her fireside. Nor had she any fear of us, to urge her to silence. They were then, it seemed, some ten hours ahead of us, and had not thought fit to brighten my hopes by halting for the night, at least not so soon. So we pressed on again as hard as we might. And then, with the rising of the sun, though veiled, towards its low winter station, and the change in the frosty air, the threatened snow began to fall.

We left the bare uplands of the Black Mountain on our right hand, and kept to the shoulder track, for much of the way in thick forest. And there we found grim traces of the fight of yesterday, though not, at first, of those we pursued. Among the bushes we came upon a riderless horse, wandering uneasily and cropping, and then stumbled upon the body of his rider, fallen weakened by loss of blood from a great lance-wound in his side, and dead of cold in the night. A second dead man, an archer, a mere hummock in the new-fallen snow, we stumbled over at the end of another mile. These, too, had fled the field and made for the distant shelter of Brecon, only to die upon the journey. We saw in many places the traces of harness flung away to lighten the load as the horses tired.

Then we sighted among the bushes a man who went sidelong and in haste from us, clutching his thigh and hobbling from a lance-thrust in the flesh there, and him we encircled and brought to a stand, and so got word of our quarry again. For he had seen them pass, as he told us readily once he found we meant him no further hurt. He was one more who had fled the field, but he did not know what had become of his lord, for in that falling night every man had made his own way as best he could. He said he had seen and heard a company ride by towards Brecon, briskly but not at a great speed, nearly an hour ago, but had not known who they were, except that there were women among them, and he thought children. We supposed they could be no other but the party we were seeking. The snow being now a fair depth, we might even be able to follow their tracks if we made haste, though the flakes were still falling, and in half an hour or so might obliterate all. They must have rested for the night, as I had hoped, but at some refuge of which we did not know, to be now so close.

We gave the wounded man the masterless horse we had led along with us, and mounted him, and sent him back to the safety of Dynevor, telling him he had nothing to fear if he would serve Meredith ap Rhys Gryg as he had served Rhys Fychan heretofore. And he went very gladly, for lamed as he was, he would have had hard work of it to get forward to Brecon or back to Llandeilo on foot, and one more night of frost might have been his death, as doubtless it was the death of many more who had scattered wounded from Cwm-du. And we hurried on, in high hopes now, and presently spied, in a place where the snow had creamed and drifted, the gashes where several horsemen had driven through the wave. The crude edges they had cut were already softening out again into curving shapes the wind might have blown, but Hywel recognised them still for what they were.

We spurred the more at the sight, and traced the same passage here and there along the forest track. Then, crossing a crest and having an outlook beyond for perhaps half a mile, and in a lull when wind and snow had eased, leaving the air almost clear, we caught one glimpse of them in the distance, as a knot of dark movement upon white, between the dappled darkness of the trees. By the same token, they glimpsed us, and knew they were followed. I suppose they had been casting glances over their shoulders at every stage of that upland journey. They set spurs to their mounts at once, for we saw their speed quicken.

So, too, did ours. Had the snow held off longer, I would have galloped on ahead alone, leaving the rest to follow me more steadily, to show that I came with no ill intent, however urgently. And I think by the time I had drawn clear of my own men and nearer to those who could very easily deal with one lone man if they so pleased, she would have considered, and wondered, and been willing to listen, even before she knew me or I could name myself to her. But I was not many paces ahead of my company when the wind rose again, and drove the renewed snow in white clouds across the forest track, so that we could see but a few feet before us, and must not only ride blind, but check our speed a little or come to grief. Nevertheless we made what haste we dared, and ours was the downhill run, while they would soon be climbing again, and I knew we could overhaul them.

But when next the torn curtains of white parted for an instant, the track before us, an uneven ribbon of white between two belts of black, was empty of them.

'They'll have taken to the forest,' cried Hywel. 'There's a track down through the woods, by the brook-side to the Usk valley. They'll be hoping for a faster and easier ride by that road, now they know we're after them. It's longer by a few miles, but better going once they're in the valley.'

We came to the dip where the brook crossed, coming down from the higher mountains on our right, and a narrow track bore away downhill to the left beside the water, which was no more than a trickle wandering through the icy stones. The snow lay more thinly there, by reason of the overhanging trees, which carried the bulk of the fall, and under the layer of white the leaves and pine needles were thick and springy, dulling the sound of our hooves, so that we hardly wondered at hearing so little from those ahead of us. We halted for a moment and held quite still to strain our ears, and caught the sharp snap of a fallen branch trampled and broken, and then the distant clash of a hoof against stones, where rock broke through the litter of needles for a moment.

'There they go!' said Hywel, satisfied. And there went we after them. The path sloped but gently at first, and was much smoothed out by the silt of years under the trees, making very passable going. And we were somewhat sheltered by the closer stand of firs and bushes from the coldest of the wind and thickest of the snow. Sometimes we caught again the sound of hooves on stones, ahead of us, or plunging dully into earth where the slope grew steep. And once, where the trees fell back, and the torn veils of snow whirled away from us for a moment, I had a glimpse of horse and rider between the trees ahead, and caught my breath in too hopeful relief, seeing the fold of a long skirt swaying beneath the hunched cloak, and above the collar, which I thought to be furred, the drift of a white scarf tied over a woman's head against the rudeness of the wind.

I said, though surely no one heard me, for we had not slackened: 'It is she! She is there ahead!' And I shouted after her against the wind at the pitch of my voice: 'Lady! Wait! Here are only friends!' But I doubt those ahead did not hear. Or if they heard, they did not trust. So we continued this strange pursuit. 'I am Samson,' I bellowed, 'the servant of your house! Wait and speak with us!'

But ahead, the trees had taken the one glimpse I had of her, and now the wind rose, and we could not even hear mark or sign that those we followed still lived and moved before us.

Then I dreaded I did wrong to follow and affright her, since she rode so fearlessly and well on this downhill path, for by her vigour and resolution it was plain that she would endure into Brecon, and I need have no misgivings concerning her. Yet I remembered Llewelyn, and the hurt he felt in being so divided from his only sister, and above all I was his man, as David had once said of me, and wanted no release from that bond. So we followed still, and harder than before, to reach her at last with voice and spur.

'Now I hear nothing,' said Hywel, checking in the middle of the way, with ears pricked and head reared. 'Halt, and listen!' And so we did, holding our breath, but there was not a sound ahead, though the wind had somewhat veered, and bled towards us. 'They must still be ahead,' he said. 'Where else could they go? The going is softer below, they'll have reached the open turf.'

So we went on, to the meadow levels nearer the Usk, where the forests fall back, and the track opened into a valley road, easy to ride. But we saw and heard no more of them.

'They'll have gained,' he said, 'once down here. We'd better ride hard.'

My heart misdoubted then that we had somehow been deceived, but we had no choice but to pursue it to the very walls of Aberhonddu, below Brecon castle, for whether our quarry had shaken us by one route or outrun us by the other, I had to know the end of it. So we galloped, for in caution there was now no gain.

Thus by the valley road we came within sight at last of the bridge over the Usk, across which was our one approach into Brecon. The snow had all but ceased then. We could see the terraces of the hills declining on our right hand towards that same gateway, and we knew that the direct track descended by that ridge. Very plainly, and much ahead of us, we could see the little group of horsemen and horsewomen – for there were several women – galloping down that pathway and on to the approaches of the bridge, where there were other horsemen waiting to receive them and escort them within. There was no longer any sense in haste, we were out-distanced. To go nearer would be only to invite pursuit in our turn.

I drew rein, and so did all those with me, and we watched that reception at the bridge-head, and it was courteous to reverence. Among the several women there I could not distinguish, from the distance where we sat at gaze in the shelter of the trees, the one I had been sent to solicit, but of her welcome into Brecon I could be in no doubt. Whether her lord was there before her was something I could not know. I knew I had lost her. But also that I could at least report her safely in haven with the children.

'In the name of God, then,' said Hywel, staring, for he had seen what I had seen, 'who was that woman we followed down the stream? And was she, God forbid, alone? For in that soft rubble and snow we could have been riding down one horseman or ten.'

I had the same thought in my mind, for it was clear enough how we had been fooled. Under cover of the squalls, and knowing that with the children to carry they must be overtaken before they could reach Brecon, the company had drawn off into the trees on the hillside above the track, while a decoy lured us away down the valley path. And when we had taken the bait and were in full cry towards the Usk, with a glimpse of a woman's cloak to keep us confident, they had returned to the hill track and ridden hard for the town. But if that was true, then one person at least had been abandoned in the forest. And if only one, then a woman. Not one of us, as we agreed, had seen a second figure.

'But more there could well have been,' said Hywel. 'Or if she ventured alone she must have some shelter she knows of in these hills, for I'm sure she's not ahead of us now. She's let us by somewhere on the road.'

I hesitated long what we ought to do. For with our errand thus completed, however lamely, we were committed to riding north to rejoin Llewelyn at Cum Hir, and our fastest and safest way, considering the weather, would have been to skirt Brecon with care by north or south, and reach the valley of the Wye, and so press on northwards by Builth. True, there were castles on the way that were held by men no friends to Llewelyn's cause, but I had companions with me who knew those ways well, and in the sheltered valley we should do better than over the wild, bleak uplands of Mynydd Eppynt, exposed to every wind. Every other road open to us was a hill road, even if we circled Eppynt by the west. But I thought it preferable, all the same, to make the blizzard an excuse for turning back to spend the night at Dynevor, and making an early start by Llandovery. To this day I do not know how far it was an honest decision, and how far a means of retracing the way by which we had come, and so keeping a watch as we went for the woman who had duped us. For if she was indeed alone and lost in the woods, with the night coming on, and the snow obliterating paths and landmarks, she was in sorry case.

So we turned back and rode along the valley with less

haste than when we had come, the leaden afternoon closing upon us. Hywel could find his way in these parts by night or day, and in any weather, we had no fear for ourselves however deep the snow. But I think that when we came to the climbing path we slowed still more, and not all in mercy to our tired horses. Also we spread out into the fringes of the trees, for there she must surely have withdrawn silently when we lost her, and let us pass without a word.

I cannot say that we found her. We had made but a quarter of the climb to the ridge track when she came out of the woods before us, slender and dark against the snow, not avoiding but advancing upon us, with her pale, bright face uplifted. Most strange, she was on foot now, and the furred cloak she had worn was gone from her shoulders. Very small and young and slight she looked, wading through the deep snow with her skirts gathered high in her hands. And as I halted my horse beside her, she said the most unexpected words I could then have heard, the first ever I heard from her:

'Sir, is there any among you is priest or clerk?'

I think we all stared and gaped for a moment, yet her face, which was oval and fierce and fair, with great eyes intent, demanded instant answer, and the questions we had for her fell by the way. I told her we had no priest among us, but I had gone some way in my boyhood towards minor orders, and knew the office. I do not know how it was, but from the moment she appeared before us and spoke so, there was no business we had of any urgency but her business. For in her face, though young and glowing with vigour, there was also, even before she spoke again, the close shadow of death.

'Come with me,' she said. 'There is a man dying.'

I lighted down and offered to lift her into the saddle, for she was soaked to the knees and pinched with cold

236

she seemed not to feel. But she shook her head, saying: 'It is not far,' and turned and plunged again into the trees, and we, picking our way and leading our horses, followed her. Snow shook down upon her and us from the trees, and she shrugged it off and paid no heed.

It was not far. Three hundred paces at the most into the thick and deepening darkness of the trees, invisible from the track, there was a wooden hut, low and leaning, but sound of wall and roof. She led us straight to the doorless opening, and I went in with her.

'He is here,' she said.

It was so dark within that but for the shining whiteness of the snow that had drifted in through the doorway I should not have been able to see him. It gave a kind of light that came from the ground upwards, not from the sky down. The first thing I was aware of was a wave of surprising warmth that met me out of the dark, and the vast, deep sound of breathing that made a part of the warmth, misty and moist on the air. She had left her dying man the great, vigorous body of her horse to warm him, wanting the means to make a fire. More, she had left him the cloak she had worn, and run out into the blizzard without it when she caught the sound of our movements below on the path. I found him by the gleam of the snow that just touched one lax hand with its feathery fringe. He lay on his back, both arms spread at his sides, his eyes wide open, for their glare had a light of its own. He made no sound, but he was not sleeping or dead, or so far gone from the world as to be indifferent to us who came in. He was stiff with agony. I quivered at the very sight of the lines of his body, straight as timber under the cloak she had spread over him.

The woman said, in a whisper for my ear only: 'He

crept here when his strength failed. I do not know how he got so far after Cwm-du. He is thrust clean through the bowels, and has a wound in the armpit besides. Take care how you touch him. He cannot last long.'

'You knew of this place?' I said as softly.

'I knew of it. He happened on it. I found him here when I came.'

I said over my shoulder to Hywel: 'Elis has flint and tinder. Get me a torch alight as fast as you can. Then find dead wood for a fire.' And they went, silently. She was quite still there, one step before my left side, her shoulder on a level with my heart, her waist almost between my hands. I said into her ear: 'Has he spoken to you?'

'Not to me! He has said: I have sinned! He is in torment. I would you were a priest,' she said.

Hywel came then at my back, very softly, with a dried branch of pine already sputtering, casting a fitful yellowish light inside that shelter, and peopling it with all its living and dying. He held it before me, stepping over the living body and reaving the torch into the rough boarding of the timber wall. The horse, steaming gently into the cold, its neck bowed meekly towards its feet, heaved up its head in mild astonishment, and stared at us with great globes of eyes. And the shape and lineaments of the mortally wounded man sprang into the flickering light, and showed me a face I knew from long since.

I went on my knees beside him on the hard earth floor littered with pine needles, and searched the visage that glared up at me with open and recognising eyes. It was more than twelve years since I had seen him, or he me, but when those great, chill eyelids rolled back he knew me as I knew him. One step from the threshold of death he was still a comely person, my mother's husband, Meilyr.

'Samson?' he said. His voice was thick and harsh from the pain he contained with so much bitter force, but it was clear enough, like the mind that drove it. 'Is it you indeed? Has she sent me her half-priest to make certain I die unshriven and unforgiven?'

Once again, as of old, I saw that for him there was but one she, in this world or another, and his whole being was still cleaving to the memory of her at the edge of death.

'Not so,' I said. 'What was there for her to forgive you but years of love never repaid? Lie still now, and let me see if there is anything man can do for you alive, for of what God in his goodness can do for you after death you need not doubt.'

He said no more for a while, only watched me at every move with those smouldering eyes of grief and rage that I remembered now far better than I could call to mind any of the blows he ever dealt me. I lifted the cloak that covered him, as gently as I might, but the clotted wreckage of his body was past any aid of mine, and the only hope was to let him lie motionless, that the riven flesh, weakening, might slacken its grip of this ceaseless pain. So I covered him again as closely as I dared, and we made a low fire between him and the doorway, so laid that it should not blow smoke over him, but give him its warmth. I took his hand in mine, and it was stiff and cold without response, and yet I knew there was still some force in the hard fingers if he chose to use it. We had wine in a flask, and gave him a little to moisten his mouth, but because of his broken belly I dared not let him drink deep. And when I looked round for the girl, who had said no word and made no sound since we came in, I saw that she was on her knees, and had taken his feet into her lap and wrapped them in the folds of her skirt, and was softly kneading and chafing them at ankle and instep. Her face was quite still and calm, and her eyes were on me. She neither offered nor asked anything, but like the angel of the archives she watched and listened, recording everything for the judgment.

Meilyr lay and suffered this handling, but nothing of him moved except his eyes that followed all we did, and the thin-drawn lips that smiled terribly at our vain endeavours. And once he said: 'You trouble needless. I am a dead man.' And again: 'Elen!' he said, as though to himself. 'She died. The only word I ever had of her, that she was dead. When I heard the girl had married into Dynevor I came to serve here, thinking I might get word ... thinking she might even come. Why try to mend me now? To what purpose? I have been a long time dead, ever since the fever took all that beauty out of the world, and my hope with it. If I ever hoped!'

But when we had done what little could be done to ease him at least of the worst of the cold and darkness, there was nothing left for us to do but stay beside him, that he might not die alone. Though if ever man lived alone, from the day that first he set eyes upon Elen's beauty the man was Meilyr. And I had thought that he wronged me, not understanding how direly he was wronged! So I sat beside him, having covered him up from the cold, and held his right hand between my palms. And as Elen had used him, so he now used me, for he neither accepted nor rejected, but was utterly indifferent.

Then remembering what the girl had said of him, that he was in torment and had cried out under the burden of his sins, I asked him if he willed to make an act of contrition and confession, for though I was no priest and could not absolve, yet the voluntary expression of his penitence was the true motion of grace.

Terribly he smiled, his eyes devouring me, and he said: 'I have sinned. Against you. When you were weak and at my mercy, I had no mercy in me. But as I did, so has it been done to me, and more also. She avenged you a thousand times over. Where is the debt now?'

'There is none,' I said. 'It is past and over, and I have forgotten it. So, too, should you.'

'Forgotten,' he said, 'but not forgiven.'

'There was no need, once I understood what trouble divided us. But if you set store upon the word, then yes, forgiven also, long ago.'

'By you,' he said, 'but not by her. When the girl came here to her bridal, she could have sent me her pardon, if she had indeed pardoned me. But never, never a word. Never any, until the word of her death.'

'You do mistake her,' I said, for I was possessed by the awareness of his anguish, and wanted nothing in that hour but to take away the great bitterness of it, if I could not take away the pain. And I began to remember all those things I could tell him truly, of how she had changed after his going, of how, with love or without it, he had become for her the single he in this world who needed no name, as she had always been for him the only woman. So I held fast his hand, and leaned over him that he might see my face by the firelight, and know I was not afraid to have it searched for truth or falsehood. And I began to tell him. Of how she froze in dread for him whenever she heard horsemen riding in, until it was certain that he had got safe away into Wales, or elsewhere, and she need fear no more. Of how she had changed, growing warmer and more like human flesh. Of how, when he was gone from her, she spoke of him constantly, and always with solicitude, troubled and anxious if the weather was stormy, grieving to know if he had a roof and a bed when the nights were cold. Of how he had only become real and close to her when he was lost to her and very far away, and only after they were parted for ever was he constantly at her side. And I said that she was strange, and it was not her fault if she could not love after the fashion of other women, but only in some secret and distant way of her own. Most women's love cries out for presence, and cannot survive without the food of glances and caresses and words. Hers awoke only in absence, and lived and grew without sustenance. I told him, last, how she had cried out like a saint at a vision: 'He loved me!' and lamented like a penitent at confession: 'I was not good to him!'

All this he heard unmoved, except to a dreadful grin of scorn, his lips drawn back from his teeth in agony. He said: 'You lie! In all her life she felt nothing for me, neither love nor hate. What you offer me is out of pity. I need no pity, and no lies. I am too far gone for lies to help me.'

Then I swore to him that all I had said was true, and I would take whatever oath he laid upon me, but still he would not believe, and at my insistence he did but turn his head away, and draw his hand suddenly from between mine, so that the movement troubled his shattered body, and he loosed a great moan. But when he was quiet again he said with certainty: 'If this were true she would have sent me a token. No, I go out of this world damned because of her. What is the mercy of heaven to me if she has none?'

I looked then from his soiled and frost-drawn face, that was growing hollower and greyer before our eyes, to all those who sat and stood around us, watching in silence, feeding the fire, and listening in dread and awe to every word that passed. And I was greatly afraid for his soul if he departed thus stubborn and mute, and greatly I cared, who once had hated him, or thought I hated him, that after a lifetime of loss in this world he should not suffer eternal loss in the next. And I thought how I had at least time left me before my going to cleanse my bosom, if I sinned now in taking his burden upon me, and how I had the means, if I willed, to try at least one more way to the heart he guarded so bitterly. Until then I had not remembered it.

'I swear to you,' I said earnestly, leaning over him so that he must see me, whether he would or no, 'by my mother's soul that I have not lied to you in any particular. And I will prove it. For she did send you a token, but not by any other, only by me. You know her, when did she ever send letters? But when I left her to go to Chester with the Lord Owen she gave me a thing to bring with me. For you! For, said she, when he hears that Owen is raising his banner, he may come, and you may meet him again. Look, do you know this for hers?'

Since I had my full growth the silver ring was tight and irksome on my finger, and I had taken to carrying it rather on a string round my neck, hidden in my cotte. I drew it out and broke it loose from the cord, and held it before his eyes. And I saw by the sudden bright, incredulous gleam in them that he had seen it among her possessions, and knew it for hers indeed. A great, strange softening came over all the lines of his face, that had been hard and white as bone. His lips fell gently apart, as though he drank and was refreshed. I think I never had seen, and never have seen since, a lie so singularly blessed. I went to take up his hand, to put the ring safely into his palm, and both his hands rose of themselves, carefully cupped as if for a sacrament, to receive it. I kept my own hands close, ready to catch the little thing if it fell out of his cold fingers, but he held it delicately and steadily before his eyes, taking it in like meat and drink both, and of the soul rather than the body.

'It is hers,' he said in a whisper. God be praised, she can never have told him how she came by it, that it was hers was all he knew, and that was enough. 'She sent it to *me*?'

I said quickly: 'You did not come, and I did not know where to find you.' For I was mortally afraid that he would turn on me and ask why I had not discharged my errand to him at once when we found him here, without such long trial before I gave him ease. But for him the act was enough, he cared for nothing more, he had his proof. So easy it was to prove with a lie what he would not believe when I told him truth!

And still he held it before his face, the little severed hand holding the rose, and his lips moved without sound, shaping her name over and over: 'Elen.... Elen.... Elen....' more blissfully than ever saint offered prayers. And then he said: 'I do repent me of all my hardness of heart, of my doubting, of my greed.... Hear me my sins, Samson!'

'In the name of God!' I said. And he spoke, and I listened. With long pauses he spoke, and for pure thankfulness I hardly knew until the close how his voice grew fainter, and laboured ever more arduously and faithfully to reach a fair end, for he was so lost in content that the feebleness of his body passed unnoticed. And greatly I marvelled at the modesty of those sins he spoke of, and at the strange depth of his humility, so long and painfully disguised within the armour of obduracy. For he was as clean as most men, God knows, and cleaner than many. I pray I may have as little on by conscience at the departing as he had, for the greater part of his burden was his own pain, and the greater part of the evil he had done was but the convulsion of resistance against the evil that had been done to him. I was assured, as I heard him out to the end, that if I could be so moved by grief and compassion for him, how much more could God have pity on his creature. And it was in my heart that Meilyr's rest was sure.

I had no power to absolve, but I said for him the prayers due to the dying, and with him the sentences of contrition. And at the end thereof I said: 'Amen!' But my mother's husband, with the ring held up before his eyes, very close because by this he saw but faintly, said: 'Elen!'

After that he spoke not at all, but he folded his hands upon the ring, and held it to his heart, for he could no longer see it, and experienced it rather by the touch of his fingers to the end of his life. With what rapture, the withdrawing exaltation of his face gave witness.

We stayed with him, perforce, through the night, keeping the fire fed, and making a bed for the girl with such dry bracken and litter as had been left in the shed, though I think she watched with us most of the time. Some bread and meat we had with us, and with the warmth of the fire and the horses and our own numbers, we did well enough, for all the snow and frost outside.

As for me, I sat all the night through by the only father I had known, and he heretofore an enemy. And in the greyness before the first light of day he died, still clasping the ring I had given him. After death, as happens sometimes, all the lines of his face, that was worn and aging, smoothed out into a marble calm and became by some years younger and fairer. And I began to marvel within myself whether indeed I had lied at all, and whether I needed to confess what I had done as a sin. For more and more clearly I remembered my mother dwelling, at my departure, on how I might well encounter

Meilyr in Chester, and how it was too late for her to send any message, for she would never see him again. And how then she gave me the ring, saying with such careful truth that it was my father's, and that – who knew? – it might yet bring me in contact with *him*. I have said she had but one *he*. So two-tongued and two-voiced are words, whoever writes or speaks them takes his life in his hand. And whether I was a liar, or had told truth believing it to be a lie, I no longer knew then, and have not discovered to this day. God sort all!

I looked at my old enemy, and he was dead and in peace, clasping the treasure I purposed never to take back from him. What was that unknown father to me, beside this father I had learned to know all too well for comfort, whether he was mine or no? Let him keep his talisman in the grave, it was of more value to him, misunderstood, than to me who knew its significance.

I got up stiffly, and went out into the forest. There was no new snow, and between the tree-tops the sky was clear and encrusted with stars.

As I came back towards the hut I saw the woman come from among the trees, and strip from her head the scarf and the wimple she wore, letting her hair stream down about her shoulders. Long and dark it was, and fell in heavy waves almost to her waist, and between the swinging curtains of silky black her oval face looked pale but lustrous like a pearl. She had not observed me, and I drew back into the bushes to look long at her without offence, for until now, though I had seen much, I had had no leisure, and no peace of mind, to realise what I saw. First she appeared like a visitant from God to demand our presence where we were needed, and that in a manner to remind us that the time of the birth of Our Lord and the apparition of angels was very close upon us. And then she had withdrawn into silence and watchfulness, unwatched, while Meilyr lived out his last hours in this world. Now at this second coming my mind was as open as my eyes. I saw her in truth for the first time.

I have said of my mother that she was beautiful, and of others have been as certain that they were not so. Of this girl I can never say whether she had beauty or no, for never could I pass beyond seeing into describing. Always there was something to arrest me and put all critical thought out of my reach. She was not tall, only a few inches higher than my shoulder, but very slender, and I thought now, for the first time being in any case to judge, that her age was no more than one or two years past twenty. She had a broad, clear forehead, with straight, thoughtful black brows, and her eyes were of a dark colouring which at a distance I took to be a very dusky blue, but which I found on closer view to be sometimes deep grey and sometimes, according to the light, royal purple, for the black of their lashes caused them to change with the changes of daylight or torchlight wherever she was. The lines of brow and nose and cheek were very pure and spare, with that lustrous sheen that came from the pearly translucence of her skin. And her mouth and chin were shapely, generous and resolute. I could never like the prim, tight, small mouths that were the courtly fashion, so that even those lavish-lipped and open by nature copied the pursed look to be in the mode. She was not so. Wide of mouth she was, and full and passionate of lip, but with such composure about her as to keep all in discipline and balance. But above all, she had a way of doing whatever she did with every particle of her attention and her being, and a way of looking a man in the eyes that both pierced him through and opened her own heart to him, if he had a mind to accept the welcome with reverence. And if he had not, she could do without him. Or if he misunderstood and presumed too far, I doubt not she could close the gates against him too tight for his unlocking.

She neither saw me nor looked round at all to see if she was seen. She stooped to the highest and purest bank of snow under the bushes, filled her hands with it, and washed her face in its coldness, her pearl-whiteness emerging stung into rose. Then she dried herself upon her scarf, and taking a comb from her sleeve, began to comb her long hair, patiently coaxing out the tangles left by her night in the bracken. When she had done, she coiled it up again and pinned it, and covered its darkness with wimple and scarf, until she was as neat as if she had slept in her own bed and made her toilet at leisure in the comfort and safety of Dynevor. And so intent was I that only when all was finished did I think to remember how she had come out here into the frosty dawn without her cloak, for still it lay with mine, covering Meilyr's body.

I went into the hut in haste, and brought out the cloak to her and wrapped it about her shoulders. She turned, holding the folds together at her throat, and looked at me, and for the first time smiled, though briefly and faintly. She shook a little with the cold, as though only now could she feel it, and hugged the fur of the high collar against her cheeks.

'It is not mine,' she said, 'but hers. We exchanged. Someone among you might have known it by sight.'

'As I remember her,' I said, 'though that's some years gone by, you are not even like. The same figure and height, perhaps, and the same bearing and gait. Yes, from behind you could pass. You are one of her ladies?'

'The least of them,' she said. And all the while that

we stood close her eyes were searching me through and through.

'Both you and she,' I said, 'mistook my errand, and gave me no chance to reach a better understanding. I was sent after the lady and her party, not to threaten or harry, but to offer her shelter and safe-conduct wherever she would be. In the name of Prince Llewelyn, her brother. But chiefly to entreat her, as he very earnestly desired, that she should place herself in his hands and come with him to Gwynedd, there to use his house as freely as her own, and enter and leave it whenever she pleased. But if she would not give him countenance, then I was to see her safely into Brecon, or wherever else she thought fit, so I could report her safe and well.'

I saw her eyes, that were large enough, God knows, in that young, weary face, dilate and glow into silvery grey within their black nests of lashes. She said, very low: 'Is that why you rode so hard after us?'

'It is. I lost my chance. And since I lost it through your gallantry and wit,' I said, 'I pray you at least to believe what I tell you of my lord's mind and my own.'

She looked at me long, and she said: 'I do believe it, if your lord's mind is as I have seen yours to be.' And after a moment, and ruefully: 'I doubt she would have rejected any advance of his, she's so set against him for her lord's sake. It is a pity!' And again, still pondering: 'It was told us of him, by messengers from Llanbadarn, that he did there no needless violence after victory.'

'I understood that she spoke, not of her own lord, but of mine, and that she wondered about him, and in particular about me, being here his envoy. For all night long she had remained silent, only warming the dying man's feet in her lap and cherishing them from movement, but there was nothing had happened in that hut that she had not seen and noted, and made more of than any man could. And I knew this of her not because she was woman, but because she was this woman. 'I see,' she said, 'that I did not at all so well as I intended, by her or by you.'

At that I shook my head. 'By me you did better than well,' I said, 'and by him that's dead within best of all. It is due to you only that he did not die alone and uncomforted, and for that I shall thank you to the day of my own death.'

Her lips moved, but upon so slight a motion of breath that I could not be sure she said: 'And I you!' But thus I think she spoke.

'And now,' I said, 'frost or no, it remains for us to bury him, and that we shall do here, where he died. But your part is done, and nobly, and I would have you safe with your own people. I will give you a reliable escort to bring you into Brecon to join your lady.'

She looked at me steadily, and jutted lip and chin for a long moment, considering. Then with a resolution as final as it was quiet, she said: 'No!'

I was at loss here, not understanding what she meant or what she wanted of me. And I began to say patiently that I could not abandon her here in the forest, or leave her to the mercy of possible unwounded and desperate fugitives from Cwm-du. Leave alone the cold and hunger of winter, her horse being in as great need as herself. And mistaking her reserve, I told her earnestly that she need have no fear of riding with my men, for I would take whatever oath she required that she should be respected in every way among us, by the last and least of our party as surely as by myself. But the dead man I must see decently into the grave here, however temporary his stay, for though he was not blood kin to me, yet in a manner he was closer than blood kin, and I would not move from this place until I had said the office over him for his rest.

She said to me, with the same still and starry face, her eyes never loosing their fixed hold of mine: 'I take your word, for all as for yourself, and I do and will trust myself with you gladly. But will you not extend to me the same choice your lord offered to my lady?'

'You do not wish,' I said, bewildered, 'to go to Brecon?'

She said: 'No!' as forcibly as before. And she said that she would have gone, with all her doubts, but for this chance that had opened for her another way. Duty she owed to her lady, and would have paid, however reluctantly. But God had brought her here to this place, and turned the world and her life about, and by that she would abide, very gladly. For she was Welsh, and of a line from which bards and warriors had sprung, and it was against her grain to flee from the Welsh and take shelter, as if by nature though against her nature, with the English, whose one aim, however they fostered one chieftain against another, was to devour Wales wholemeal.

'Then is it your wish,' I said, 'that we should see you safe back to Carreg Cennan, into the household of Meredith ap Rhys Gryg?'

'Not that, either,' she said. 'I have no father or brother left there to make me welcome, and I think it no wise move to put myself into the protection of a lord like Meredith, with grown sons around him. If I am to beg shelter and refuge, I'll beg it from the highest. If you will take me, I will go with you to your Prince Llewelyn, and if there is a place for me about his court, in service among his womenfolk, I will fill it as well as I may.'

I was taken full aback at this resolution in her, and yet I did not question or advise, hardly knowing then why. It was not long before I knew. For on the face of it this was folly, for her to venture afield into Gwynedd, the one woman among ten men, and for us to burden

251

ourselves with her when our passage might not be without troubles. And this folly I accepted and embraced, never asking a reason of myself or her. I asked her only: 'Do you mean this in earnest? And is there none left here at all who deserves and waits for news of you? Not one person to be in distress for you?'

'To the best of my knowing,' she said steadily, 'not one.'

So then I knew, by reason of the great flood of hope and joy that filled me, why I had no desire to examine or consider all the difficulties that might face us on her account, or the need we had of haste to overtake my lord. And I said to her only: 'Come, then, if that is your wish.' For God he knows it was mine.

We buried Meilyr, my mother's husband, in a deep hollow of the ground among the trees, where the mast and mould of years from the branches had made a loose, crumbling soil that would not harden like the open ground, even in the frost. We broke the soil with our daggers and hands to get deeper, and since we could make no very profound grave without better tools, we prised up rocks from the bed of the brook to pile over him, for fear wolves or foxes should dig him up again. Later we sent word to the canons of Talley, to bring him away and give him better burial. That day there was none but myself to speak the words over him. Yet I think he has not slept less well for that. Could I have laid him with my mother, I would have done it. As it was, I took her ring, when we moved and composed his body, for his hands had loosed their hold of it, and threaded it upon his little finger, that he might not lose it in the earth.

The woman stood with us by that graveside, not heeding the cold or the wind. And when I rose from kneeling beside him, I looked at her, and her eyes were wide and fixed, staring upon the silver band on his finger, where the little engraved hand held the rose. In her face there was nothing to be read, except the rapt solemnity of death's presence, for to be brought face to face with another man's death is to meet one's own death in the way, and this touched her nearly, for she had been the instrument of God in blessing his departure, and I think she grieved and marvelled, as at the loss of something she had not known until then for hers. And that was my case also.

Nor had dead Meilyr yet ended his work with me. But that I did not know when we piled the icy rocks over him, and left him to his rest.

We rode back into Dynevor as the light was beginning to fail, and made a stay overnight for her sake. And in the morning we took fresh horses and set out for the north.

Refreshed and resolute, she rode beside me out of the gatehouse and down the track from the mound. With kilted skirts she rode, astride like a man, and booted, for I think she was determined that she would not be a drag upon our speed, but keep mile for mile with us, untiring. All she had with her was a thin saddle-roll with a few clothes in it, and whatever else women will not leave behind when they leave most of what they possess. And since for the first few miles we faced the east and the dawn, there was a lustre upon her face and a brightness in her eyes, for the sun came up red and splendid across the wasting snow.

It came upon me suddenly that I did not even know her name, for though she must have gathered many of ours from our utterances, there had been no one to speak hers before us, and so positive was her presence that until then I had felt no need to find a talisman for her,

253

as though such a woman could be shut into a charm and held in the hand. But now, realising, I spoke my astonishment aloud, and she looked round at me, and deep into me, as was her way, without a smile.

'Yours I know,' she said. 'They call you Samson. You are the private clerk and close friend of Llewelyn ap Griffith. And well I know I should have told you more of myself than I have, though God knows I have told you true. My name is Cristin, Llywarch's daughter, who was Rhys Mechyll's bard until his death.'

'I have heard him spoken of,' I said, 'many a time.'

She gazed straight before her into the rising sun, and said: 'There is more. Among the men who went out from Dynevor to meet Llewelyn at Cwm-du there was one Godred, a younger son of one of Rhys Mechyll's knights, in Rhys Fychan's service now. Like many another, he has not come back. They have no word of him here at Dynevor, except that one who did come in safely from that fight saw him unhorsed and fallen in the forest, and doubts if he got away with his life. Yet some will make their way alive into Carmarthen, surely, and some into Brecon, and only God knows the names of the spared.'

She turned her head again to look at me, and her eyes in the low, radiant light were burnished silver-grey, and large as moons, but her face was quite calm and still.

'I am Cristin, Godred's wife,' she said. 'Or his widow.'

CHAPTER IX

In the cantref of Gwerthrynion we found the traces of Llewelyn's passage clear, for he had possessed himself of most of that goodly land, ripping away all the western borders of Roger Mortimer's lordship on the march. And only this cantref, out of all he had taken into his power that winter, had he retained for himself, using all the others to bind various of his allies to him, that it might be seen that the deliverance of Wales would be also the enlargement of all those who took part in it. So we passed in peace, with remounts where we needed them, and lodging at request, and came to the Cistercian house at Cwm Hir, always dear to Llewelyn Fawr, and always loyal to his line.

They were gone from there before we came, but only by one day. So we took a night's rest, and went on after them. It was then some five days before the Christmas feast.

Cristin, Godred's wife, rode with us grimly, without complaint or flagging, though often I know she was very weary. At every halt I took care to make provision for her privacy and rest, and at every uprising she came forth fresh and neat, with her youth like armour between her body and any failure or faintheartedness. For she was a very strong-willed lady. And though there was much about her I did not understand, I understood only too well that it might be my irredeemable loss if I questioned her concerning what she had seen fit to tell me, and afterwards had told me no more. And whether she had loved this Godred, and been happy with him, I could not know, for on that subject she had closed both her lips and her heart. But chiefly I told myself that she had cause to believe the word of the soldier who had reported him fallen and wounded, and was sure in her own mind that he was dead, and that being so, she wished to escape from the scene of her loss, being now utterly alone, into some new expectation of life in another country. But whether I believed this because it was the most probable truth, or because I greatly desired it to be so, that I do not know. I do know that daily I prayed earnestly without words that I might be delivered from the sin of praying for his death.

And yet in those days we rode together in such precious comradeship as I had never known with any woman, or ever thought to know. And being forbidden by her silence to speak of her secrets, I found no such prohibition upon my own. In the hospice at Cwm Hir, before I left her to her rest, we sat some while together, and were at peace, and suddenly I desired above all things to tell her all that she must, in her heart, desire to know about the man she had helped to die in blessedness in the foot-hill forests of the Black Mountains. And I told her all the story of my mother and my mother's husband, and my mother's brief and nameless love, out of which I was born.

'I knew,' said Cristin, 'that it was no simple matter of an errand undertaken, or you would have given him the ring at once, as soon as you knew him, and so discharged it. Then you have sacrificed to his peace of mind all those hopes you had of finding a place for yourself among your father's kin.'

'I sacrificed nothing,' I said. 'I gave him, with good-will, what he valued and needed more than I. As for the hope that I may some day find someone who is kin to me, what have I lost by the gift? I shall not forget the hand and the rose. If I see it again, I shall know it.'

'But you have buried,' she said, 'the only proof you had to give you rights among them, even if you find them. Have you thought of that?'

I had not, for the truth was that long ago I had let go any ambitious idea I had had of establishing myself with my father's house. For now that I had a place in Llewelyn's confidence and an ambition all the dearer and more consuming because it was his, and mine only in reflection from him, I had no need in this world of any other kin.

'Well for you,' she said, watching me with deep gravity, 'if you bury with the ring everything that it signified, and rest content with the present and the future, forgetting the past. What need have you of any man's hand to raise you, when you have a prince as lord and friend? And what of brothers when he uses you as a brother? You have made for yourself a valuable and enduring place which you owe to no man's patronage, and no man's merits but your own. And you tell me you would not change, and have no regrets. Cut off the father you never knew, for he will only eat away a part of your mind that you cannot spare. Better to think rather of sons.'

I said that she was surely right, and to say truth I was shaken and moved that she felt so deeply and spoke so earnestly of my affairs. Indeed there was nothing left in me of feeling towards my lost father, by this time, but a small, disturbing core of curiosity, for from him I had in part the blood that ran in my veins, the impulses that drove me, the wits with which I served my prince, and some share in my face. Desiring knowledge of him was desiring knowledge of myself.

But as for any need to make claim upon his blood and his household, if I did discover it, or to make myself known to any scion of that house, I felt none. The most I wanted of them was to know, not at all to be known. And so I said.

'You are wise,' she said, and I thought she drew breath as though in ease of mind, and let fall a long, soft sigh.

We overtook Llewelyn and the main part of his force at Bala, for there he had halted to disperse for Christmas those of his army companies recruited from Penllyn and Merioneth, before the ranks from the north moved on to their homes. He had kept his word to bring the young men of the four cantrefs back safely, almost to a man, and many of them with booty to show for their campaign. And at Bala, before the chieftains separated, they held council concerning the next moves, for it was certain that the force and impetus we had gained ought not to be allowed to die down again while the winter season again grew wet and wild, with little frost. Even if harder cold should come, we now held the whip hand where food supplies were concerned. By the time my party rode in, the princes had agreed among them how soon they should muster again, the place and the target.

It was my intent to go alone to Llewelyn before I presented Cristin to him, for the sight of a straight and comely young woman entering the hall with me would surely raise his hopes that it was the Lady Gladys I brought to him. But someone had observed us before ever we reached the gate of the llys, and carried him word, and he came out in haste from the high chamber to meet us. He had just come in from riding, and now came from the fireside, unarmed, belting his gown about him, and he was flushed and bright from his exercise. At this time, shortly before his twenty-eighth birthday, he had let his beard grow, being much preoccupied with other matters in the field, and thereafter he kept it so, but close-cropped so that it left his mouth bare, and drew golden-brown lines along his upper lips and round the strong, sharp bones of his jaw, as though some cunning artist had engraved him in bronze. In his eager expectation his eyes also had centres of gold. And even when they lit upon Cristin he was still in hope and in doubt, for he had not set eyes upon his sister for fifteen years and more, and any woman riding in with me then, young and slender and dark, could have passed for the Lady Gladys. Nevertheless, he was quick to perceive that this one was too young.

I lifted Cristin down, and she made a deep reverence to him, but he stopped her quickly, taking her by the hands and raising her, for the courtyard was muddy with melted snow. He said that she was welcome, and turned to embrace me.

'I am glad to have you safe back with us,' he said. 'I feared you might have run your head into more trouble than I bargained for when I sent you out. You've had no losses?'

'None, my lord,' I said. 'Delayed we were, but not by any disaster to ourselves. And though I'm sorry I could not bring you the Lady Gladys, yet she is safe in Brecon with her children. And someone else I have brought, who can give you more news of her than I can, for she has been in your sister's service, and was of her party when she left Dynevor. This is Cristin, daughter of Rhys Mechyll's bard Llywarch. She is left without a protector, and has chosen to be of your party rather than take refuge with the English.'

'This is a story I must hear,' said Llewelyn, 'but out of this cutting wind. Come in to the fire, and I'll have meat and drink brought for you.' And he took her by the hand and led her through the hall of the llys to his own great chamber, where there was warmth, and furs to nest in, and the soft grey smoke of the brazier drifting high in the roof.

'So you have chosen to be wholly Welsh,' he said, when she was seated close to the fire, a horn of wine in her hand and the glow of warmth bringing a mirrored glow into her face, 'when my own sister fled from me. I grant you she might well feel she had good cause. But you, it seems, were not afraid to venture.'

'There is more in it than that, my lord,' she said. 'I fear I have been the cause of your plans going awry, for it was I who drew off Master Samson's pursuit and let my lady get safe into Brecon. As he will tell you. It was well-meant, but I have deprived her of the choice of which I was only too glad to take advantage, and I fear you may think less well of welcoming me when you know all.'

'That,' said Llewelyn, eyeing her steadily, 'I doubt. But if you want Samson to be your advocate, you could hardly do better.'

So I told all that story, how Cristin had played the hart to our hounds, and then gone to earth in the forest, how we had ridden on, in time only to see the Lady Gladys and her company cross the bridge into Brecon, where we could not follow, how we had returned by the same road to look for the woman who had deceived us, and how she had come forth to us out of the woods to lead us to a dying man. There was very little Llewelyn did not know of my grief with Meilyr, and his with me, for in these years of our close companionship we had talked of everything that linked and divided us in the past. He sat listening very intently as I told him of that death and burial.

'Rhys Fychan and I between us,' he said soberly, 'have much to answer for. That was cruel waste at Cwmdu, of Meilyr and many another. Meredith has promised to send me a courier if anything is heard of Rhys himself, whether he lives or is slain. We found some wounded, and a few dead, on our way north again from Dynevor, but of Rhys no sign. For my part I think he was luckier than this man of his, and is with the English now, somewhere in one of those castles they hold along the Towy. I wish he had seen fit to come in with us and own his Welsh blood, and spare so many deaths.'

Cristin looked up with the flush of the wine in her face, holding off sleep now that she was in from the cold, and said doubtfully: 'But as we heard it in Dynevor, you came south to set up Meredith in all his own lands and Rhys's, too. To cast out Rhys as Rhys cast out his uncle.'

'It need not have been so. To set up Meredith again in his own, yes, that I had sworn and have kept. But there was enough there once for both, and could be so again. The tale of their holdings in Cantref Mawr and Cantref Bychan is long enough, and the vale of Towy could very well hold both, if they would but be allies instead of enemies. But a brother who takes the English part when he has a choice I will not endure there. He made his own decision.'

She said: 'I think, none too happily. Between the upper and the nether millstone a man feels his bones turning to powder. I think he chose what he took for safety, thinking the English stronger than you. He may well have other thoughts now.'

'Late,' said Llewelyn, 'for such as Meilyr.'

'Too late,' she questioned persistently, 'for such as Rhys?'

He looked at her with a long, wide-eyed look, taking her in with more attention than before, and slowly he smiled. 'I see that you are a loyal liege-woman to your lord and your lady, as well as a patriot Welshwoman. I cannot answer for what Rhys has done, nor guess what he may do. But I am mortal and fallible enough myself, God knows, to be very ware of damning a man for choosing wrong once out of fear for his life and lands, or shutting my ears to him when he turns and says: I was craven and I own it, and now I have done with it. Closing and locking one's doors may keep many a good man out, and that would be pity.'

For all the cloud of weariness and warmth that was closing her eyes, she was very sharply aware of him, and I knew that he had won her. And that pleased me, having so high a worship for both. She wanted, as I think, to give him pleasure in return for the hope he had freely given her for the prince she had served, for she began to tell him of her lady and her young sons, and to reassure him of their good health and high spirit on the ride to Brecon, the children taking it as a new game. The elder, Rhys Wyndod after his father, was nearly eight years old then, and very like his mother, she said. And the younger, five years of age, was named Griffith for his grandsire.

'And there is more to tell,' she said, 'that a brother may like to know. My lady is again with child. No, you need feel no guilt or fear for her, she was in excellent health when she rode out, and only two months gone. She is strong and takes childbirth easily, and she will do very well, wherever she brings forth her third son. I do but tell you that you may take it into account, in whatever dealings follow. For I am sure Rhys Fychan is not set against you or against Wales, but only vexed for his failure against you, as is only human, and very perplexed as to what is best to do for his life and the good of his line. And if he comes to, she will never be far behind.'

Now this was surprising to me in my lord, whom I believed I knew so well, that he was so much charmed by this news, and asked her so many questions, he who had taken no thought at all for his own succession, and never seemed to see woman unless she spoke out with a voice as profound and shrewd as man. So utterly was he absorbed in his passion for Wales. And surely Wales is also a woman, being in all things both capricious and durable, tyrannous and lovely, harsh and gentle, wayward and faithful. To Cristin, in this first meeting, he spoke as to his match, and me he forgot, and I did not grudge being forgotten, for I greatly desired that she should make safe her place in his court, and be at rest there.

If she had forgotten me, that I might have grudged, but she did not. In all she had to say to him, I was a presence. There was no need to tell me so.

When they were done, for he saw that she was very weary, he said to her: 'Madam, my steward's lady here will make proper provision for your rest. Tomorrow we ride for Aber, and if you are not too tired with your long journey I would have you travel with us, for Goronwy's wife at Aber will welcome you, and I shall be glad to have you keep the feast with us there. If you prefer it, we will provide you a litter. Make your home in my household as long as you please, and use it as your own. And beyond that, is there anything I can do for you, to set your mind at rest?'

She looked up at him out of the cushions and skins that cradled her, and the heavy lids rolled back from her eyes, that were like violets, if violets could be lighted by candles within them. Her face was suddenly so still and so pale that for a moment she ceased to breathe, and all her bones shone white through the skin, as though smitten by frost. One glance she cast at me, and then looked back to him.

'There is something,' she said, 'since you have asked

for word from Meredith ap Rhys Gryg of the dead and the living. Of your kindness, will you ask him also for any news of one Godred ap Ivor, a landless knight in Rhys's service? For I am his wife, or his widow, and I would fain know which.'

'That I will do,' he said to her, as gravely and simply as he would have said it to a man. 'God forbid that I should have cost you so high, beyond my repaying. But whatever I can get to hear from Dynevor of Godred ap Ivor, you shall hear the same hour.'

Then he committed her to my care, to see her safely bestowed with the steward's wife, and she and I went out from him together in silence, her arm against mine. I had no word to say. For fear of the wrong answer I could ask nothing. But ever I watched her face as we went, while she looked not at all upon me, but straight before her, and was still white as ice with her own fear, the fellow to mine or its counter-balance, and which I dared not guess. For greatly she had steeled and mastered herself to ask that thing of him, wanting certainty instead of doubt, but there was nothing in her manner to me, then or after, to tell me which certainty it was she dreaded, to hear again of Godred living, or to receive assurance he was dead.

She rode with us next day, fresh as a flower, and now more decorously as a woman should, in a gown I had not seen before, for we were safe in our own country, and there were other women of the party, coming with the court from Bala to Aber to keep the feast. There was no great haste, for messengers had gone before to make preparation for the prince's coming, and we could ride at ease, sparing our horses and ourselves. So it was a pleasant and merry cavalcade that made its way through the mountain roads by Dolwyddelan and on to Bangor, where we halted for the night, and the next morning took the coast road east to Aber.

David had gone on before with the vanguard, to disperse those levies from the parts about Bangor and Carnarvon, and he met us at the crossing of the river Ogwen on that final morning ride, to escort his brother with fitting state to Aber. He had shed his mail, and blossomed in brocades and furs, very handsome and handsomely adorned. And when he had kissed Llewelyn's hand, and been warmly embraced, he fell into our line where it pleased him, exchanging greetings here and there with all those he knew best, and so ranged through the whole length of our procession until he came to me.

'Samson!' he cried, throwing a boisterous arm about me and all but wrestling me out of the saddle. 'I'm glad to see you back with us whole and safe. You were so long, faith, I almost feared we'd lost you. But I hear you had no luck with my sister.'

I owned it, and told him how it had befallen, and when he heard of that last encounter with my mother's husband, and of his death, he was cast into a sadness as true as it was brief, as when he himself had broken to me the news that I should not see my mother again.

'He was a dour fellow,' he said, 'this Meilyr, but never less than patient with me, when, God knows, I was trial enough even to longer-suffering souls than he. It was Meilyr first taught me to ride. I am glad, Samson, that you were brought to him so strangely, and he did not go solitary. Shall we not send word to Meredith to fetch him away to proper burial? For you say the place is marked with stones.'

I said it was already done, for we had sent a messenger from Dynevor to the canons of Talley, with an endowment for his disposal at the abbey. Though doubtless, for all the devout searches they made for others of the

265

fallen, many a man died there in the forests after Cwm-du, and wore away to clean bones undiscovered. And in the justice of God I think their unblessed sleep could not be held against them.

But when I went on to tell him how Cristin had rejected escort into Brecon, and chosen to cast in her lot with a free Wales, David's face lit like a sunrise with startled joy, and he looked round to search among the womenfolk for this new countenance.

'You have brought her here with you? She's among us now? Bring me to speak with this young she-warrior! I did not know my sister had such resolute maidens.'

'She is not a maiden,' I said drily, 'but a wife. Or a widow by now, maybe. Her husband was a knight in Rhys Fychan's bodyguard, and she's had no word of him since Cwm-du.'

'And she is under your protection,' he said, gently mocking me, 'and I am warned to keep my distance, am I?' I was silent, for I had not thought to have given him even so much enlightenment, and I feared to betray myself further. Even so, he grew serious again, and eyed me intently as we rode, not concealing his thoughts, but not plaguing me with them, either. 'I'll never add to her troubles,' he said, 'but you'll not grudge me a word with her, and she so gallant a guest of our house, and so wholehearted a Welshwoman.' His tone was light and a little mocking still, but his curiosity and his eagerness were real enough, and since there was not a personable young woman in any of the courts of Gwynedd who was not known to him, he could hardly fail to find the new face for himself in very short order. I thought it as well to bring him to her myself, and did so as we rode.

Cristin lifted to him her pearl-clear face, faintly flushed with the sting of the cold air and the exercise of riding, and opened her grey eyes wide upon his beauty. It seemed that she was undisturbed, for her serenity never quivered. It was he who lost the thread of his easy banter for a moment, and let a silence fall like a drift of snow between them. She had that kind of assurance, rooted in a personal pride quite without arrogance, that can endure such silences and feel no need to fill them. It was not often that David found himself at a loss with a woman, and I think the novelty of that experience did not at all displease him. He was much taken, and rode by her the rest of the way to Aber, not exerting himself to charm, for he had never found that there was any need, but rather taking pleasure in being charmed.

I let them alone on that journey, and what they said to each other, he questioning and she replying, I never knew, though I am sure it was formal enough and civil enough, the expected exchanges between princely host and respected guest. When we rode into the maenol at Aber it was David who took her waist between his hands and lifted her down, and did it with little haste and much delicate care, I think partly for pure mischief because I was close, and could not choose but see what pleasure it gave him.

Afterwards he came into my little office and flung his arm about my shoulders in his usual impulsive way, and: 'Find me another such phoenix,' he said, 'since it seems you have the happy gift of plucking them out of the snow. For I won't wrong you by taking yours.'

'She is not mine,' I said patiently. 'She is waiting for news of her husband, and the prince has promised all possible efforts to discover whether he lives or not. With half of Rhys's force gathering alive and angry in Carmarthen and Brecon, there's every chance Godred ap Ivor is somewhere there among them, and waiting for news of her as she is for news of him.'

So I said, though it made my throat stiff and sore to

utter such things reasonably, as though I hoped for them, and daily it became harder not to wish her landless knight dead and buried.

'Waiting, perhaps,' agreed David, 'but not greatly exerting himself, surely? Look, this lady was not scattered and lost from a confused fight, as the men were, she rode with my sister's party for Brecon, and left it only to ensure her companions should get safely within. She knew of a hut in the forest, where she could take shelter. Do you suppose Gladys did not know the whole of it, where she would be, where to send for her? You were lucky they left you time for that dawn burial, I dare swear they were not far behind you when you left. If this Godred of hers is in any one of the royal castles along Towy, then long before this he knows what befell her, he'll know what they found in the woods, the ashes of your fire, the staff of your torch, the droppings of your horses. He'll know, or as good as know, since she is not in any of the English fortresses, nor in Dynevor or Carreg Cennen—'

'He may be too notoriously of Rhys's party and in Rhys's former counsels to go asking questions in Meredith's castles now,' I said.

'He would not need to. My sister could and should be doing it for him, under safe-conduct. What's to prevent? So since he must know she is not there, what's left but that she rode north with you, willing or unwilling? He could very well have got Gladys, or Rhys if he lives, to send an envoy here to ask for news of her, who would grudge it? No, either this is a very indifferent husband for such a spirited wife,' he said warmly, 'or else he's dead indeed.'

He stirred out of his serious reasoning suddenly, and looked at me along his shoulder with a sharp and challenging smile. 'Have I comforted you?' he said.

Doggedly I answered him: 'I wish her whatever is for her happiness. Why should I take comfort in any man's death?' But even that was to say too much, for David was very wise in me. Always he knew my mind earlier and better than I knew it myself, except, perhaps, for what I thought and felt concerning him; and even there I would not be certain he was often deceived.

'I know of several reasons,' he said, still smiling. But he did not think it needful to name them. He got up from sitting beside me, leaving a hand upon my shoulder, and its grip was warm and vital, as though some part of his superabundant life flowed through his sinews into mine. 'Take heart!' he said. 'Your Cristin may yet find herself a free woman.'

'She is a free woman now,' I said obstinately. 'And she is *not mine*.'

He was moving towards the door then. He turned with it open in his hand, and the wintry light spilled over him from outside, glittering and chill, turning his smile to a starry brightness, as pure as ice.

'You think not?' he said, and closed the door softly between us.

Nevertheless, as I know, on the eve of Christmas Eve, after the harpers had played us into a daze in hall, and the wine and the wood-smoke had made us slow and heavy with pleasure and sleep, David did make a certain advance to Cristin, I think without expecting more than a refusal. Perhaps even for the strange, sweet sensation of being refused. I saw him draw up a stool at her shoulder at high table, and lean upon the board beside her, speaking long and persuasively into her ear. And I saw her smiling and calm, no way displeased or tempted, replying to him gently without turning her head. He kept up his siege for a long time, and when he left her at last he took up her hand, that lay easy and empty upon the table, and kissed it with his usual considered and winning grace. Then she did look up at him, with that wide and generous glance of hers that went in deep through a man's flesh to his heart and spirit, and serenely she smiled.

When he had left her, I got up from my own place and went and sat beside her, which I felt to be folly but could not forbear. It was growing very smoky and a little drunken below the fire in the great hall, and there was some singing between the offerings of the bards, and some coupling in the dark corners or where the hangings were ample. Cristin looked round at me, and understood my coming very well.

'Do him justice,' she said, low-voiced and wryly smiling, 'he takes no for an answer. Ah, you need not be anxious for me, not with your foster-brother.'

'He is not used,' I said, 'to being refused.'

'The better for the first to refuse him,' she said. 'But you trouble needless. I am not so beautiful that he need strain against his usual habit to win me, and he has no will to pursue those who are unwilling. Why should he, when he has only to lift a finger to draw nine out of ten after him?'

So much she had learned of him in hardly more than a day, and yet she was the tenth, no, the thousandth, woman, and he moved her only to an open and uncritical liking. But of his complacency I was less sure than she.

'You need not trouble about Prince David,' she said, 'while he has his hands full with work that stretches him mind and body, fighting or ruling or hunting or what you will. But when he has not enough work he will turn to playing. And his games could be dangerous. Oh, not to women! The only grief he will ever cause to women is the grief of losing him. But to you, to his brother, to all those nearest and dearest to him, he could do great damage. And to himself. To himself most of all.'

The women were leaving the high table then, and she also rose to go to her bed. I went with her down through the hall, and out into the frosty courtyard, for her lodging, like mine but in another direction, lay in the sheltered dwellings along the curtain wall. It was the eve of the eve of Christmas, as I have said, and sharply cold, and those who left the warmth of the hall to seek their rest crossed the rimy spaces quickly, huddled in their cloaks. But we two slowed and went side by side out into the centre of the courtyard before separating, as though we had both more to say before we could part, and found no right words. There was bright moonlight once we were out of the shadow of the hall, that silvered her from head to foot, like a virgin saint on an altar.

I said, not subtly, for I was in torment: 'And did you truly feel no desire to go with him, as he wished? For all that beauty and vigour and grace of his, no desire at all?'

She halted, and stood still before me, within reach of my hand if I had but stretched it out from my side. With her great eyes dark and clear upon my face she said: 'None.'

'God knows,' I said, 'you need hardly wonder or blush if you had. When he wills, there are few can resist him.'

'You forget,' she said, 'that I am already bespoken.'

'Your heart also?' I asked her, low and hoarsely.

'My heart first, most, and for ever,' she said. And all the while she gazed unwaveringly at me with that mute face and those searching eyes. So then I had my answer.

I lowered my eyes from her, her brightness and stillness gave such pain. I said my goodnight, softly and faithfully, for she did me no wrong, and even to have known and served her was great joy. And I went away from her to my own small chamber, there to pray for continued grace to serve her still as best I might, and to wait with patience and resignation for news of the man who had her heart. For still, if he was dead, for which I must not hope, some day there might be for me the grace of a nearer service. But when I looked back out of the sheltering shadow under the wall she was still standing where I had left her, and looking after me, and only slowly, now that I had vanished, did she also turn away to her own place.

So we kept our Christmas feast with great reverence and gratitude for victories won, hearing service daily in the royal chapel of the llys, and at night we drank deep and heard noble singing to the honour and praise of Llewelyn and David and their allies. And on the last day of the old year came a rider from Meredith ap Rhys Gryg, bringing word that Rhys Fychan was known to be alive and well, and reunited with his wife. The messenger brought also a list of those of his chief tenants, officers and knights to be with him under English protection. But the name of Godred ap Ivor was not among them. Of him nothing was known.

So the hope I would not recognise, since it was the death of her hope, thrust up its head again as often as I ground it underfoot, and grew like a weed.

CHAPTER X

———————

We marched again, one week into the new year of twelve hundred and fifty-seven, and I left her behind at Aber with Goronwy's wife. I say 'I left her' as though she had given me some right to hold myself responsible for her safety and well-being, but indeed she was her own mistress, and I had no more rights in her than any other among us. The only thing I had that was mine alone concerning her was the memory of the journey north together. Not even she could have taken that from me, even had she wished. But she was always my sweet friend, and cherished, I think, those same memories for kindness' sake, if she had no love left to give. So it was well for me, however deep the hurt, that I should leave her for a while.

We mustered at Bala, for this time Llewelyn was bent on settling accounts with Griffith ap Gwenwynwyn of Powys, who in every dissension was unswervingly on the side of England. After the winning of the two Maelors from that other Griffith, Madoc's son, at the beginning of our winter campaign, those mishandled neighbouring lands of Powys Gwenwynwyn stuck sharply into our eastern flank, at once a knife ready to disembowel us and a barrier against our free movement southwards. Moreover, this was the most obstinate and renegade of all our chieftains, a Welsh hater of the Welsh, and his example was a danger to Llewelyn's cause as long as he remained immune.

We struck, therefore, by way of the Tanat valley to

the Severn, that great river, and then swept southward, upstream, along the valleys of Severn and Vrnwy both, seizing and settling as we came, until late in the month we reached Griffith's town and castle of Pool. The castle lay between town and river, and escape over the water into England was never difficult for him and his family. We burned the town, but by the time we fought our way into the bailey Griffith was away with his wife and children to the protection of the lady's father, John Lestrange, and appealing also for help to John FitzAlan, who was lord of lands at Clun, and held Montgomery for the king. Though it did him little good, for we pushed on still to the south on our own side the water, and though we did not take the castle of Montgomery itself, for it stands upon a great rock on the English side, in so strong a position that men might waste hours scaling the mound, and attack with mangons and trebuchets is impossible, there being no comparable height convenient to mount them, yet we did sack and lay waste the town below, for a memorial to our visit. All that Lestrange and FitzAlan and Griffith could do between them was to hold the castle itself, for the force they sent out against us we shattered in the fields between Severn and Berriew, and sent them scurrying back up the hill to the shelter of their stone walls.

After this Llewelyn thought it high time to be seen and felt in the south again, for he well knew it would be harder for a prince of Gwynedd to hold together that fragmented region, so strong in marcher castles and so parcelled out among many sons, than to keep a firm hand upon the north, where the sun of his countenance and the shadow of his justice were always close at hand. Before the English had recovered from the shock of Montgomery we were joining forces with Meredith ap Rhys Gryg in Cantref Bychan, and sweeping on towards the sea between Towy and Tawe. Before the end of February we were in Gower, where many of the Welsh tenants of the de Breos lands rose to join us in great joy, and we not only ate away the borders of this Norman barony, but did as much for the power of the king's seneschal in that region, Patrick of Chaworth, the lord of Kidwelly. Not for many years had those two great men been penned within their own fortresses, as they were then, or seen so many of their possessions lopped like branches from the trunk, and been powerless to prevent.

In the month of March we had proof positive of the alarm we had caused in King Henry's court, for a letter came from the king's brother, Earl Richard of Cornwall, requesting Llewelyn to receive a deputation of Dominican friars who would present to him the earl's protestations and proposals for an end to this warfare, and offering him a safe-conduct to meet with them.

'I see,' said Llewelyn, amused but thoughtful, 'that Henry thinks his brother's influence may carry more weight than his own, now Richard has one foot on the steps of the imperial throne.' For this Earl Richard, whose general good sense and steadiness were by no means to be despised even for themselves, was come into a greater title this year, having been elected king of the Romans – that is to say in plainer terms, king of Germany – and emperor-elect, though for all I could see, very little practical gain ever came of it.

'Will you go?' asked David doubtfully. 'Better Richard's good faith than Henry's, I grant you, but I would not stake my life on either.'

But Llewelyn said without hesitation that he would go, and replied courteously to the invitation, accepting the place appointed, and the date. 'For if they are come to the point of being willing to talk,' said he, 'there's a chance at least, if no more, that we may secure everything we have gained. If they'll offer peace on present terms, so much the better. Even a truce would give us time to consolidate.'

David was in some doubt still, for he felt we had not yet gone far enough, and that we should gain more by continuing this impetuous invasion than by halting to strengthen our hold on what we already had. Nevertheless, Llewelyn went to the meeting, for I rode to the earl of Gloucester's castle of Chepstow in his train, as his clerk and secretary, while David, with Meredith ap Rhys Gryg, maintained our proper presence in arms in Gower.

Now on this ride we passed through the whole wide land of Glamorgan, and used our eyes along the way, too, to good effect later in the year. For nothing well learned is ever wasted. But very little else came of the meeting, if nothing was lost.

Earl Richard had sent a long and reasoned letter, very persuasively worded, but its effect was but to appeal to Llewelyn, in the name of the treaty of Woodstock and of right relations between our two countries, to restore the four cantrefs of the Middle Country to Prince Edward's control. And though it was suggested that such a conciliatory move would produce a worthy return, nothing was precisely stated of its substance. Nor did it seem that the Dominican brothers who came as envoys had any authority to bargain beyond what Earl Richard had set out in his own hand, which did not carry us far.

Llewelyn sent by them a long and courtly reply, which we took pleasure in composing, rejecting the argument that he was acting against the interests of his fellow-princes in Wales, for on the contrary, what he had done and was doing had the backing of all of them, with a very few exceptions, and represented the true will of the

276

Welsh people. He said he could not surrender any part of his conquests, for all were Welsh land, though he was prepared to agree that the commotes of Creuddyn and Prestatyn should remain as yet under English control. Which was a mild irony that may have tasted sour to the court, for though these commotes were indeed theoretically dominated by the castles of Diserth and Degannwy, still garrisoned by the English, the garrisons hardly dared put their heads out of door now that they were isolated among free and vengeful Welshmen. And to sum up, Llewelyn would be very willing to discuss a permanent peace on the basis of his present position, but short of that would agree only to a long truce on the same basis. For neither of these courses, it seemed, were the English yet ready. So nothing more came of this visit, and we returned to rejoin David at Carreg Cennen, and went home to Gwynedd for the Easter feast.

There were daffodils in the grass when we came home to Bala, and by the lake the catkins danced in the hazel bushes, for it was a most lovely spring, the renewal of all life. And Cristin was there, for she had ridden down from Aber with Goronwy's wife and children to meet us, and the llys was prepared for the festival with young branches and green reeds and the yellow and blue field flowers, kingcup and violet, and the chapel decked with fresh embroideries.

I had thought on the way, those last miles, that I would avoid her company, for the sweet of that season was so sharp that I could not well bear it. But she was coming down the meadows as we rode in at the gate, with her skirts kilted out of the dewy grass, and her hair down in two loose braids over her shoulders, and her stride was long and lithe, like a boy's, and in her arms, very lightly and easily balanced against her shoulder, she had a new, speckled lamb, still damp and curly from its dam, one of the laggard comers of that spring. One of Tudor's little boys, the youngest, ran and dawdled and ran again behind her, with a wand of willow tufted with yellow catkins in his hand.

Thus at every return she came back into my life, and I was stricken afresh with that extreme quality she had, whether it should be called beauty or by some other name, so that the breath stopped in my throat for pure wonder. So lovely did she seem to me that I knew at last how my mother had appeared to dead Meilyr, and his image rose within me and filled me with that same unendurable pain he had suffered, the chiefest sorrow of the human heart, to love and not be loved in return, to love and know oneself unloved.

I understood then those things he had known, how the sweet and bitter of the beloved's presence are so finely balanced one against the other that the lover can neither live with his darling nor without her, and is forever torn in two by the impossibility of decision, going back again and again to suffer the same anguish, again and again withdrawing only to find the void outside the range of her looks and words a living death. So Meilyr had his full revenge on me at last.

'Bala has a new shepherdess,' said Llewelyn with admiration, reining in beside her. She greeted him only with an inclination of her head, to avoid shifting the weight of the lamb, and said simply: 'The ewe has a second one still coming. Morgan will bring her down with the twin when she's safe delivered. There are hawks hovering. I thought well to get this one into the fold and leave him free. She was very late, he had some trouble with her.'

'You have unexpected skills,' he said, smiling.

'I learned more than needlework,' said Cristin composedly, 'in my father's house. We had sheep, too.' Her eyes were fixed and urgent upon his face, but she would not ask. 'I give you joy, my lord,' she said earnestly, 'of your triumphs won, and wish you all the blessings of this feast.'

'I would I could have brought you joy,' said Llewelyn. 'But of your husband there is still nothing known. I am sorry!'

I saw for a moment that sharp whiteness and tightness of fear in her face until he spoke, and then the softening that was rather of resignation than relief or despair. 'I am grateful for your care of me,' she said steadily. 'I can wait.' And she turned her head a little, and looked at me.

So it was always. Her love I could not have, but her dear trust and companionship I could not forswear, for that would have been a great and undeserved injury to her. And in those bright spring days I learned to keep fast hold of the hope I still had in her friendship, to savour the joy it was to be with her, and to contain the sorrow. For there was promise in her words, and I could wait, too, half a lifetime if need be, to have her mine at last. If she preferred my company, if she confided in me, if she put her trust in me, surely that was immeasurable blessing, even if in the end I gained no more.

Thus I did not avoid her, but made myself ever ready and willing when she sought me out, as often she did. And if there was great pain, there was great bliss, too, such bliss as Meilyr never had from my mother. And we came by a way of living side by side that was gentle and cordial and close, working together in accord, speaking freely of all the daily affairs of the court, but never now of Godred or of ourselves, while we loved and waited, she for him, and I for her.

*   *   *

There was little real fighting in the north that summer, only a reordering of the establishment of those parts of Powys we had taken from Griffith ap Gwenwynwyn, and once in May, to trim straight a position that somewhat irked our forward movement, the taking of one more of his castles, at Bodyddon, which we stormed and razed, not caring to garrison it ourselves, for once emptied of his power it was of no significance to us.

It was elsewhere that the great things were happening, and so suddenly that Llewelyn had no warning, and no time to be upon the scene himself, for the best was over before we even had word of any action in the south.

It was in the evening of the fifth day of June that a courier rode into the llys at Bala, where we still made our headquarters at this time, and made himself known for one of the officers of the war-band of Meredith ap Owen, Llewelyn's ally in Builth and Cardigan. We knew the man, Cadwgan by name, for he had fought with us at Llanbadarn in the autumn, and he was a strong, seasoned man in his fifties, who had served his lord's father before him. He would neither eat nor drink until he had told his tale, though he had ridden since morning without rest or food. We brought him in to Llewelyn in the high chamber, where he was in council with Goronwy and Tudor, and David came running after the rumour of news as eagerly as a boy.

'My lord,' said Cadwgan, when he had bent the knee to Llewelyn and kissed his hand, and hardly waiting to rise again before he began, 'we have won you and Wales a great victory, and dealt King Henry a formidable blow. Three days since, on the Towy, we routed the king's officer and a great host, pricked off their baggage horses, looted their stores, and smashed their army to pieces. What's left has made its way back into Carmarthen, but it's no more than a remnant.'

'They came out after you?' cried Llewelyn, taking fire from this jubilant outcry. 'What possessed them, out of the blue, without fresh offence? I looked for Henry to call out the host against us this year, but here in the north, not on the Towy. Nor has he sent out any such summons, we should have heard of it long before.' Which was true, for his intelligence by now was efficient and swift, and the feudal host ground out to its muster commonly with a month's warning and often more.

'No, my lord, this was a great force, but made up from the garrisons of many castles and from the marcher lordships, and great gain that will be to us, God willing, for this defeat leaves many a good fortress but wretchedly manned, and ripe for taking. But hear me how this fit began, for it concerns your own kinsfolk, and it ends not at all as it began, but with some strange reversals. It's for your lordship to determine how best to use it to your gain.'

Always the first to leap to a hazard, David cried: 'Rhys! I see the hand of Rhys Fychan again in this coil. Who else could have set them on?'

'Hear me the whole story,' said Cadwgan, flushed and grinning, 'and judge. We got word only two days before the end of May that there was great activity about the castle of Carmarthen, and levies coming in from many parts there, so we made our own preparations. My lord, with Meredith ap Rhys Gryg, made all fast at Dynevor, and also placed all their host, a great number, about all the hills around, overlooking the river valley, with all the archers we could muster. But we did not know until they moved that Rhys Fychan was with them, with his own forces, nursed all this while under English protection. We have the truth of it now, past doubt, your lordship will see why. Rhys had talked the king's seneschals in the south into taking up his cause and setting out to restore him to his own. They put their heart into it, too, it was a great host that came along the valley to Dynevor the last day of May, with the king's own officer leading them, Stephen of Bauzan.'

'I know him,' said David. 'The king sets great store by him. He was his governor in Gascony aforetime.'

'He'll be less in the royal favour now,' said Cadwgan heartily, 'for he's lost King Henry a mort of men and great store in horses and goods. They came and took station around Dynevor to storm it, and we let them spread out about the valley meadows that evening as widely as they would, for well it suited us they should feel sure of their ground. We were sure as death of ours. The castle was held well enough to sit out the storm, and we others, the most of us, were all round them in the hills, and had had time enough to choose our cover and our field for shooting. We let them stir in their camps in the dawn of the first of June, and then we opened on them at will with arrows and darts, wherever a man came within range. And from all sides. They could not attack one way without exposing themselves on either flank, and all that day they spent trying to assemble into better positions, and to bring up their engines to break into Dynevor. We knew by then that there were Welsh with them, and they could only be Rhys's men. So then we knew what was afoot.'

'If they set out in such numbers, and so equipped,' said Llewelyn, concerned, 'it could still have been a grim business.'

'So it could, my lord, and we were taking it grimly, I warrant you. Not a man of us thought we should break them as we did, but we trusted stoutly enough we should keep them out and cost them dear. But hear what happened! At earliest dawn on the second day of June our lookouts suddenly cried a marvel, and we looked, and saw a small body of horsemen, who had gathered apart in cover of trees, ride out full gallop straight for the castle gateway, the foremost of them carrying a white surcoat threaded on the point of a lance. And it was Rhys and his Welsh knights, crying to the castellan to open quickly, and let them in, for they were sickened of their servility, and begged to be of our part, free Welshmen like us.'

David uttered a shout then that was half excitement and half derisive laughter. 'And he did it? He opened the gates to such a bare-faced trick? How far were the English behind?'

'My lord, I well understand you,' owned Cadwgan warmly, 'and I would not for my life have been in the castellan's shoes, for he had but a matter of minutes to make up his mind. You say right, the English had the measure of what was happening by then, and they came like devils after. But it was they who turned the trick, for by the very look of them Rhys would not have lived long could they have got their hands on him, and he had good need to batter at the gates and cry to have them opened. It was that, and knowing Rhys well by sight, and some of those with him, too. Whatever settled his mind for him, he opened the gates and they came tumbling and hurtling in, and he got the gates to again in time, and loosed every archer he had until the English drew off. But the cream of the jest – and it was a good jest! – is that they had come out only to put Rhys back into Dynevor, and back in Dynevor he was, and the gates made fast behind him, so what were they doing there in the valley, on a fool's errand, and getting picked off by our bowmen as often as they stirred out of cover? I swear to God, if they had taken it the opposite way, and attacked then in a fury, we might have been hard pressed. But the ground had been cut from under them,

283

and they let themselves be confounded. They began a retreat. And that was all we needed. All along the valley they drew off to Carmarthen again, and all along the hills on either side we went with them. First we cut off the heavier and slower, the baggage and the engines, the sumpter horses, and any stragglers who tired. And about noon, at Cymerau, where the Cothi comes down and empties into the Towy, we thought it time to make an end, for fear too many should get back to Carmarthen alive. We were either side of them, and our horsemen had followed lightly along, and were fresh, with the slope in their favour. We made our attack there. It was a slaughter.'

'How many,' asked Llewelyn, glowing, 'got safe away?'

'My lord, if you mean in order, as a body of fighting men, none. As headlong fugitives, running every man for his own life, perhaps one in five who set out from Carmarthen won back to it alive.'

'And de Bauzan?'

'We rode him down. I saw him unhorsed, I thought him wounded, and sorely. They got him away with them. It was the one ordered thing they did. But alive or dead, that we cannot know. They left arms and harness littering the fields. We made a great harvest.'

It was indeed a victory. My eyes were on David's face, and it was torn between delight and outrage, all his bones starting in golden tension, for the summer had gilded him over like precious metal. His eyes, blue and light and stony with rage, grieved helplessly that he had not been there at Cymerau, and I think in some sort blamed all of us for his loss. And I thought then that what Cristin had said of him was wise and true, that unless he was spent recklessly and constantly in action and passion he would turn that same wealth to bitter mischief, to his own hurt most of all.

Llewelyn was other. He could take pleasure in another man's prowess, and never grudge that it was not his own, nor value it the less in the common cause because its credit shone on other men's arms. He sat with his chin on his fists and his eyes wide and thoughtful, and asked questions very much to the point.

'And your losses? Our losses?'

'My lord, a nothing! We were never exposed but in the last onslaught, and then we had the advantage. I count but eleven men dead, no more than twenty-five wounded.'

'Good! And this force was drawn from the castle garrisons in those parts? How far afield?'

'As far as the coast, my lord. There were men there from Laugharne and Llanstephan. What remains of their force is in Carmarthen, and that they did not leave too ill-provided. Being so near us.'

'But the others! Meredith is following up his victory?'

Cadwgan laughed gleefully. 'My lord, by now I think we should hold Llanstephan at least, and some of the others will not be far behind. But Carmarthen we've let alone.'

'It was well done,' said Llewelyn, and thought for a moment in silence. 'And Rhys Fychan and his knights?'

'They sat comfortably in Dynevor,' said David bitterly and scornfully, 'and had no fighting to do. And you, brother, are expected to extend your clemency to this so sudden change of heart.' His voice was like an edge of steel, but more with his own deprived discontent than with any true hatred of Rhys or his sister. He could not endure that there should have been so glorious a turmoil, and he not in the centre of it. I could see with his eyes at that moment, and see the whole of our careful month's work, stiffening the bones of what we had won, drained of any worth or satisfaction for him.

Llewelyn said mildly: 'I asked a question of Cadwgan, lad, not of you,' and looked at the messenger.

'We also have been in great doubt,' said Cadwgan honestly. 'But one thing is certain. This rout would never have taken place but for what Rhys Fychan did. For it wholly overturned the minds of the English, and caused them to act like men defeated before defeat. And that I hold in credit. But what we should think of him, I vow to God, we cannot agree. And we would fain have you come and judge. But as for the present, he and his knights are honourably lodged in Dynevor, and have not been used against the English. Nor,' he said frankly, 'let out of the gates or out of sight.'

'Wisely!' said David. But Llewelyn took no heed of him.

'Nor disarmed? Nor in any way confined, apart from being kept within the gates? And my sister has not been sent for, wherever she may be?'

'Not yet, my lord.'

'That was also wise,' he said with a wry smile. 'We can ill afford to embrace false allies, but still less to discard true ones.'

'True?' cried David, smarting. 'Need you debate concerning Rhys, after all that has passed? There is not a grain of truth in him!'

'There is not a man on earth,' said Llewelyn sharply, 'of whom I would say such a thing. If we are never to write a quittance for things past, which of us will be out of prison?'

He spoke still frowning over his own thoughts, and never so much as glanced at David, and I knew he meant no reference at all to what he had endured and forgiven from his brother. It was David's own heart that wrung the too apt sense out of the prince's words, and cast the hot colour suddenly upward from chin to brow in a burning tide. He was silenced. But Llewelyn was not looking, and noticed no change in him.

'Say to your lord,' said Llewelyn, when he had made up his mind, 'and to Meredith ap Rhys Gryg also, that they should continue to hold Rhys Fychan and his men in honourable liberty within Dynevor, but allow them as yet no part in their campaign. He will know very well he is on probation, you may discover much by his bearing in the meantime. Before midsummer day I'll be with you. Until then he is, let us say, neither ally nor prisoner, but a guest, he and all his. So deal with him. Now take rest and refreshment, and I will write to Meredith.'

Then Cadwgan went away, content, to eat his fill, Goronwy taking charge of him, and Llewelyn sat down with me to write his letters to both Merediths, for he was always aware of the need not to set one before the other of those two kinsmen and neighbours, though indeed they worked in harness singularly well, as Cymerau was the proof. But David lingered, very pale now with intent, and very grave, and came and sat down fronting his brother across the table.

'Hear me a word,' he said. 'In season, this time! I know all too well I often speak out of season. I felt, as I deserved, that sting you gave me, minutes ago. Who am I to deny any man a right to grace?'

'Sting?' said Llewelyn, astonished and gaping at him, half his mind still preoccupied. 'What sting? I know of none. And surely I intended none!'

'You sting best,' said David with a rueful smile, 'in innocence, and in your innocence I do willingly believe. But what you said concerning man's need of forgetfulness and forgiveness both, whether it touched Rhys Fychan or not, touched me shrewdly. I have taken much for granted these past months, God and you did well to remind me.'

Understanding dawning on him then, Llewelyn said in indignant amazement: 'I meant no such nonsense! What devil possessed you to take me so amiss?' And he reached across the table, and cupped a hand round the nape of his brother's neck, and shook him heartily, until the black hair fell down over David's eyes, and though reluctantly, he could not help laughing.

'Fool!' said Llewelyn, releasing him, 'I have *your* past deeds in very good remembrance – seven months of hard campaigning, and never a sour word. You have earned the same right as any other to speak your mind in my counsels, and argue against me wherever you think I am going astray.'

'And so I will,' said David, pushing back his disordered hair from a face wiped clean of laughter, 'though forgetting nothing now. I tell you that you go astray, or may do so, in forgiving too easily, and settling accounts too cheaply. Think about it! I say no more.'

He rose, and turned abruptly towards the door, but there as suddenly he halted and looked back. 'Yes, one more thing, the gravest. I pray you believe and remember that in saying this I do not speak only of Rhys Fychan.'

Then he went quickly away, and left us to our letters.

One week more we spent in making secure those lands in Powys, and then left Goronwy to continue and complete that necessary work, while Llewelyn and David took the greater half of the army south through Builth to Dynevor as he had promised. But before we left we had already received a message from the horse-doctor in Chester, no way surprising in its tidings, but useful in its detail. King Henry, shocked out of his querulous attitude of protest and disbelief by Cymerau – for there had been no such disastrous blow to royal power in South Wales in his lifetime – had sent out his writ to call out the feudal host for a campaign in full array against us. The muster was set for the first day of August, and the meeting-place was Chester.

'There's no justice in the man,' said Llewelyn, reading. 'It seems he's giving me the credit for what the two Merediths have done against him, for it's still at me he aims. They'll be complaining of that, small blame to them.'

In the event, as we learned later, King Henry himself, while knowing well enough by this time who was the head and spirit of Welsh rebellion against him, was torn two ways as to how he might make the best use of his projected muster, and later amended his writ to divert a minor portion of his knight force to the south, though their enterprise there never came to anything.

'We have time,' said Llewelyn, 'to get through a deal of work before the beginning of August.' For he was certain that this time the king would contrive, whether on borrowed money or his own, to mount the great assault he planned, the Welsh situation being now even more desperate for him than in the previous autumn. And even if there were great difficulties surrounding and hampering him, we dared not take the threat lightly. Therefore the prince sat down with Goronwy and his council, before riding south, and worked out most thorough plans for placing Gwynedd in a state of readiness for siege. Our common defence of goods, gear, stock and people was to remove all into the mountains, an operation to which our folk were accustomed, and which could be accomplished in very short order. Other measures were considered this time to frustrate all movement on the enemy's part. Bridges could be broken, tracks and meadows ploughed up, mills and such establishments destroyed, even fords turned into death-traps by excavating great pits in the hitherto safe shallows, which the water would conceal. All these things were planned in detail, together with instructions to those men of the neighbouring trefs who would carry out their execution, but nothing was to be done until shortly before the day fixed for the muster. Events sometimes change even the plans of kings, and we wanted no wasted destruction. Indeed, Llewelyn had encouraged in Wales, after his grandfather's example, the new centralised institutions which must perforce be borrowed from the English in order to resist the English, the use of money and trade, the exaction of feudal dues in return for land, even the founding of a few towns and the award of charters and markets, so that we had more to leave than aforetime in these withdrawals into the hills. But still we could do it at need, and as quickly as before.

Then, having confided this system of defence to Goronwy, and left him to send out the necessary orders in our absence, we rode for Dynevor.

Meredith ap Rhys Gryg came out to meet us as soon as we were heralded, and was close at Llewelyn's side, and voluble, all the last mile of the way. It was no marvel that he was anxious to get in his word first with his over-lord, for he was the uncle and rival of Rhys Fychan, and all those good lands in the vale of Towy had been bandied about between those two with equal violence and injustice, each when in power depriving the other, though for Rhys Fychan it had to be said that his uncle had been the first to do unjustly, and for Meredith that he had never yet gone over to the English against his own people.

So Llewelyn was faced with no easy judgment here when he sat in council in the great hall of Dynevor that evening of our coming, with all his allies of the region about him, and their stewards and officers and clerks at their backs to speak in their support. Already there was none in the whole of Wales who disputed his supremacy, but there never was Welshman yet who was not prepared to argue his case endlessly even in the teeth of his lord, and I knew we should have a long and contentious session. Next to David at Llewelyn's right hand sat Meredith ap Owen of Builth and Cardigan, and he was both strong in his prestige from Cymerau, equal to that of Meredith ap Rhys Gryg, and free of those motives of personal greed and personal venom that were likely to unbalance his namesake's opinions. On this able, faithful and incorruptible man Llewelyn greatly relied.

It was, I think, his uncle's doing, since this castle was now in his possession which had been by inheritance the nephew's, that Rhys Fychan was brought into the hall only when the whole council was assembled, as though he had been a prisoner coming in to be judged, which by his bearing he surely felt to be true. Though Llewelyn greeted and seated him courteously, there was no help for it, he knew the business before us set his liberty and possessions at risk, as well as his honour, and it was a very pale, defensive and erect Rhys Fychan who sat down in our circle to weather the storm.

It was the first time I had ever set eyes on the Lady Gladys's husband, and I studied him with much interest while the castellan, who had taken the responsibility of admitting him with his following, set forth the bare facts of his coming. Rhys was some three years older than my lord, which made him at that time thirty-one years of age. He was medium tall, and of a good, upright carriage, his hair and his short beard of a light brown, and his features fair for a Welshman, and well-formed. He looked both proudly and fearfully, which was no marvel in his situation, and the set of his mouth I judged to be at once resolute and resigned, as though, no matter what we made of it, he had taken the step

291

on which he had determined, and was prepared to abide the consequences. He did not therefore have to accept them with any pleasure! And I take it as no reproach to him that he was afraid, and as credit that he gave no expression of his fear. I saw how David watched him, with drawn brows and jutting underlip, and I think his interest was engaged by Rhys's bearing as was mine, and his mind, however doubtful, was open.

When the castellan had ended his brief recital, Llewelyn asked him of himself: 'And you ... I judge what your opinion was from what you did, for indeed there was heavy responsibility upon you, and yet you did open the gates. Tell me, were you formerly in the service of the Lord Rhys, when he held Dynevor?'

'No, my lord,' said the knight simply. 'I am from Dryslwyn, I came here as the Lord Meredith's man, and his man I have been all my days.'

'Then you took this risk upon the evidence of your own eyes and senses, without prejudice or favour. That I find impressive.'

'My lord, it was plain to me they were in fear, and the English who came after them were in great fury. There was no doubt in my mind the Lord Rhys did what he did without their knowledge and against their interest. I could not let Welshmen be cut down under my walls and never raise a finger to help them.'

'My lord,' said Meredith ap Rhys Gryg roundly, 'there's no dispute over letting them in, and we can take it as true, as my man swears, that this was no plan to bring in his English masters with him. I can think of other motives no more noble, and no better calculated to make us accept him back into our ranks. And the simplest is that he changed his coat because he saw the old looking somewhat threadbare. He was not the only one taken aback by the reception we gave them. De

Bauzan liked it no better, but he could hardly run for the gates and demand to be taken in. No, there's no mystery here. Rhys found himself of the losing party, and had no appetite for our archery. He made a leap for safety and the winning side. It's a landmark, I promise you. We've reached the point of being successful enough to draw in the waverers. You'll find he'll not be the last. The fealties that swung slavishly over into King Henry's purse when we were down, will be swinging back, mark me, now we're up again with a vengeance.'

I confess there was something in this, as we found thereafter, not to our surprise. Yet to come back to one's allegiance cautiously, after due approaches and guarantees given, is one thing, and to tear oneself out of the ranks in the field and make that exchange without guarantees of any kind is quite another. And Rhys was not such a fool as to suppose that he would be welcomed with open arms. I expected the prince to ask him at once to speak as to his own motives and in his own defence, but he thought it better to let those who carried grievances and had doubts speak them out now and get relief, before he brought the matter to the issue.

So he called on one and another, and brought them gradually to the point of declaring whether Rhys should be fully accepted into the confederacy or not, though not in such positive terms that they could not veer later if they so wished. And some said one way, and some the other, Meredith ap Rhys Gryg the loudest in opposition. It was not all a matter of the castles he would be required to restore, but also of the long enmity between them, and doubtless some genuine mistrust.

'All we have risked our lives and fortunes,' he said, 'to bring Wales into this ascendant, while he has pledged and maintained his allegiance to England all these years. And are we now to take him into favour, and restore him all that was his? At a gesture, at the first word of repentance, without one act to give it substance? I say no! We cannot throw him back to the English, but we need not therefore embrace him as a brother. What has he done to deserve it?'

Llewelyn looked then at Rhys, who had sat with a face of ice to listen to this, and asked him equably:

'What have you to say in answer?'

Rhys opened his lips as though they were indeed stiff and cold, and said: 'That what my uncle says is just. I pledged fealty to King Henry eleven years ago, when I saw no security and no hope anywhere else. If that was a craven act, then we were many craven souls in those days. That I have maintained what I undertook ever since, for that I make no apology. I was taught to abide by my word, and so I have done, until loyalty seemed to me worse than treachery. Now I am doubly a traitor, and not proud of it, and all I want is to change my coat no more. Whether you accept or reject me, I am back among my own. Here I will die.'

Llewelyn looked quickly from him to Meredith ap Owen, that grave, quiet man, and again back to Rhys. 'And in the future,' he said mildly, 'I doubt not you will offer us acts substantial enough, to pay your indemnity?'

'If you accept me,' said Rhys Fychan, 'the event will prove all. All I have to offer is the man I am, and my intent. Take it, or leave it.'

I looked at David then, for this, however effortful, weary and sad, was talking after his own fashion. And I saw that he was moved and hopeful, though he hesitated still.

There passed another such understanding glance between the prince and Meredith ap Owen, and Meredith said, in his great, gentle voice, that was deep as an organ: 'I think I may point to one act already done, which has greatly aided our cause. Rhys has not claimed it, but I make the claim for him, if he is too proud to vaunt his own skills. Ask him, my lord, if he did not make the plan for this great victory we have claimed as ours. Who brought the English to Dynevor in such high hopes, and ensured we should have due warning of their massing at Carmarthen? Who saw them encamped here in the valley at our mercy, and then forsook them and sent them haring back to their castle under our hail of arrows? Ask him, my lord, if we do not owe to him the whole triumph of Cymerau, which we never let him share!'

There was a sharp and wondering silence round the hall at this, while men looked at one another questioning and marvelling, before all eyes turned back to Rhys. And Llewelyn looked at him also, with a veiled smile, and said softly:

'Well? Answer the question! Was this indeed how, and why, you came back to us?'

What colour was left in Rhys's face drained out of it, and left him white as wax. I saw the cold sweat start on his forehead and lip, and for a long moment he struggled with his tongue and his silence, aware that on what he answered depended his whole fate, and feeling in his blood and bones what those about the table wanted from him. For most men see but a little way before their noses. He drew breath very slowly, but his voice was loud and firm as he said: 'No!'

'You have more than that to say,' said Llewelyn when the stone-hard silence grew long. 'Say on!'

'I did not plan this slaughter,' said Rhys, the blood flowing back hot and desperate into his face now that he had cast his die. 'Nor would I, I pray, so use any company that had received me into itself. I asked the English to help me win back what was mine, since I had lost it for their sake. If you think I would so betray any man

295

who put trust in me, then kill me, and be done! Nor did I think Dynevor would escape and triumph, or I would have stood by my own error to the end. No, I believed you were lost, and then I knew you for mine, and I despaired, and willed to be lost with you. My heart sickened, and I could not bear it longer that I was Welsh and traitor. I called up my knights, and we came to die with you. And that is truth, as God sees me! As for your victory, it was yours, none of mine, to my grief. And since I did not wilfully betray my companions,' he said, looking full at Llewelyn, 'as you would have had me do, and since I have given you the wrong but the true answer, do with me whatever you see fit. I have finished!'

He was so blind by the end of this that he could not see that Llewelyn was smiling, that David was glowing like a rose. But there was no silence at all after Rhys made an end, for Llewelyn rose from his place and went round the circle to where Rhys sat, took him by the hands, raised him to his feet, and kissed his cheek. He had to stoop a little, he was the taller.

'You have given me both the true and the right answer,' he said heartily. 'God forbid I should take into my love any man who would sell his friends, however mistakenly cherished, into so fatal a trap. I would you had come to us earlier and more happily, but with all my heart I welcome you, and call you my brother.'

Then David uttered a muted shout of surrender and acclaim, and bounded up from his place to embrace his sister's husband in his turn, and give him the kiss of kinship. And after him, though more soberly still with right goodwill, Meredith ap Owen, for he, too, was of the royal blood of Deheubarth, his father Owen being a first cousin of Rhys's father.

Rhys Fychan himself, thus passed from hand to hand in welcome where he had looked only for rejection and ignominy at the worst, and at the best a long and hard probation, was so stunned and at such a loss that I think he hardly knew what was happening to him, or what the gathering murmur of approbation meant. For though some, no doubt, had reservations, and a few, had they not known themselves so greatly outnumbered, would have refused him countenance, yet when Llewelyn asked if any man had matter to urge against, no voice was raised.

'Never hold it against us,' said Llewelyn then, smiling, 'that we tempted you so grossly, since the issue has shown you are not to be tempted. And now sit down with us in full council, and no more glancing behind, for there are matters arising out of this return which should be settled among us at once.'

But before he would do so, Rhys went on his knees before the prince, and lifted his joined hands, offering homage and fealty after the English fashion, as he had formerly pledged them to King Henry, in token of the severance of all those English ties which had bound him so many years. Publicly and voluntarily he did this, for Llewelyn would not then have asked of him any such gesture. And he did it with a burning face but a bright and steady eye. 'And this,' he said, rising, 'shall be my last allegiance, and this I will never take back.'

Then all present accepted his willing act with acclaim, though it may well be that Meredith ap Rhys Gryg found his assent sour-tasting in his mouth, for he stood to lose by his nephew's gain. And of this Llewelyn needed no reminder.

'Two matters chiefly remain to be dealt with,' he said, resuming his place and his authority, 'now that the main is settled. For this castle of Dynevor, and Carreg Cennen also, were from his father's death the inheritance of the Lord Rhys, and must return to him now. And I have ever in mind the great services of the Lord Meredith ap Rhys Gryg, which must not be slighted. Yet I think there was a time when both lived here, and for both there was room in the two cantrefs, and so there should be again.' Then he went on to show that he knew, by reciting the list of them, how the properties in Ystrad Tywi had been distributed between those two in the days before Rhys expelled his uncle and drove him to take sanctuary in Gwynedd, thus reminding both that if one had grievances from the past, so had the other, and silence and reconciliation might be best.

'It is my hope and counsel,' he said then, 'that you should agree to return to that division, remembering this, that even if you, Meredith, are losing something by Rhys's return, yet you have both not only a common enemy close at hand, but also, together, the means of extending your common estate at the enemy's expense, not at each other's. To cling to a castle and thereby lose an ally with whose help three castles more might be won, is very poor policy. Together you are far stronger and can do far more than the two of you apart could master. And be far more than double the value to the cause of Wales.'

Rhys, who was still dazed and open to emotion with the joy and relief of his reception, offered his hand warmly to his uncle, and promised that for his part he forsook all enmity against him, and begged forgiveness and forgetfulness of his own revenges mercilessly taken when the advantage was with him. And Meredith perforce accepted his hand, though with less enthusiasm, and conceded that the past was past.

'That being so,' said Llewelyn, 'we have here a greater and more effective army by the addition of Rhys and his knights, and an enemy greatly weakened, and fortune waiting only for us to move. You,' he said to the two

Merediths, 'have made good use of Cymerau by storming the castles it left empty of men, and it is for you to hold and garrison Laugharne and Llanstephan and Narberth as you see fit. But there's more to be won yet. If they drew on those households, so they will have done on others further afield. What's to prevent us from driving west into Dyfed, and shocking de Valence and Bohun and FitzMartin?'

There was no man there but agreed to that gladly, and as long as he could hold them together with the prospect of action and booty he had them in the hollow of his hand.

'My Lord,' said Rhys Fychan, 'with your leave, we can add to our numbers yet, if two or three days can be spared. There were foot soldiers of mine left to fend for themselves when I was let in here. God he knows they could not be blamed for what I did, but considering what followed, I doubt there were many left by the time they reached Cymerau. They know this country, and by then it was a headlong flight, they could as well slip away into the hills, every man for himself. Give me two days, and I'll get word out to enough of them to reach the rest, and bid them home. If I call, they will come.'

'Well thought of!' said Llewelyn. 'Do so, while we make ready. And one more thing, not the least. Where is my sister? Were you forced to leave her in English care, in Brecon or Carmarthen? It may not be so simple now to get her safely out, but it shall be done.'

'By God's grace,' said Rhys thankfully, 'she is not in any of their castles. Two weeks before we massed at Carmarthen I took her away to a hermitage of women near Hywel, with her maids and the two boys. For she was drawing near her time, and had some women's troubles that frightened her a little, and was not willing to risk bearing her child there in Brecon without me. Thank

God the boys would not stay behind, as then I would gladly have had them do. There is a holy woman among the anchoresses at Hywel who is very expert in childbirth, my lady has visited her before, and wanted to be in her care. We can reach them without hindrance, and bring them safe home.'

'Let be until she is delivered,' said Llewelyn, 'if she puts such trust in this holy woman. If need be, we can set a guard about the place, but I think awe of the anchoresses might serve even better to keep her secure until her waiting's over. But then,' he said, 'you have been a long time without news of her, and she of you, that's an ill thing at such a time. Send to her and set her mind at rest, and I hope your own, also.'

And thus it was done. And Rhys Fychan with great joy and fervour went about resuming the control of his own castle, and making lordly provision for his guests.

We reckoned then that we had but three weeks, or four, to spend here in the south, before we must turn homewards to meet King Henry's threatened muster. So after two days we sallied forth again from Dynevor, my lord with his brother, Rhys Fychan and the two Merediths, all at one and in high heart. Rhys's messengers had shaken out the word of restoration and the Welsh alliance through the forests and hills and along the vale of Towy, bidding all who welcomed it pass it on still further, and we had the first-fruits of that sowing already in our ranks when we rode, good lancers and bowmen who had been in hiding since Cymerau, until they should discover which way the wind blew.

We drove west from Cantref Mawr, passing to the north of Carmarthen, and swept into Dyfed, in this summer season a most lovely country, where the clouds ran like new lambs over clean green hills. We ravaged and looted the borders of Cemais, doing great despite to the lands of the lord William de Valence, who was King Henry's half-brother, being one of the sons of the king's mother by her second marriage to the Count of La Marche. This William was lord of Pembroke in right of his wife, and greatly hated in the whole of Dyfed, even by many English barons and marcher lords, so that few tears were shed over what we did to his barns and stock and manors. But our time being limited, we seized a foothold in Cemais by storming the castle of Newport, where Nevern comes down to the sea, and from there made heavy raids southward into Rhos, and came near enough to Haverfordwest to set up a great flutter in Humphrey de Bohun's garrison there. Thus we continued until the first week of July, for the grip of the English marchers was strongest of all in this corner of Wales, and what damage we could do to that stranglehold in so short a time we did. Then we drew off in good order, leaving Newport garrisoned in fair strength, and made our way briskly back to Dynevor.

There was no more bustle than usual about the baileys when we rode in, and we had no warning, except that there was a young woman who came out at the clatter of our arrival to see what was happening, and then clapped her hands and ran into the great hall to carry the news. And we were but dismounting in the inner bailey when another figure appeared in the broad doorway, and came slowly and carefully down the step towards us. She was very richly and gaily dressed, her coiled hair uncovered to the sun, and there was about her an air of joy and solemnity, as though she kept a festival of her own. By the black of that coiled hair, that was almost blue in the sun, like David's, and by the beauty of the face she raised only when she reached the foot of the steps and stood on level ground, I knew her. Those same long lashes and dark eyes she had raised upon King Henry's face, and dazzled him, long ago in the guest-hall of Shrewsbury abbey. True, she was not now so slender as then, her body was thickened with maturity, and with the bearing of two children. Of three, rather, for she went with such care upon the steps, and looked up only when she was on level ground, by reason of the infant she carried in her arms. The Lady Gladys had brought her third child home as soon as she was strong enough to bear the journey, impatient for the happy reunion her husband's messengers had promised.

Rhys saw her and gave a cry of triumph and joy, and dropping his rein before the groom could reach him, ran like a deer to embrace his wife and child, which he did, after the impetuosity of his approach, with slow and reverent care. He kissed her above the child's head, tender of its smallness and softness, and then with a timid hand put back the shawl from its face and looked at it in wonder, as though he had not two children already, but this were the first ever to be born, and a miracle.

He looked round then at us, and laid an arm about his wife's shoulders, and brought her to Llewelyn, who stood motionless where Rhys had left him, watching them draw near. At her face he gazed with earnest searching and deep wonder, as Rhys did at the child. He had not seen her for sixteen years, and through most of those years all he had known of her was her implacable enmity towards him. He had everything to learn. Something she had already learned, or so it seemed by her smile, which was faint, mysterious and radiant.

'My lord,' said Rhys, 'I think you have long desired to be better known to your sister, who is my wife. She is here, and hale, and desires as much of you.'

She was the elder by a year, and a woman, and moreover, a woman of great assurance, like her mother, yet even she did not know how to begin, for everything that had passed lay between them now, not as a barrier to be stormed, only as a ruinous waste to be clambered over before they could reach each other, and it was hard to find a way through without stumbling. David, who would have clasped and kissed her without a thought, stood back behind my shoulder and let them alone. I felt his hand close upon my arm as he watched them, and I knew that he was smiling. David had many smiles. This one, withdrawn and still, womanishly tender against his will, belonged only to Llewelyn. But it never lasted long.

The child was their salvation. The prince looked down curiously at the tiny head, covered with dark hair, and the crumpled face all new infants wear, and said: 'I am glad to see you so well and happy, and safely delivered. It is another son?'

'It is,' she said.

'And healthy and strong? I grieve that it was I who sent you running from Dynevor with him, when most you needed to be safe at home.'

'He has taken no harm,' she said, 'and neither have I. He is whole and perfect.' And she parted the shawl to show him, and Llewelyn touched the shrunken pink cheek with a large, marvelling finger, and then thrust the same finger delicately into the minute, questing fist that groped in the air. The child's fingers closed on it strongly, and clung. Thus held, he looked at her with innocent pleasure, and asked, as men do over children, valuing symbols: 'What will you call this one?'

'He is already named,' she said. 'And I trust he will grow up as gentle, valiant and magnanimous as his namesake.' She looked up into her brother's face, and said, flushing deeply: 'His name is Llewelyn.'

CHAPTER XI

I came to the Lady Gladys in the evening, when she had withdrawn to the high chamber and left the lords to their wine, and spoke to her of Cristin, for I thought it no blame to Llewelyn if he forgot this one small pledge among all his triumphs and cares of that day. And she was soft and warm and gracious, who had been a proud girl and a prouder woman, for she was much moved by what had passed, and utterly disarmed by all her husband had told her of Llewelyn's dealings with him. She spoke of her brother with wonder and gratitude, and said that she was glad he had by him so loyal and true a friend as I. And she talked of the years of her estrangement as of an ill dream past with the night.

'Had we but met,' she said, 'I could not have held out against him all this time. I must surely have seen him as he is, honest and generous, better than wise. Oh, Samson, how strange a childhood we had, that separated us so far and sent us into the world by such different ways. Ways,' she said, 'of which only he chose his own, and against great pressures, as now I see.'

I told her that exactly so he had spoken, grieving that she was his only sister, and he did not even know her. And she smiled, and said: 'That shall be remedied.'

Then I asked her if my lord had thought to question her, or Rhys, as he had not until this visit had opportunity to do, concerning a certain landless knight who had been in Rhys's service at Cwm-du, one Godred ap Ivor. She said that he had not, which was small wonder considering the excitement they had been in, and their total absorption in each other. But even had he so remembered, she said with regret, she could have had nothing to tell him, for though many of Rhys's household army had made their way to one or another of the English-held castles in Ystrad Tywi, and thus the tale of the survivors had gradually been made up, and the war-band reformed, yet nothing had been heard again of Godred. True, she said, there were some of the fugitives from Cwm-du who were thought to have drawn off over the wilds of the Black Mountain, southwards, and placed themselves in the hands of Earl Richard of Gloucester, and possibly some had stayed and entered his service in Glamorgan, but if Godred was among them, that she could not say.

'And surely,' she said, 'if he lived he would have appeared again by now. I knew the young man well, for his wife was one of my women, and dear to me. And to speak truth, I might well say I am glad, if that is not a sin, to think that Godred may be dead, and grateful that I need never meet him face to face and have to answer his questions. For his wife,' she said heavily, 'died in the forest after we fled to Brecon, and I cannot get the load from my heart that her death lies at my door. I should never have let her take so mad a risk for me. It has been heavy on my mind ever since, and will be as long as I live.'

At this I was so stricken with wonder and so moved that I trembled before her and could not speak for a while. For this was one reason I had never thought of, why the lady had not sent after to enquire about Cristin. She had believed from the first that there was no need of questions to which she already knew the answer. Though what had so persuaded and convinced her I was foolish and slow to imagine.

'Madam,' I said, as softly as I might, 'if you can find

heart-room for one more joy in this day without surfeiting, I believe I can supply yet one more. With your lord, your possessions, your child all secured, your brother restored, can you yet bear another gift?'

She could not fail to see where I led her, and her dark eyes grew great with incredulous wonder. She said: 'No one ever died of joy. If you mean what you seem to mean, oh, Samson, quickly, tell me so! Is she truly living? Cristin, Llywarch's daughter?'

'Living, and well,' I said, 'and safe under Llewelyn's guardianship in the north. We have been making enquiry after her husband for her sake all this time, but could not reach you in Brecon, to pair our half of the story with yours. And now for my life I do not see how you came to be so sure that Cristin was dead.'

'But they came riding hard after us,' she said, bright and fierce with remembrance, 'through the snow in the early morning. They were gaining on us, we should have been ridden down before ever we could reach the town, and Cristin offered to lead them off by the valley path and leave us free to go forward in safety if the ruse succeeded. She knew of a hut in the woods where she could hide from them and let them by. All this she did for me, and did well....'

'I know it,' I said, 'for I was captain of that company that pursued you, and God knows for no ill purpose.' And I sat down with her and told her all that story, while she sat still and silent, listening. And at the end she said, in a very low voice: 'How strangely we deal with one another! Such horrors as I imagined, and yet they were only ordinary men who rode after, not monsters. If I had known that it was you, I should have been calmed and ready to trust. And yet I had not such trust in *him*. And you know and I know that such things as I imagined have happened, and will happen again, wherever there is warfare. It is not so great a step from man to monster. And what I afterwards believed was not so hard to believe. For you see, she did not come. She said that if the way was clear, and the hunt passed by the hut without pausing, she would return to the upland way and follow us. She knew the country as well as any among us, and she was not afraid to ride alone. But if she had cause to feel it dangerous to come out of hiding, she would bide the night over, if need be, and wait for us to send for her. And in Brecon we waited, but she never came.'

'But in the morning,' I said, 'you did send out for her?'

'We did. And surely you remember what there was for us to find?' She gripped her hands together in her lap and wrung them, remembering, for in grief remembered and changed to rejoicing there is very painful pleasure. 'In the hut, the ashes of a fire, and the trampling of many feet, and blood. But no Cristin. Round the hut the hoof-marks of many horses. And when they hunted further afield round that place, there was the hollow silted with leaves and mould, and in it, covered over with stones, a new grave....'

'You thought it *hers*?' I cried, suddenly pierced through and through with understanding.

'What else could we think? It seemed as clear as day, and as black as night. We thought she had taken shelter there as she intended, only to be discovered by the men she had decoyed away from my trail. Oh, Samson, can you not see how it would have been, if they had been what I supposed? Cheated of their success, with their lord to face after their failure, and this creature in their hands, the girl who had made fools of them and loosed me safe away! We thought they had had their sport with her through the night, and at dawn killed her and buried her. Such things have been and will be again, to all ages. You know it as well as I,' she said.

I owned it, for it was truth. Though by the grace of God there may some day come a time when such things will cease. But in this world? Who knows!

'You did not disturb the grave?' I said. For that also mattered to me.

'We did not. And for two days thereafter there was heavy snow in the hills, and it was a week or more before we could go back there. That time I went with them. The grave had been opened. The stones were laid aside in a cairn, and the hollow was empty. The religious from Talley and Llywel and Llangefelach had been busy collecting and caring for the dead, and this was the work of men of reverence. We did not question any more.'

'He is buried at Talley abbey,' I said, 'Meilyr, my mother's husband. Where I pray he rests in peace, and his soul in bliss, for he had little enough bliss in this world. But Cristin is alive and well in Bala, or perhaps at Aber if Goronwy's family have moved there, and you need not mourn for her any more. If we come safe out of this summer's campaign, and if that is what she wishes, and what you wish, then she shall come back to you.'

And she was so glad, and so moved, that my own resolution to silence was shaken, and I would have told her, I know not how barely and poorly, something of what I felt for Cristin, Llywarch's daughter, as never yet had I told it to anyone, even Llewelyn, who knew the inmost of my heart upon every other matter. But while we were thus rapt into our remembrances and dreams, she most grateful and tender, I most in peril of self-betrayal, Llewelyn came in with his arm about Rhys's shoulders, and after them David with Rhys's second son riding on his back and driving him like a curvetting horse, and Rhys's eldest son, also Rhys, plucking at his brother's ankle and doing his best to bring him down. And there was so much laughter and noise that we were delivered from all solemnity until the children were borne away to bed, very unwillingly. David had always a charm for children, as for their elders. All the more if they were women, but men had no remedy, either.

But afterwards we told this story over again to those three princes. And Llewelyn, counting days, said that we had still time to make some small foray into Glamorgan, not merely to carry the word to any men of Rhys's bodyguard scattered there, that they might return to their allegiance at Dynevor without fear if they would embrace the Welsh cause with their lord, but also to send a very different message to Earl Richard of Gloucester, who had lived too easy and too undisturbed a life heretofore in his southern lordship. And so it was agreed, though we were drawing near to the middle of July now, and the muster was called for the beginning of August at Chester.

'We made full provision before we came south,' said Llewelyn, unperturbed, 'and Goronwy will have seen all carried forward ready for the day. We have still time for one more fling before we go to stand off King Henry and his host. And though I think it a very slender hope, if by some chance we can recover a lost husband for our shepherdess of Bala, that would be a fitting ending to this campaign, and a goodly gift to take back with us.'

But David was silent, who would commonly have been the first to applaud any such audacity. And his eyes were fixed upon me, as I knew before ever I glanced at him, and they had a chill and rueful blueness, and saw, as always they did, too much, too clearly, and too deep.

Howbeit, we went, leaving Dynevor two days earlier than we should otherwise have done, to the disappointment of the Lady Gladys, who had found great joy in this unlooked-for reunion with her brothers. For there was something in her of David, without his penetration, in that everything she did was done with her might, whether it was loving or hating, and gratitude came as impulsively to her as either of these, so that after his generous and skilful championship of her husband's cause among his peers there was now no one in the world for her like Llewelyn, against whom she had once been implacable.

We went south by Carreg Cennen to Neath, and from there ranged for two days eastward along the fringes of the earl's honour, sacking his manors and levelling his defences, with little resistance. So unprepared for us were they – for I think they had believed us already on our way north again, the king's threat being now so close – that we were able to split our forces into two, and even three, parties, and so range further afield than we could have done with a single army, though not attempting any fortified place while we were so divided. Then we met together again for an attack upon the earl's castle of Llangynwyd, finding it close at hand and in no great state for standing us off, for though well-manned it was in some disrepair.

The garrison put up but a very brief fight. I think a number of them were Welshmen not greatly affected to their lord. Then, when we pressed home our attack, many of them escaped by a postern and fled into the valleys of the small rivers that flanked the castle, where there were woods to give them cover, and so scattered to take refuge in two or three fortified manors belonging to the earl, which could be reached quickly from that place.

Llewelyn was not slow to consider that those who ran might well number among them some of Rhys's men, not yet apprised of the change in their lord's fortunes, and none too happy in the service of the English earl. Therefore he detailed off three small parties of us to beat the woods in the direction of those manors, and take up, if we could, such stragglers as would accept Welsh service in its place, while he and the greater part of our host laid waste the defences of Llangynwyd, to make it untenable against us for some time in the future. Of these three parties he gave me one, and we rode due east, down from the highlands where the castle stood, into a river valley well-treed and rich and beautiful. We were but seven men with myself, and we had orders not to adventure against any companies in arms, but to use our Welsh tongues to lure the Welsh, and let the English alone. And so we did, and sent several promising fighting men back to Llangynwyd with tokens from us to ensure them a welcome.

We had reached the limits of our territory, and camped for the night before returning, for the weather was hot and kindly, and we had ample provisions, and good horses if we should need to elude some unexpected attack. Against such possibility we put out two pickets, and took our rest by turns in the grass under the trees. We were not far from one of the small, clear rivers of that country, which covered us by the south approach with a coil of its waters, and at earliest dawn, awaking, I thought with pleasure on that cool stream, and walked down to its banks to bathe. The river-bed being stony and turbulent where the curving channel was worn, I thought there might well be a quiet, spreading pool below, where the ground opened out a little, though still well wooded, and so walked down in that direction, and found it to be as I had supposed. I shed my clothes in the grass among the trees, and was about to cross the open sward to the gently-shelving bank, when I heard a light splash as of a big fish rising, or a diver entering

311

the water, and froze where I was, still within cover. And in a moment I heard someone before me, at no great distance but hidden beyond the silvery alders, begin to sing, by watery snatches as he swam, a light love-song.

A high, pleasant voice it was, and it sang in Welsh. I was in two minds whether to go back and put on my clothes, but here was an evident Welshman, and as evidently alone, for no man sings like that but for his own private pleasure. And if this was one of those scattered souls I was seeking, I could hardly affright him if I came to the bank as I was, or have much to fear in my turn from his nakedness. Then I thought to draw nearer to him, still in cover, for I judged he had entered the water from my side of the river, and somewhere nearby he must have discarded his own clothing. So I went softly between the trees, and found he had left more than shirt and chausses unguarded, for there was a horse grazing on a long halter in the sward, and saddle and leather body-harness and lance propped against the bole of an oak. His sword lay there beside, and a saddle-roll with his cloak strapped to it. This one had not fled from Llangynwyd entirely unprovided!

Coming thus between him and his armaments, I was at advantage over him, and had no need to demonstrate it by any show. I went down through the trees to the bank, which sloped down to a little sickle of gravel.

He was there in midstream, turning and plunging like a gleaming fish, and as I watched he struck out almost silently for the bank opposite, reached two long, muscular arms out of the water, and hauled himself up to turn and sit in the short turf, dangling his feet in the shallows. In the act of turning thus, he saw me and was abruptly still and silent, though for a moment only. It was not surprise or fear, but the wild wariness of

woodland animals that gazed across the river at me,
measured and weighed me, and was assured of being
able to outrun or outwit at need. He laughed and said:
'Goodmorrow to you, Adam! But I had rather it had
been Eve who came.' And he drew up one long leg out
of the water, and wrapped his arms about his knee
and studied me as I was studying him, with his wet hair
plastered over his forehead and temples, and the drops
running down through the golden-brown curls that
matted his chest.

He was younger than I by a few years, and very finely
and gracefully made, for a Welshman uncommonly fair.
The streaming locks on his brow looked no darker than
wheat, even thus full of river water, and when dry
showed almost flaxen. He was gilded round the jaw
and lips with a short, bright stubble, but clearly he went
normally shaven clean like a clerk. Under easy golden
brows he gazed at me with round brown eyes, for as yet
I had not spoken, and what is there in a naked man to
make clear if he is English or Welsh? I had it in my
mind that this debonair and gay young man had all
those lean, long muscles braced for action, for all his
smooth face. But whether he had more reason to fight
shy of English or Welsh I could not yet be sure.

'You need not trouble yourself,' I said in his own
tongue, and watched his shoulders relax and his smile
widen, 'at least I'm no serpent. Your beast and your
gear are safe enough for me, but lest you should entertain any thought of meddling with my goods, let me tell
you we are seven, and a whistle would fetch the rest
running.'

'Also Welsh, like you?' he said.

'Every man.'

He jutted a thoughtful lip at me, and said with certainty: 'But *you* were not at Llangynwyd, that I know!'

'Then your knowledge is at fault, for I was, and so were we all. But of the other party. And be easy, we mean no harm to any man who ran from there, not if he be Welsh. We have a message to you. Where were you meaning to head now? For one of Gloucester's manors?'

He did not answer that at first, but laughed to himself, and slid down into the river again. 'Come in,' he said, making strokes just strong enough to hold him motionless against the current, 'since I take it that's what you came for. There's water enough for two, and on my part no haste.' And he rolled over and plunged out of sight, to reappear on my side of the deeper passage.

So I leaped in and joined him, and we swam a while, and lay in the shallows together after, letting the cool of the flow stream over our shoulders and down our loins. He lowered his head back into it until only the oval of his face broke the surface, and his hair stood wavering out from his temples like yellow weed or pale fern.

'To tell truth,' he said then, 'I was wondering myself what the next move was to be. For I was never much enamoured of Earl Richard's service, and in any manor of his I might find my welcome altogether too warm. For I reckon I was the first out at the postern at Llangynwyd, and with horse and harness that were not mine until yesterday. And though I have a brother who is lord of a manor in Brecknock, I fear I made that sanctuary too hot to hold me some years ago, his wife being young and pretty. And I can hardly go back to my old service at Dynevor, since Rhys Fychan was thrown out of it, for his uncle Meredith is no friend of mine.'

'Then you've not heard the news,' I said. 'For Rhys Fychan is back in Dynevor, and in pledged allegiance to Prince Llewelyn and his confederacy of Wales, and the very message I had for you is that the door's open to any who care to go that road with him. You may ride back when you will, and the gift of one of Gloucester's horses won't come amiss there, either. Or you may go partway with us, for we go back to Llangynwyd, and then northwards for Gwynedd.'

'No!' he cried between delight and disbelief, and rose in a fountain of sparkling drops to stare at me. 'Is that true? Rhys has changed sides, and been well received? How did this come about? I thought that was an irreconcilable enmity on both sides.'

I told him briefly the way of it, and he sank into the water again with a crow of joy. 'I am glad of it!' he said, lying still and straight there like a drowned man. 'I was Rhys's man until Llewelyn broke him, and I'd as lief be his man again, all the more if he's quit his English allegiance. Right joyfully I'll ride with you. You said truly, no serpent but an angelic voice! May I know who it is comes to point me my way? Surely no two friends ever saw more of each other at first meeting!' And he laughed. His was a face very well acquainted with laughter, by the lines of it.

I told him I was Samson, Llewelyn's clerk, and asked his name in return. In utter innocence I asked it, so pleasant and strange was this encounter, with some quality in it of dreaming. Until then, when I awoke.

He said, easy and content, with his eyes closed: 'My name is Godred ap Ivor.'

The bright, bracing chill of the water was suddenly harsh as ice flowing down breast and belly and thigh, the blood so stayed in me at the name. And he lay soothed and smiling and blind beside me, his head tilted back, the large, lace-veined eyelids bland and still.

I rose with infinite care upon my elbow and looked

315

down at him, thus oblivious, never knowing what he had done to me, feeling nothing of the immense loss and grief that weighed upon my heart, filling me slowly like pain poured from a vessel. I looked about us, and there was no man to see and no man to hear, no man to know that I had ever met him in this place. And all I had to do was fill one hand with that floating hair, drag his head down under the water, and roll over upon him to hold him under until he drowned. And no one would know. What would he be but a fugitive knight who had left horse and harness lying, and gone to bathe in a river whose currents he did not know? For months we had written him down as dead. So brief and easy a gesture now to make it true, and Cristin would be free.

That was so terrible a moment of temptation, and came upon me so like a lightning-flash out of a clear sky, that I cannot bear even now to remember it. I do believe with all my heart that there is no man who cannot kill, given the overwhelming need and the occasion. And if I did not, it was not out of any honourable resistance on my part, it was because of Cristin, who did not want him dead, but wanted him living.

And he lay by me in his comely nakedness, the worst offence of all, arrogantly sure of his safety, feeling nothing, fearing nothing.

'Get up, then, Godred ap Ivor,' I said, when I could speak without suffocating or cursing, 'and set about getting dry, while I tell you something that concerns you nearly, and only you. For that name I have known now for many months. I have been looking for you all this time.'

At that he opened his eyes wide, in surprise and interest but without disquiet, and leaping up in a great wave of water, waded ashore to where the risen sun gilded the grass, and for want of cloth or kerchief to dry himself, began to dance and turn about in the sunshine. I followed him ashore more slowly. Even the night had been warm and gentle, and the morning came in quivering heat. It was no labour to dry off in that radiant air.

'I feel,' said Godred, clapping his arms about his shoulders, 'the honour of having had your attention. But how or why is mystery to me. What is it you have to tell?'

'You had a wife,' I said, the words coming thick and slow upon my tongue, 'who was in the Lady Gladys's service, and fled with her from Dynevor last December.'

'I had,' he said, suddenly still, and looking at me with a reserved face and narrowed eyes.

'Did you never seek to find her, after that flight? It is a long time now, seven months.'

He must have felt some censure in my tone, for his voice was defensive as he said: 'At first I had no chance, for I was two months sick of my wounds after Cwm-du, and knew very little of where I was myself, or what was being done with me. Afterwards, yes, I sent out everywhere message of mine could go. They told me in Brecon she was dead.'

'So they believed in Brecon,' I said.

'You mean she is not?' he said slowly, staring.

'She is alive and well. She is in Gwynedd, living at Llewelyn's court and under Llewelyn's protection.'

He hesitated, frowning, watching me very intently. 'You mean this?' he said. 'She is truly alive? But why should you lie to me!'

'I would not. She lives, and no harm has come to her but the harm of not knowing whether you lived or died.'

'But how?' he cried. 'How did this come about?'

I told him, as barely as it could be told. 'Mercy of God!' he said, like a man rapt in wonder. 'How strangely providence does its work. She mourning me, and I mourning her, and suddenly this return to life! Take me with you to Gwynedd! One more in Llewelyn's army will not be amiss, with the host called out in two weeks' time, and the cause of Wales is the same now north or south. Let me ride with you to fetch Cristin home!'

I said that was our intent, and that he was welcome, I, who had crooked my fingers so short a while before, to drag him under water by the hair and there drown him. That sin was past, and could be confessed and repented. As for the awful sin of wishing I had done so, that would remain with me and be repeated endlessly for many years, if his youth was not cut off by some accident of war to spare me murder.

'And we had better be moving,' I said, to make an end, 'or we shall miss the best of the day.'

He took that for acceptance enough, and went to put on his clothes, and so did I. In a little while he came leading his horse through the trees to me. Clothed, he looked slighter and frailer than I had seen him to be, and younger, for his was a face that would always keep its boyish look. As lightly as he had sung, before ever I set eyes on him, so now he came whistling. He fell in beside me, the horse pacing between us, and began to speak of Cristin, as though her miraculous recovery were the only source of his exultant lightness of heart. Yet constantly I felt that he was ever so by nature. Howbeit, he spoke of her very winningly, having a feeling for words that would have done credit to a bard. His voice, too, was one of his chiefest graces, that pure, high voice for which the men of music love to make songs.

Being still full of a personal and bitter curiosity concerning him, for he had taken away all my present hope and all my peace of mind, and shown me to myself as a murderer by intent, I was observing whatever I could see of him as we walked, and since the led horse was

318

between us I had but glimpses over the swaying neck of his yellow hair crisping into curls as it dried, and paling to the colour of wheat stalks just before ripening, of his face in profile now and then, eager and open, and under his horse's round belly of the lithe, easy stride of his long legs. And after these, I looked upon the left hand that was visible to me, holding his bridle. Brown and strong it was, with broad knuckles and a powerful, flat wrist, good enough for a bowman. And upon the little finger he wore a ring. A plain silver ring with an oval bezel for a seal. This I could see clearly, for it rode close beneath my eyes, so that there could be no mistaking the deeply incised pattern of the seal, a little hand severed at the wrist, holding a rose.

Then I knew what Cristin had known, when she looked upon the ring I gave to Meilyr, and when afterwards, on the ride north together, I told her how I got that ring, and what it meant to me. And I understood at last why she had urged me to put away all thought of the father I had never known, and think no more of the hand and the rose. 'Well for you,' she had said, 'if you bury with the ring everything it signified, and rest content with the present and the future, forgetting the past.'

And I knew at last, too late, hearing her voice in my memory so urgent and passionate, how I had fooled myself and failed her, so grossly mistaking what she meant when she told me I need have no fear of her armour against David, for she was bespoken, heart and all. And yet, she was a wife, and what could she or I do but remember it? Whether we would or no!

But no part of all this coil and tangle of sorrow was his fault, and he, too, had rights, this young man who walked stride for stride beside me, so closely matched, in whom I could not doubt I beheld at last my stranger-father's youngest son. It was not only the ring that told me so, though the ring was the key that unlocked my knowledge. No, for I knew, now, what had been so disturbing to me about that meeting of two naked bathers, facing each other across the river, about that face and its shaping, those eyes and their arched brows. For though he was fair, and I dark, he well-favoured and I homely, he too light of mind, and I too grave, we were sealed and signed as from the same mintage, mirror-images one of the other, my brother Godred and I.

I told him nothing of my birth, I asked him nothing of his. I brought him back to Llewelyn at Llangynwyd, and presented him as a miraculous mercy, a bountiful act of God. My lord's pleasure in this return of the lost was all the pleasure I expected to get from it. For to him it was indeed not only an unlooked-for grace, but a favourable omen.

'Now I will believe,' he said, greeting Godred, 'that the blessing of God is with our arms, now that this one hopeful aim has been happily achieved, that was not desired for our own glory. Small right we had, after so long, to expect to find you, and you are here. A living encouragement to hope for everything, even the impossible.'

So he saw it, and for him I was glad, for we were going back to Gwynedd, whither David was already gone before us with the vanguard, to face an assault by forces greater in numbers and equipment by far than our own, and it was well that we should go in high heart. And that we did. And I must own that Godred had all the graces and attractions a young man should have, all his bearing, his eagerness now to reach his wife, his gratitude for her restoration, all were right and proper, and moving to behold. All through that journey to the north he spent much time with me, and I could not well forsake or avoid

320

him, to make known to others the contention I felt within myself.

Thus we came again into Gwynedd by the twenty-seventh day of July, and at the fords of the rivers we began to meet with custodians who sprang up out of hiding at our approach to show the safe way across, for the principal fords had already been pitted, and some of the more vulnerable bridges broken. Many of the lowland trefs had been abandoned, the inhabitants with all their gear removing into the mountains. It seemed that Goronwy had done his work thoroughly, and there was little for Llewelyn to do but place his forces where most he wanted them, and have them ready for action.

'They'll come by the north route,' he said, 'near the coast, for he'll want above all to relieve and re-provision Diserth and Degannwy. And that, seeing he cannot stay camped there for ever, or leave his south coast fleet there, either, we'll let him do. It would not be worth good men's lives to stand too stubbornly in his way. Once he's gone we can break again any supply chain he can leave behind him.'

I had expected and dreaded that Cristin would be still at Bala, but all the women of the court had been withdrawn into the castle of Dolwyddelan, high in the mountains of Snowdonia. When we came into those parts Llewelyn, having determined on making his base and headquarters at Aber, whence he could hold the north coast, gave Godred his leave and blessing to ride direct to Dolwyddelan to be reunited with his wife, and either bide with us or take her home to the south with him, according as they chose together. The prince gave him a guide to bring him there the more readily, since he did not know our tracks in the north, and that duty, naturally enough, he assigned to me. In pure goodwill he said that I alone had deserved it. And in my own heart

I confessed to God that it was true, and only fitting punishment that I should restore to my dear love the unloved husband of whose death my will was guilty, but not yet my hand.

Then we rode together and alone, and Godred was assiduous in his civil attention to me, and I, in my private bitterness, attributed to him all manner of motives which perhaps never were his: as, that he courted me because he had ambitions in this new service, and had seen that I was close in Llewelyn's confidence, and might advance him; or, that I might, if he did not win my favour, do him harm there; or, that he felt I had some reservations about him, and desired to allay them. But never, which may well have been the truth, that he felt real friendship and gratitude to me, and showed it like any other man.

For I knew that I was unjust to him. I knew I had no grounds for holding against him my resentment or my pain, and yet my ingenuity kept finding me just such grounds. I remembered things about our meeting which had then meant nothing, and in all likelihood meant nothing now, and found them meanings. I recalled the lightness of his mood, as though he had no care in the world, he who had lost Cristin, the treasure I had never possessed, and never now should possess. But he was by nature of a light mind, which is no sin, and had accepted the fact of his loss many months before, was he to weep all day and every day? There was also that thing he had said concerning a brother – my world was now populated with brothers! – who had a manor in Brecknock to which Godred could not go because of some small matter of his brother's young and pretty wife. But whatever that harked back to might have happened before Godred's own marriage to a wife who had more than youth and better than beauty. Indeed, it might never have happened at all, it was such a loose vaunt as gay young

322

men may well use before a stranger, not desiring to give away too much of their true and perhaps anxious selves. It could not seriously be counted against him.

It did not dawn upon me until we were nearing Dolwyddelan that there was some other particular troubling me, with better reason. Something was amiss in his account of his own proceedings since Cwm-du. For he had said in his own defence, when I questioned him about the efforts he had made to find her, that for two months he had lain very sick of his wounds, scarcely alive enough to think of such a quest.

But I had sat naked beside his nakedness in the water, had watched him turn and leap as he swam, and stretch out his arms to the sun as he dried himself. And nowhere on all that fine, athletic body was there mark or scar or pucker of even the smallest wound. Not one blemish in his smooth whiteness.

At the outer ward of Dolwyddelan we were challenged and passed within, over the ditch defences, and up the rocky mound to the inner ward and the hall. The place was seething with activity, and well garrisoned, since so many of the noble women were there for safety in this perilous month. And now that we we there, Godred fell silent and almost abashed, as near as he could get to that state, and left it to me to go first and order all that passed. Llewelyn's castellan came out to us as we dismounted, recognising me, and I told him our errand was to Cristin, Llywarch's daughter, but not what it was, for I desired with an intolerable, burning desire to know the best and the worst, and that I could learn only from her face, when she came in innocence to see who called for her. And if this was a cruelty I pray it may be excused by the cruel need out of which it sprang.

And by reason of this same desperate need I would not

go within, but waited for her in the blanched noon sunlight of the ward, that there might be no shadows to hide from me any quiver of motion and feeling that passed over her muted but eloquent face. If Godred wondered at this, small blame to him. But I think he did not wonder, for in that summer he lived willingly out of doors, and could have been content like a bird, without roof or nest after the brooding of the spring. On other matters perhaps he did wonder, for he watched the doorway as insatiably as did I. If he had not been so blithe and sunlit a creature I would have said he was nervous of his welcome.

The great doorway of the hall showed black like the opening of a cavern, the sun being at an angle that slanted across the opening but fingered only a pace or so within, where it had nothing on which to rest, until she came. Thus she blazed suddenly out of that darkness like a star, so impetuously that her skirts danced as though in a fresh wind, and being dazzled by the flood of light in her face, as abruptly halted and stood stock-still on the upper step until she had her sight again. And having regained it, she looked for me.

There was not left one grain of caution in me to doubt it, for I saw her close and clear, and doubt there was none. So bright she was, there was no bearing her radiance. When she was called forth to a messenger, she knew what face the messenger must wear. She stood smiling in happy expectation, and her gaze swept across the court like a beam of the sun itself, and lit upon me, and was satisfied. She took one flying step to meet me, and her hands came up as if to fill themselves with warmth and light. Then, having found me, she found him beside me.

I cannot say the sun went out, for she was so gilded she could not but be golden. But she was a carven figure, who had been only an instant since a sparkling flame. A second time she was still, and the airy flying of her garments settled about her into carven folds. In her eyes the fire turned to ash. On her mouth the smile was petrified into stone. Yet she kept her countenance. In truth I never knew her to lose it, only to close it like a marble door, as then she did.

It was not with any hate or fear she looked at him, only with the dulled remembrance of old things past, which she, like me, had never thought to see move and breathe again. I would not have said, then, that there was anything amiss with him but that he was not Samson, and that he stood between Cristin and Samson like a great stone wall, long as the world and high as the sky. And God knows, sorry as I was for myself, I was sorrier yet for my secret brother, so comely and so light, quivering here beside me for dread of this meeting after eight months of absence, and not loved as I, God help me, was loved. Whatever he had been and done, he had not deserved this, nor was he at all armed to resist and conquer it. He did not move until I laid my hand on his shoulder and thrust him towards her. Then he went forward, slowly at first but with a quickening step, his hands held out to her.

And she, too, moved, slowly that woman of golden ice moved and came down the steps to the beaten earth of the courtyard, pale as clay in the rainless midsummer. She did not extend her hands, they were tightly linked under her breast, as if to hold in the heart that cried and fluttered to go free, like a mewed hawk. He went to her and folded his arms about her, and strange it was to find him clumsy about it. And over his leaning shoulder she looked constantly at me, and her eyes were great lamps that had all but gone out, only the last glimmer of a flame alive in them, even while her hands stole about his body and lay like delicate, inert carvings under his shoulder-blades, clasping him with resignation to her heart. Even when he stooped his head and kissed her, I swear she never took her eyes from me until his nearness cut me off from sight. And then she closed them.

As for me, the kiss was more than I could endure. I, too, turned my eyes away. I had my bridle rein still in my hand, I span round upon it like a hanged man spinning upon the cord in the convulsion of death, and groped my toes into the stirrup and mounted, and the horse veered under me, feeling my disquiet and despair. I rode through the dark archway from the inner ward, across the ditch and out by the great gatehouse, and never looked back. At a heavy, languid walk we went, for there was no haste to be anywhere, only to be away from that place. But all down the slope to the roadway I could feel the strings of my heart and hers drawn out infinitely fine to breaking with every pace I took away from her. For now indeed I knew the best and the worst of it, and they were one, and in this world, short of murder, which it seemed was not among my skills, there was no remedy.

I rode for Aber by way of the Conway valley. At Llanrwst they told me that the host was already mustering in strength at Chester, according to the king's decree, but Henry had not yet arrived in that city. At Caerhun, before I struck off to the left over the old Roman road across the high moors, I heard it rumoured that the Cinque Ports fleet was on its way coastwise to Anglesey, and that help had been promised from Ireland. Truly a formidable army threatened us, and a fleet far stronger, if not more manageable in our waters, than the small craft Llewelyn had built and gathered together in defence. Where I appeared, there I was known for his right-hand man, and eagerly apprised of all that went forward, and no man saw anything wrong in me, neither in my bearing, nor in the way I received and responded to the news. So does the impetus of habit continue to carry us when the heart has ceased to put forth any power or passion. For I was an empty shell, too numbed as yet to be fully sensible to the pain of my loss.

That came later, and with the suddenness of lightning flash or flight of arrow, when at Aber I left my horse to the grooms, and asked after Llewelyn. They said that he was in his royal chapel, and there I went to seek him.

Had I come by daylight he would have known the moment of my entrance by the light entering with me, though the chapel was withdrawn beyond a small ante-chamber. But it was late evening, and the light of the one altar-lamp within, though dim and red, was greater than the last remnant of twilight without, and the door was curtained, and opened silently, and there was no sound to disturb him. Thus I came into the chapel with him, and he did not know he was not alone. And seeing him thus on his knees before the cross and lamp at the altar, I drew aside and stood in the darkness, unwilling to touch with movement or sound so profound a stillness and concentration as I beheld in him.

His eyes were open and his head erect, his hands pressed palms together before his breast. His sword, the one he commonly preferred and carried, was laid upon the altar. I think there was not one tremor of movement in all his braced body and reared head, not even the quiver of a hair. He was always plain in his attire, less from humility than indifference, never feeling any need of trappings or jewels to make him royal, who was royal from head to foot and from the heart within to the hand without. But his blessed plainness kept him man among men as well as a prince among his people. He was twenty-eight years old and in the rising prime of his vigour and

power, and I saw his profile drawn in red by the light
of the lamp, the spare, cropped beard no more than a
heightening of the lean lines of his bones, and saw in
that face, in its stillness and unawareness of me, what
was not to be seen in the bright mobility of his daily life.
There was an ordinary man's solemnity and dread in
him, beholding as he did with wide-open eyes the immen-
sity of the burden that lay upon him. And upon him
alone, for there was no other being in all this land of
Wales who could lift any part of that load from him. He
knew it without pride, and accepted it without reluctance,
but the weight of what he carried was a fearful and a
wonderful thing.

I do not know what prayers he made, for aloud he
made none. Whatever was said was said within. I do
know that I beheld in him so fierce and purging a flame
of resolute love, and so deep a recognition of the perilous
nature of his pilgrimage towards the Wales of his desire,
that I was suddenly enlarged out of my cramping shell
of self, and understood the nature of love, and felt its
pain, in such measure that it was hardly to be borne.
And all the more, being thus enlarged, did I burn in
anguish for Cristin, and for myself, and for Godred
whose grief was different but surely no less, and for all
poor souls under the skies who bear in silence and fortitude the sorrows of man. For only in beholding something greater did I realise how great was my own scope,
the well of passion within me how deep.

I crept into the darkest corner there, and waited out
with him the term of his vigil. After a while he stirred
and rose from his knees, and lifting his sword from the
altar, kissed the cross of its hilt and shot it back into
the scabbard. Then he went out, still unaware of me, a
shadow among the shadows.

I went forward then and took his place before the

altar, for I was no longer an empty shell, but a fountain of feeling and longing, overflowing without restraint, and there was a great need in me of a channel into which I could empty all the passion with which I was charged, for even my pain was power, and pure, and could not be left to run to waste.

What befell me there in the chapel was not so much prayer as a wild disputation with God, before the stream I fed had a bed and banks, and ran with the force of a mountain river. And sometimes the voice that argued against me and for me seemed rather to be the voice of Meilyr, my mother's husband, demanding, for so he had a right to demand, of what I complained, for I loved, which is great blessing, as now he himself knew and acknowledged, and I was loved, which is great blessing also. And who has two such dowers may not cavil because he has not the third, to see his happiness fulfilled in this world. For love is a joy and a force of itself alone, looking for no advantage.

But still rebelliously I complained of my pain, for it was very great, and so clamoured in me that I knew it for a daunting and formidable thing, either for good or evil, and what was I to do with it, to make living still possible, even profitable?

Then that with which I contended said to me that I must offer it to God as an earnest, as a weapon, as the squire proffers his lord a sharp lance in a just cause. And so I did at last, embracing it ungrudgingly and offering it with a whole heart, for such a cause I had, the cause of my lord. This and more I will bear, I said in my soul, and never speak loth word, so my prince speeds well in this coming storm. Let every pain of mine count to him as one step on the hard road to his vision of Wales free and glorious. Transmute my every darkness into a light on his way. For this door closed against me, open to him the door into his heart's fulfilment, and if need be, let my death pay to prolong his life until his work is accomplished.

When I was eased of my too much fervour, I went in to him in the high chamber, where he was closeted with Goronwy and Tudor and a messenger newly in from Chester, from our smith who went in and out as doctor to the garrison horses. Llewelyn rose and embraced me, and was altogether as I always knew him, practical, alert and unassuming. I looked upon him with earnest attention, for I had just accepted him as my reason for being, the one pure purpose and justification I had, having acquiesced in the loss of everything else. And I saw that he was enough, and my life would be filled having nothing more.

He asked me of Godred and Cristin, and I told him, without stumbling, how I had left them embracing. And all must have been well with my voice and face, for he was glad. And in the midst of much perplexity and pain I was glad of his gladness, and even the lie of my content which I offered in his service I commended to God as one grain towards my lord's harvest.

So ended that journey. And so began the campaign of that August and September, for the news from Chester was that King Henry was arrived in the city, and slowly all that ponderous mass of engines, foot-soldiers and cavalry was toppling into motion and rolling westwards like a flood tide to overwhelm us.

CHAPTER XII

The host moved upon us on the nineteenth day of August, crossing into Tegaingl the same day, and upon Welsh soil they lumbered westward like a mountain moving, as heavily and as terribly. We took the field the next day, but divided into raiding parties, not as a massed army, and with orders to hold off from any major engagement, but miss no opportunity of picking off any who strayed unwisely from the host. If we were forced to mass and meet them, we could move far more quickly than they could. But as we had expected, they kept to the northern ways, being bent on relieving Diserth. The ships from the Cinque Ports, for which the muster had been waiting, had by this time made the voyage round to our north coast, and with their cover from the sea the castle was relieved. We thought it no good sense to interfere with this operation, which could be no more than a temporary ease unless the whole of the Middle Country could again be occupied and settled, and this they made little attempt to ensure. So we contented ourselves with penning them securely into these northern lands, and we knew we could isolate Diserth just as effectively a second time as soon as they drew off.

They crossed the Clwyd into Rhos near to Rhuddlan, and among these rivers they lost a considerable number of horses and men, and especially baggage beasts, in our pitted fords. But still we forebore from encountering them in pitched battle, which would have been their desire and gain, their superiority in numbers being so great. So they came, the ships keeping pace with them, along the north coast to Degannwy by the twenty-sixth day of August, and lifted the siege of that castle also, as Llewelyn had foretold they would and allowed them to do. One ship at least they lost for some days, grounded in Conway sands, until a high tide lifted her off, though only at the cost of throwing overboard much of the provision she carried, in order to lighten her. And there at Degannwy King Henry camped ingloriously, and sat inactive day after day until the fourth of September. We could not make out why they should sit there so still and ineffective, but it seemed that they were waiting for their promised reinforcements from Ireland, and these never came. Nor did we see any sign of ships in the offing, our sea patrols off Anglesey keeping constant watch, for we were determined not to lose our harvest in that island granary without a fight. But the need never arose. The weather then was breaking, and on the fifth of September the English struck camp, and began the long withdrawal to Chester, with little accomplished.

For Llewelyn these were ideal conditions, for there is nothing better suited to our Welsh manner of fighting than a retreat in formal order by a larger force. Withdrawal then can easily be turned into rout, measured speed harried into flight, and order broken apart into disorder. But here we attempted not too much, but only hung on their skirts all the way back to Chester, lopping off such as fell behind or ranged too far ahead. And on the hither side of Dee we drew off and let them go.

'He calculates too warily,' said Llewelyn in judgment on the king, without prejudice or malice, 'he begins too late, he gathers way too slowly. In short, he is not a soldier. There are things he does excellently well, but not this.'

Thus ended King Henry's last great expedition into Wales, with little gain and less glory. All those too thorough preparations we had made were needless, though the experience was useful. The mountains of Snowdon remained inviolate, and our women and children and old men came cheerfully back to their villages in the lowlands before the autumn descended. Llewelyn's conduct of this defence, though not gravely tested, had been immaculate, sparing of our men and resources and countryside, and even chivalrous towards the enemy, for we could well have done them far greater damage at little more cost to ourselves. But the prince would not have it so, being more intent on conserving our own forces than destroying theirs.

All this time, as we moved about the Middle Country on the fringes of the English host, I had half-expected Godred to appear among us and offer his lance to add to ours, but he never came. And when the enemy had all crossed the Dee and withdrawn into Chester, there to disperse, and I returned with Llewelyn first to Aber, and then to Dolwyddelan, we heard there from the castellan left in charge that Godred had taken his wife, and ridden south for Dynevor.

'For though the knight would rather have stayed and come to Aber to join you,' he said, 'the lady strongly entreated that he would take her home, and could not wait to be away.'

'It's no marvel,' said Llewelyn. 'She has suffered anxiety and sorrow among us – what could we do against it, until Samson found her husband for her? But surely she'll be glad to be home with him, where she has been happy, and with my sister who values her. And a good lance in the south is as sound value to us as a good lance here in Gwynedd. It is all one.'

As for me, I said not a word.

So was I sealed into my own silence that I wanted for

fellows, as though a curtain had been drawn between me and other men, and it was both affront and relief when that one creature came back, some ten days after us, from whom nothing that passed within me was secret, and to whom nothing was sacred. For I had seen little of David while the fighting lasted, he having his own command and I being always with Llewelyn, so that when he rode into Dolwyddelan from Chester he had still all to learn concerning the coming and passing of Godred, and having learned some part of it in easy innocence from Llewelyn himself, kept his mouth shut upon his thoughts, but came flying to me. I was at my work, and had not known of his arrival, but before I could rise to greet him – and indeed I was glad of him – I saw that he was in a great rage with me.

'What's this I hear,' he said, 'of Cristin leaving us? You've let her slip through your fingers, after all this coil? And you – can it be true? – *you* brought the fellow here to fetch her away? Fool, did I not as good as tell you, the first time I set eyes on the pair of you together, that she was yours for the taking? And when you were too deaf and blind to take the drift, did I not *show* you she was steel proof against all others, and would go with you to the world's end if you lifted your finger? When she would not give one thought to me, but followed you into the snow as she had followed you from Brecon to the north? Could you never conceive, in your priestly modesty, that a woman might set her heart on you for her own good reasons, and throw the rest of the world to the winds? One night it took Cristin to make up her mind, and a year was not enough to open your eyes! And now see what you have done to her!'

I was startled and stricken out of all conceal, and told him, as though confessing a sin, that I had had no choice, that even if I had known then what her true desire was – though he had no right to name it for her with so much certainty! – yet it was the will of God that I should chance upon the man, and that finding him alive I could do no other but tell him truth, and render up his wife to him again. But strangely, the pain David gave me, and that without mercy, was like a reviving fire, and to have that spoken of which could not be spoken of with any other was a deliverance like the escape from a dark prison.

'No choice!' said he with furious scorn. 'No *choice*! Had you not a dagger you could have slipped between his ribs there in the forest, and no one the worse or the wiser? Wives can become widows overnight. If you are too nice to do your own work, there are others could do it for you—'

'Never speak so to me!' I said. 'I have been that road, and stopped in time. I will not have you or any other walk it for me.' But I did not tell him, not even David, that Godred was my brother, my father's lawful son.

'Well, as you will! What profit now in harrowing over old ground, what you've done is done. But, man, what you have thrown away! Llewelyn knows nothing, surely, of all this? He seems to take this reunion as a blessing from God! And you have left him in that delusion?'

'I have,' I cried, flaring back at him in my turn, 'and so must you. The prince has great matters on his heart, and a great undertaking one long stage towards its accomplishment, and I will not have even so slight a shadow as my distress cast athwart his brightness, nor one thought of his mind turned aside from the enterprise of Wales to be spent upon me. Is that clear enough?'

At that I saw the flames in his eyes grow tall and pale in the old fashion, and steady like candles in still air as he peered through and through me, half in jealousy, half in impatience, wholly in rage. 'Still his man, I see!' he said. 'As deep committed as ever. What, do you even believe you can buy him a smooth walk through this world by swallowing your own tears? Fool, do you really think God should be grateful to you for flinging his good gifts back in his face? But if you want me silent, I'm silenced. I'll not overcast my brother's sunrise. And since you're such a chaste and upright fool, I have done. I wash my hands of you!'

And he flung out of the room and left me quivering to the racing of my own blood and the sharp, indignant vigour of my own breath, a man alive again. But in a little while he was back, just as impetuously, to fling his arm about my shoulders and ask my pardon for things said and not meant. And whether in anger or in affection, his was a life-giving warmth.

'God knows,' he said, 'you do exasperate me with your too much virtue and devotion, but who am I to be the measure? If *I* tried to close such a bargain with God, he might well strike me dead for my impudence, but *you*.... Who knows, he may have taken you at your word! What would you say if there were signs and omens I could read for you, earnests of heaven's good intent?'

I looked at him speechlessly, and waited for his word, for though his voice was light again and his smile indulgent, he was not in jest.

'Omens come in threes,' he said. 'Two I have brought with me from Mold, one I find coming to birth here. First, Griffith ap Madoc of Maelor has withdrawn his fealty and homage from King Henry, and pledged it henceforth to the confederacy of Wales, like his fathers before him. There is but one Welsh prince now who still denies his blood and clings to England, and that's Griffith ap Gwenwynwyn of Powys, and between my brother and the men of Maelor his chance of holding Powys much longer is lean indeed. Second, King Henry has proposed a truce to last through the winter, and better news to us even than to him, a truce there will surely be. Time to mend all our sheep-folds and sharpen all our swords. And the third – Llewelyn may have opened to you already the scheme he has in mind, of approaching the Scots with a proposal for an alliance?'

I said that he had. For the king of Scots was a boy of fourteen years, and married to King Henry's daughter, a circumstance which had offered a means of placing a great many of Henry's henchmen, both English and Scots, close about the boy's throne, and greatly incensed and alarmed those patriot lords who feared the growth of English power. Two countries threatened by the same encroachment may well make common cause against it.

'Think, then, that if such an approach is to be made, it must be made not for Gwynedd, not for Powys, not for Deheubarth, but for Wales! And all those voices that speak for all those princedoms must be united into one voice, and given utterance through one overlord. I prophesy,' said David, taking my head between his hands and holding me solemnly before him, 'that in the new year the summons will go out throughout this land, to every prince and magnate, to an assembly of Wales, where that one voice will first be heard to speak, and that one overlord will be acknowledged and acclaimed. And his name,' said David, 'I think I need not tell you!'

As he had prophesied, so it befell.

Not many weeks into the new year we rode to that assembly, of all the lords of Wales from north to south, from the marches to the sea. From Gwynedd we came in a great party, David the foremost at his brother's side. Rhodri also came, though Rhodri kept much to his own lands, and had stayed out of trouble and out of the battle-line in the lands of Lleyn while we waited for

337

King Henry's attack, I think not so much out of fear as out of a narrow and suspicious jealousy that he was not prized enough or sufficiently regarded, which kept him usually in a huff against one or other of his brothers, and caused him to refuse such openings as they would have offered him, while complaining that they did not advance him to greater things. As for Owen Goch, he was still prisoner in Dolbadarn, and so continued many years, though with a lightened captivity once his first intransigence ebbed and allowed it. But Llewelyn would never trust him loose again.

Of those others who came, from the south I mention Meredith ap Rhys Gryg of Dryslwyn and Rhys Fychan of Dynevor, from the west Meredith ap Owen of Uwch Aeron, from central Wales Madoc ap Gwenwynwyn of Mawddwy and the three grandsons of Owen Brogynton, Owen ap Bleddyn and the two sons of Iorwerth, Elis and Griffith. From the marches to the east came Griffith ap Madoc of Maelor, with his brother Madoc Fychan, Owen ap Meredith of Cydewain, and the three sons of Llewelyn of Mechain, themselves Llewelyn, Owen and Meredith. In great state they came, and all the noble guest-house of the abbey was filled with their splendour.

There my lord made known his mind concerning the future of Wales and its union under his leadership, and in council there was no dissenting voice. With one accord they accepted him as overlord, on royal terms of protection and justice upon his side, and fealty and service upon theirs, consenting also to the despatch of an envoy, in the name of this new Wales, to compound an alliance with Scotland, for the better guarding of both lands from the encroachments of English power. And Gwion of Bangor was chosen and approved as envoy to the Scottish patriots.

To this day I remember, above all, the burning whiteness of my lord's face when the hands of the last of his vassals were withdrawn from between his hands, and there was a silence, every eye hanging upon him. For he was so pale and bright with desire and resolution and the pride of great humility that he seemed to be as a lamp lit from within. And I remembered that we were born within the same night, perhaps the same hour, and his stars were my stars, and I thought how therefore there might be indeed a logic in this, that whatever I paid in sacrifice might justly weigh to his gain, and it followed that there was nothing for grieving even in my grief.

I will not say that it ever seemed to me that Cristin's coin could justifiably be spent like mine, but Cristin I could neither help nor save. God would surely some day fill up for her the void where she had poured out her love to no avail. As for myself, I thought I was well spent and well lost if I bought one more gleam of lustre for this my prince, who thus spoke to us:

'My grandsire Llewelyn ap Iorwerth took to himself the style and title of prince of Aberffraw and lord of Snowdon, and did great honour to that name. But both these are names of the north, and Gwynedd is but one member in this land, and though I was born there, and of that same line, yet you have laid on me now the right and duty of speaking for north and south alike, for east and west, and of maintaining the rights of all. I think it only fitting that this all should be one. And with your consent I choose to be known henceforth as Llewelyn ap Griffith ap Llewelyn, prince of Wales.'

Every man there, to the last and least of us, caught up the breath from his lips and cried his title back to him with acclaim:

'Llewelyn ap Griffith ap Llewelyn, prince of Wales!'

When we rode from Strata Florida it was a winter

339

dawn, but of sparkling beauty, for there was a clear sky and light frost that silvered the bushes over and rang the branches like bells. For the first mile of this journey of the first true prince of Wales we rode due east, and the sun came up before us into its low zenith vast and glorious, the colour of red gold, as it might have been an orb presented at a coronation.

GLOSSARY

---

ap: son of

brychan: plaid or blanket of homespun, and by extension the truckle beds so furnished

cantref: hundred: regional division of land, literally 'hundred hamlets'

castellan: custodian of the castle

clas: monastic community of lay canons under an abbot, and including at least one other priest

commote: division of land, smaller than the cantref, on which the courts of justice are based

crwth: small stringed instrument, played with a bow

distain: steward, the chief official of a principality

edling: the official heir, nominated by a prince in his own lifetime and accepted by his people

fawr, mawr: great

fychan: lesser: attached to a name often distinguishes son from father

goch, coch: red

llyn: lake

llys: court: the royal seat in each region of a principality *maenol:* manor; in particular the fortified dwelling of a chief

penteulu: the captain of the prince's permanent household army

saesneg: English: thus Maelor Saesneg is the commote of Maelor which thrusts into English territory

talaith: the gold diadem of royal office

teulu: the prince's household army

tref: homestead or hamlet

ynys: island

ystrad: valley: Ystrad Tywi is the Vale of Towy